Tom Bradby has been a correspondent for ITN for almost two decades and is currently ITV News' Political Editor. He is the author of five thrillers: *Shadow Dancer*, *The Sleep of the Dead*, *The Master of Rain* (shortlisted for the Crime Writers' Association Steel Dagger for Best Thriller of the Year 2002), *The White Russian* (shortlisted for the Crime Writers' Association Ellis Peters Award for the Best Historical Crime Novel of 2003) and *The God of Chaos*.

D1147391

Also by Tom Bradby

SHADOW DANCER
THE SLEEP OF THE DEAD
THE MASTER OF RAIN
THE WHITE RUSSIAN
THE GOD OF CHAOS

and published by Corgi Books

BLOOD MONEY

TOM BRADBY

CORGI BOOKS

TRANSWORLD PUBLISHERS
61–63 Uxbridge Road, London W5 5SA
A Random House Group Company
www.rbooks.co.uk

BLOOD MONEY
A CORGI BOOK: 9780552153089

First published in Great Britain
in 2009 by Bantam Press
an imprint of Transworld Publishers
Corgi edition published 2010

Addresses for Random House Group Ltd companies outside the UK
can be found at: www.randomhouse.co.uk
The Random House Group Ltd Reg. No. 954009

The Random House Group Limited supports The Forest Stewardship
Council (FSC), the leading international forest certification organisation.
All our titles that are printed on Greenpeace approved FSC certified paper
carry the FSC logo. Our paper procurement policy can be found at
www.rbooks.co.uk/environment

Typeset in 11/15pt Sabon by
Falcon Oast Graphic Art Ltd.
Printed in the UK by CPI Cox & Wyman, Reading, RG1 8EX.

2 4 6 8 10 9 7 5 3 1

To Claudia, Jack, Louisa and Sam.

Wall Street, 21 October 1929

Rock-a-bye, trader, on the tip top.
When the board meets, the market will rock.
When the rate rises, quotations will fall.
And down will come trader, margins and all.

Wall Street Journal

CHAPTER ONE

THE MAN'S ARMS WERE STRETCHED WIDE, FINGERS pointing to the heavens, as if in prayer. But wherever God was shining his light that Monday morning, it sure as hell wasn't here. His blank eyes stared at a dull grey sky. His cheeks were fleshy and lips full. A derby sat close by his left hand, as though he'd clutched it as he fell. It had landed rim up and filled with water.

A flashgun exploded in the morning gloom.

'Hey, get lost!' Quinn straightened and pushed back the photographer. 'Officer! Get this sap out of here.' He snapped up his collar against the rain, which fell in heavy drops that rolled down the back of his neck. His trenchcoat was too thick for such unseasonable weather; his palms were clammy and his chest prickled with sweat. He pulled out a handkerchief and wiped his forehead.

A Buick tore down from Old Slip and took the turn fast into Wall Street. The crowd scattered, but too late.

A group of First Precinct station-house officers brushed rainwater from their uniforms and yelled at the departing driver.

Normal activity on the street had ceased. Newspaper vendors and shoeshine boys, who'd long since abandoned their stalls, jostled to glimpse the flattened corpse. A man clambered onto a chair outside a barbershop, his chin covered with thick white foam.

Caprisi stood a little apart. He was recording witness statements in a rain-sodden notebook. The guy was thorough, Quinn had to give him that. He crouched again and ran his hands through the dead man's pockets, pulled out a wallet containing a thick wad of notes and some loose change. In the trouser pocket he found a single ticket for the latest Gloria Swanson picture, showing at the Rialto uptown.

'The shoeshine kid on the corner says he landed just like that. *Thwack* . . .' The rain ran in rivulets down Caprisi's slicked-back hair.

'What's his name?'

'I don't know yet, but the uniform boys say he's from this building. Number eighty, top floor.'

'Did the kid see anything else?'

Caprisi shook his head. 'He didn't look like he wanted to hang around.'

'Any sign of an argument?'

'No. But it was raining real hard. The kids had taken shelter.'

Quinn thrust his hands deep into his pockets. It was damp there, too. 'What do you think?'

'About what?'

'Kind of odd he landed face up.'

Caprisi's brow furrowed.

'How many people have you seen jump off a roof backwards?'

'Maybe he was scared of heights.' Caprisi's face remained impassive.

'Very funny, Detective. How come he's got his hat and coat on?'

'It's raining.'

'Who puts a coat on to kill himself?'

'Maybe he didn't like to get wet.' Caprisi lowered his voice. 'Watch out, Schneider's here.'

Tall and slightly stooped, the deputy commissioner made his way through the crowd. His glasses had steamed up. 'I told McCredie to send Brandon.'

'The Bull was stuck over in Brooklyn,' Quinn replied, 'so—'

'Mr Brandon to you, rookie.'

Quinn removed his hands from his pockets. 'Sir, I've been a precinct detective for more than—'

'If you're new to us, kid, you're a rookie. Head-quarters is different, and the sooner you learn that the better.' Schneider glanced at the body. 'Clear this up. Put the corpse in the back of a van and get it out of here. And make sure you scrub the street.'

'Sir—'

'That's an order.'

'Shouldn't we wait for the doc?'

'No.'

Quinn glanced at Caprisi for encouragement, but received none. 'It just seems curious he landed face up, sir. I mean, suicides usually land face down. Maybe we should hang on.'

Schneider took a pace closer. 'I'll tell you what's curious, Detective. We have an election in ten days' time and our balls are going to be busted from here to Ellis Island and back again if the mayor doesn't win. Are you invested in this market?'

'Er . . . no, sir.'

'Then you're the only man who isn't. Have you seen the crowd outside the Exchange?'

'Yes, sir. We saw it on the way up.'

'Have you taken a look in a brokerage window this morning?'

'Yes, sir.'

'Then tell me how much we need a corpse lying in the middle of the street here.' Schneider pushed his glasses back onto the bridge of his nose. 'Clean it up, and do it quick, or you can take the caning from the mayor yourself.'

'What should I put in my report?'

'I don't give a damn. Take a hike up to the guy's office. Find someone who'll tell you he couldn't take the pressure and sign it off.' Schneider turned away, then checked himself. 'You're Quinn, right?'

'Yes, sir.'

'I was sorry to hear about your mother. She was a good woman.'

The sudden change in tone caught Quinn by surprise. 'Thank you, sir.'

Schneider strode away.

'I'll get the uniform boys to sort it out,' Caprisi whispered.

Quinn stared again at the body, then looked up and spotted a familiar figure in the crowd. He hurried over. 'Dad . . .'

'Did Martha tell you she'd changed jobs?' Gerry Quinn removed his cap and brushed the rainwater from its peak. 'She was working for the guy who jumped. It's Moe Diamond's outfit.'

'Well, Moe's family, so I figured—'

'Moe hasn't been family for more than a decade!' Gerry glared at him. 'I knew there'd be trouble when he turned up at your mother's funeral. Who in hell invited him? I didn't pick Martha out of the Bowery so she could fall in with a man like that.'

Quinn didn't answer. A decade's unasked questions crowded in.

'I thought she was working for La Guardia,' Gerry said.

'She was, but Moe offered a hell of a salary.'

Gerry Quinn put his uniform cap back on and bashed it down. 'I want you to take her home.'

'I can't.'

'Aidan's over in Jersey at the main dealership.' Quinn's elder brother was a salesman for Ford motor-cars.

'I'll get her a ride.'

'I want someone to keep an eye on her.' Gerry had lowered his voice an octave, which accentuated his Belfast accent.

'Dad, the deputy commissioner was here. He wants the street cleaned up real fast.'

'I saw Schneider. I heard what he said. You want my advice, you should do yourself a favour and get the hell out of here.'

Quinn frowned. 'What do you mean?'

'Take it from a guy who's been around the block a couple of times.'

'But I have to—'

'Do as I say, son.'

Quinn sighed. 'Where is she?'

'The roof.'

'What's she doing up there?'

'Needed some air, I guess.'

CHAPTER TWO

QUINN'S ADOPTED SISTER STOOD CLOSE TO THE LIP OF THE roof, silhouetted against a brooding sky. She looked cool and imperious in a cloche hat and the fashionable patterned Chanel coat he'd bought her from Wannamaker's the previous Christmas. 'You okay?' he asked.

'No.' Martha's skin was luminous and a smouldering anger radiated from her fiery blue-green eyes.

'I have to take you home.'

'Moe needs me.'

'He'll get along without you today. Dad's upset. We need to go.'

Quinn offered her a cigarette, cupped his hands and lit a match. They listened to the steady drumbeat of the rain. 'Is that your new partner?' She pointed at Caprisi, who had followed Quinn onto the roof.

He nodded.

'He's nice-looking, for a guinea.'

'He's from the Rat Squad.'

'So Italians are only good for busting other cops? Is that it? Well, he looks okay to me.'

Quinn waited. 'We should go in.'

'The air's cleaner up here.'

'You'll catch a chill.'

'I'll live.'

The rain slowed to a fine drizzle, swept across the rooftops by intermittent gusts of wind. A seaplane buzzed overhead and looped around the East River. The clouds broke and thin slivers of sunshine danced across the water.

Quinn flicked away his cigarette and went to join Caprisi at the other end of the roof. From there, the body down in the street looked like it was floating on a sea of umbrellas. He turned around. Martha was watching him intently.

A Salvation Army collector broke into song outside the Cocoa Exchange on Pearl Street, with all the cheer of the last waltz on the *Titanic*.

Quinn walked along the parapet. The gravel underfoot was soft and had turned to mud where the water collected in small pools. He bent down. 'Hey, Caprisi, take a look at this . . .' He pointed towards a semi-circular imprint.

'Detective! What in hell are you doing?'

Quinn snapped around. Schneider stood by the entrance to the roof. 'Sir, I—'

'I just got back from the Exchange. The body's still there.'

'The uniform boys are bringing a van around from the station house,' Caprisi said smoothly.

'When?'

'I told them it was urgent.'

Schneider didn't look convinced. 'If they're not here inside five minutes, you'll have to move the body yourselves. And make sure they take it to Centre Street. Have Doc Carter call me.' He moved towards Quinn. 'His name was Charles Matsell. Go down to his office, have someone confirm his state of mind, then head straight back to Centre Street. I want the report on my desk by lunchtime.' He looked at Martha. 'Who's the broad?'

'She worked for him.'

'Then talk to her.' For a moment his gaze lingered on her. 'On second thoughts, she's probably the reason he jumped. Get one of his partners on the record.'

The Unique Investment office wasn't your average Wall Street joint. A gloomy corridor with an iron hat-stand and a noticeboard with the latest stock prices gave way to four doors. Quinn sat Martha down and told her he would be no more than ten minutes. She didn't seem to hear him.

An officer from the First Precinct stood guard outside the dead man's room, which was closest to the entrance. It was spacious and airy. The walls were covered with baseball souvenirs. A silver-plated bat in a glass frame hung directly above the desk, alongside a photograph of Waite Hoyte and Babe Ruth. A copy of the *New York*

Times lay open on the desk. Matsell had circled a series of stock prices. There was nothing else of interest, unless you counted a few market reports cut out of the financial pages of previous editions.

Quinn opened the drawer. It was full of stationery and neat piles of typed stock summaries. He flicked through them. There was a lot of stuff about companies he'd never heard of. A photograph slipped out and landed face down on the floor. He reached for it, touched its edge and flipped it over.

Martha was lying on a bed. A smile played on ripe, barely parted lips. Her hair was tousled and her legs and arms were stretched languidly across the satin sheet. Quinn glanced at the discarded jersey suit beside her and the neat triangle of dark hair that showed tantalisingly beneath her garter belt.

He slipped the picture into his inside jacket pocket, where it burnt his chest. He loosened his collar and breathed in deeply. He stood, momentarily unsteady, then stepped into the corridor.

Martha gave him a nervous, vulnerable smile. 'You okay, Joe?'

'Yes. You?'

'Fine. Just fine.'

'You sure?'

Her brow furrowed. 'Sure.'

Moe's voice boomed from the landing. He burst into the corridor. His stomach, framed by a pair of wide red suspenders, poked through a starched white shirt undone at the belly button. His nose was broad and his skin pockmarked, but his face lit up when he laughed and, since he liked to think of himself as everyone's favourite uncle, he laughed often. 'Joe and Martha! My two favourite kids!' He slapped Quinn on the shoulder and pushed past him into Matsell's office.

He rifled through the cupboards on either side of the desk, couldn't find what he was looking for and led Quinn down to the far end of the corridor. He pulled a bottle of bootleg whisky from beneath his own desk, poured a couple of large slugs, shoved a glass into Quinn's hand, and gulped from the other. Quinn hadn't seen him since his mother's funeral six months ago and noticed that he had aged considerably. His eyes had lost their sparkle. 'Jesus, Joe.' He reached for a brass ashtray and lit a cigar. 'He didn't deserve it. I mean, Christ! None of us does.' Moe glanced out at Martha in the corridor and closed the door.

'Didn't deserve what?' Quinn asked.

'To end up like that!'

A third man entered the room. His cool green eyes rested steadily on Moe. The newcomer was tall and slim, with a thin, angular face and a nose filled with hair. 'Dick Kelly,' he said, without offering his hand. 'Charlie was our partner.'

'I'm sorry,' Quinn said.

'We might hold the department responsible for a great deal, Detective, but we can hardly blame you for his suicide.'

'Did you have any idea—'

'What gets into a guy's mind? What makes him scared

21

of his own shadow? It's kind of a sickness, right?'

'So you thought he might do something like this?'

Quinn had directed the question at Moe. Since he was now studying the floorboards, Kelly picked it up. 'We didn't, but maybe we should have.'

'Why was that?'

'Once a guy goes a little crazy . . .'

'A little crazy?'

'He tortured himself with threats that didn't exist.'

'What kind of threats?'

'He thought someone was out to get him.'

'Someone in particular?'

'We should have gotten him to a doctor.'

'He mention anyone by name?'

Kelly shook his head. 'He figured he was being chased by his own shadow.'

Moe leant forwards. 'You know how it is, Joe, better than any of us . . .'

Quinn didn't answer. He pulled over a chair and picked up the overnight edition of the *Sun* that lay on it. 'TIGER, ON OFFENSIVE, RIPS LA GUARDIA', ran the banner headline. 'TAMMANY OPENS GUNS ON HISTORY OF GOP NOMINEE'. He glanced at the photograph of Babe Ruth above Moe's desk.

'Hell, there's an exception to every rule!' Moe laughed. 'You don't have to be a Yankee to admire the bambino!' Moe had been a lifelong Giants fan.

'Has McGraw seen it?' Quinn asked.

'He'd forgive me.'

John J. McGraw had been the Giants manager during

their glory years, but he'd also owned a billiard parlour next to the old *Herald* building, where Moe had been a pool-table hustler. Maybe he still did. Moe had once taken Quinn there to witness Rothstein's legendary thirty-four-hour battle against Conway, which McGraw had finally closed out at four in the morning.

'Moe, why did you say Matsell didn't deserve it?'

'I didn't say that.'

'It was the first thing you told me when I walked in here. "He didn't deserve it. None of us does." '

'Hell, it was just an expression.'

'But why did you say, "None of us does"?'

'Joe . . . I told you already. Who in hell wants to end up like that?' He paused. 'You're at Headquarters now?'

'Yes.'

'When did you start?'

'Last week.'

'Didn't I say you'd make the big-time?'

'Moe—'

'Dick, the kid's smart. Always was. Crazy in the head and as reckless as a lion cub but smart, like his mother. He and Martha made a hell of a pair! The kid and his shadow . . .'

'Moe—'

'That was before she grew into a goddamned swan to torture us all!' He hitched up his pants and wiped his nose on his sleeve. 'But, sure, it's ba-ba-boom time for you, Joe. Headquarters is big bucks. You know that.'

23

Quinn tried not to think of how Moe used to stick his stubby fingers down Martha's pants.

'You want to end up a pauper, like your old man?' Moe asked.

'It's a good thing he's not listening to you say that, Moe. I've got to do a report, so I need to know if Mr Matsell was upset about something.'

Moe Diamond shoved the fat stub of his cigar between his bloated lips. He had recovered a little of the old self-confidence. 'Charlie was kind of secretive, Joe. He did his work. He was good at hooking in new clients. But outside of meetings we didn't see too much of him. He wasn't one of us, if you know what I mean.'

Kelly nodded in agreement.

'Was there something on his mind?'

They shrugged.

'Did he seem like he was depressed?'

'Not that we could see. But, you know, Joe, sometimes it's hard to tell.'

'Did he have trouble with a broad?'

'We all got trouble with broads, Joe.'

'I mean . . . a particular girl?'

Moe frowned. He looked at his partner and they shook their heads.

'Did he get on with Martha and the other girls in the typing pool?'

'Hell, Joe, you name a man on this earth who doesn't like Martha!'

Quinn bit the inside of his cheek. 'Was he close to any of them?'

'There are only two broads in that office and Charlie dealt with Martha.'

'Who's the other?'

'Stacey. She was real upset at the sight of the body so we sent her home.'

'It's not possible that he was—'

'C'mon, Joe . . . Stacey's like Martha and if you think I'd let one of the guys fool around with your little shadow . . .'

Quinn bit back his response. He looked around. This place was a sign of how far they'd all come: pool-table hustling had become Wall Street broking. He'd missed a large part of Moe Diamond's life. 'How come you guys got together?'

'Dick and I set the place up. Charlie had just arrived in the city from Minnesota and had a bankroll. I'd seen him up in Saratoga in the old days, so I knew he was on the level.'

'Did you help him lose his bankroll?'

'Hell, no! Joe, I told you at your mother's funeral, you want to tip me the wink, I'll make you a rich man. That's guaranteed.'

Quinn recalled the conversation all right, but every fix and venture Moe had ever entered into was 'guaranteed'. 'Why do you figure he *might* have wanted to jump, Moe? I need to put something down here.'

For a while, neither man spoke. Then Kelly said, 'We don't know what to think. Other than running away from his shadow, he didn't have a reason in the world to kill himself.'

'It's always hard to tell, Joe,' Moe said. 'You know that better than—'

'Did you see him outside of the office?'

'No.'

'Was he married?'

'No.'

'Did he have a regular girl?'

'Not that we knew of.'

'Did he . . . ?' Quinn hesitated. 'He and Martha weren't close?'

'Joe, c'mon . . . What's eating you? I already said—'

'You just said she's a beautiful woman. So maybe he—'

'Joe,' Moe said, 'Martha's family, you know that. We take care of her. You shouldn't listen to your father. He can't keep her locked up until she's an old maid.'

'Charlie gambled,' Kelly said. 'That's all we've been able to come up with. We thought maybe he'd got himself in too deep somewhere.'

'Who did he play with?'

'We don't know,' Moe said. 'It was just what we heard.'

'Where did you hear it?'

'That's kind of private.'

'Did he know Rothstein?'

They shrugged, which meant the answer was yes.

Quinn moved to the window. It had stopped raining and he watched a few thin rays of sunshine glimmer on the water by the pier. 'Moe, did Charlie Matsell have any visitors this morning?'

'None that we knew of.'

'Did you see him go up to the roof?'

They shook their heads again.

There was a knock and Caprisi nudged the door open. 'You got a minute?'

Quinn stepped into the corridor.

'Charlie Matsell had a visitor,' Caprisi told him. 'The man came in around nine fifteen, just after the rush-hour. The security guard at the front desk recognized him. Apparently he'd been here before. He was a real fancy guy in a fifty-dollar suit. He stayed about half an hour.'

'He left before Matsell fell off the roof?'

'Yeah.'

'You figure he could have been a broker calling the guy in?'

'Maybe, but Schneider won't want that in the report. He told me it would be best if it turned out Mr Matsell's girlfriend had left him.' Caprisi raised his eyebrows. 'We'd better go. They're moving the body now and he's hovering. He wants us out.'

CHAPTER THREE

THEY EMERGED AS THE CORPSE WAS BEING LOADED INTO the back of a van, so Quinn took hold of Martha's arm and guided her to the passenger seat of the Gardner. It was a brand-new black sedan, with a sleek hood and gleaming headlamps, but she didn't appear to be impressed. She glanced up at a huge poster plastered across the wall beside them, which carried La Guardia's latest advertisement written in the manner of a newspaper headline: 'GOP Slams Building Scheme, Challenges Mayor Walker on Tammany Receipts'. It had been repeatedly defaced. The Democrats' New York party machine still had plenty of defenders.

Quinn watched a seaplane turn in towards the city. The pilot circled once and dropped onto the choppy waters of the East River. The engines roared as he swung around tightly in front of a car float inbound from Jersey City. The sun shimmered through broken rainclouds over the staid residences of Brooklyn Heights on the bluff. A group of boys kicked their legs against the stone jetty and watched the fishing smacks and scows plough upriver, apparently immune to the discordant cacophony of blasts and whistles from the nearby steam shovels.

Quinn fired up the Gardner and swung it onto South Street. The road was thronged with sailors in peajackets, workmen in dungarees and shabby drifters who hung about the warehouses in the hope of finding work. He sounded the horn to clear them out of the way and eased his foot down on the gas pedal. Rain began to fall again, blown in waves off the river and pelting the Gardner's windscreen.

Caprisi lolled back in the rear seat, eyes closed.

Martha adjusted her hat and stared intently at the truck ahead. 'There's nothing you could have done,' Quinn said.

'There's always something that could have been done.'

'Not this time.'

'What do you mean?'

'There were two sets of footprints on the roof. The set closest to the edge faced backwards.'

'I don't understand.'

'His heels had dug in. I'd say he was pushed.'

There was a long silence. 'That's impossible.'

'Why?'

She didn't answer.

'He had a visitor this morning. Do you know who?'

Martha seemed mesmerized by the rivulets of water

running up the windscreen. 'Joe, do you mind if we don't talk about this now?'

Quinn turned into Seventh Street and let the Gardner ride to a halt. Old women wove along the sidewalk beneath battered umbrellas and stall-keepers crowded beneath the shelter of narrow awnings. Two sparrows picked at manure left by the old clothes man's horse. Grandpa Santini, dressed in droopy pants and an old country undershirt, watched them mournfully and tugged at his long moustache, while his tall, curly-haired grandson shouted a familiar curse from inside the hood of the family's new covered van: 'Sonamabeetch!' He gave its side panel a good, hard kick.

'I'll take you up,' Quinn said. He turned to Caprisi. 'Give me a minute.'

Martha's eyes were on wisps of smoke that billowed from the hat factory at the end of the row. They drifted, stagnant in the damp sky, before bunching together to ride the wind over to the Jersey shore.

Fall had come late this year, but now the jingling ices wagon, with its coloured bottles, had disappeared and the ice-box man had pulled on his beanie and put on thick boots. Butchers hung the grey, stretched bodies of hares in their windows, while the warm-skinned fruits of summer had given way to cool apples and round purple Concord grapes heaped in slatted baskets. Pretty much everyone in the tenement used the grapes to make wine and the acrid aroma oozed down the stairwell.

'Let's go,' Quinn said.

She didn't acknowledge him, so he got out of the Gardner and went to open her door. She muttered something inaudible and, before he could dissuade her, set off down the sidewalk to the butcher's on the corner.

The store was warm and light, its shelves stacked with glistening entrails. Behind a giant meat-grinder, hearts and livers hung from hooks on the ceiling. Martha was served by the man with bushy eyebrows who looked like the huge cop in the Chaplin movies. 'You want breast?' he asked her. 'Me too, *tsotstele*.' It meant 'cutie', but today Martha wasn't in the mood to smile.

Quinn took her arm as they emerged onto the sidewalk. He gripped it tight.

'Joe, you're hurting me. What's wrong?'

He eased the pressure.

'I'm all right,' she whispered.

Despite the rain, Mr Roth sat in his usual place on the stoop, in dark, shapeless pants and a collarless shirt, buttoned up tight to his throat. He patted the shiny old derby on his head, but Quinn ignored his attempt at conversation and guided Martha up the stairwell. The doors to each apartment would have been wedged open in the summer to draw cool air from the stone landings, but now they were shut tight against the anticipated onset of winter.

As they climbed higher, Yosele Rosenblatt's ululations drifted through the air. Quinn wondered if Mr Herman, who lived in the apartment below them, ever took the recording off his Victrola. They reached the top floor and Quinn let Martha into their apartment. He took off her coat, shook it carefully over the mat and hung it on the stand in the corner. They moved to the front room and listened to the rain fall upon the roof. The furniture smelt of lemon-oil polish and the curtains had been newly starched. As his mother had, Martha kept the place immaculate.

She took off her cloche hat, hung it on the rail by the bathtub and shook out her wavy dark hair, which had been cut fashionably short. She was wearing a pleated skirt and a jersey top which bore an uncomfortable resemblance to the one Quinn had seen discarded in the photograph in Matsell's desk.

'Was this guy Matsell a friend?' he asked.

'No.'

'You didn't like him?'

'Not much.'

'You weren't close?'

'No.'

She tried to move past him, but he held her arm. He could feel her breath on his cheek. 'You sure about that?'

'Certain.'

A tap dripped. A dog barked and was quieted with a fierce command. Martha freed herself from his grasp and sat, head in her hands, in Ma's old wooden chair.

Quinn edged closer.

'You'd better leave me, Joe.'

He didn't move.

There was a crash from the courtyard. Quinn went to

his bedroom and opened the door to the iron stairwell. He stepped out as skinny Sarah clambered past him on her way to the roof. Sarah was a lithe eleven-year-old, whose favourite trick was to steal from a woman downstairs who was too fat to chase her around the stairwell's tight corners. The woman hammered a saucepan against the railings in protest and demanded Quinn pursue the girl.

It was only a few paces to the roof, but by the time he got there, Sarah had long since skipped over the brick partition and set off down the block. She was supposed to be in school, or at least at the orphanage, and had no intention of sticking around for any kind of argument.

Quinn watched her go. As a child, this had been his domain, a playground of black tar and low brick dividers, which ran all the way to the end of their stretch of Seventh. He walked to the edge. The image of his mother lying face down on the street was as crisp as the day it had happened.

He went back to the iron stairwell, where the window to his father's apartment banged in the breeze. He stepped in to close it against the rain. He had not been inside his parents' bedroom since the day his mother had jumped and his father had moved to the box-room. Everything was as neat and tidy as she would have wished; the white linen cloth over the small iron bed, the enamel wash-bowl, the crucifix on the wall.

The room smelt of detergent. The old man had scrubbed the floors and walls clear of the stench of stale booze. The air was still. The room was dominated by a photograph of the couple on their wedding day. His father's steady eyes seemed to follow Quinn as he moved. He looked at his mother. She gazed back at him.

He stepped towards the shelf in the corner and picked up a painted box he had made for her at school, now chipped with age and use. He took down a cream-cheese tin of baseball cards, and a crude ferris wheel he'd bought on a Sunday outing to Luna Park with Sergeant Marinelli, one of his father's junior officers. Quinn spun the wheel. It didn't turn freely because Aidan had squashed it on the ride home.

He bent down to wipe the dust from the top of his father's accordion. The memory of happier years tugged at him, of the Irish rebel songs his father had loved to play and of his mother's laughter, which had once rung to the rafters.

He caught sight of Martha in the doorway. 'He never comes in here,' she said. 'It's usually locked.'

Quinn heard a footfall in the corridor. 'Dad?' He joined Martha in the doorway as a man in a trenchcoat and Homburg hurried past.

CHAPTER FOUR

BY THE TIME QUINN REACHED THE LANDING, THE MAN WAS in full flight. Quinn clattered after him. He passed Mr Roth in the hallway and careered out onto the slippery stone stoop. The man leapt onto the running board of a waiting Chevy, which roared off.

Quinn reached the Gardner and slid into the driver's seat. He fired the engine, stamped on the pedal, swung the wheel around hard and put his palm flat on the horn.

'Anything I should know about?' Caprisi asked.

'The guy was in my father's apartment.'

Caprisi whistled quietly. 'They only just pulled up. I saw them outside the place on Wall Street.'

Quinn swerved to avoid skinny Sarah, now playing jump-rope with two friends on the corner. He put his hand flat on the horn again to clear the teeming streets. 'Are you sure?'

'Sure I'm sure.'

Quinn tore after the Chevrolet all the way to the fish market on the corner of South and Fulton where it tried to swing right in front of the stubby trawlers and draggers berthed along the pier but crashed into the stalls. Boxes of fish and ice flew across the bonnet and windscreen. Men in rubber boots who had been stacking crates into lines of refrigerated trucks darted for cover, forcing Quinn to swerve violently, then reverse out, by which time the Chevy had made its break westwards. The man on its running board kicked away stray fish and climbed in through the window.

'Drop back,' Caprisi said. 'They'll never outrun us.'

Quinn eased his foot off the gas. It was true. The eight-cylinder Gardner had been bought as a pursuit vehicle and could touch a hundred.

Quinn kept his distance. As they reached the far side of Manhattan, the Chevy turned into West Street and headed north again, along the Hudson. The river was hidden behind an unending line of bulkhead sheds, cranes and warehouses, and a surging mass of back-firing, horn-blowing, gear-grinding trucks.

The Chevy tried to lose them, but it never stood a chance. It hit a taxi and nearly mowed down a slow-moving group of seamen pouring in and out of the cheap lunch rooms and tawdry saloons along the front. It overtook a truck, almost smashed into one coming the other way, then disappeared.

'Close up,' Caprisi said.

Quinn put his foot back on the gas. They tore down Hubert, took a right and headed back along Beach. They turned south. The driver in front must have had his foot flat down. They swung onto the lane by the piers and sped past a row of warehouses. The narrow strip was packed with freighters, trucks and dock workers. A truck nosed out and the Chevy had nowhere to go. The driver swerved, hit a stone bollard and went straight into the Hudson.

Quinn stopped the Gardner. For a moment, the Chevy wallowed, the great lamps on its hood pointing towards the Jersey shore. Then it began to sink.

The men inside were trying frantically to open its doors. Quinn slipped off his suit jacket and holster and climbed down a ladder at the side of the pier.

'What the hell are you doing?' Caprisi shouted.

The Chevy was almost completely submerged. Quinn balanced himself and dived into the ice-cold water. He kicked out and reached the car just as it disappeared beneath the surface. He took a deep breath and held on. A white face appeared and fingers scrabbled behind the glass.

Quinn gripped the door handle with all his strength until his lungs gave out. Pain seared his chest and his thick worsted pants dragged him downwards. He kicked hard, somehow broke the surface and threw himself back, gasping for air. He breathed in a lungful of oily, effluent-laden salt water and coughed and spluttered as he swam to the pier.

When he reached the top of the ladder, Caprisi pulled

him onto the road and stood over him. 'What in hell did you do that for?'

Quinn struggled for breath. They were surrounded by a crowd of curious onlookers. 'Thanks for your support. I appreciate it.'

'You must be out of your mind!' Caprisi's face was puce with rage. 'Schneider will kill us. We'll have to send divers down. Do you know how much they cost?'

'Caprisi—'

'We're supposed to go right back to the office and file a suicide rap. Instead, we've chased a bunch of guys halfway around the city and now they're at the bottom of the Hudson.'

'Calm down.'

'Calm down? I've got less than two months to go before I'm out of this viper's nest and back home to an honest living with a pension to tide me over. I can't afford a disciplinary.'

Quinn had recovered his breath. 'You saw the footprints. The guy was pushed. That makes it a homicide.'

'No, it does not. It's a suicide. That's it. You heard what Schneider said.'

Quinn looked at the pierhead warehouse. The mayor grinned down at them from a billboard; he wore a morning coat, spats and his top hat. Quinn coughed up a mouthful of river water and watched the pools spread around his feet.

CHAPTER FIVE

QUINN HAD DRIED HIMSELF OUT AS BEST HE COULD, BUT HIS shoes still squelched and left a soggy trail. McCredie bellowed with laughter. 'Been swimming, Detective? On police time?'

'The suspects went into the water.'

'*Did* they?'

'Yes, sir.'

'And how in the hell did they do that?'

'They were trying to outrun us and took a wrong turn down a lane by the piers on West Street. They swerved to avoid a truck, lost control and went over the edge.'

'So, why didn't you let them drown?'

'They did.'

'Good!'

'I wanted to question them.'

'Well, that was very noble of you.'

Assistant Chief Inspector Ed McCredie was a big man with an expressive, cheerful, lived-in face and eyes that sparkled with humour. He wore a thick winter suit, fashionably cut with wide lapels, and a garish tie loose at the collar. He went everywhere with his hands thrust deep in his pockets, jingling a bunch of coins. He'd held sway over the main detective squad at Headquarters for nearly two decades and, to most of the men and women who worked here, he was more or less equivalent to God.

McCredie stood in front of the glass door to his corner office. He was smoking a cigar. 'Listen, I need to talk to you without that guinea bastard getting in the way. Who was the guy down on Wall Street?'

'His name was Charlie Matsell,' Quinn said quickly. The brevity of his superior's attention span was legendary. He handed over the business card he'd taken from Matsell's office. 'He worked in Moe Diamond's outfit and we figure he was—'

'Hey, Mae,' McCredie shouted. 'What's happening?'

'Still falling, sir. The ticker's running way behind, sixty minutes or more.' Mae Miller shot Quinn a grin.

'You hear that, boys?' McCredie said, to no one in particular. 'It's a goddamn disaster. You in the market, son?'

Caprisi joined them. 'No, sir.'

'You should be. You want to live on a detective's pay all your life?'

'Er—'

'Have you talked to Brandon?'

'Not yet.' There was no light on in the glass office behind him. Sightings of Johnny Brandon, the head of

40

the homicide bureau, were rare. 'The way I see it,' Quinn said, 'Matsell—'

'Mae, what's happening on Murray Street?'

'No news. They're still not moving.'

McCredie ushered Quinn into his office. As Caprisi made to follow, he blocked his path. 'You got a report to finish, Detective. Schneider wants it.'

Caprisi glanced at Schneider's office. He flushed.

'Sir,' Quinn said, 'Detective Caprisi has a lot of the detail that we need to—'

'Tell that to Schneider.' McCredie closed the door and watched Caprisi retreat. 'We've surrounded a bunch of armed robbers down on Murray,' he said absent-mindedly. He stubbed out the cigar on a dented ashtray and leant against a glass cabinet, filled with boxing trophies from his youth.

There was a poster on the bench. 'MISSING!' it read. 'Since 16 October, AMY MECKLENBURG.' The photograph showed a girl clutching a small white dog.

'Cute kid,' McCredie said. 'If we're not careful, La Guardia's going to have a field day.'

'Who is she?'

'Decent family. Went missing in Brooklyn.'

'Are we putting out an alert?'

'Not yet. Byrnes is on her trail. He figures it's some-one in the family, but if he doesn't get to her soon, we'll have to start pasting these things up and that'll be hellish painful.' McCredie lit another cigar. 'So, what happened? Schneider will hit the roof when he hears we've had to send divers into the Hudson. I need to

41

work out how to stop you getting your ass whipped.'

'Some guy broke into my father's apartment so I—'

'What were you doing there?'

'My sister – well, she's my brother's fiancée – worked for the dead man. I gave her a ride home.'

'So what's the big deal?'

'Caprisi saw the guys in the Chevy parked up on Wall Street, so they must have followed us.'

'And why do you figure they wanted to do that?'

'We're trying to work it out.'

'Your old man runs the First Precinct station house?'

'That's correct, sir, yes. You might remember—'

'Sure, I remember Gerry Quinn. Who could forget him? So, you chased the guy?'

'Sir, there was something else. Back at Wall Street, I sneaked a few minutes on the roof and it was real clear Matsell was pushed.'

'Says who?'

'There were two sets of footprints in the gravel, and if he jumped, he went off backwards. I mean, suicides . . . Well, people who jump land face down.'

'I'm sorry about your mother, son. I haven't said that before. I should have. She was a good woman.'

'Thank you, sir. I didn't realize anyone here knew her.'

McCredie coughed. 'Yeah, well, I understand where you're coming from, but guys getting ready to kill themselves do all kinds of dumb things. I wouldn't read too much into it.'

'He had a visitor just before he . . . jumped.'

'Who?'

'We didn't have time to find out.'

McCredie sighed. 'Moe Diamond always was a crook, but much as it pains me to admit it, Schneider is right.'

'But—'

'Listen, son, I've got the shit going down on Murray, and if Byrnes can't trace this girl's uncle, I'm going to have to watch the gentlemen of the press wade in with another white-slave scare. So if Schneider *says* it's a suicide, right now it *is* a suicide.'

'But it isn't.'

'You know what's going on here, son?'

'No, sir.'

'A goddamned election, that's what. And since you're new to us, I'm going to give you a real simple guide to what's at stake. It may not have escaped your attention that we failed to bust the Rothstein case.'

'Of course, I read about—'

'So now Major La Guardia and all his little Republican buddies are alleging that the *reason* we haven't solved the murder of the city's most notorious hoodlum is because Mayor Walker, the entire Democratic machine and every single cop in this place are so bent they're in the pocket of one organized crime faction or another. Do you understand, son?'

'Yes, sir, I know, but—'

'Hold on a minute,' McCredie interrupted. 'So, if Major La Guardia can whip up any kind of controversy with ten days to go until polling day, we're all finished

– you, me, Tammany, the commissioner, the mayor. Because, believe me, if Major La Guardia does win this election, he ain't going to hang around to sort the good from the bad in here or anywhere else.'

'Sir, a man was murdered. What does that have to do with organized crime?'

'Nobody was murdered, Detective. But I'll lay out ten bucks that the guys you chased into the Hudson this morning turn out to have had connections we'd rather not read about in our morning newspapers.' He shook his head. 'The folks over at City Hall are nervous. So is the commissioner. If we give them controversy, they'll come looking for scapegoats.'

'I do appreciate that, sir, but—'

'You know what Schneider wants, son?'

'No, sir.'

'He wants me dead in the water. That's why he moved his office down here next to mine. Once upon a time, he was just a small-time pen-pusher from New Jersey installed on the top floor to count paper-clips. But then he decided he wanted a cut of the action so he spun the commissioner a line about busted budgets and gave himself an office in Vice. Now he's got that wrapped up with Fogelman in the chair, he's moved down here to get on my nerves. Homicide, the safe and loft division, burglary, street crime, the central pool – he wants to control the lot. I wouldn't put it past the little shit to have tied up a sweetheart deal with our friend Major La Guardia already, because he wouldn't understand the meaning of "loyalty" if it was branded on his goddamned backside.'

'But, sir—'

McCredie smiled. 'Relax, son. I like you. I figure you're going to be one of the good guys. I know you're keen and you'll get your chance, but this is just some dumb Joe who killed himself over a broad. That's it.' McCredie laid a hand on Quinn's shoulder. 'Once we've got you through probation, you can ditch that guinea bastard.'

'Caprisi seems like a good guy.'

'He's from the Rat Squad. He's spent his life snitching on fellow cops. And if O'Dwyer fries, I'll make sure he does too.'

'Sir,' Mae had put her head around the door, 'they just called in from Murray. They're about to go in.'

'Tell them I don't want a screw-up. Any mistakes and I'll kick Sullivan's ass all the way back to Jersey.'

When it was clear his audience was over, Quinn headed back to his desk.

Caprisi handed him a cup of coffee and cut him dead when he started to apologize. 'I'm doing a preliminary report for Schneider. He wants us to run him through it.'

Quinn glanced at the deputy commissioner's office. Its glass door was always shut. 'The boss thinks the guys we chased into the Hudson were strong-arm hoods for one of the crime set-ups.'

'You don't say? I had them all figured as altar-boys.' Caprisi peered at him. 'Did you know them?'

'No.'

'You sure about that?'

'Yes.'

'Wall Street's your father's precinct, though, right?'

'Sure.'

'And it was his apartment that guy was in?'

'What's your point, Caprisi?'

'Nothing. Just getting the facts straight in my head.'

Quinn watched his partner. 'Did you work on O'Dwyer?'

'No.'

'But it was a Confidential Squad bust?'

'I thought you guys liked to call it the Rat Squad? It was Valentine's bust. Maybe that's why they had it in for him.'

'When's O'Dwyer up for clemency?'

'Soon, and he won't get it.'

Quinn sat on the edge of the desk. 'You figure he should fry?'

'O'Dwyer beat a man to death, Detective, and thought it a damned good joke because that man was a Negro.' Caprisi sipped his coffee. 'What did McCredie say?'

'Nothing . . . I mean, not much.'

'O'Dwyer was one of his Irish gang. He took it hard when Valentine reeled him in.'

'You figure loyalty is such a bad thing, Caprisi?'

'It depends what kind.'

'Hmm . . .' Quinn noticed a pile of posters of the missing girl on a desk behind him. 'What's the score with this girl?'

'Which one?'

'The one who went missing in Brooklyn. Byrnes has the case. How come, if she disappeared in the middle of last week, we didn't get assigned to help him?'

'It's someone in the family. The uncle disappeared at the same time.'

'Then why is it a Headquarters case?'

'Because if it *isn't* her uncle, the newspapers will say it's white-slave traffic and the commissioner will feel the heat from City Hall. Look, I've got to organize the divers.' Caprisi disappeared down the corridor.

Quinn took a couple of sips of strong, dark coffee. As the most junior – or least consequential – members of the main squad, they had been placed in the corner by the hat-stand. The walls around them were plastered with official orders. Quinn adjusted the books on the shelf. From his last job as the senior detective in the Bronx, he'd brought with him Phelps on wounds, Bundage on toxicology and Tanner on poisons.

He watched Schneider come out of his office and disappear into McCredie's. It looked from this distance as though they might be arguing. Once or twice, McCredie glanced in his direction.

Quinn picked up the telephone and gave the operator his home number. He waited. 'Martha?'

'Joe? Is that you? Everything's fine.' Her voice was strained. 'He's here and he wants to speak to you.'

'Joe?' Now his father was on the line. 'What happened? Did you get him?'

'The driver lost control and went into the Hudson. None of them got out, so we've sent down divers.

47

We won't have any leads before tonight at the earliest.'

'Did you get a look at him?'

'No. But it seems like he followed us from Wall Street.'

'Everything's under control here. Nothing stolen.'

'I'll come down and—'

'Stay where you are. We're okay. We'll see you tonight.'

The call was terminated before Quinn could insist. He replaced the earpiece.

He lit a cigarette and watched the smoke drift up towards the wooden fan. Two boys from the safe and loft squad gathered around a wireless set.

Mae caught his eye, sauntered over and sat next to him. She'd had her blonde hair fixed up, he saw. 'What's that about?' He gestured at McCredie and Schneider.

'You know what they're like. One day I swear they'll kill each other.' She watched them for a minute. 'If you ask me, the boss wears it pretty well.'

'How's that?'

'This is supposed to be his floor, isn't it? Schneider seems to think that the man who controls the budget should control everything else, but what does he know about being a cop? I've no idea how the boss puts up with it.' She smiled at him. 'But he likes you and at least you got a run out this morning.'

Quinn offered Mae a swig of coffee, but she wrinkled her nose. 'It's different here,' he said.

'You don't say.'

'Over in the Bronx, everything was straight down the line. Here, it's . . .'

'It's early days, Joe.' She smiled. 'It can only get better, right?'

O'Reilly rounded the corner, carrying a red bucket with a picture of a grinning Mayor Jimmy Walker plastered to its side. He rattled it under their noses. 'Cough up, Detective.'

'I'm supporting the major.'

'Very funny.'

'No, I am.'

There was warning in Mae's eyes.

'It's five dollars *minimum*.'

'I gave five dollars last week, and I'm supporting La Guardia.'

O'Reilly rattled the bucket. 'Cough up, wise guy.'

Quinn reached into his pocket, peeled off a dollar and threw it into the bucket.

'You're new here, Detective,' O'Reilly said, 'and the boss likes you so I'm going to forgive your lousy sense of humour.'

Quinn chucked in a five-dollar bill.

'We'll expect your support on election day,' O'Reilly said.

'You only have to ask.'

O'Reilly moved away.

'You shouldn't rile him, Joe. He's a bully-boy. And everyone is nervous La Guardia will win.'

'He won't.'

She leant forward. 'What about the photograph?'

'Which one?'

'The one the newspapers keep talking about – the

49

picture of the mayor and Rothstein standing together like bosom buddies. If they print that, Jimmy's finished.'

'What does the boss say? Does it exist?'

'He says he'd like to think Jimmy Walker's too smart to allow himself to be photographed with a man like that.'

'But he's afraid he's not as smart as he looks?'

'Exactly. He doesn't have a very high opinion of our friends at City Hall.'

'If they had it, the newspapers would have printed it already. And since Rothstein has been dead almost a year, I don't see them getting their hands on it now.'

'Mae!' One of the other stenographers waved at her. 'It's Sullivan from Murray Street.' Mae raised her eyebrows and went back the way she had come.

Quinn stubbed out the cigarette and drained his coffee.

CHAPTER SIX

DOC CARTER WAS A FOPPISH YOUNG MAN IN FANCY SHOES, grey suit pants, a tennis shirt and sweater. He looked like he'd walked right out of Fitzgerald's *The Great Gatsby*. Quinn wondered why he wasn't in private practice, then caught a whiff of his breath. 'I was on a day off,' Carter said. His eyes narrowed. 'Have you been swimming, Detective?'

'That's very good, Doc. Why did they interrupt your tennis?'

'Berkowitz is ill. It seems strange that he's always unwell on a Monday, wouldn't you say?'

'I've never met him.'

'Ah, I forgot, you're new.' Carter washed his hands and eyed him with suspicion. They had met only once previously, on Quinn's induction day. 'Why are you here?'

'I wanted to take a look at the autopsy on the guy from Wall Street.'

'Which guy?'

'The uniform boys brought his body in about two hours ago.'

'Oh, you mean the jumper.' Carter shook his head. 'I haven't done him yet.'

'When do you think you'll get around to it?'

'Later.'

'Any idea what time?'

A thin sheen of sweat glistened on Carter's forehead. 'There's no hurry.'

'Doesn't Schneider want it? He told us we needed to sign the report off by lunchtime.'

Carter waved a hand. 'He's got it.'

'He's got what?'

'He has what he needs.'

'So, you have done the autopsy?'

'Not in full.'

'But, Doc, you've either opened the guy up or—'

'For God's sake, Detective, I gave him what he wanted. Any fool could tell it was suicide. Schneider was in a hurry.'

'Oh . . . okay.' Quinn acted as if he understood all too well. 'Mind if I take a look?'

'I do, yes. I have a luncheon appointment and a couple of dead armed robbers to cut up.'

'Humour me. It'll only take a few minutes.'

'Come back later.'

Quinn moved in the direction of the laboratory. 'He'll be in the refrigerator, right?'

'Hey!'

Quinn ignored the warning and strode through the doorway. 'What do you want to look at him for?' Carter tried to position himself between Quinn and the iron door in the corner.

'McCredie wants more detail. You know how it is. I don't want to get caught between them.'

'McCredie doesn't think it's a suicide?'

'Sure he does.' Quinn gave the doctor a reassuring pat. 'I've just got to bang in some extra detail so we're covered.'

Carter did not look convinced, but he helped himself to a slug of whisky from a coffee cup on the shelf and pulled an iron trolley out of the refrigerator. No one wanted to get caught between McCredie and Schneider.

Matsell seemed much bigger than he had on Wall Street, but maybe that was a trick of the light. Quinn checked the pockets again and flicked back the coat and jacket. Both had been tailored by a Jacob Zwirz.

Matsell's nose was too big, his cheeks and lips bulbous. The back of his skull had been concertinaed in the fall. Quinn opened the shirt and checked the chest for bruising. He picked up a set of pincers and tapped the man's incisors through his half-open mouth. 'A lot of expensive gold crowns . . .' He caught sight of something embedded in the back of Matsell's throat, probed deeper and pulled out a thick plug of cotton wool. He held it up to his nose.

Carter's face drained of colour.

'You want to explain to me, Doc, why a suicide victim would have a ball of cotton wool soaked in chloroform shoved right down the back of his throat?'

Carter did not look as if he wished to know the answer to this particular question. 'Perhaps he was trying to dull himself to the pain.'

'Of what?'

'He placed a pellet in his mouth just before he fell.'

'Sure he did. But you might want to do the autopsy now. I'll wait.'

'I'm too busy.'

Quinn gave him a withering stare. 'Doc, we can hold the line on your verdict, but this is unfinished business.'

Carter took a blood-spattered white coat from a hook behind the door. 'This had better be a good idea, Detective.' He put on his glasses, took down a long butcher's knife and a hacksaw and set to work.

Quinn forced himself to watch and was pleased that he only felt nauseous once, when Carter cut open Matsell's head and shards of skull, with congealed blood, flicked against the white-tiled wall.

Out of the window Quinn could see blurred figures hurrying through the shadows below. The headlamps of passing automobiles occasionally cut through the gloom. He moved closer and pressed his nose to the glass. A small child struggled with an umbrella, and he remembered being picked by his mother to run down to the El station to await his father's return, armed with an old Chinese parasol. He would kick his heels beneath the giant stone pillars with the other kids from Seventh and skip all the way home, singing out a hundred questions about life as a Headquarters detective.

His old man would put an arm around his shoulder.

Quinn indulged himself with the memory of the father he'd once known. He tapped a nail against the glass and traced a rivulet with his index finger, reminded now of that summer on the covered porch at the *kuch alein* guest-house on Coney Island where they had listened anxiously to the urgent patter on the iron roof until it ceased and they could head back down the boardwalk to the beach.

Carter stood before him with a glass tube and a syringe. His face was grave. 'This is most un-satisfactory,' he said.

'What is, Doc?'

'I was looking for a clear sign in the tissue that he'd been rendered unconscious shortly before his death. But whatever happened to this man, he was fully conscious when he came off that roof.'

'So . . .'

'The chloroform must have been administered after his death.'

'He was killed *before* he fell?'

'No, he certainly died in the fall.'

Quinn shook his head. 'I'm confused.'

'The plug of chloroform must have been placed in his mouth *after* he came off that roof.'

'That's impossible.'

'Illogical, but not impossible.'

Quinn took hold of the tube. 'So . . . you've tested what? His blood?'

'The tissue in his brain. There is no sign of chloroform anywhere in his system. Therefore he died before it was administered. Someone stuck the cotton wool in his mouth after the fall.'

'Why?'

'I have no idea.'

'Is it possible you're mistaken?'

'No.'

'What's the explanation?'

'I don't have one.'

'Think of something.'

'That's your job. There's no medical mystery to be unravelled. I have established the facts.'

'So,' Quinn said, 'someone wanted to make it seem as though—'

'I have no idea. It remains a suicide. I shall simply put—'

'Doc, you can't put this down as suicide.'

Carter flushed. 'Be careful what you say, Detective. There was no interference with this man before his death. What may have happened afterwards is no concern of mine.'

'But—'

'That's your job.' Carter moved to the side and took another long slug of whisky. They stood together, staring at the body.

'Thanks,' Quinn said. 'If you think of anything else, I'd appreciate a call.'

Maretsky sat behind a tall wooden desk in the basement, deep in a novel. He didn't look up as Quinn approached.

'Is Yan here?' Quinn asked. Stefan Yanowsky was the friendly giant who ran the Criminal Investigation Bureau.

Maretsky glanced into the small back office and raised a heavily tufted eyebrow. 'Have you been swimming, Detective?'

Quinn grimaced.

'It's hardly the weather for it. You'll catch a chill.'

'Good advice.' Quinn paused. 'Maretsky, you came from Shanghai, right?'

'St Petersburg, which they now call Leningrad. If you're not careful, they'll take over Manhattan. People don't believe it, but I tell you—'

'I figure the commissioner has it in hand,' Quinn said. One of Grover Whalen's first moves as head of the NYPD had been to set up a Communist Squad to combat the Red menace.

'The commissioner is a smart man. People should listen.'

'But you lived in Shanghai?'

His face puckered. It made him look like a swamp rat. 'It's not a secret.'

'And you worked in the police department there?'

'I may have done.'

'Did you know Caprisi's brother?'

Maretsky shifted uncomfortably. 'I'm not so sure.'

'You're not so sure he was there or you're not so sure you knew him?'

Maretsky didn't respond.

'What was he like?'

'Foolish. Impulsive.' He gave Quinn a significant look. 'Like all young detectives.'

'What happened to him?'

'Why do you want to know?'

'I heard Caprisi lost one brother in Chicago and another in Shanghai. He seems kind of intense. What happened in Shanghai might have had something to do with that.'

Maretsky slid from his stool and all but disappeared. 'What did you come down for, Detective?'

'I need to check if we have anything on a Charles Matsell.'

Maretsky shuffled away between the rows of box files. 'You think the commissioner will survive if La Guardia wins?' he asked.

'La Guardia won't win.'

'You never know. People are tired of scandal.'

'People never tire of scandal.'

'Maybe they're fed up with swell Jimmy and his crowd feathering their nests.'

'Don't count on it.'

'That Major La Guardia is smart, you mark my words. From the way he's talking about it, he *has* got this photograph of Jimmy and that hoodlum Rothstein together and he'll whip it out just before the big day. Maybe that'll convince people at last that Jimmy has his snout in the trough.'

Quinn listened to the Russian's feet padding through the warren of shelves. Maretsky finally returned with a dusty red folder. The name 'Charles Matsell' was stamped on the front. Inside there were notes on two traffic violations, which had been discharged five months previously. Quinn turned the file over. It had been signed out more than twenty times. Among the names on the list were Schneider, McCredie and Commissioner Whalen. It had been taken out the previous day by Johnny Brandon. 'That's a lot of interest in a pair of traffic violations.'

The Russian stared at him.

'You got any idea why, Maretsky?'

'No.'

'You want to take a guess?'

'No.'

Quinn tapped the desk. 'Check two other names for me, will you? Moe Diamond and Dick Kelly.'

Maretsky went back into the warren and returned a few minutes later. 'Nothing.'

'You sure?'

'Yes.'

Quinn looked him in the eye. 'Okay. Thanks.'

CHAPTER SEVEN

MOST OF THE OFFICE'S INHABITANTS WERE HUDDLED around wireless sets. Caprisi was at his desk, hammering at his typewriter – the other detectives wrote out their reports by hand and passed them to the stenographers, but Caprisi preferred to do his own.

'Can I take a look at your notebook?' Quinn flicked through the pages. 'Did anyone get close to Matsell after he fell?'

'Just a cop. He went off to call the precinct.'

'Who was he?'

'I don't have a name. Why?'

Quinn sat. 'Charlie Matsell had a chloroform-soaked bud of cotton wool in the back of his throat. It was put there *after* he fell.'

Caprisi was clearly bewildered by this.

'The bureau has a file on Matsell. It's been signed out around twenty times – by Schneider, McCredie, even the commissioner. Johnny Brandon took it out only yesterday. All it contains is two traffic violations.'

'Very interesting, Detective. But we can't put any of that in the report.'

'Why not?'

'We just can't.'

'Aren't you curious?'

'No.' Caprisi turned back to his typewriter.

'That's a shame,' Quinn remarked. 'I heard you were once a good cop.'

Caprisi spun around. 'And I heard you were a maverick hothead who was real lucky to get his shot at Headquarters.' He glared. 'An ambitious maverick. That ought to be a contradiction, but I guess you figure you'll end up as a top-dollar celebrity cop, like your father – or Johnny, the "Bull", over there.'

Quinn glanced at the head of Homicide's empty office. 'I'm just trying to do a job, my friend.'

'And so am I.' Caprisi pulled the sheet off the roller. 'Schneider wants to see us. Don't breathe a word of this or you'll screw us both.' He marched over to the far side of the room.

Schneider's office was larger than McCredie's and more handsomely furnished. The deputy commissioner was seated behind a wide mahogany desk, adorned with a single photograph of his wife and two grown-up sons. Without his derby and overcoat, he was several sizes thinner. His dark hair receded across a wide forehead but his face was so narrow it looked as if someone had sucked air from it with a foot pump. Bright blue eyes sparkled behind rectangular steel-rimmed glasses.

The budget lists he used as a weapon to subdue the department were scrawled on giant boards across the wall. The word 'Divers' had been written in ominously large letters alongside today's date.

He read Caprisi's report slowly. 'What did Dr Carter have to say?' Schneider didn't engage in small-talk.

Caprisi looked at Quinn expectantly.

'He just confirmed what we already knew, sir.'

Schneider's eyes narrowed. 'Why did you feel the need to go see him?'

'I was curious,' Quinn said. 'I figured there might be some extra detail to flesh out the verdict.'

'And was that curiosity satisfied?'

'Yes, sir.'

'Dr Carter tells me you not only badgered him into performing tasks he considered unnecessary but also picked up a set of pincers and probed the body yourself. Is this correct?'

'Well, sir, I—'

'Do you wish to become a pathologist, Detective?'

'No, sir.'

'Would you welcome Dr Carter's involvement in your work up here?'

Quinn shook his head.

Schneider's eyes were fixed on him. 'I'm told you found a plug of cotton wool soaked in chloroform in the man's throat.'

'Yes, sir, I did.'

'And what was the explanation for this?'

Quinn glanced at his partner for support, but

Caprisi's eyes were focused on the wall. He breathed in. Hang it. 'You see, sir, it's like this. We saw two sets of footprints in the mud at the edge of the roof. It looks like Matsell went off backwards, which means he was pushed. Add in the chloroform plug . . .'

'Perhaps it was to dull the pain of impact,' Schneider suggested. 'Had you considered that?'

'No.'

'Why not?'

'The doc confirms the cotton wool was placed in Matsell's mouth *after* he landed.'

'Anything else?' Schneider's expression combined distaste and incomprehension.

Quinn glanced at his partner again. Well, he'd come this far. 'There's sure been a lot of interest in Mr Matsell's file,' he said. 'They must have been controversial traffic violations.'

'What do you mean?'

'It's nothing, sir,' Caprisi said. 'Joe's just been covering every base . . .'

'I commend you on your enthusiasm,' Schneider said, 'but deplore your indiscipline, Quinn. You are a new boy here. You are on probation. And right this minute I would rate your chances of avoiding a return to the precincts at around zero.' He tapped his silver pen against the desktop. 'Now, I don't know what was ailing Mr Matsell. I imagine that, had we the time and the resources to investigate, we'd discover he'd been jilted. But whatever idiosyncrasies you may feel you've uncovered, that's all they are and all they will remain. Is that clear?'

'Yes, sir.'

'This city leads the world, Detective. Millions look to us. We cannot – we *must* not – falter. To say the atmosphere down on Wall Street is febrile is an insult to the meaning of the word. The newspapers have their story and, though it serves us ill, it's brief and straightforward. We will move on. Is that understood?'

'Yes, sir.'

'I hope so, Detective Quinn.' Schneider crossed his legs beneath the desk. His shoes had been immaculately polished. 'I have taken the liberty of pulling in some of your reports from the precincts, and I don't like what I read. I confess myself surprised that Chief McCredie gave you a berth here, though perhaps I shouldn't be since he has turned promoting his native kind into an art form. I shall be watching your progress with interest.'

'With respect, sir, a suicide wouldn't explain why a bunch of hoods tailed us uptown and broke into my father's apartment.'

Schneider's cheeks coloured. 'That seems to me to be a matter for you and your family. I don't see it has any bearing on this case.'

'It sure seems like it does to me, sir.'

Schneider's eyes glinted with fury. He took Caprisi's report, slid it into a buff folder, marked it 'Closed' in bold letters and placed it in his out-tray. 'You'd better go home,' he said. 'You'll be reassigned tomorrow after line-up. Good day.'

* * *

Halfway back to their side of the office, Caprisi said, 'Congratulations. You just screwed your career in two minutes flat. What in hell were you thinking?'

Quinn took his jacket from the back of the chair. 'I'm heading back down there.'

'You're kidding?'

'There's something wrong about this. You know it as well as I do. It was *me* the guys in the Chevy came after. I need to find out why.'

'Schneider just told us to close the case. Besides, it's my wife's birthday and she'll kill me if I'm late home.'

'Schneider's not the chief of detectives.'

'McCredie said something different?'

'He's more . . . flexible.' It was a straight lie, but since he'd come this far, Quinn figured he might as well keep going.

'He asked you to go back to Wall Street?'

Quinn perched on the edge of his partner's desk. 'He wants us to report in to him.'

Caprisi's gaze was steady. 'You want to tell me what he really said?'

'He—'

'This is about your father . . .'

Quinn frowned.

'Don't take me for a fool, Quinn. This is your old man's precinct. It was his apartment the guy broke into. Your sister was the last person to see Matsell alive and, by the look on your face this morning, I'd say you're pretty darned certain she knows more than she's letting on.' Caprisi watched him. 'Tell me something else. Do you know why your father turned his back on life in here as the city's number-one celebrity detective?' He reached for his coat. 'I thought not. I have a feeling I'm going to regret this.'

They strode onto the landing and banged the elevator button.

'Joe?'

Quinn swung around. A tall, stooped figure stood in the doorway. The man wore an overcoat and fedora over a neatly pressed tan suit and highly polished shoes, but his face was white, his eyes puffy and his handsome features drawn. Quinn grasped his arm. 'Are you all right, Ade?' They stood together awkwardly. 'Hey, this is my partner, Caprisi. Caprisi, this is my brother, Aidan.'

The two men shook.

'I'll see you down in the hall,' Caprisi said.

Quinn guided Aidan to a recess at the top of the stairs. 'What is it?'

Aidan's wide blue eyes glistened. He slipped his hands into his pockets, then took them out again. His brow was furrowed and his lips tight, as they always were when a situation had moved outside his control.

'What's happened? Is this about Martha's—'

'She called me at the dealership and I came home. She says she's fine.'

Quinn waited. 'You want coffee?'

'I have to go back to work.' He stared at his feet. 'I'm sorry, Joe . . . I don't know where else to turn.'

'What's going on?'

66

'It was stupid. Jesus, I'm on a good salary, there's a bonus coming at Christmas. I should have been content with that . . .'

'But?'

'I wanted more for her, Joe. She deserves it. We've talked about getting away, starting over . . . somewhere new – Kansas maybe, or out west. Somewhere we could leave the past behind. You know how it is for all of us.'

'What did you do?'

'There's a guy at work who's made a mint. He's got a system, swears by it. He's a salesman, but he's no fool. He said it was easy. Just watch for the stocks being tipped by the Wall Street columnists and make sure you head in big on the first day. That was the secret. Borrow hard and go in big on margin. I didn't listen to him at first but, heck, he's gotten a new Pierce-Arrow Roadster, a weekend place on Long Island. I watched him for a few weeks and saw him rake in the dough. It seemed like a real good bet.' Aidan forced a smile. 'You know me, Joe, I never cross a road without checking both ways . . . One day, he tipped me and I went for it.'

'But it didn't go up?'

'At first it did. So I held on. Jimmy Pike and I talked about opening our own showroom next spring. I figured I could make my stake on one bet. Then, before I'd even noticed, it fell again. "Don't sweat," my friend said, "it'll come back." But it didn't, Joe. And it hasn't. I'm down. Real down. Far down. And they're calling me in.'

'So, tell them you don't have the dough.'

'I can't do that.'

'Why not?'

'The bank wouldn't lend me the cash and my broker wouldn't let me take that much margin.'

'Jesus, Ade, you didn't—'

'Ben Siegel's boys just shook me down on Fulton. They've given me twenty-four hours,' Aidan told him mournfully. 'I didn't know it was him. This guy from the showroom said he knew a fellow on Delancey who worked with Wall Street types and was used to taking the risk. No one told me he was one of Luciano's boys.'

'Did they come looking for you earlier on Wall Street?'

'No. Why?'

'Did they talk to Dad?'

Aidan's eyes widened with alarm. 'No – why would they?'

'It's nothing. We had a tail from Wall Street to the apartment.' He squeezed his brother's shoulder. 'Relax. It must have been about something else.' Aidan's features crumpled and Quinn felt the sting of his brother's humiliation. Aidan was the sensible one. He paid the bills, negotiated the rent. Just lately, he was the only thing that had held the family together. 'What are you going to do?' Quinn asked softly.

'You could warn them off, maybe, buy me some time. I didn't want to talk to Dad. He has enough on his plate right now.'

'Ade . . .'

'I'm so sorry, Joe. I shouldn't have come.'

'How much do you owe?'

'It doesn't matter. I'll go.'

'I'm your brother,' Quinn remonstrated. 'If it wasn't for you, we'd have gone under. You know that. Tell me.'

Aidan shuffled uncomfortably. 'Three thousand . . . four, all in.'

'Where are you going to get that kind of dough?'

'When the market turns I can sell out. This stock's bound to come back. If you could buy me a little breathing space, that's all I need.'

'Times have changed for Ben Siegel and his boys.'

'I know that.'

Aidan had spent most of their childhood rescuing his fiery younger brother from the consequences of his determination to take on the world. The only other time he had ever needed Joe's assistance was when he'd taken a punt on a neighbourhood craps game. He'd gone in too deep, lost out and got into a fight. Joe had settled the score by knocking the gang's leader out cold. That boy's name had been Ben Siegel.

'I'll be okay, Joe. I shouldn't have troubled you.'

'You're my brother, Ade,' Quinn reminded him again.

'Will you tell Martha?'

'Are you kidding?'

Aidan looked relieved. 'Thanks, Joe. I'm sorry.'

Quinn hurried on down the stairs. The marble hallway below was deserted, save for a sad-looking woman, who watched him pass.

He smiled at her, but she didn't smile back.

CHAPTER EIGHT

QUINN AND CAPRISI RODE TOWARDS WALL STREET IN silence. The rain had ceased and slivers of late-afternoon sunshine glinted off waterlogged sidewalks. When a trolley-bus accident on Park Row forced them to cool their heels in a jam, Quinn watched people flood in and out of the offices of the *Sun* and the *Tribune*. On his first day in the job, Frank Dillon of the *Sun* and Bob Burke of the *Mirror* had called him up with more or less the same pitch: we like to catch detectives on the way up, they'd said, so let's share a beer some time. He'd been flattered. None of the big crime reporters had ever called him in the Bronx.

'Thanks,' Quinn said to his partner. 'I appreciate this.'

Caprisi's eyes were locked on the road ahead.

The Gardner edged forward and Quinn examined the walnut dash and leather upholstery. That was another thing about the Headquarters squad: you could demand

– and *get* – the best. As a detective in the Bronx, you'd wait a thousand years to drive a car like this, but the Gardner had been requisitioned from the traffic division simply because Headquarters was short.

'Is he older or younger?' Caprisi asked.

'Who?'

'Your brother.'

'Oh, two years older.'

'He's the sensible one, right?'

'How did you guess?'

'Because it sure as hell can't be you.'

Quinn thought of all the days – so many more of them – when Aidan had been chosen to run down and meet their father at the El station. Good brother, bad brother, Moe Diamond had once told him. Moe had never bothered to take Aidan out to the pool halls. 'What about you, Detective Caprisi? I heard . . . I mean I was sorry to hear about your brothers.'

'It was a long time ago.'

'You were close to them?'

'Like I said, it's in the past.'

'Sure. I understand.'

They turned off Park Row and wound their way down to Wall Street via the East River. As Caprisi pulled up the Gardner, Quinn gazed up at the great stone monoliths: temples to power, wealth and certainty. Flags snapped urgently against their poles along the street as men and women in grey raincoats flocked, like anxious worker ants, to join the crowd outside the giant pillars of the Exchange. A movie

71

camera was perched on the steps of the Subtreasury Building and the banner headline on the newsstand screamed: '6,000,000 SHARE PANIC; LATE RALLY STEMS LOSSES'.

A paper boy in an eight-panel cap shoved a midday edition of the *News* at them. 'There's support on the way, *organized* support.' The kid's voice was breathless. 'They say Morgan's buying. He's taken ten thousand US Steel.' Caprisi handed him a nickel.

Quinn was accosted by a pair of street kids. 'We'll look after your car, mister.'

'Sure you will.'

'It'll cost you a dollar.'

'No, it won't.'

The taller of the two boys took a step closer. His expression was filled with theatrical menace. They were such dead ringers for himself and Aidan a few years ago that he struggled not to grin. 'It's real dangerous round here, mister. Man's gotta watch out for his tyres.'

'It's okay, son. We've got a big guard dog in the back.'

'Does he put out fires?'

Quinn laughed and palmed the kid a pocketful of dimes. 'Now scram before I box your ears.'

They belted away down Pearl Street.

Quinn saw that Caprisi's face had paled. 'What are you in on?' he asked.

'I've got a guy who says the market needs a shakeout. The tip is, buy Wright Aeronautics and Du Pont.'

'Which guy?'

'He's been right before, that's all I'll say. He shouldn't tip me off, but he's doing me a favour.'

'You invest your paycheck?'

'Wise up. I'm in on margin, like everyone else. I've taken as much credit as my broker will give me. You?'

'No.'

'You should be. You want to be a goddamned cop all your life?' Caprisi gave him a thin smile and strode off in the direction of the Exchange. After a few minutes it was clear why: the shoeshine boy who'd been set up outside number eighty had drifted down the street in search of new customers. Quinn helped his partner talk the kid into a street-level café and bought him a cup of hot soup with a soda. Caprisi slipped him a dollar for his time. 'We need to ask you a few questions.'

'Mister, I already told you—'

'There's no trouble, son,' Quinn said easily. 'Finish your soda and we're out of your hair.'

'Do you know Johnny the Bull?' the kid asked.

'Sure we do.'

'He's one hell of a tough cop, right?'

'He certainly is.'

'You work with him?'

'We do, son.' Quinn propped an elbow on the table. 'But how about the guy who fell off that roof – you know him?'

The boy eyed them. 'He never gave me any business. Ethel – she works in the café behind my pitch – she said he was as Irish as Paddy's pig, but I told her, "That's wrong, it's the other guys, the big fat one and—"'

'Moe Diamond and Dick Kelly?'

'I don't know their names. The fat guy gives me some tips, and on Paddy's Day he palms me a dollar.'

'The dead man's name was Charlie Matsell.'

'I only knew his face.'

'Did you see him arrive at the office this morning?'

'Sure, in a big black Buick. I don't get to pitch because he comes right to the door.' He gestured despairingly. 'A lot of the rich fellas don't stop.'

'What time?'

'In the rush.'

'Did you see him again before he landed on the street?'

The boy pushed away his soup. 'No.'

'Did you see anything *before* he fell?'

'No . . . It was like he dropped right out of the sky. One minute, nothing, the next . . .'

'Must have been quite a shock,' Quinn said gently. 'It's okay, son. We're not trying to trick you. Just relax and think back. You're talking to a regular and polishing his shoes. Suddenly you hear a thud and a guy's landed in the middle of the street. Everything stops. Nobody knows what to do. What happens next?'

There was a long silence. 'I guess the cops came.'

'The guys from the precinct weren't called for twenty minutes,' Caprisi said.

The kid stared out of the window.

'Who went to him first?' Quinn asked.

'I don't know.'

'A cop?'

74

'Yes!'

'What did he look like?'

'He wore a uniform. I didn't see his face.'

'Where did he come from? Did he walk out the same building?'

For a moment the boy didn't answer. Then, 'He wasn't the first,' he said. 'There was another man. He barged right past me to get a look at the body.'

'Can you describe him?'

'He had on a trenchcoat . . . and a Homburg pulled over his eyes. I saw his face, but . . .' The boy shrugged. 'He was kind of thin.'

'Did you see him put anything in the dead man's mouth?'

The boy frowned.

'Think back. The guy barges past you, he crouches down next to the body. Then what?'

'I saw him put his fingers to the man's neck. Then he stood up and pushed past me again.'

'He say anything?'

'He might have said he was going to call an ambulance. Or maybe that was some other guy.'

'When did the cop turn up?'

'A few seconds later.'

'What did he do? Exactly.'

'The same thing.'

'He put his fingers to the dead man's neck?'

'Yeah.'

'Anything else?'

'I – I don't know. I don't think so.'

'Did you see either of the men put something in the dead man's mouth?'

The boy shook his head.

Quinn took out another dollar bill, pushed it across the table. 'Thanks.'

CHAPTER NINE

OUTSIDE, THE CROWD HAD SWELLED. CAPRISI STOOD ON tiptoe to see what was happening by the Exchange but he still wasn't tall enough. Quinn stopped in front of a brokerage window and peered in through the steamed-up glass at the prices being marked on the blackboard. Caprisi started walking again and they wound their way back through the crowd to number eighty. Caprisi headed to the guard at the front desk while Quinn slipped through to the back to check the stairwell. The door to the street was locked. He climbed the first flight of stairs and hung out of the window. Easy enough to drop out unseen, he thought, but no way *in* without access to the door.

He returned to the lobby, waited until his partner had finished, and then they rode the elevator.

'He's sticking to his story,' Caprisi said. 'He says no one left the building in the few minutes after the guy fell. He was in the doorway. They'd have had to shove right past him.'

'The rear door's locked, though it would have been easy enough to drop out the first-floor window. What did he say about the guy in the fancy suit who came in to see Matsell just before he was killed?'

'He claims he doesn't know who that was.'

'Do you believe him?'

'I don't know.'

'How come the cops didn't arrive for twenty minutes?'

'Everyone in the street assumes the uniform guy on the scene is going to call around to the precinct house, right? So nobody else does.'

'Maybe.'

'But he doesn't.'

'Hmm. I'll check it out.'

They got out of the elevator and climbed the stairs to the mezzanine level. The office of Unique Investment Management was locked. 'Maybe the guy downstairs has a key,' Caprisi said.

Quinn tested the hasp. It was loose, so he put his shoulder to the door and shoved. On the second attempt, it gave. He flicked on the lights. There was a single overcoat on the hat-stand, a real fancy one. The label said it had been hand-tailored by Jacob Zwirz.

'Moe?'

Caprisi was already at Matsell's desk so Quinn went down the corridor to Moe's office. The filing cabinet was packed with newspaper clippings, but apart from a pen, a pot of ink and a few paper-clips, the desk was empty. There were no memos or letters. In fact, no clues at all as to exactly what line of business Unique Investment might be in. Quinn rifled the filing cabinet again.

After a few minutes, Caprisi appeared in the doorway. 'I checked in with the precinct. Nobody can remember who called in the incident.' He held up a sheet of paper. 'I found this bill next door. It seems our friend Mr Matsell lived in a suite at the Plaza.' He slouched against the frame. 'What do you figure this outfit does? What does your sister say?'

'She's only worked here a few months. She said it was a brokerage firm.'

'But there are no clients, letters or bills . . .' Caprisi pointed at the open drawers of the cabinet. 'That's the only storage in the place. Anything there?'

'Newspaper clippings.'

Caprisi took a seat. 'So, we've got a dead guy who lived at the Plaza and a company that doesn't appear to do any business. You want me to go talk to your sister?'

'No. And she's – she's not my sister. She was adopted when we were older.'

'Your folks wanted a girl?'

'It wasn't that.'

'So . . .'

'It's a long story.'

'They're the kind I like.'

'Her mother lived in the cellar of our tenement.'

'You stole her?'

'No. She – I mean the mother – wasn't a good woman. Martha is . . . She's engaged to my brother.'

Caprisi whistled quietly. 'Okay. Are you going to ask her about this?'

'Of course.'

'You sure it wouldn't be easier to have me put a few questions?'

'Yes.'

Caprisi raised his eyebrows. 'Whatever you say, Detective.' He lit a cigarette and threw the pack at his partner. 'Tell me about this guy Moe Diamond.'

'What do you want to know?'

'Who is he?'

'Moe's not a killer.'

'I didn't say he was. But he has to be a suspect.'

'He's a hustler. He was a friend of my mother's family back home in Ireland – he and she were second or third cousins. He came out on the same ship as us and we used to see quite a lot of him as kids. He worked the pool rooms at McGraw's place. McGraw was the manager of the—'

'I'm from Chicago, not China.'

'Well, McGraw had a billiard parlour, next to the old *Herald* building. Moe used to take on all comers. He knew Rothstein and sometimes they played together, though Rothstein was the better shot. They ran a place after that in an old warehouse on Water Street, mostly dice games and poker.'

'He was a friend of Rothstein?'

'Associate. Rothstein didn't have friends. They used to go on the train together up to the racetrack at Saratoga in the summer. After that, he kind of disappeared. I heard he'd made a pile of money and shipped out of town. No one knew where he'd gone. My mother said Cuba, but there were others who said Chicago or out west. The next time I saw him was at my mother's funeral about six months ago. He offered Martha a job with good money.'

Caprisi stubbed out his cigarette in the ashtray. He moved to the edge of Moe's desk and pulled open a drawer. 'What do you figure he's up to?'

Quinn scanned the room. He wondered if he'd been wise to admit he knew Moe. 'There must be a safe. Moe was like Rothstein – always has a bankroll, so he'll have somewhere to keep it.' He checked behind the filing cabinet and the framed photographs along the wall. They shunted the desk aside and pulled up the rug on the floor. Then they worked through each office in turn, moving furniture and running their hands along every wall in search of a loose panel. They drew a blank.

Quinn seated himself at Martha's desk. He opened the central drawer. There were a few bills and neatly typed stock reports, beneath which he found a photograph of his mother in her prime, long dark hair tumbling over slim shoulders. He put it carefully aside. There was a tangled collection of hairbands and makeup in the drawer to his left, all purchased at Wannamaker's. Then he found a blue box, sealed with a lilac ribbon, and a letter addressed to him at Centre Street. He placed the box on the desk and untied the bow.

Inside, carefully rolled into a scroll, there was a collection of letters and mementoes he had sent her. She had kept the baseball cards he'd given her the first Christmas she spent with them and the picture of a snow wolf he'd drawn for her eleventh birthday. At the bottom of the pile was the letter of congratulation he had written on her engagement to Aidan.

It had taken two hours to complete, but ran to only two lines. Quinn stared at the words; they might have been written in blood. Then he picked up the envelope addressed to him. It had not been sealed.

Dear Joe,

It has taken me many hours to pluck up the courage to write, because I know the effect this will have. However, the tension between us has reached such an unbearable pitch that I can delay no longer.

You said in your letter that what happened two months ago was an expression of the most deeply held feeling, but you were wrong. It was just a kiss, an exhausted, half-crazed reaction to the tragedy of your mother's death. I was tired and miserable, my mind not a little cloudy from the effects of your father's home-brewed whisky. It was a moment of madness that must be forgotten.

You said that I do not love Aidan; that is not only untrue, but a statement of the most breathtaking arrogance. How do you know what I feel? Upon what do you base this assertion? Aidan is kind and considerate. He is steady and loyal. He has looked after all of us these past few months in a manner that is above reproach. Your father, you, me: all of us have

needed his care in our own ways. Without him, Joe,
you should recognize that you would have done your
best to pick a fight with God and pretty much anyone
else you could reach. He is a good man, with a good
job and good prospects. He is supportive of my work
at the refuge and enjoys helping children whom, Lord
knows, have little enough going for them. He is not
concerned at the effect that some of my 'political
associations' might have on his career. He has been
very loyal to me through the past two months, which
have been, on occasion, abjectly miserable. Not that
you would have noticed.

Most of all, he is the man best placed to deal with
the dark side of my experience.

Nobody wants to talk about that. Nobody should.

For this reason, I must insist that you forget what
happened that night. It was complete madness.

Please let us never speak of it again.

Love, Martha

'Are you all right, Joe?'

Quinn started.

'Something spook you?'

Quinn folded the letter and slipped it back into the
pile. 'Just bills and stock reports.'

'What do you want to do?' Caprisi asked.

'I . . .'

'You want to leave it? Maybe we should head down
to the Plaza, see what we can turn up there.'

'No. Not yet.'

Quinn returned to Moe's office. He gazed around the walls and put pressure on the floorboards. He tried to concentrate. 'Moe has to have somewhere to hide his bankroll.'

'Maybe he takes it with him.'

'He'll have hidden it somewhere he figures no one will think of.' Quinn looked up at the ceiling. His mother had always concealed her valuables in the roof space; she'd claimed it was a trick from the old country. He took a chair from behind Moe's desk and pushed at the panels. None would budge until he reached the corner. 'Give me a hand,' he said.

Caprisi moved over to the chair and Quinn clambered onto his shoulders.

'You weigh a ton,' Caprisi groaned.

Quinn fumbled in his pocket for a box of matches and lit one. 'There's something here.'

Three dust-laden boxes were hidden in the corner of the roof. He climbed in, dragged them over and handed them down to his partner.

The first box was filled with statements, all stamped 'Bank of America'. Quinn didn't have to look far. The top page listed a transfer of a cool two million dollars.

'No wonder Matsell could afford a suite at the Plaza,' Caprisi said. 'We should go down, see what he left in his room. I'll call them.'

Quinn sat at Moe's desk and flicked through the statements. When Caprisi had hung up he flipped back to the top page and circled the entry for two million dollars. 'This is their business. The cash comes in here.

Then, over the next four or five weeks, it's paid out in smaller amounts to *this* account, here. Four weeks later, it's paid back. Except now it's more than three million. Unique deducts a healthy commission, and some expenses, and the rest goes back to the original investor.'

'That's one hell of a trade.'

'This must be the broker's account.'

'So what are they buying and how can we get some?'

Quinn's eyes narrowed. Whatever they were doing certainly involved big sums, but there was nothing to prove it was illegitimate. He took a thick wad of statements, folded them and slipped them into his pocket. 'They won't miss these for a few days.'

CHAPTER TEN

AS QUINN GAZED OUT OF THE GIANT WINDOWS AT CENTRAL Park, its colours still vibrant even in the fading light, he thought of his mother. What she'd have given to spend even one night in a suite like this. The hotel had been one of her obsessions. If she had been talking about rich people from overseas or out of state, they were 'the kind who stayed at the Plaza'. A fancy girl disporting herself in a Fifth Avenue store was 'the type who gets married at the Plaza'.

They'd once called his mother 'the Princess' because, rain or shine, she would never show her face on the street unless she was decked out in her Sunday best. It was an image he clung to, far removed from the incontinent, booze-soaked shadow lying on the sidewalk, nightgown askew, that haunted his dreams.

It was hard to mourn someone who had really died a long time ago.

Quinn adjusted his jacket and touched the edge of

the photograph of Martha that still seared his chest.

The past pressed in on him. Close to the south-west corner of the park, children played among the fall leaves. One was eating an ice-cream of the kind Sergeant Marinelli used to buy them on the Sundays their father had promised to take them to Coney Island. Marinelli was from Vice and had dragged them around houses where the women wore a lot of makeup and told them they must be proud their dad was the most famous cop in New York.

'It's a swell room,' Caprisi said.

Quinn turned. The Plaza's English manager, Mr Templeton, stood beside him, arms crossed behind a perfectly tailored back. He claimed never to have spoken to Matsell, but was understandably nervous about word leaking out that one of his guests had been murdered.

The fifteenth-floor suite comprised a bedroom, bath-room and living room. A fire flickered in the hearth. 'Do you have his registration card?' Quinn said.

'Yes, of course.' The manager turned to an assistant, who produced a sheaf of papers. 'These are his monthly bills.'

Quinn took them and sat at the desk. Charles Matsell had arrived on 1 November the previous year from Havana. 'What was he doing in Cuba?'

'I'm afraid I couldn't say.'

'How long had he been there?'

'I have no idea.'

'Did he stay here before he left for Cuba?'

'Not that I am aware of, but it was before my time.'

'How long have you been here?'

'Two years.'

'Check your records, would you?' Quinn smiled at him. 'I'd like to know if he had stayed here before.'

Matsell's monthly bills were unremarkable. He rarely used the telephone and never appeared to eat dinner in the hotel. The sole extra expense – apart from breakfast – was a nightly bar bill. 'He was a regular in the bar?'

'I understand he was fond of taking a whisky in his room.'

'Alone?'

'Yes.'

'Did he ever . . . entertain?'

'I'm not quite sure I catch your meaning, Detective.'

'Broads.'

The manager cleared his throat and tugged at one end of a slim moustache. 'Mr Matsell was a valued guest. We would not have pried into his private life.'

'So, the answer is no?'

'Detective, I—'

'Yes or no, sir. It's a simple question.'

'No. I do not believe he . . . entertained anyone in that fashion.'

'Did you know him well?'

The manager seemed embarrassed. 'We do have a number of long-term residents. Naturally, if he had had a particular concern, I would have been delighted to address it, but Mr Matsell wished to keep himself to himself. We respect that here at the Plaza.'

Quinn looked at him. 'Mr Matsell was in a very lucrative line of business. It seems to us he could have bought the hotel. Do you have any idea what that business might have been?'

'Naturally, we don't make a habit of—'

'Maybe you should go talk to your staff. We'd like to know what kind of visitors he had.' The man's face reddened. 'In fact, better still, bring the guys on the front desk back up with you.'

'What – all of them?'

'Yeah. The telephonists, too.'

'But I'm not sure if they'll be in the hotel. I mean . . .'

Quinn glanced at the clock. 'It's the same shift, right?' The man turned away and Quinn waited until he heard the door click shut, then said, 'Pompous ass.'

'Doesn't mind if his guests get stiffed,' Caprisi said, 'just as long as it doesn't cause embarrassment.'

Quinn slipped through to the bedroom. Another door, which led back to the corridor, stood ajar. There was a brass clock by the bed, alongside a copy of the previous day's newspaper and a well-thumbed dime crime novel, *The Long Island Affair: A Detective Carraway Mystery*. Quinn slipped it into his pocket. He checked the drawers, which were packed with shirts, underpants, suspenders and socks. The cupboard was filled with suits. In one, he found a roll of greenbacks, which he took out and counted. More than ten thousand dollars. He threw the money onto the bed.

Like Moe Diamond's overcoat, all the suits had been tailored by Jacob Zwirz. The bedside cupboard was empty and the bathroom yielded only a set of expensive toiletries. When he returned to the window, Quinn noticed the corner of a brown leather suitcase above the closet. He threw it onto the bed, forced the lock and flipped back the lid: thirty thousand dollars in three bricks, and a large quantity of pornographic photographs. He picked up one of two girls together and another of a woman with two men. His throat was dry.

He sifted through the rest carefully. There were no pictures of Martha, half naked or otherwise. He turned one over and held it up to the light. It was just possible to make out 'Delaware Photographic. 202 Westgate Avenue, Delaware'. Quinn took out the picture of Martha. The same wording was printed faintly on the back.

He picked up the telephone by the bed and instructed the hotel operator to put him through to Headquarters. He asked for Mae Miller. 'I know it's clocking-off time, but would you be able to put something down the wire to Delaware? Tell them I need to know about a company called Delaware Photographic. I figure it makes photographic printing paper and, if that's right, I need a list of every studio it supplies in Manhattan.'

'Jesus, Joe. That could take a while.'

'Mark it down as a multiple homicide wrap, ongoing, and say I need the reply by seven a.m.'

'They'll never do it by then.'

'Mark it "critical, ongoing".'

'Is that wise? If the boss finds out, he'll—'

'If we do it any other way, I'll be lucky to get the reply by Christmas. Thanks, Mae, I owe you.'

'Sure, Joe, I'll . . . I'll do it, for you.' She severed the connection.

Caprisi walked in with another roll of dollar bills. He dropped it onto the bed and took a seat.

'How much you figure is there?' Quinn asked.

'Fifty thousand at least.'

Quinn passed across the pictures. 'Maybe these will take your mind off it.' He upended the suitcase. At the bottom, he found Charles Matsell's passport. He flicked through it. 'The guy's been everywhere – France, England, Germany, Switzerland, Cuba, Colombia, Argentina, Brazil . . .' He threw it to his partner.

There was a faint knock on the door and the manager glided in. One hand pressed the ends of his moustache. He stopped dead, mesmerized by the dollar bills.

'Fifty thousand or more,' Quinn said. 'In his case, his pockets, the closet and the drawers.'

'But we have a safe downstairs. We could have . . .' The man's eyes were popping, and he was struggling to maintain an air of distant superiority. 'I have spoken to the front desk, to Security and the chambermaid who does the afternoon and evening shifts on this floor. None of them can recall Mr Matsell receiving any guests. Nor had he stayed here previously.'

Quinn handed him one of the photographs. 'You sure there were no broads?'

'Yes.'

'Did you bring up the guys from the front desk?'

'I asked them to wait in the corridor, but I can assure you—'

'Bring them in.'

Quinn watched the two women and three men file through the door. 'Thanks for coming up. I figure you all know that our friend Charlie Matsell met with a real unpleasant end this morning.' They were silent. 'So, we need to ask a couple of questions. Did any of you see him last night?'

The eldest of the group nodded. He wore a uniform with shiny brass buttons. 'He came to the desk to get his keys.'

'What time?'

'It would have been about eight o'clock.'

'Did you speak to him?'

'No more than to say good evening.'

'Was he usually more talkative?'

'No, sir, I can't say that he was.'

'Did anything strike you as out of the ordinary?'

The man shook his head.

'Were there any visitors? Phone calls? Requests for assistance?'

'No, sir.'

'He didn't order room service?'

They all shook their heads.

'So he came in about eight, but that was the last anyone saw or heard of him. And he didn't make any phone calls.'

'I did take a message for him, sir,' one of the telephonists said. 'At least, I think it was for him. It gets so busy at that time, it's hard to—'

'Who was the message from?'

'I . . .' The woman blushed. 'I'm sorry, sir. It was a gentleman, but I can't remember who.'

'It's okay,' Quinn said gently. 'What was the message?'

'It was just . . . I think it was just that someone called, but would call again.'

'But no one did?'

'No . . . I mean, yes, that's right.'

'What happened to the message? Did you write it down and slip it under the door to his suite?'

'All messages are written out and taken to Reception straight away,' the manager said. 'He would certainly have received it.'

Quinn faced the guy from the front desk with the shiny brass buttons. 'Do you recall giving him the message?'

'I don't, sir, but I'm sure I would have. I'm certain it would have been there.'

Quinn double-checked the desk and the trash can next to it. 'Was the room cleaned today?'

The manager looked surprised. 'No. As soon as we heard, I ordered that it should not be touched.'

'Good.' Quinn found another trash bin by a lamp in the corner. There was nothing in it. He pushed back the furniture and checked behind the desk. He went through to the bedroom and located a third trash can half hidden behind the bed. In it was a piece of screwed-up paper, upon which was written: 'Mr Scher called again.'

'Is this it?' Quinn asked. 'That's your hand?'

The woman nodded. 'Yes, sir. I remember now.'

'What did it mean, "Mr Scher called again"? When did he call before?'

'I believe he had telephoned earlier in the day. At least, he said he had.'

'Was his a name you recognized?'

'No, sir.'

'Did he say anything else?'

'No, sir.'

Quinn turned to the manager. 'Have you heard the name before?'

'No.'

'Okay. That will be all for now.'

The manager took one more look at the cash and they all turned away. Quinn scooped up the money, the photographs and the passport and put them back in the suitcase. He picked it up, walked to the elevator with Caprisi and they rode down in silence.

The lobby was thronged with wedding guests, the men in morning suits and top hats, the women dressed as if for the world's last waltz. Somewhere close by, a swing band was playing 'Ain't Misbehavin'', which Louis Armstrong had just turned into the hit of the year. Quinn spotted Mayor Jimmy Walker behind a palm tree.

They made for the exit, but the mayor blocked their way. He was dressed for the wedding, with a silver-topped cane under one arm. 'Gentlemen.' He flashed them his trademark smile. 'You're the new detectives on the Headquarters Squad.'

'Yes, sir,' Quinn said.

'This is my assistant, Spencer Duncan.' The tall, lugubrious man resembled a bloodhound. 'Deputy Commissioner Schneider has told me about you. I wanted to offer my gratitude for the way you handled a difficult circumstance this morning.'

'Thank you, sir.'

'Spencer and I are great supporters of the police department, as you know. We shall be watching your career with interest. Your father was once, after all, a man to be reckoned with. Is that not so?'

'Yes, sir – I mean, I believe so.'

Someone else was waiting for the mayor's attention, so he moved on. Duncan didn't budge. 'Did your report throw up anything, boys?'

'We're still working on it, sir.'

'Did one of the guys at Headquarters speak to you?'

'Er, you mean—'

'McCredie's in charge, right?'

'Yes, sir.'

'But I bet Schneider had a word with you too. He's an ambitious guy.' It was said without wholehearted approval.

Neither Quinn nor Caprisi replied.

'It's a sensitive time, the way Wall Street is. You're smart enough to understand that.'

'Yes, sir.'

'This election could be tighter than people think. If we screw up, we'll all be out of a job.'

'Yes, sir.'

'Just as long as you get that.' Duncan patted Quinn's shoulder and edged him towards the street, which was a sea of gleaming metal. A row of finely polished automobiles disgorged more wedding guests. The women glittered under the street-lamps, dripping diamonds and decked with feathers.

'What was that about?' Quinn asked.

'I've no idea.'

'How did he know who we were?'

They watched a couple of tourists climb into an open carriage for a tour of the park. Quinn checked the time. 'I'll go and see if they've identified the guys in the Hudson. See you tomorrow.'

'I'll come with you,' Caprisi said.

'I thought you said it was your wife's birthday.'

'It is.'

'Then go home. Take her a present. I'll call you if anything shows up.'

'I want to keep an eye on you.'

If this was a joke, Caprisi's expression remained funereal.

'You really are a tough nut to crack, Caprisi, do you know that?'

CHAPTER ELEVEN

MCCREDIE HAD HIS COAT ON WHEN QUINN PLACED Matsell's open suitcase on his desk. Outside, the office lights had been dimmed and most of the detectives on the floor had long since departed; only Caprisi was left, hunched over his desk. Somewhere a wireless had been left on and the upbeat sound of a steel band floated down the corridor.

'I thought I told you this case was closed,' McCredie said. 'Schneider's been busting my balls all afternoon about you going to see Doc Carter. What's this?'

'I figured if he committed suicide, we ought at least to clear his place out.'

'Did you find anything else?'

'No, sir.'

'How much did you take?'

'Nothing.'

'C'mon, Detective. We don't believe in fairy tales here.'

'We haven't touched it.'

'You frightened of the guy from the Rat Squad?'

'No.'

McCredie stepped over. He picked up a couple of the photographs and examined Matsell's passport. 'He got around. Have you counted it?'

'Not yet.'

'You should.' McCredie handed Quinn the pictures and the passport. He shut the case. 'I'll make sure it gets into the benevolent fund, if no one claims it. And for Christ's sake don't tell Schneider or we'll never see it again.'

'But should I—'

'I wouldn't trust the little shit to take out my trash. How do you figure he can afford an estate out on Long Island? So, count it and bring it back with a note of how much is inside. I'll make sure it doesn't go missing.' He picked up his own briefcase. 'I've got to get out of here. Mrs McCredie wants to take in a show. Have you spoken to Yan?'

'No.'

'Give him a call. At this time of night, you'll probably get that Polish dwarf of his.'

'Maretsky's Russian, sir.'

'Well, they're all damned Poles to me. God knows how the basement got so full of them.' He tutted. 'We've got an ID on one of the guys from the Hudson. He's a guinea hood. Yan was trying to dig something up. We need to come up with a reason why you should have chased those guys off the pier or Schneider'll be

busting our balls all week about the cost of the divers.'
McCredie opened the door and reached for his hat. 'I'll
be home around eleven. Give me a call if Yan turns
something up.'

'Yes, sir, but—'

'What, Quinn?'

'It's just . . . You must have worked with my father.'

'Of course, son.'

'I wondered if—'

'All that's in the past. But you've a great future, so
don't worry about it.' McCredie stepped out of his
office. 'Cheer up, son. Tomorrow is another day.'

Caprisi was hammering away at his typewriter, so
Quinn slid past him and walked down the stairs to the
basement. Yan was still at his desk, devouring a sandwich like it was the last food left in Manhattan. He was
a big man, with a jovial, lived-in face and a clipped grey
moustache. Yan thought Gloria Swanson, Babe Ruth,
Ronald Colman and (especially) Commissioner Grover
Whalen overrated, but would happily have laid down
his life for the Brooklyn Dodgers.

Quinn knew all this because Yan loved to talk. He
lived in Brooklyn, surrounded by Newfoundlanders
who ran fishing smacks out of Sheepshead Bay. Quinn
had once busted a group of them for running stolen
bank bullion up to Boston, which had made them firm
friends. Yan didn't seem to like his neighbours very
much, or Maretsky, or most of the other central
Europeans he stuffed his department with.

It was an achievement to get in and out of his bureau in less than half an hour. 'Hey, kiddo,' he said, folding his newspaper. 'Is this the hero detective who chases hoods into the Hudson? You'll wish you hadn't when you see this!' He pushed a file across the desk. Pinned to the front was a photograph of a man with a thin face, large eyes and bushy brows. His name was Paulo Vaccarelli and he was a strong-arm hood for Charlie Luciano and Ben Siegel.

Quinn stared at the photograph. It was true, he'd had better news. 'You know anything else about this guy?'

'Not much.'

'Can I take a look at the files on Luciano and Siegel?'

'Be my guest.' Yan lifted the flap to allow Quinn through and led the way to a large, well-lit section close to the fingerprint division. A sign above it read 'Rogues' Gallery'. 'Welcome to the men who run the greatest city on earth.'

An entire wall was devoted to Arnold Rothstein.

Yan caught the look on Quinn's face. 'You could never have enough files on AR. He was in on everything. The bad news for you is that Charlie Luciano's his natural heir and you just gave one of his guys an early bath.'

The section on Luciano was to their left. Quinn ran the tip of his finger along the line of files and pulled out the one marked 'Charges'. It was as thick as the Bible, but there weren't many convictions. Charlie Luciano had been done for shoplifting as a kid and spent five months in a corrective penitentiary as a teenager for peddling heroin, but every charge since then – and they were numerous – had been marked 'dismissed' at a preliminary hearing. In each case, bail had been posted by the Detroit Fidelity and Surety Company and guaranteed by Arnold Rothstein. On each occasion, an assistant district attorney had reported that there was insufficient evidence to prosecute.

'Did Charlie Luciano work for Rothstein?' Quinn asked.

'Nobody worked *for* Rothstein. He was a loner. But if you want to understand who Luciano is, what he does, and what position he occupies in this city, then you first have to understand the life and times of Mr Arnold Rothstein. He was king of the underworld and link-man between organized crime and the fat-cat politicians who have their snouts buried deep in the Tammany trough. Or so it is said.' Yan smiled, with heavy irony. 'His death created a vacuum. I'd say Charlie Luciano is working hard to fill it.'

Quinn moved backwards along the line of files. 'Rothstein / Chicago Club / Saratoga'; 'Rothstein / Gambling Commission / Bag Man'; 'Rothstein / World Series Fix' . . . He took down the World Series folder, but only out of curiosity. It was part of the thrill of making it to Headquarters that you could leaf through the details of a case that had shocked America. 'What kind of guy wants to fix the World Series?'

'A guy like Rothstein.'

Quinn replaced the file and looked further along the

line: 'Rothstein / Idaho Copper'; 'Rothstein / Colombia Emerald Company'; 'Rothstein / File# 77'; 'Rothstein / Wall Street' . . . He pulled out the Wall Street file.

'Anything I can help with?' Yan asked.

'The dead guy was pushed off a building on Wall Street.' For once, Quinn was in no hurry to get away. 'When Caprisi and I left the scene, Luciano's men followed us up to my place on Seventh. Why?'

Yan pursed his lips. 'Rothstein had Wall Street connections, but not Luciano – at least, none I've ever heard of.'

'What's this file for?'

'They were bucket-shop swindles, probably before your time. Rothstein was always in the background, but we never pinned anything on him.'

'A bucket shop?'

'It's like a betting shop for stocks. They've turned into brokerage houses now, but six, eight, ten years ago, they used to have boiler rooms out back packed with salesmen trying to peddle worthless stock to suckers on a tipster list.'

'And the suckers lost everything?'

'Sure they did. Rothstein provided the bankroll, but the fixes were set up by a guy called Rice. He got folks to pile into worthless companies like Idaho Copper and sold out his own stock for an enormous profit.'

Quinn leafed through the file. George Rice had set up a newspaper called the *Iconoclast*, which had been sent out to three hundred thousand investors on a mailing list bought from a racing tipster. He had urged his subscribers to invest first in the Colombia Emerald Company. A Colombian priest, he alleged, had discovered an ancient map that had led him to a mine abandoned by the Incas, which had started producing emeralds valued in millions. Investigators had discovered no such mine existed and taken out an injunction to prevent sale of the stock, but not before Rice had made a mint.

A few months later he had tried the same fix again with a company called Idaho Copper. The file contained the headline on the front page of the *Iconoclast*, which urged its readers to 'SELL ANY STOCK YOU OWN AND BUY IDAHO COPPER. WE KNOW WHAT THIS LANGUAGE MEANS AND WE MEAN IT'.

Quinn shut the folder and slipped it back on the shelf. 'Did Luciano have any connection to this stuff?'

Yan shook his head.

'But now Rothstein's dead, he could have moved into this world?'

'He could have.'

'And he's the king now, right? If anyone was going to fill Rothstein's shoes, it would be him?'

'In theory, he still works for Joe the Boss, the man who likes to think he's the big guy. But Luciano is a maverick. That's why they cut him up.'

'Who cut him up?'

'Nobody knows. About two weeks ago, someone took Charlie for a ride out to Staten Island and left him for dead. Now they're calling him "Lucky".'

Yan disappeared into the warren of shelves and

emerged with a slim folder. Inside it was a photograph of Charlie Luciano with a vicious gash across his cheek. '*Salvatore Lucania*', it read, '*known as Charles Luciano. Born Lercara Friddi, Sicily, 11 November 1896. Staten Island Report.*'

'Those bastards out at Tottenville can't write English,' Yan grumbled.

He wasn't wrong. The stenographers couldn't type, either, or spell. Tottenville appeared with four *t*s and a single *l*. The facts appeared straightforward, though. A few weeks ago Charlie Luciano had presented himself, exhausted and covered with blood, at the front booth of the Tottenville Precinct and demanded the uniform cops order him a taxi. They'd taken him to the hospital, where his cheek had been sewn back together. The doctors said they'd overheard him say the wound had been inflicted with an ice pick.

'So, who cut him?' Quinn knew a little of this world, because he'd tried to nail Ciro Terranova, a thug who headed up operations in the Bronx and Westchester. Frankie Yale was liege lord of Brooklyn and overseer of the produce markets, while Masseria, Luciano, Lansky and Ben Siegel ran a central office in Little Italy.

Yan shrugged. 'Maranzano.'

'Who the hell is Maranzano?'

'An old moustache Pete. They sent him over from Palermo to be the boss of bosses, but Joe the Boss and Charlie Luciano told him to go fuck himself.'

Quinn thought about this. 'The point is, Charlie Luciano has to have a connection to Wall Street. That's why his men were there and that's why they followed me.'

'Well, it would be news to me.'

'Maybe he supplied the dough for these guys to play around with. Maybe something went wrong. Have you ever heard of Charlie Matsell?'

Yan shook his head.

'He was the swell who got pushed off the building this morning. His file only contained a pair of traffic violations, but it sure attracted some attention upstairs.'

'Why do you think that was?'

Quinn smiled. 'I was hoping you might tell me.'

'I have no idea, Detective.'

'If you had to speculate . . .'

'I've been here long enough to know speculation is bad for my health.' He walked briskly down the line of shelves. 'If you need anything else, come back to me.'

'There is one more thing. Do you have a file on a guy named Scher?'

Yan kept walking. 'First name?'

'We haven't got it.'

'Hold on a minute.'

He disappeared from view. A few minutes later he returned empty-handed. 'Nothing.'

'Nothing at all?' Perhaps it was Quinn's imagination, but Yan seemed older suddenly, the grime of the city etched into his forehead and the lines around his eyes.

'That's correct.'

'Does the name sound familiar to you?'

'No. Why?'

'Somebody left a message for Matsell in the hotel last night. It's maybe nothing. Thanks for checking.'

'Watch yourself, kiddo.' Stefan Yanowsky's gaze was steady.

'Sure . . . Thanks, Yan.'

A couple of steps down the corridor Quinn ran into Schneider. 'Good evening, sir.'

'Quinn. How've you been getting on?' Schneider's brow was furrowed.

'Fine.'

'I hear you've got an ID on one of the dead men?'

'Yes, sir.'

'He's one of Luciano's?'

'It seems like it.'

'That doesn't justify your actions.'

'Er, no, sir.'

'I understand you're ambitious, but charging across town in pursuit of a tangential connection to a clear case of suicide is nothing short of reckless.'

'Yes, sir.'

'Do you have any idea how much those divers cost?'

'No. I mean, not exactly.'

'They were *very* expensive. Chief McCredie may have hoodwinked the commissioner to the point where he is at liberty to play fast and loose with our budget, and plenty else besides, but I intend to see *that* changes.'

'Yes, sir.'

'This matter is now closed. You will be reassigned in the morning.' Schneider stepped back to allow someone through, then came forward again. He was not the kind of guy who was inclined to respect another man's personal space. 'Have you spoken to your father about this?'

'About what, sir?'

'The suicide.'

Quinn stared at him. 'No.'

'He's the precinct captain?'

'Yes.'

'You haven't talked to him about the incident?'

'No. I mean, not in detail.'

Schneider leant close enough for Quinn to smell the remnants of his lunch. 'What about the cash?'

'Which cash, sir?'

'I'm told you picked up a suitcase of dollars at Matsell's place?'

'Oh . . . yes.'

'You and your Irish buddies planning to walk off with it?'

'No, sir, of course not.'

'Where is it?'

Quinn hesitated. 'McCredie has it.'

'Right.' Schneider marched off.

Quinn slumped into his chair and glanced at Matsell's case beneath his desk.

'Schneider was looking for you,' Caprisi said.

'I saw him downstairs. He is one strange guy.'

Caprisi thrust a sheet of paper at him. 'I typed up a new report, which he wants to see in the morning. Matsell took his own life after a gambling quarrel. Case closed.' He pushed across a correcting pencil. 'I'm sensitive about spelling.'

'Spelling's the least of our problems. They found an ID on one of the guys they dragged out of the Hudson. His name was Paulo Vaccarelli and he was one of Luciano's strong-arm men.'

Caprisi raised his eyebrows. 'This just gets better and better.'

'Moe Diamond knew Charlie Luciano in the old days. They were enemies, but they knew each other. So, if one of Charlie's guys followed us up from the office, I figure—'

'It was Luciano's money they were fooling around with?'

'I guess.'

'Swell.' Caprisi stood and put on his coat. He pulled a bag onto his shoulder. 'But we don't need to amend the report.'

'The report says suicide.'

'It does.'

'And you figure that's right?'

'No, but I know trouble when I see it. Why do you think Schneider's so keen to have it that the guy jumped?'

'I don't know.'

'Exactly. And we shouldn't want to know. The mayor congratulates us on our excellent handling of a sensitive situation. That's enough for me.'

'Caprisi—'

'What is it, Quinn?'

108

'If I got pushed off a building, I'd want someone to ask a few awkward questions.'

'So now you're the dead banker's Good Samaritan? That is real affecting.' Caprisi stepped closer. 'I'll tell you where we're at. I saw the expression on your face when you were around that broad. Adopted sister or not, you looked like you wanted to eat her for breakfast. Well, fine. But I've got two months till I get out of here with a pension and I'm not going down with you.'

He stalked out.

Quinn pulled over Caprisi's report and read it. It was clear enough. It was what they wanted.

He drummed his fingers.

He got to his feet, put on his own coat, walked onto the landing and down the stairs. The same woman was there, waiting in the hall.

She watched him pass without a word.

CHAPTER TWELVE

THE ENTRANCE TO MCGRAW'S BILLIARD PARLOUR WAS tucked away down a dark alley next to the old *Herald* building. A single lamp created a dull cone of light, and it was so quiet that Quinn could hear rats scurrying in the trash.

The door was opened by a six-foot-five gorilla in a trenchcoat.

'This is still McGraw's place, right?'

'It might be.'

Two more men loomed from the darkness. A lot of security for a billiard hall.

'Is President Hoover here?'

'Beat it, wise guy. We're closed.'

'I'm here to see Moe.'

'He's not expecting guests.'

'Tell him it's Joe Quinn.'

'No.'

'I'm family.'

'You could be his long-lost goddamned sister for all I care. You ain't gettin' in here.'

'Just do yourself a favour and tell him it's Joe Quinn.'

The man moved towards him. 'Listen, fella, I ain't gonna say this to you again. We're here to make sure Moe don't receive any visitors. So beat it, okay?' He screwed up his face. 'You smell like a cop.'

Quinn took a step forward, so that they were nose to nose. 'I am a cop. So tell my uncle Moe that I'm here or you'll spend the rest of the night cooling off in the Tombs.'

The gorilla edged back. He glanced at his colleagues, who shrugged. 'Stay here,' he said gruffly, and disappeared.

In the gloom, Quinn could just make out the photographs from the Giants' glory years that lined the corridor. 'How long you had security on the door?'

'That's none of your business.'

'You work for Moe?'

'That's none of your business, either.'

'You guys always this talkative?'

They glowered at him. The head gorilla came back and nodded for Quinn to follow him.

The parlour was almost deserted. Moe was in the back, playing pool with the barman. He was bent over the table, his gut resting on the corner pocket. 'Evening, Joe.' He took a shot. The balls cracked loudly, but missed the far pocket. Moe puffed his cigar, sipped from the mug of ale beside him and threw Quinn a cue. 'Take Billy's place. He's no challenge.'

111

Quinn walked around the table, lined up a shot, fired and missed.

Moe surveyed the state of play for a few moments, then cleared the table. When he had finished, he took out a black triangle. 'Again. Try harder this time. Billy, get the boy a whisky. On the rocks.'

'I quit drinking, Moe. It's against the law, remember?'

'You're kidding me.'

'Of course.' Quinn took the drink and lit a cigarette. He sat on a bar stool. 'How many times am I going to have to watch you clear the table?'

Moe filled the triangle. 'You start.'

'I know that trick. You break them up.'

Moe hammered the white into the colours. Two went into the pockets, one spot, one stripe. 'Damn.'

Quinn lined up a spot. He put it down. 'You ever heard of a guy called Scher, Moe?'

'Why?'

'He called Charlie Matsell at the Plaza last night.'

'Never heard of him.'

'You figure Charlie had some dealings you and Dick didn't know about?'

'I doubt it.'

Quinn straightened up. 'How long you had strong-arm guys on the door?'

'Not long.'

'Who are they?'

'Does it matter?'

'I guess not. Where's McGraw?'

'I bought him out.'

Quinn's eyes roamed over the line of empty pool tables. 'So, it's like a private club?'

'Take the shot, Joe.'

Quinn missed.

Moe chalked his cue and circled the table.

'Did you figure out that Charlie was murdered?' Quinn asked. 'Is that why you put gorillas on the door?'

'Who says he was murdered?'

'I say he was.'

'You got any evidence?'

'There were footprints on the roof, two sets. Charlie was pushed. And someone put cotton wool soaked in chloroform in his mouth after he hit the street.'

Moe puffed at his cigar. 'That's wild talk, Joe.'

'It's in the autopsy.'

'Yeah? Who fished out the cotton wool? Some washed-up doctor who was half cut when he dropped it in and didn't remember?'

'I found it.'

Moe squinted at him through the smoke. 'Charlie was a messed-up sonofabitch.'

Quinn took out Matsell's pictures and placed them on the edge of the table. He'd been careful to keep them separate from the photograph of Martha, but he still needed to check that it was in the other pocket of his jacket.

'You trying to sell me some dirty pictures?'

'We found them in Charlie's suite at the Plaza,' Quinn said.

'So what?'

113

'Have you seen them before?'

'No!'

'You figure it's possible he took them himself?'

'How in hell should I know?' Moe threw the photographs back across the table.

'Maybe he knew some of the girls.'

'Wise up, Joe. You can buy a set like this on any street corner.'

'Charlie Matsell took a closer interest.'

Moe chewed his cigar. He pocketed a ball. 'What makes you say that?'

'There's evidence to suggest he did. You think some of the women were tricked?'

'Does it look like it?'

'Did he ever see the girls in the office after work?'

'Ah . . .' Moe chalked the end of his cue again. 'Since I figure you have only a limited interest in Miss Stacey Burrows, what you're really asking me – *again* – is whether Charlie had something going with Martha.'

'Did he?'

'He'd have liked to. Wouldn't we all?'

'That's not an answer.'

'Is this a professional enquiry, Joe?'

'I'm just asking a question.'

'Sure you are. But you forget I knew you when your little dark head barely reached my knee. I've seen the way you and that girl are together.' Moe came around the table. He sat on a bar stool, still holding his cue. 'Joe, I don't know if Charlie had a thing going with Martha. I sure doubt it. But she's a grown woman and

114

you're family, so I say as your friend that you've got to think about this. It wasn't just what her mother did. Your old man took Martha in after he found her selling *herself* on the Bowery. If you didn't know that, you should. So maybe none of you'll ever turn her into the Virgin Mary. Not you. Not Aidan. And especially not your old man.'

Quinn stared at him. 'You've got no call to be saying that, Moe.'

'It's the real world, kid. And I'll tell you something else. Your mother—'

'Leave her out of it.'

'Yeah? Well, I was sure sorry for what happened to her. She was real sick by the end, that's all you can say. She'd faded so far. But she was once a very beautiful woman – you know that?'

'Did Charlie ever take Martha out after work?'

'Relax, Joe. This is headed nowhere.'

Quinn slipped off his stool and scooped up the photographs. 'Moe, if you want to tell me what's going on, maybe I can help you.'

'Nothing's going on.'

'Then how come you've got three five-hundred-pound gorillas on the door?'

Moe put down his cue. 'You should tell your old man. Maybe he'll think about it.'

'Think about what?'

'Getting himself some protection too.'

'Why?'

'You just tell him your uncle Moe said, "Watch out."

He'll know what I'm talking about. That's all I've got to say.'

'What do you mean?'

'I'm not saying anything else, Joe. You just tell him that. And if you won't, then get Aidan to. He'll listen to your brother.'

'What am I supposed to warn him about?'

'He'll understand.'

CHAPTER THIRTEEN

QUINN LOOSENED HIS TIE AND SLIPPED OFF HIS COLLAR. 'I'M not listening!' he called.

'Liar! You can hear every word.'

He pulled a thick sweater over his head. On the dresser, there was a line of fresh starched collars. Since he didn't like to wear a shirt and collar so stiff they could have patrolled the streets alone, Quinn had offered to iron his own, but she would have none of it. This was the way his mother had always done things and there was no way on earth that Martha would try anything different.

'Joe!' she called, but he didn't move. 'If you look at yourself any longer you'll shatter that mirror.'

He wondered if he still knew the man staring back at him.

He ducked through to the main room. She was bent over the hob. He nudged her aside, picked up the coal shovel and fired up the belly of the stove. 'You should use the gas,' he said. But he knew she wouldn't because his mother had always insisted it was too expensive.

'I didn't have any dimes.'

He reached into his pocket, found one and pushed it into the meter. He saw there was a pile in the jar.

'You should put something on your hair,' she suggested. 'That way, you could hold the tufts down.'

'I like tufts.'

'Then no wonder you don't have a girl.' She laughed at him, but her smile faded as she read his expression. She stirred the stew in the pot and brought the spoon to her lips. 'It tastes okay,' she said, with ill-disguised surprise. 'You want a soda?' Before he could answer, she picked up the newspaper. 'See here? They chose my question.'

'What question?'

'I sent in a question for "The Inquiring Photographer". I got five dollars! Are you ready?'

'Shoot.'

'What is your pet driving peeve?' She rolled her eyes and put a hand on her hip. 'That is the question our enquiring photographer put to people today, sent in by Miss Martha Quinn of Seventh Street.'

'It's a fascinating question.'

'It is. Mr Royal W. Healey, the manager of the Astoria Hotel, says that "It is the fellow who drives right down the centre of the road at a speed of twenty miles an hour and refuses to move over to the right side of the road so the faster-moving automobiles can pass. The name for such a driver should be 'roadhog'." '

'Amen.'

'Are you a roadhog, Joe?'

'Sure.'

'When are you going to take me for a ride in that new Gardner?'

'Soon.'

'What about Mrs E. L. Bouchet of Flushing? "I am annoyed most by the motorcycle cops who hide around corners and behind bushes, waiting to give someone a summons for going thirty or thirty-two miles an hour. I don't mind the manly cops who stay out in the open as a protection to other drivers." ' She looked at him. 'Are you a manly cop, Joe?'

He wondered who she thought this performance was kidding. 'Yeah,' he said.

'And finally, there is Mr Anthony Di Leonardo, who "doesn't like the fellow in back of me who honks his horn continuously, particularly when I'm doing the right thing and there is nothing else I can do. It makes me feel like getting out of my car, ripping his horn out and hitting him on the head with it." '

'Easy, Mr Di Leonardo.'

They lapsed into silence. Quinn watched her catch her reflection in the mirror. Martha flushed. She hated to display a trace of vanity. 'Please put on the wireless,' she said.

Quinn reached behind him and flicked the switch. It was tuned to WABC and the sound of a concert band filled the room. He nudged down the volume.

Martha closed the newspaper and dropped it on the

table. She looked at the headline. 'You should buy on the dip. That's what everyone's saying.'

Quinn thought of the fear on Aidan's face as his dreams of impressing her dissolved. 'I wouldn't sink a dime on Wall Street.' He sat down. 'You want to tell me about Charlie Matsell?'

'No.'

She tried to get past him, but he gripped her arm. 'You sure about that?'

'I wrote you a letter.'

'I don't want a letter.'

'I'll send it to you. It's better that way.'

'For whom?'

'Joe . . .' She shook herself free.

'You ever hear of a guy called Mr Scher?'

'No.'

'He didn't call your office?'

'No, he did not.'

'Who was the man who came in to see Charlie just before he died?'

She looked as if she might deny any such visit. 'I don't know.'

'Did he have an appointment?'

'No.'

'Had he been in before?'

'Maybe. Mr Matsell was secretive about his appointments.'

'What did this guy look like?'

'He wore a suit.'

'Was he tall or short, fat or thin?'

'Tall.'

'Describe him.'

'Oh, hell, I don't know . . . He was kind of heavy-set. He had baggy cheeks, like a bloodhound.'

Quinn leant forward. 'Say that again.'

She hesitated. 'What?'

'He had cheeks like a bloodhound, right? That was what you said.'

Martha turned away from him so that he couldn't see her face. 'Well . . . yes. I mean—'

'He was tall, slightly stooped?'

'I – I'm not sure. Why?'

'I was thinking about someone who expressed a sudden interest in the case tonight. You know who I mean by Spencer Duncan?'

'He's the mayor's aide. He's in the newspapers.'

'You figure it could have been him?'

'No.' She shook her head emphatically. 'No.'

'Do you know what he looks like?'

'Yes. I mean, no, not exactly.'

'You figure Charlie Matsell could have been connected to the mayor's office?'

'Of course not.' Martha stirred the stew again, making sure her back was to him.

'Did Charlie Luciano ever pay a visit?' he asked.

'No – I mean, I have no idea. Mr Matsell kept his cards real close to his chest. I told you already, he didn't want me to discuss his business.'

Quinn watched her. 'How did you get mixed up with these guys, Martha? What was it they wanted from you?'

'They didn't want anything.'

'You figure this performance is going to convince me? Is that it?'

'I don't know what you're talking about.'

'Oh, I think you do. And sometimes it's hard to figure you out.'

She spun around. 'How could *you* possibly be expected to do that?'

'I know what you've been through.'

'Do you? I doubt it. Your idea of hardship is a father who won't stroke your ego now you've made it to the big-time.'

'Cruel.'

'True.'

Her eyes bored into his. The tempo of the concert band changed and Martha reached forward and twirled the volume button. She came across the room and took his hand. 'Come on, I'll pretend you're Ronald Colman.'

'You're not fooling anyone, Martha.'

'Just dance.'

She guided him around the tiny room and the wooden floorboards creaked beneath their feet. There was a thump on the ceiling below and Martha stamped hard in return. She leant her head back and pretended she was Gloria Swanson. It was a long-standing joke, but neither of them laughed.

They twirled faster and, as they danced past the coal fire, beads of sweat crept onto his brow. Her warm body pressed close to his. The tempo slowed. He closed his eyes and tried to shut his mind to the scent of her. His fingertips tingled and he could feel her breath on his cheek.

They turned and turned again.

They moved slower still.

There was a tap on his shoulder. 'Mind if I step in?'

Aidan's smile was thin. Their father stood behind him in the doorway.

CHAPTER FOURTEEN

MARTHA SWITCHED OFF THE WIRELESS. GERRY TOOK OFF his overcoat and placed it carefully on the hat-stand. He smoothed down a few strands of hair and sat at the far end of the dinner table. Quinn took his seat opposite Aidan. There was a lamp on the wall behind them, but Martha lit a candle. She took down some bowls and filled them with stew, then placed a glass of ale in front of each man. She busied herself tidying up.

'Sit down, woman,' Quinn's father said.

Aidan loosened his tie and sipped his ale.

The room was silent save for the sound of cutlery scraping against china. Gerry wiped his mouth. 'Aidan's trying to sell me his new model: the Dry Lakes Roadster! He says refined folk upgrade their automobile every two years. Should I believe him?'

Nobody answered.

'You see, Ade? We ain't convinced. Or maybe we're just not *refined*.'

124

Martha sat down. She kept her eyes firmly on the table.

'I figured Schneider and the boss might kill each other today,' Quinn said. 'Mae says that now Schneider's wrapped up Vice with Fogelman in the chair he wants to hound Ed McCredie off the main detective floor.'

Everyone else stared at their food.

'I thought McCredie was a legend as chief of detectives, so how come Schneider's got in there? Why doesn't the boss just tell him to go back to counting paper-clips?' Quinn persevered.

'Nobody wants to talk about this at table,' Gerry said.

'I just figured—'

'Nobody wants to talk about it!'

Quinn stared at his father. 'I saw Moe tonight.'

Gerry continued to eat. He did not meet his son's eye.

'He had three five-hundred-pound gorillas on the door; said you should do the same.'

'Has he just got out of the asylum?'

'He was rattled.'

'He has plenty to be rattled by.'

'I figure Charlie Matsell's murder must have got to him.'

'He wasn't murdered.'

'Can you two quit the shop-talk?' Aidan said. 'Martha's had a hell of a day.'

'Did you hear about the report on the chloroform?' Quinn asked his father.

'C'mon, Joe . . .' Aidan said.

'I can speak for myself, Aidan,' Martha replied.

'What chloroform?' Gerry asked.

'Somebody put cotton wool soaked in chloroform in the guy's mouth after he fell.'

Gerry frowned.

'That make any sense to you?'

'No.'

Quinn looked at each member of his family in turn. No one would meet his eye. He finished his stew. 'I figured, Dad, that you might be able to give me a few tips here. You worked for McCredie. You knew Schneider. You were the number-one detective. Everyone says so, even the mayor. Some of the old-timers like Yan asked to be remembered to you.'

'I don't want to talk about Yan.'

Quinn had lost count of the number of times he'd tried to talk to his father about Centre Street. 'I know it was a long time ago, Dad, but there's a bunch of guys still there you'd know.'

His father's face was stony. 'I said I don't want to talk about it.'

'Okay . . .' Quinn agreed. 'But I've worked for this chance, so I guessed you might want to—'

'That's your concern.'

'What is?'

'It's your affair.'

'Why do you say that?'

'Joe, the place is so bent they shit crooked.'

They were silent again. Then, 'Dad, I slogged my guts

out to get there, so is there any chance you could at least offer a little advice?'

'You wanted a shot at the big-time.' Gerry sighed. 'I'm sorry you didn't see through it. If you want to hang out with a piece of trash like Moe Diamond and listen to his scheming, malevolent nonsense, then that's your business, but don't bring it to this table.' He put his spoon down and scooped up the rest of the stew with a hunk of bread.

Aidan and Martha still avoided Quinn's eye. 'Oh, I get it.' He pushed his chair back. 'You know, just once in your life, it wouldn't have killed you to offer a few words of encouragement,' he told his father, then retreated to his room, closed the door and lay on his bed.

The apartment fell silent. Laughter echoed in the stairwell. He closed his eyes. After a few minutes, he heard the door go and listened to their footsteps on the stairs. His father and Aidan would be in McSorley's now until gone midnight.

Quinn picked up the dime novel he'd taken from Matsell's room at the Plaza and leafed through it. He lost interest and listened to Martha doing the dishes. He moved to the doorway.

'I'm not going to take your side,' she said.

'I'd never ask you to. But it wouldn't have killed him to wish me luck.'

'Maybe he's right.'

'About what?'

'Headquarters.'

'Times change, but he doesn't.'

'He's been a cop thirty years, Joe. He knows a thing or two. Maybe he expected you to ask his advice before you applied.'

'When has he ever been interested?'

Martha shot him a sideways glance. It was true that whatever support and encouragement had been available was directed at her: the finest clothes, a handsome allowance, trips to New Haven and Washington . . .

'I don't care,' he said. 'It's just a fact.'

'You do care. And you don't see the way he talks about you when you're not around. If you did, you'd never say such a thing.'

Quinn stepped forward. He picked up a dish-towel.

'Leave them,' she said.

'I'll give you a hand.'

She took a plate from him. 'I don't want help.' She finished stacking the dishes and turned to Aidan's collars, took them down from a peg and pulled out a bottle of Lintel's starch.

'I'll turn in,' he said.

'Goodnight.'

Quinn washed his face and brushed his teeth at the sink in the corner, which, with the bath, was screened from the main room by a curtain. He walked down to the men's room on the floor below, then went back to his room, switched off the lamp and lay down.

Moonlight illuminated the wall above him, which was covered with scenes his father had painted from Mark Twain's *Huckleberry Finn*. In the first, Jim, the runaway slave, helmed the raft down the Mississippi while Huck sat trailing his feet in the water. Then there were the two grifters, the 'lost dauphin' and the 'English duke', being tarred and feathered by the townsfolk after their dismal performance of the *Royal Nonesuch*. And, finally, Jim's attempted rescue, complete with Tom Sawyer's bleeding leg . . .

Quinn closed his eyes. He and Aidan had lain there half dead as their father painted these scenes and their mother sat reading the story in a voice shaking with emotion. It was 1918, the year New York had succumbed to an epidemic of Spanish flu, with all the fear and hysteria that can only be engendered by the sight of corpses piling up in the streets. The diagnosis of a school doctor one afternoon in December had been considered a death sentence. He and Aidan had been taken to a special sanatorium created in the assembly hall, convinced they would see neither parent again.

But their father had ignored the instructions on quarantine procedures – he certainly didn't take orders from anyone but himself. That night, as Quinn and his brother had fallen prey for the first time to the sweats, Gerry had stormed in, scooped them up onto his broad shoulders and carried them home through the cold, gloomy streets.

For four days they had remained locked in this room while both parents fought to keep them alive. At night, when he was conscious, Quinn would watch his parents sleeping on the floor beside him. Sometimes, when he had the strength, he would reach down and touch his father's hand.

He rolled over now to face the wall.

On the fourth day, the sweats had broken and his parents' careworn, exhausted faces had been transformed by joy and relief. The Christmas that followed had seen an explosion of happiness: the four locked inside, staging mock battles with Gerry's army of lead soldiers, drinking and eating, laughing, Gerry belting out songs on his accordion as their mother stood on the table to sing . . .

Quinn opened his eyes again. It was the time before his father had left Centre Street and his mother had got sick.

It was the time before Martha had come.

He listened to her moving about next door. She was starching the shirts. Then he heard her filling the bath.

She slipped into the tub and lay still, scooping handfuls of water over her body.

A dog barked. There was an altercation on the street outside, discordant voices rising to a crescendo, then falling swiftly away.

He heard her stand to soap her body. He placed a pillow over his head, closed his eyes again and tried to think about something else.

He sat up, lit a candle, reached for his jacket and pulled out the photograph. Martha's lithe body appeared arched, her breasts high and proud.

His hand would not steady so he sat up and placed the picture on the bed. He tried to look past the supple limbs and luminous skin. The edge of a briefcase was visible, perched on a mahogany chair, and a pile of rumpled sheets. It looked like the chair he'd seen in Matsell's suite at the Plaza, but it was hard to be sure. In one corner he made out the tip of a man's shoe and the turn-up on his pants.

He closed his eyes briefly, then looked again. A bead of sweat trickled down his forehead. There had been at least two men in that room.

He put the photograph on the floor and lit another candle. He looked in the dark corners and made out something else: the tips of a pair of fingers on the far side of the bed.

Three men . . .

His gaze returned to the centre of the frame. Her eyes were closed, lips parted. A sheen of sweat glistened between her breasts. The jersey suit spilled onto the floor. A buckle hung loose on her garter belt. He heard Moe's voice: 'None of you'll ever turn her into the Virgin Mary.'

Quinn put the photograph face down on the chair beside him.

He stood and moved to the door, then slipped quietly into the main room.

She was kneeling in the bath, visible through a slit in the curtains. She rinsed her shoulders, half in profile, her hair matted and damp, the curve of a breast glowing in the candlelight.

She turned slowly. Her hand fell from her shoulder as her eyes met his.

131

Neither moved.

There was a shout from the stairs, distant, but enough to shatter the spell. Quinn snapped around and walked away. He shut his bedroom door and lay on the bed again.

CHAPTER FIFTEEN

IT WAS NOT A WARM NIGHT, BUT THE AIR WAS CLOSE. HE heard Martha drain the bath and tidy the apartment before she retired to the small bedroom next to his. Once or twice a soft footfall strayed close to his door. He imagined her lying only a few feet from him, on the other side of the wall.

He got up and tugged back the curtain. A man smoked a cigar and stared up at the clear night sky from the outside stairwell of the building opposite. Quinn drew up his own window and climbed up to the roof. A gust of wind tugged at a line of washing. Sheets flapped. He sensed movement. 'Sarah!' He caught the girl as she tried to bolt out of the rear of her makeshift shelter alongside the skylight. She didn't have the grace to look ashamed. 'I thought we had a deal.'

Defensive brown eyes beneath a thick mop of hair gazed up at him. 'I don't like Mrs Brackenridge.' Mrs Brackenridge was the large class teacher who liked to stroke her breast while reading *Hiawatha*.

'Martha will kill us both,' Quinn said. The deal had been that Sarah went to school during the day and stayed at the orphanage on week nights so that they could officially sign her out at weekends. 'Why didn't you go?'

'I did.'

'Then why didn't you stay?'

'I don't like her.'

'We've had this conversation.' At least a dozen times, Quinn thought.

Sarah didn't answer and Quinn met her blank stare with barely concealed irritation. Martha had found Sarah trying to sell herself on the Bowery. After three months at the refuge, she had registered with an orphanage from which she constantly ran away. So, unless she was stealing roasted potatoes – mickies – from the Irish boys along Seventh, or following Martha around town like a shadow, she was mostly to be found in the shelter she had built for herself up on the roof.

'What are you going to do tonight?' he asked.

'I'll stay here.'

'You can't. It's sure to rain again.' Quinn grabbed her tattered sweater. It was soaked. 'Martha will go crazy. I'll have to take you back to the orphanage.'

'No!'

'Sarah, it's been raining all day. It's wet as hell up here.'

'I'll go to school tomorrow.'

'You've broken that promise a million times.'

'I'll keep it this time.'

'You didn't this morning.'

'I will so!'

Quinn sighed.

'Maybe we could go out to Coney Island tomorrow,' she said.

'I have to work.'

Whenever he and Martha took the kid out it was always to Coney Island, where she would accept a cool drink and disappear into the crowd. It didn't take a genius to figure out what she was looking for. Quinn had watched her trail soldiers the length of the board-walk. He'd searched military records across the United States for anyone who shared Sarah's surname, and had even written to a sergeant in Iowa.

The girl sat down, pulled her legs tight to her chest and stared at her shoes. Her faraway expression reminded him of the days soon after they'd found her. Quinn bent down and touched her shoulder. He knew from bitter experience that further argument was point-less. Sarah curled up in the corner of her den like a dog.

Quinn sank down against the wall and lit a cigarette. 'You know, Sarah, life is easier if you play by the rules.'

'Do you play by the rules, Joe? Do you?'

Quinn blew a thick plume of smoke into the night sky. He felt a few spots of rain on his cheeks.

'You love her, don't you?' Sarah said.

Quinn didn't answer.

'Do you think she loves you, too?' Sarah threw a stone over the lip of the roof. 'I figure she does.'

'It's not as simple as that.'

'Why don't you—'

'Do you still trail her around town?'

'No.'

'You follow her to work?'

'No.'

'It could be important.'

'That's when I'm supposed to be in school. There'd be big trouble if she caught me.'

'There's going to be big trouble anyway.' He looked at her. 'You can't stay here.'

Sarah curled up tighter. 'She didn't come to see me.'

'She won't always be able to see you, Sarah.'

'What do you mean?'

'She'll go away, maybe. Have you thought of that? Aidan wants to take her to Kansas.'

Sarah thought about this. 'She wouldn't go,' she said finally. 'She'd never go with him.'

'They're engaged.'

'I know, but still . . . She'd never leave the refuge. And she thinks La Guardia will be mayor one day.'

'She stopped working for him months ago.'

'No, she didn't.'

'What do you mean?'

'She had a cup of coffee with him last week. I saw her.'

'Where?'

'Just by the Cocoa Exchange.'

'I thought you said you didn't follow her to work?'

'I don't . . . It was just that time.'

'Did you ever see her with anyone else from her office?'

'No. I only followed her that day.'

'Sarah . . .'

'I swear it!'

'Do you have any idea what she and Major La Guardia talked about?'

'No.'

'Did you ever see her go to a hotel? Did you ever see her go to the Plaza?'

'The Plaza?'

'Yes.'

'No . . . no.'

'Sarah, tell me the truth.'

'I swear!'

'It's important.'

'I followed her that one time when she met Major La Guardia. She didn't go to a hotel.'

'What about other times?'

'I only followed her once.'

'But you've seen her at the Plaza?'

'No. Never. I swear.'

'She might have gone there with Mr Matsell.'

'I never saw it.'

'If she's in trouble, Sarah, you can help her.'

'I didn't see nothing.'

Quinn sat back. Sarah's relationship with the truth was so inconsistent that it was hard to be sure when she was hiding something. 'Did you ever see her go to a photographer's studio?'

'No. Why?'

'She didn't go there after the Plaza?'

'I've never been to the Plaza. I didn't see her there. But why?'

'It doesn't matter. And don't tell her I asked.'

'Why?'

'And don't ask so many questions.'

'Why?' She gave him a grin.

He clipped her gently around the ear.

Quinn smoked his cigarette to the stub and flicked it across the brick divide. 'Are you hungry?'

'I took some food.'

'I know.' Quinn stood. 'If I tell her you're here, she'll be mad at you.'

'Please don't tell her.'

'You can't live your life up on this roof.'

'Maybe I'll be a detective, like you.'

Quinn ruffled her hair. 'Yeah, maybe you will.'

He awoke to the sound of a heavy footfall upon the stair, then muffled voices. A few moments later, Aidan stumbled in. 'Joe,' he said, 'are you awake?'

'I am now.'

'I'm sorry.' Aidan took off his suit and lay down on the bed. Quinn sensed the tension in him.

'Forget what I said earlier, Joe. It's my problem.'

'I said I'd take care of it and I will.'

'I shouldn't have got you involved.'

'I've got the money.'

Aidan was silent. 'That's not possible.' He sat up again. 'Joe, I only told you this afternoon. Where did you get it from?'

'It's under your bed.'

Aidan swung his feet to the floor and flicked on the light. He pulled out a small wooden box and looked inside. He stared at it for a long time. Then he came over, sat down, wrapped his arms around his brother and hugged him. 'Joe . . .'

'It's okay, Ade.'

'No, it's not. I don't deserve a brother like you.'

'Sure you do.'

'I don't.' He paused. 'Where did you get it?'

'You don't need to know that.'

'Will there be trouble for you?'

'No.'

'Are you certain?'

'I'll handle it.'

Aidan closed the box and pushed it back beneath the bed. 'I owe you.'

'You owe me nothing. You're my brother.'

'Do you think Dad knows about this?'

'No.'

'Will you tell him?'

'Of course not.'

'He'd say I was a fool.'

'He thinks we're all fools.' Quinn turned over. 'And he'll be right if we don't get some sleep.'

A door slammed in the courtyard below.

'I love her, you know. I just wanted to do something

special, something she wouldn't expect. She's been through so much, I figured it would—'

'I know, Ade.'

'We sure were blessed the day she came into our lives.'

'Ade, I really have to get to sleep.'

'Sure, Joe. I'm sorry.'

Quinn stared at the wall briefly, then closed his eyes.

'Joe, will we ever stop trying to impress the old man?'

Quinn contemplated this in silence. 'He's already impressed by you.'

'But he loves you.'

Quinn opened his eyes and focused on the paintings on the wall above him. He traced the one of Jim and Huck on the raft with his finger. 'Do you remember Dad making these pictures?'

Aidan didn't stir.

'Ade?'

'They're still there, aren't they?'

'Do you remember the Christmas afterwards, when it was just the four of us? You, me, Mom, Dad . . .'

'Of course.'

'You ever wish we could go back to that?'

'What are you trying to say, Joe?'

'It's just—'

'I know you had an argument with Martha. But don't take out on her your frustration with Dad. Nothing has been her fault.'

'We never talk about what happened. Why did it go wrong?'

140

'Mom got sick, Joe.'

'You ever ask yourself why?'

'She drank too much.'

'But why? She wasn't sick before that Christmas. You were there . . . you know what she used to be like. You remember.'

'She never liked us to talk about the past. You know that. It made her worse.'

'But she's dead now.'

Aidan sighed. 'Come on, Joe.'

'The year after that Christmas, Mom and Dad started to argue, he left Centre Street, we took in Martha and Mom got sick.'

'Mom got sick because she drank too much, Joe. Now she's dead. Who wants to talk about that? There's no point harking back to a day when it was just the four of us. That was a long time ago. We can't have it back. Dad is different. We're all different. Even talking about it . . . Well, that's just hard on Martha. Nothing's her fault. So thanks for helping me out with the dough, Joe, but goodnight.'

Aidan switched off the light. A few minutes later, he was snoring softly.

CHAPTER SIXTEEN

THE FIRST SPLINTERS OF SUNLIGHT PIERCED THE WINDOWS high in the walls of the Grand Street gym as Quinn danced from side to side, pounding the punch-bag with increasing ferocity.

After a few minutes, he let the pace slacken. Sweat poured from his half-naked body. A movement on the far side of the hall caught his eye. He had thought the gym was empty, but now he saw that his father was sitting on one of the benches, watching him. Quinn fought to catch his breath. Gerry stood up and walked to the podium. 'I thought I'd find you here,' he said. He pulled on a battered pair of gloves, climbed up and took a stance.

'I'm done, Dad.'

'C'mon. You won't kill me.'

Gerry danced forward and tried to land a punch but, instinctively, Quinn ducked away. The older man came again, with a swing to the stomach and a jab to the face, which his son easily blocked. Quinn counter-attacked and broke his father's defences, but stopped short of a strike.

They floated around the podium in the dappled pools of sunlight. Quinn parried everything his father threw at him. After a few minutes, Gerry's wide forehead glistened with sweat. He took off his gloves and laughed. 'You haven't lost your touch, Joe.'

Quinn lobbed his own gloves onto a bench. They climbed off the podium and he slipped on his shirt and jacket.

'Aren't you going to soap yourself down?' Gerry said.

'My partner can't smell.'

'The guy from the Rat Squad?'

'Yeah.'

'What's he like?'

'Intense, but thorough.'

'Good cop?'

Quinn shrugged. 'The other guys hate him.'

'Do *you* think he's okay?'

'I don't know. Yeah, I guess so.'

'That's all that matters, then, right?'

Quinn didn't answer.

'He married?'

'Sure.'

'Kids?'

'One, I think. A boy. Why?'

They lapsed into silence. Quinn went to his gloves, bashed them together and watched the dust rise. He slipped on his leather boots and put the ones he used for

143

boxing on the rack. 'Schneider was there in your time, right?'

Gerry swung a leather bag over his shoulder. He watched a couple of kids slip through the far door. 'Yeah.'

'Did you get on with him?'

'Nobody gets on with Schneider.'

'How about the Bull? You get along with him?'

Gerry put his own gloves back on the shelf and picked up a small holdall. He stopped in the corridor and glanced at the noticeboard. He was one of the directors of the Grand Street gym. 'We're getting a new canvas.'

'Who's paying for that?'

'Tammany.'

Big Mick Murphy stopped to buttonhole Gerry about the drains. He was a stooped giant, with cheeks like balloons and long white whiskers. Gerry promised to lean on the committee to make sure they were fixed. He stepped out onto the sidewalk and looked up at the sky, now heavy with rain. 'I'm sorry, son. I know I've been . . . difficult sometimes.'

'We understand, Dad. It's only been a few months.'

'I don't just mean since your mother died.'

Quinn waited. He felt light-headed.

'You don't have to prove anything to me, Joe.'

'I know.'

'I just wanted to say that.' The old man took his arm. 'Give me a ride home. There's something I'd like to show you.'

144

They drove the short distance in silence.

The dining-table in Gerry's apartment was covered with lead soldiers, which had been newly repainted. They had once used them to re-enact the battle of Saratoga, with red-coated British regulars, German mercenaries from Brunswick in blue, Canadians, Loyalists and a wild band of Iroquois Indians on one side, and the patriots who had flocked to Gates's standard from Vermont, Connecticut, Massachusetts and New Hampshire on the other. Gerry had even mended the model of Neilson Farm, which he had once placed atop an imaginary Bemis Heights.

Quinn was entranced. 'Where did you find them, Dad?'

'In the attic. I figured one day you'd have a son and . . .' He shifted from one foot to the other. 'They're for you anyhow. Take them when you're ready.'

'What about Aidan?'

'I asked Ade. He said you should have them.'

Quinn sat by the table and weighed a soldier in his hand. He wasn't sure he understood the message. He touched his boot against the door of the cupboard where his mother had hidden her booze and thought of the times he'd seen his father's hunched shoulders in the half-darkness as he carried her, inert, addled, to the bedroom.

'I'm sorry if I made Mom sick, Joe. I never meant to.'

'You didn't.'

'I did.'

'How?'

Gerry didn't answer. The void opened between them again, and Quinn didn't know how to fill it. He examined his father's brushwork on the soldiers; he had always done such things with meticulous care. Gerry took his uniform raincoat down from the peg and made for the door. 'Good luck, son.'

'Dad, hold on a minute. I'll give you a lift to the precinct.'

But he was met only by the sound of receding footsteps on the stairs.

Quinn kicked his heels and watched the dark clouds chase each other across a brooding sky. He bought a couple of apples from a stall, then a cup of coffee and a morning newspaper from the Italian hole-in-the-wall grocery store.

By the time he reached the Gardner, a bunch of kids had surrounded him. 'Give us a ride, mister!' He let them stand on his tailgate halfway down Seventh Street, then put his foot on the gas and tipped them off.

As Quinn arrived Caprisi checked his watch. 'McCredie brought the meeting forward half an hour because of this business in Murray Street.'

Quinn took off his overcoat, hung it on the stand and followed his partner down the corridor to a packed briefing room. Mae Miller and Kitty Barry, the only female detective at Headquarters, leant against the back wall. Kitty nodded to him but, like the others, avoided Caprisi's eye. Quinn went and stood beside them.

146

Mae leant over. 'I got an answer from Delaware, Joe. They gave us the name of their agent in New Jersey. He supplies all the stores in Manhattan.'

'Thanks. Stick the number on my desk and I'll call him.'

'You've enough on your plate. I'll get onto him as soon as he's in.'

The commissioner and Schneider strode through the doorway, Johnny Brandon and O'Reilly hot on their heels. As the newspapers never tired of pointing out, New York's foremost detective was movie-star handsome: Brandon's square jaw, straight nose and penetrating eyes showed to particular advantage alongside O'Reilly's slack, pockmarked features. The two men shot hostile glances at Caprisi.

'Okay, girls.' McCredie stepped in front of the blackboard and scanned the room. 'Where's Byrnes?'

'He went up to Syracuse last night,' O'Reilly said. 'I'm doing the brief for him.'

'Okay, listen up. We've got a big slate this morning. For those of you who don't read the newspapers, or are too idle to ask your colleagues what's happened in your absence, we broke the siege in Murray Street last night. Two of the guys are laid out and two more have taken a trip to the Tombs. I want all of you to make sure you get down to line-up this morning. Take a good look at the guys we brought in. We've got nothing on file and Yan doesn't recognize them, but we figure they must have a record somewhere. Those of you with recent experience in the precincts need to pay particular attention. Maybe they're small-time local hoods. We have one still on the run.' McCredie held up a crude drawing. 'This is all we've got until we can persuade the others to assist us. Take a good look. Finding this jerk is today's priority and I want him nailed by sundown. Any of you have anything to say, bring it straight to me. The men hired a black Cadillac sedan from K and B Auto Rentals at one twenty-three Suffolk Street. The plate number is on here. It's not been returned, so maybe our man has it. O'Reilly?'

'Yes, sir.'

'On your feet.'

'Yes, sir.' O'Reilly shuffled a piece of paper in front of him. 'Okay. For anyone who wasn't around at the end of last week, this kid Amy Mecklenburg went missing Wednesday morning on the way into town. Her uncle is a garage mechanic in the Bronx and he failed to show for work the same day. The girl's mother said she believed he was due to go to Syracuse for the weekend and the local boys up there have someone matching his description getting off the train on Thursday with a girl. But we've found no sign of them. We've checked the hotels. Danny went up there last night with some of our uniform boys to oversee a door-to-door.'

'Anything else?'

'Yeah. I'll mark the plate number of the guy's old Ford on the board, just in case the train story is wrong. We've put out an all-stations alert.'

'What happens if it's not the uncle?' Kitty asked.

The room was silent.

148

'Time's running out, right?' she went on. 'If it's somebody else and we don't get to her soon, she's dead meat.'

O'Reilly looked about him for support, but most people in the room were stony-faced. 'We're pretty sure it is the uncle,' he said.

'But what if it isn't?'

'We're checking out every lead we have. Danny's in Syracuse. I'm working this end with the rest of the boys.'

'Her mother is down there in Reception, waiting. I saw her again this morning. They seem like a nice family. Why would the girl have run off with the uncle?'

'There's nothing more we can do, Kitty,' McCredie said.

'We can go public. I'm sure Mr O'Reilly will have no trouble speaking to his friends at the newspapers.'

O'Reilly glared at her.

'Kitty,' McCredie said, 'you know what's happening here.'

'Sure. We're going soft on it because there's an election.'

'We're not going soft on it.'

'Then let's put out a call for help.'

'If we don't find her by Wednesday, we will.'

'She could be dead by Wednesday.'

'We can't go public with every goddamned girl who goes missing for five minutes.'

'She's been missing five days.'

McCredie glanced over his shoulder at the commissioner. 'We figure it's a domestic case and we'll proceed on that basis until something shows us otherwise. We've got a lot of guys on it, so it should all happen pretty quick.'

'So, City Hall doesn't want a pretty white girl missing in the middle of an election. Shall we tell her mother that?'

'That's enough, Kitty.'

She threw up her hands in disgust.

'Right.' McCredie cleared his throat. 'Those are the two big-ticket items for this morning. Anything else?'

No hands went up.

'Okay, anyone who's got time, pitch in to help find this guy from Murray Street.' He slammed his book shut. 'That's it. Don't forget line-up, which will begin in five minutes.'

The men pushed themselves to their feet. O'Reilly made his way over to Quinn. 'You've got their pulses racing, son.' His breath stank of whisky.

'About what?' Quinn asked.

'The mayor was in here this morning to talk to McCredie and the commissioner. Johnny figures it was about your suicide.'

'Why?'

'You tell me. Maybe the dead guy was a big shot. Oh, and by the way, I should stay away from the dyke.'

Kitty grimaced in his direction. 'Get lost, O'Reilly, you great fat baboon.'

CHAPTER SEVENTEEN

A SHORT MAN IN A SLOUCH HAT STOOD CENTRE STAGE.

'Vita Morello,' Chief Inspector James Pyke called from the lectern. 'Arresting officer, Michael Sullivan. Mr Morello says he's from Bridgeport, Connecticut, but they've got no record of him there and neither do we.'

'He's just off the boat,' someone shouted at the front. 'New muscle.'

Morello glowered at the roomful of detectives and uniforms.

'Mr Morello,' Pyke went on, 'was arrested at eleven p.m. last night while in the act of holding up a hole-in-the-wall grocery store on Twelfth Street.' He flipped the chart. 'Anyone got anything on him?' He glanced around the room. 'Moss, quit gossiping. Take a good look, gentlemen. I've got a feeling this may not be the last we'll see of Mr Morello. Next . . .'

Caprisi was propped against the wall in the far corner of the gymnasium, a cigarette stuck to his lips and his

151

hands stuffed deep in his pockets. Quinn pushed through a group of uniforms to get to him. 'How much longer?'

'Four more.'

'Have we had the guys from Murray Street?'

'They were first up.' Caprisi let the cigarette fall from his lips and ground it into the floor.

'Right,' Pyke continued. 'Shut up, all of you. This sorry piece of humanity here is Pierre Devlin, a gentleman of Belgian extraction. Lives at two twenty-three, Twenty-third Street. Arresting officer, Swire. Offence, attempted abduction of young female and involvement in the white-slave trade.'

One of the officers at the front shouted something, but Pyke ignored him. 'Take a close look, gentlemen. Mr Devlin has not been very enthusiastic about assisting us with our enquiries. We believe he's linked to the dance-hall ring we busted two weeks ago. Mr Devlin was running the girls down to Philadelphia and St Louis in a sheep truck and bringing others back to brothels in Red Rock. He operated out of the same dance hall on Coney Island as Mick Cleaver who, you may recall, is currently a guest in the Tombs for selling his own sister. There's also a possible link with the case in Brooklyn – the missing girl went for an interview out on Coney Island the day she disappeared. Maybe her uncle was plugged into the ring.' He surveyed the room. 'I suppose it's too much to ask for Byrnes and O'Reilly to show up—'

'I'm here,' O'Reilly shouted. He was with Brandon

and the other big guns in the squad. 'And I'm sober.'

Pyke gave a sigh of disgust. 'Any of you seen this man before or know anything about him, go straight to McCredie, because O'Reilly's too damned stupid to make sense of it. Next . . .'

'If there's a link with Coney Island, how come they're so confident it's the uncle?' Quinn whispered.

'I don't know, Joe,' Caprisi said. 'It's not our case.'

'Why is it such a big deal for City Hall?'

'La Guardia told the *Sun* last week that underworld figures were behind these abductions. First Rothstein, now your friend Luciano.'

'Yeah, but Kitty has a point if—'

'C'mon, Joe. O'Reilly's a buffoon, but Danny Byrnes is a good cop when he wants to be. And, like I said, it's not our case.'

Quinn swung back to face the room. There was a good turn-out this morning, maybe two hundred detectives in all, plus the uniformed officers who'd made the arrests. The purpose of this gathering was to check if anyone recalled questioning a culprit in another context. McCredie and the big shots thought it was a waste of time, but no commissioner had had the balls to abolish it.

The detectives always gathered in groups. The safe and loft boys stuck together; so did the men from the pickpocket division. Kitty usually stood on her own, though she was sometimes courted by the more junior guys in the main Headquarters squad. Fogelman and the men from Vice were on the left, close to Schneider.

McCredie, Brandon, O'Reilly and the other old-time Irish cops were gathered to the right, just visible through a thick fog of cigarette smoke. Hegarty stood with them in shirt-sleeves and vivid red suspenders, a cigar pressed to his lips. As Centre Street's powerful press spokesman, he'd helped turn his old pal Johnny Brandon into a star. He'd already offered to do the same for Quinn. *You've got potential, kid, I'm telling you.* Quinn found it hard not to be flattered by that.

Brandon glowered in their direction.

'What's eating the Bull?' Quinn said.

Caprisi grunted.

Quinn slipped through the crowd to intercept the chief of detectives as soon as the line-up was finished. 'Excuse me, sir.'

'Quinn . . . yes?' McCredie's expression made it clear this was not a wholly welcome encounter.

'I wondered if I could have a word.'

'Sure.' McCredie didn't move as Brandon and the others came up alongside him.

'I mean in private.'

He raised his eyebrows. 'Okay, but maybe later. Is it urgent?'

'No . . . no.'

'Come see me at clocking-off time.' McCredie strode away and took the stairs three at a time.

Caprisi and Quinn were a few paces behind Brandon, O'Reilly and Hegarty. As they approached the lower landing, all three slowed. O'Reilly turned first and, with two great fists, took hold of Caprisi's collar and swung

154

him around. As soon as his feet hit the floor, Hegarty punched him square in the face and Brandon spun him through a door into the equipment room.

Caprisi recovered, landed a punch and retreated. O'Reilly stood in the doorway and barred Quinn's path. 'This isn't your fight, kid.'

'What the hell are you doing?'

'We just heard O'Dwyer's going to the Chair for killing that nigger, so the guinea here is going to pay for it.'

'He didn't have anything to do with O'Dwyer.'

'He worked for Valentine.'

'Then go after Valentine.' Quinn heard a groan. He saw Caprisi double up. Brandon towered over him with a nightstick. Hegarty spat out his cigar and rolled up his sleeves. 'Get out of the way,' Quinn said.

O'Reilly grinned. 'Scram, kid.'

Quinn lowered his voice an octave. 'Get out of the way. And that's your last warning.'

O'Reilly laughed. 'My last warning? Did you hear that, boys? Take it from me, kid, you need to get the hell out of here.'

Quinn punched deep into O'Reilly's belly. The big man crumpled forward, eyes popping with surprise and pain, so Quinn set him up with a left and finished him off with a powerhouse right. O'Reilly flew backwards, bounced off the door and skidded along the floor.

Quinn stepped into the room. Brandon and Hegarty towered over Caprisi, nightsticks raised. 'Get out of here, kid,' Hegarty said. 'We've marked you out for the top. We're going to make you a star. You don't have to soil yourself with this rat.'

Caprisi struggled to his feet, bloodied but not beaten. 'Listen to what Mr Hegarty says, rookie,' Brandon told Quinn. 'Back off or we'll break your neck.'

The room was full of metal cabinets. Nightsticks and bulletproof vests were stacked three deep. Discarded shirts and jackets hung from pegs or were strewn across wooden benches. The room stank of sweat and boot polish. 'Leave him alone,' Quinn said.

Not a single hair on Brandon's handsome head was out of place. Vivid blue eyes fixed Quinn with a steady gaze. The Bull darted forward, but Quinn easily side-stepped the blow. Caprisi struggled to his feet and landed a punch on Hegarty, who stumbled back into a cabinet. Brandon swung the nightstick again and this time Quinn felt it whistle past his ear.

'Aren't you going to even things up?' Brandon asked. He pointed to a nightstick, which had clattered to the floor.

Quinn made to reach for it, then danced forwards instead and jabbed viciously with a left and a right. Brandon staggered back, dazed. Hegarty landed another blow on Caprisi, who fell to his knees in the corner.

Brandon leant against a shelf. He had a cut to his right eye and a tuft of hair flopped over his forehead. He feinted one way, then swung again. Quinn ducked. He jabbed twice to the stomach and followed with an uppercut to the chin. The Bull's head snapped back and he flew over a bench.

Caprisi was on the floor now and Quinn saw Hegarty bring his stick down across his back. He moved quickly. Brandon was barely on his feet, but he kicked him in the shins and gave him three swift blows to his solar plexus and jaw. The Bull went down hard, banged his head against the edge of a bench and lay still. O'Reilly watched from the doorway, but didn't intervene.

Caprisi pushed himself unsteadily to his feet, and somehow ducked another blow from Hegarty's nightstick. Quinn kicked the back of Hegarty's right knee, pulled his shoulder around and struck him square on the nose. The press chief squealed like a stuck pig and tripped over his friend, so that they lay across each other like a pair of circus clowns.

Caprisi dusted himself down. Quinn picked up his partner's wallet, which had spilled onto the floor, and slipped a photograph of an attractive dark-haired woman and a small boy back inside it.

'You'll pay for this,' O'Reilly said, but he made no move to block their path.

'No,' Quinn said, jabbing him hard in the chest. '*You*'ll pay for it. Don't ever come near either of us again.'

The Irishman didn't respond.

'Have you got that, O'Reilly?'

'Sure.'

'And you can give your buddies the same message when they wake up.'

'Sure, Joe.'

Caprisi was out in the corridor, walking with

difficulty. They reached the men's room and examined themselves in the mirror. Caprisi had a cut lip and a bruised cheek.

'Is your back okay?' Quinn asked.

'No.' Caprisi ran a tap and began to clean himself up.

Quinn offered him a handkerchief. 'It's been washed.'

Caprisi dabbed his lip, which was swelling rapidly. He arched his back and grimaced with pain.

'You want me to take a look?' Quinn asked.

'What are you – a goddamned nurse as well as Jack Dempsey?'

'Maybe they broke something.'

'It's bruised is all.'

'You should tell the doc.'

'Where in the hell did you learn to fight like that?'

Quinn examined his fists. He didn't have a scratch on him. 'You think we should tell McCredie?'

'About what?'

'About what just happened.'

'No.'

Quinn hesitated, but the question had to be asked. 'You reckon he knew about it?'

'Of course.'

Caprisi washed and dried his hands. 'You want to go take a look at Charlie Matsell's bank accounts, right?'

'Sure I do.'

'What is it you figure you're going to find?'

'I don't know.'

'I don't believe that, but seeing the way you fight, I'll take it on trust you know what you're doing. So, let's go. And welcome to the wilderness, by the way. You just fought your way out of the Irish in-club.'

They walked downstairs to the central hall. The woman Quinn had seen the previous day was still sitting there. She watched them pass.

'Is that the mother?' Quinn asked, as they came out onto Centre Street.

'Yeah.'

'Goddamn.'

'Exactly.'

When they reached the Gardner, Quinn didn't get in. 'She looked sick. Did you see her eyes? We should check she's all right.' He retraced his steps.

'I thought you wanted to go back to Wall Street.'

'In a minute.'

'C'mon, Joe, she's O'Reilly's problem.'

'We both know how reassuring that must be.'

The woman turned slowly towards him as he approached.

'Ma'am, are you okay?' She made no response. Quinn crouched down beside her. 'Ma'am . . . Mrs . . .'

'Mecklenburg,' Caprisi said softly.

'Mrs Mecklenburg, are you okay?'

'Has there been some news?'

'No, ma'am. We're not working on your daughter's case. I just wanted to check you were all right. I saw you sitting here last night and again early this morning.'

'Isn't everyone working on it? I thought nearly all of your officers would be.'

'A whole lot of them are. You've seen Detectives O'Reilly and Byrnes and their team.'

She was shaking now. The tremor had begun in her hands and spread quickly.

'Ma'am? Mrs Mecklenburg?'

People waiting in the lobby were staring. Quinn and Caprisi helped her to a bench at the back of the hall by the telephone booths, out of sight.

She was oblivious to them. 'Get Mae,' Quinn whispered.

It seemed, for a moment, as if grief would consume her, but she fought to regain control. She wiped her eyes. Her forehead was damp with sweat. 'It'll be all right,' she said. 'I'm a foolish woman. Detective O'Reilly said he'd find her.'

Quinn crouched down again. 'Ma'am, has anyone been looking after you?'

'Detective O'Reilly says they don't believe that . . . There's nothing to suppose that . . . It'll be a misunderstanding, won't it? Girls can be so . . . silly sometimes.' She tried to laugh. 'Do you have children, Detective? You look too young.'

'I sure hope she's with her uncle, ma'am.'

'With *Peter*?' She frowned. 'No. I've told Mr O'Reilly that he would never do such a thing. I mean . . . I cannot . . .' Tears rolled down her cheeks. 'Why would anyone say such a thing? Peter's a good man. He's kind and gentle. I don't understand. He was always due to be away this weekend. I told Mr O'Reilly that.'

'Ma'am, did Detective O'Reilly ask someone to come down here and take care of you?'

'He said I should go home but . . .'

'When we're done here, I'll go upstairs and see if I can find anything out.'

'Perhaps there's been an automobile accident. Maybe they're in hospital and unable to place a call.'

'Could be.'

She pulled a photograph from her pocket. Her hand shook so much that it fluttered to the floor. Quinn picked it up. 'She's a beautiful girl, ma'am.'

'That's the little dog I bought her for her thirteenth birthday. I've asked the neighbours to look after him. He'll be so happy to see her back.'

Mae appeared with Caprisi. She touched the woman's shoulder. 'Mrs Mecklenburg, I'm sorry to see you like this. Please, come with me.'

'Where will you be?' Quinn asked, as Mae led her gently away.

'Downstairs.'

Quinn watched them go, then went to the central staircase.

He found his quarry in the corner office. O'Reilly was alone. He stood up and backed away. 'Jesus, Joe . . . the Bull's with the doc.'

'I'm after some extra dope on this Brooklyn case.'

'What – what do you want to know?'

'The girl's mother's downstairs. She's not well.'

'I told her to go home.'

'Yeah? Well, she didn't take your advice. She says it

can't be the uncle. Have you got anything else? Any other leads? Anything at all we can give her?'

'They always say that, Joe. The guy was supposed to be in work Wednesday and Thursday but never showed up. Johnny's about to talk to her. He'll be down as soon as he's finished with the doc.'

'I thought Danny Byrnes was handling it.'

'He is, but McCredie's getting nervous and wants it cleared up real quick.'

'Mae's with her,' Quinn told him. 'Do me a favour and go give her an update. I'll check if she's all right later on.'

'Sure, Joe.'

CHAPTER EIGHTEEN

THEY WALKED DOWN TO THE GARDNER WITHOUT speaking, climbed in and Quinn headed south past the Tombs and City Hall. There had been an accident in front of Jacob Leisler's oak, so he took a side road and worked his way back towards Broadway. Leisler had been hanged by the British for opposing colonial rule, and Quinn had never been able to ride past the tree as a kid without being told his story. Sometimes he'd thought it was the only thing that made his father, an Irish rebel to his core, feel at home.

'Why'd they do that?' Quinn asked. 'Just leave her there . . .'

Caprisi sighed. 'It's O'Reilly. What more can you say?'

It had started raining again and great fat drops bounced off the hood.

'Kitty's on the money. Imagine how bad it'll look if it comes out we didn't find the girl in time because of a bunch of politics.'

163

'Like I said, Danny Byrnes is a reasonable cop. McCredie's bound to go with his judgement.'

'Hmm. I still say it's a mistake.' The traffic was slow. 'Tell me something,' Quinn said. 'How come you joined Valentine? I figure you're smart enough to do anything you want.'

'It was a chance to get to Headquarters.'

'That was it?'

'Yeah.'

'Do you regret it?'

'No.'

'What was he like?'

'Honest.'

'It must be kind of hard nailing other cops, though. Look how our friends back there took the news on O'Dwyer.'

'It's not so hard when you see how it all ends up.'

'What do you mean?'

Caprisi arched his back and grimaced again. 'You know our friend Charlie Luciano? Valentine estimated he made upwards of ten million dollars last year from liquor alone. How do you think he got away with that?'

'So, there are a few precinct captains who—'

'A few precinct captains? C'mon, Joe, you're smarter than that. You think all those Headquarters boys are going to pass up the chance to take a cut of some of that action?'

'Who's on the payroll?'

Caprisi dabbed his lip with the handkerchief.

'O'Reilly?'

'Maybe they all are.'

Quinn snorted. 'Even McCredie and the commissioner? Give me a break.'

'The commissioner got rid of Valentine.'

'Only because everyone hated the snooping. You can't run a force if every single cop is looking over his shoulder the whole time.'

Caprisi shoved the handkerchief into his pocket.

'I'm not condoning it,' Quinn said, 'but are you going to tell me it's the end of the world if O'Reilly or even the Bull turns a blind eye to the liquor business? Don't you take a drink?'

'You can be a naïve bastard, do you know that?'

'Hell, just because I—'

'You want to know what it means? I'll tell you. Imagine you're just an average guy. Not a cop, or one of those corrupt sachems who run Tammany Hall, just an ordinary, average swell. You go out to a bar one night and you find that one of these hoods is sitting at the next-door table. He likes your wife, thinks she's real pretty, and he has to have everything he wants. On the way home, he tells his boys he'd like to borrow her. She puts up a bit of a fight, so when they're finished, she's all messed up. They decide it's easier if she takes a ride to the bottom of the Hudson.'

'Okay—'

'No, it's not okay. That was a real case. I had to look into it. The precinct cops, whose job it was to bust the guy, were so bent they could have pulled a cork. Now we've got rid of Valentine there's nothing to stop them.'

They pulled up outside the Bank of America branch on Broadway, just south of Exchange Alley, but Caprisi wasn't finished. '*That*'s why I joined Valentine and *that*'s why I'll defend him.'

'I get the point.'

'Maybe up in the Bronx or over in Long Island, it doesn't matter. Maybe it's a while since you had any dealings with the likes of Charlie Luciano but, trust me, down here it's different.'

'You're telling me that even Commissioner Whalen is—'

'I'm telling you I don't know anything for sure any more. If you want the dope, Valentine thought Schneider and the Bull were probably taking the liquor dough. But that's not the point. If it turns out we're on Luciano's tail and we piss him off, you'll take a bath in the Hudson for good and there'll be nothing I can do about it.'

'Maybe things will change.'

'Don't hold your breath.'

'La Guardia's making a hell of a play for City Hall. People say he's straight.'

'He hasn't a goddamned chance. Not unless you believe in miracles.'

Quinn looked out at the entrance to the bank. 'So, do you think we should drop this?'

'I didn't say that.' Caprisi pushed open the door and ducked out into the rain. 'Don't put words into my mouth.'

'Relax. I'm not trying to get you into trouble here.'

'You may not be but, believe me, trouble is where we're headed.'

The Bank of America, Lower Broadway, teemed with people, mostly women. As Quinn waited in the hall, young girls in tight-fitting skirts hurried around them, attending to the crowd by the counters. He looked up at the vaulted ceiling. Everything about the bank smacked of power and wealth, from the gleaming brass ashtrays to the spotless carpets and finely polished mahogany desks.

Caprisi returned with an attractive blonde. Quinn grinned at him, but he didn't respond. The woman led them up to the first floor and along a narrow corridor to an office overlooking Broadway.

The manager of the branch was an Ivy League type, big and heavy-set. His tailor-made suit was a little too snug, and his thin moustache and wavy hair, thick with brilliantine and combed back off his forehead, failed to hold back the years. Quinn put him at a shade over fifty. His conspicuous, shallow charm reminded Quinn of Commissioner Whalen. 'Benjamin Francis,' he said, reaching out a hand. 'Violet said you require some assistance.' His smile faded as he caught sight of Caprisi's face. 'Are you all right, Detective? I can get Violet to—'

'I'm okay.'

'You want a drink – a cup of coffee, some water?'

'No.'

Caprisi placed the statements they'd taken from

167

Matsell's office on the desk and Francis sat down. Quinn noted the thick carpet and the fancy paintings on the wall. This wasn't your average Bank of America branch. 'Nice place you have here, Mr Francis.'

'Thank you.' He waited for Quinn to say something. 'Are you folks from Headquarters?'

'Homicide.'

Francis picked up a silver box and offered them both a cigarette. They declined.

'I guess you have a lot of Wall Street clients,' Quinn said.

He flashed them a salesman's smile. 'That's why we're here.' He tapped a cigarette against the box and lit it. 'How can we help?'

'Well,' Quinn began, 'the problem we have, sir, is that someone pushed one of your clients off a roof.'

'Good Lord.'

'His name was Charlie Matsell.'

'Matsell? I'm not sure I know him.'

'He was a partner in Unique Investment Management, based at eighty Wall Street.' Quinn pushed a sheaf of bank statements across the desk. 'They received some real big sums from this account here, which looks like it's also held with your bank. We need to know whose name is on the ticket.'

Francis's cheeks coloured. 'Well, I—'

'You could be of great assistance to us, Mr Francis. You understand that, where such serious sums of money are involved, we're bound to examine anyone connected extremely closely.'

Francis looked from one to the other and back again. Quinn suspected he knew perfectly well who held the account, but allowed him to go through the charade of leaving the room and reappearing five minutes later with a name written upon a piece of headed paper: the Olive Oil Company.

'The Olive Oil Company?' Quinn said. It had to be a joke.

Francis wasn't laughing. 'According to our records.'

'And who owns it?'

'I'm not sure that I—'

'Does the name Luciano mean anything to you, Mr Francis?'

'No . . . I mean, yes, I'm aware of who he is.'

'Does he have an account here?'

'Not to my knowledge.'

'Does he own the Olive Oil Company?'

'I don't believe so . . . I don't know.'

'Mr Francis, do you figure someone like Luciano would have wanted to invest in Unique Investment Management?'

'I . . . I have no idea.' Sweat glistened along his hair-line.

'Sir, we've a lead here that we need to follow,' Quinn said.

'Of course. Whatever we can do.'

'We'd appreciate it if you'd let us have a look at *all* Unique's statements for the last two years.'

'Detective, I cannot do that.'

'Sir—'

'Ben – please call me Ben.'

'Okay, Ben.' Quinn moved to the window: indistinct figures traipsed down the rain-sodden sidewalk. 'This is a homicide investigation.'

'I know that, but all our accounts are confidential. You must understand—'

'Sure, Ben. But the problem is, we can't take no for an answer here.'

His forehead creased. 'Then you must get legal authority. I cannot simply—'

'We don't have time for that.'

Francis tried to get up, but Quinn put a foot behind his chair, then sat on the edge of his desk. 'Ben, you know as well as I do that there's something wrong with these accounts.'

'I know no such thing.'

'Sure you do. I can see it in your eyes. Unique isn't your regular kind of company, is it?'

'I have no idea.'

'I think you do, Ben. I figure you knew something was wrong the moment we walked in here. And, seeing the look in your eyes, I'm betting you also know all about the Olive Oil Company.'

'Detective, I really must insist—'

'Don't make us loosen your memory in the Tombs, Ben.'

'Are you threatening me?'

'Yeah.'

'I shall call my lawyer.'

Quinn clamped his hand on the telephone. 'Ben, you

don't want us to march you out of here in front of all those clients, do you?'

Francis swallowed hard.

'Now, the Olive Oil Company is a Luciano concern. Isn't that right?'

'I'm not sure that I . . .' He shook his head. 'I don't know. I cannot say.' His face had flushed bright red. They heard the honk of a departing ferry. 'I have never met Mr Luciano. I have only ever dealt with Mr Lansky.'

'Mr Meyer Lansky?'

'Yes.'

Quinn removed a pen from his pocket. He pointed at the statements. 'Take a look at these. You'll see a pattern. The money – here it's two million dollars – comes across from the Olive Oil Company. Unique trades it. I'm betting these transfers are to a broker's account. A few weeks later it comes back. But now – abracadabra – it's more than three million.'

Francis stared at the figures.

'Here's what we need, Ben. All the statements that relate to Unique's accounts since the day they were opened. We'll have to find out if these transfers *are* to a broker and, if so, which one. And we'll want all the statements you produced last year for the Olive Oil Company.'

'I can't do that!' Francis took out a handkerchief and wiped his brow. 'You must understand, these people enjoy client privilege. You don't have a warrant. I cannot simply let you—'

'And these transfers here, the regular ones, relatively small sums, but they're always going to the same accounts. I need to know who the accounts belong to.'

'Gentlemen, please, be reasonable. I cannot provide you with clients' private details.'

'Ben, we've been over this.'

'Even so, it's just not possible to—'

Quinn smiled. 'You know what they do to men like you in the Tombs?'

'I'm calling my attorney. You came marching in here—'

'By the time you get hold of him, you'll be wishing you'd never been born.' Quinn grabbed his wrist. 'Ben, you're withholding important information in a homicide investigation. Don't make us spell it out for you.'

Francis pulled his arm free. He rubbed his hands together. A muscle twitched in his cheek. With clients like his, Quinn didn't blame him for being nervous. 'No one will know, you say?'

'That's right.'

'No one? That's a promise?'

'Not a soul.'

They all knew the consequences of crossing a man like Luciano, and it said something about Ben Francis that the distant threat of discovery and punishment by the Mob was less frightening than the shame and discomfort of a more immediate trip to the Tombs. 'You'd better make sure I don't regret this,' he said. He opened the door. 'Violet, could you come in here a moment, please?'

The willowy blonde hurried in. It was clear from the way Francis talked to her that she was used to ministering to his needs.

Once she'd gone, the banker stood brooding by the window. Once or twice, he made a desultory attempt at conversation, but they fell quickly back into silence. When Francis went out to the bathroom, Caprisi put a hand on Quinn's shoulder. 'You're a cruel bastard,' he said approvingly.

Violet placed the first box on the desk and smiled at Quinn.

'Please,' Francis said. 'Help yourselves.'

'You weren't interested in how they made so much money, Mr Francis?' Caprisi asked.

'I don't . . .' He looked from one to the other. 'If you need anything else, I'm sure my secretary will be able to assist you.'

'I'm sure she will,' Caprisi muttered.

Quinn leafed through the Unique statements. Periods of inactivity, when only the regular monthly outgoings persisted, were followed by a series of transactions of the kind they'd already witnessed. Over the eighteen months since the account had been opened, the sums being paid in by the Olive Oil Company had grown every quarter, starting at a couple of hundred thousand dollars and rising to the final investment of three million.

Violet came in with another box containing the Olive Oil accounts. She put it on the floor beside Quinn's chair. 'There are three more. Do you want them all?'

'Sure. Oh, Violet?'

She turned back.

'Did Mr Francis tell you about these other accounts?'

She shook her head.

Quinn picked up one of the sheets. 'On the Unique statements, there are monthly payments to a series of accounts. Here – you see? We need to know where these were held and in whose name.'

'Yes. I'll – I'll see what I can do.'

'You can do that, right?'

Violet made sure she wasn't being observed from outside the room. 'He said everything but those accounts,' she said.

'Why do you think he said that?'

'I don't know.'

'Then you'd better go and—'

'I'll get them,' she said. She took the sheet and smiled at him again.

Quinn flipped open the top of the new box. 'Jesus . . .' He scanned the figures on the first page. 'How much do you guess the Olive Oil Company has in its account, to the nearest hundred thousand?'

'Five million.'

'*Twenty-seven* million.' Quinn paused, astounded. 'Twenty-seven million dollars. There are almost no debits, just credits.'

'Except to the guys at Unique?'

'Yeah.'

'No wonder our friend Ben didn't want us in here.'

Quinn whistled. He looked up at the portrait that

dominated the wall above the desk. 'Twenty-seven million,' he said.

'I told you they were rich.'

'You saying they got all this from liquor?'

'Why not?'

'I don't know. I just figured . . .'

Quinn turned his attention back to the pile of statements and worked through them. Once in a while there was a debit on the account, but mostly it was a long record of cash sums paid in. 'Why do you think they were in bed with Matsell?'

'Unique had a good proposition. They saw a chance to bring some of their dough above board and make it clean.'

'You think the Olive Oil Company has ever even seen a bottle of olive oil?'

'No.'

Violet shimmered in. She had a pad of paper in her hand. 'I have the information for you.' She pushed her glasses to the top of her nose. 'I'm afraid the first two numbers are for accounts at different banks, but these two are held here.'

'Go on,' Quinn said.

'One of the gentlemen is a Jeremy Norton; the other, Simon Rosenthal.'

'Rosenthal is a columnist,' Caprisi said. '*Daily News*.'

'What does he write about?'

'He picks stocks, right?'

They looked at Violet, who nodded.

'Who's Norton?' Quinn said.

'I believe he works for the *Tribune*, but you'd have to ask—'

'He also picks stocks?'

'I believe so,' she said.

'Sounds something like the old Wall Street fixes Rothstein used to run,' Quinn remarked to his partner. 'You buy up stocks, then pay columnists to write them up.'

'What? A guy from the *Tribune*?'

'Why not? Maybe Yan's wrong.'

'About what?'

'Luciano *is* muscling in on Wall Street.' Quinn stood. 'We need to ask him how he was making so much dough.'

'No, we do not,' Caprisi said, but Quinn was already halfway out of the door.

CHAPTER NINETEEN

THE ENTRANCE TO LUCIANO'S HEADQUARTERS WAS sandwiched between a chop-house and a drugstore. Only the tiny peephole in the door hinted at something more interesting within. Quinn knocked, and they waited in the drizzling rain. A couple of kids eyed them from further down the sidewalk.

The flap on the peephole was whipped back and an eyeball surveyed them. 'What do you want?'

'We've an appointment with Mr Luciano,' Quinn said.

The peephole was bolted shut and they heard footsteps fading into the distance. A couple of minutes later, the door swung open. The man who faced them was built like a wrestler, with a broad face and a neat Adolphe Menjou moustache.

They followed him down the hall, past a Negro porter and up the wide staircase to a gilt ballroom, which sparkled with novelty lights. A hundred tables, each decorated with a single gardenia and a crisp white linen cloth, faced a jet-black stage ringed with palm trees. A bar packed with liquor bottles and cocktail shakers ran along one wall. A voluptuous woman with riotous auburn hair stepped aside to let them pass. 'Hello,' she said.

Luciano, Owney Madden, Ben Siegel and Meyer Lansky were at a table, deep in conversation. Madden broke off in mid-sentence and turned towards Quinn. He flashed a grin. 'What do you know? If it ain't the kid himself!'

Madden stood and offered Quinn his hand. Luciano and the others didn't budge. They stared at him as if he was excrement on the soles of their shoes. 'You two know each other?' Luciano asked. He had a ghastly, vivid gash across his cheek, which made one eye droop. The wound wept clear liquid and he dabbed it repeatedly with a handkerchief.

'Sure we do,' Madden said. 'You want a drink, Detective? You are a detective now, right?'

'No, thanks.'

'Take a Scotch highball.'

'I'm okay.'

'Sure you're okay, kid, but we all need a drink.'

'No thanks, Owney.'

'How come you know each other?' Luciano asked Madden.

'Relax, Lucky.' Madden took a sip of his liquor and pulled out a fat cigar. 'Joe here's okay. He's a fighter. I spotted him pounding the ring down at Grand Street and offered to make him into something. I fancied he could knock some sense into that nigger Johnson, until Willard got there first.' Madden sat back. 'Jeez, you could have been great, kid! But he turned me down, said he wanted to be a cop, just like his pa.'

'Is this your place, Owney?' Quinn said. Madden was an old-time gangster and he was surprised to find him in Luciano's company.

Caprisi looked like he wanted to bolt for the door.

Madden waved a hand dismissively.

'I heard you were in down at the Cotton Club.'

'Maybe. Have you been to take a look?'

'No.'

'I'll fix you a table. You ever heard Louis Armstrong?'

'Only on the wireless.'

'He's playing next week. I'll get you a table.' Madden lit his cigar and pointed at Caprisi. 'Your uncle Moe hangs out there most nights. You should see the broads, Joe. The tan bitches are the best you'll ever find. It's even better than Lucky's place.' Madden spat out some tobacco. 'You still fight, kid?'

'No.'

'You ever change your mind, come find me and I'll make you a fortune.'

'What the hell does he want?' Luciano growled.

'There's no belly on you – like Lucky here. You want to take a seat?' Madden clicked his fingers at the girl they'd passed on the stairs. She had perfect, bee-sting lips and dark, kohl-rimmed eyes. 'This is Talulah.' He chuckled to himself. 'And you should hear her sing.'

'I need to talk business with Mr Luciano, Owney.'

'In a minute. Relax.'

'We need to talk now.'

Madden glared at him. Then he pushed himself to his feet. 'You always had balls, kid, I'll give you that.' He turned towards Caprisi. 'How many people do you figure turned down the chance to box for Owney Madden?' He grinned. 'I seem to recall you gave Lucky and Ben a whipping. Isn't that right?'

'We were kids,' Luciano said, without humour. The men around him shifted in their seats. Madden laughed again and walked out.

'Do I need to frisk you?' Luciano asked.

'No.'

The Sicilian nodded at the bodyguards and indicated with a flick of a hand that they should follow him.

They went out the back, past the kitchens. A blonde in high heels smoked a cigarette by the rear door. She gave them an anxious smile.

Luciano led them up a narrow staircase. The walls were black and covered with pictures of singers who'd graced the club's stage: Helen Morgan, Phil Baker, Sid Silvers and Marian Harris. 'You ever heard Libby Holman?' Luciano pointed to the photograph at the top of the stairs.

'No.'

'You should. She's playing Saturday night. Bring a girl. I'll have them reserve you a table.'

Quinn neither accepted nor rejected the offer. As a young man, Luciano had exuded a kind of edgy bonhomie, but having his face cut open by fellow hoodlums out on Staten Island had clearly soured him.

They turned the corner into a room with giant windows overlooking a warehouse. A two-way radio stood on a sideboard below a navigation map, which displayed liquor lanes from Nova Scotia. Luciano did not appear to appreciate the incongruity of inviting policemen into his lair.

Lansky and Siegel slipped in behind them. Quinn and his partner were surrounded. 'You've got business?' Luciano asked.

'We've come about Charlie Matsell.'

'Who in hell's he?' Luciano's eyes narrowed. Lansky circled them. He was a small, slight man, with large ears and, like Madden, he moved softly. He lit a cigarette. He didn't bother to introduce himself to Caprisi.

'You know Charlie Matsell,' Quinn said, 'because you and Meyer invested in his company. You pumped in millions from the olive-oil business and made a killing.' He waited for a response. None was forthcoming. 'How d'you do that, Mr Luciano? You pump it into stocks and pay some columnists to ramp the price, like the fixes Rothstein used to run?'

'It's not against the law,' Lansky said.

'You don't deny it?'

'You want to get to the point, Detective?' Siegel said. 'Mr Luciano's a busy man.' His blue eyes sparkled with life and a smile split his handsome face. He had a quick temper and a reputation not just for resorting to violence but relishing it.

'Where money's at stake,' Quinn said cautiously, 'people fall out.'

'You think we whacked Matsell?' Siegel blurted.

'He jumped.' Lansky dropped his cigarette and crushed it beneath his boot.

'He was pushed.'

'And you figure that's the way we settle our business?'

'Vaccarelli worked for you. Why was he following me?'

'Why don't you ask him?' Lansky said.

'You know why.'

'I heard some cop chased him into the Hudson,' Siegel said.

'A lot of people work for us,' Luciano added.

'Vaccarelli was one of them.'

'And?' Lansky shot Luciano a warning glance.

'Why was he following me?' Quinn said again.

'If you've got an accusation to make,' Luciano replied, 'make it.'

Quinn glanced at Caprisi, then back at Luciano. 'Maybe we can help each other. You had a fix going with Matsell and it'd be bad news for everyone if we blew it, but there's no need for that to happen. Matsell was making you millions, but someone pushed him off a roof. If it wasn't you, who was it? Maranzano?'

There was a long silence. Each seemed to be waiting for another to make the first move. 'That's a real interesting question,' Lansky said. He glanced at Luciano, who nodded. 'Look, fellas,' he went on, 'you're smart guys and we shouldn't get off on the wrong foot here.' He sauntered across to the other side of the room and took down a glass. 'You want something to drink?'

'No.'

'Whisky?'

'No, thanks.'

'Lucky and I, we figure we need a couple of good detectives on the books, intelligent cops who know their way around town and don't owe any favours. Guys we can rely on.' Lansky shook his head mournfully. 'You're not planning to retire on a cop's pay like your old man, are you, Joe? Because we figure you're smarter than that.'

Quinn didn't answer.

'Good. We can use a pair of guys like you.'

'No, you can't.'

'Five hundred a week says we can. Each. Until you retire. And we'll pay a handsome Christmas bonus, so you can buy your girl something real special.'

Quinn said nothing.

'We figure you could use the dough, Joe. Rumour has it your big brother's on the rack.'

'Leave him out of this.'

'If he figures he can wait for the market to turn, he might be in for a surprise,' Lansky said. 'We'd hate for anything to happen to him.'

'Is this what you do now? You buy cops? Who else have you got on your ticket? Schneider, Fogelman and all the guys from Vice? Johnny Brandon?'

'It's a good offer for a Mick bastard,' Siegel said. 'You should be grateful.'

'Easy, Ben,' Lansky breathed.

'We offer the creep more money than he'll earn in his whole damned life and he insults us.'

Lansky held up his hand. 'I'm sure he didn't mean any harm.'

'You figure it was your girl, Detective?' Luciano asked. 'Is that what's bothering you? I heard she was Matsell's broad. You figure she pushed him off the roof?'

Quinn met his gaze. Luciano smiled.

'We can maybe help you out, Joe,' Lansky said, 'but we've got to know you're on our side. We can do a deal. If he was banging your girl, I can understand you're upset, but we figure that makes her a suspect and it makes you one too, along with your stupid brother.'

'Don't talk about him like that.'

'What you going to do, Detective? Ride to his rescue like this was some argument over a craps game? Grow up.'

'Okay,' Luciano said. 'This interview is over. You think about our offer and get back to us. But don't leave it too long.'

Quinn leant against the Gardner. A passing trolley car sent a wave of water cascading over the sidewalk and he jumped onto the hood to let it pass, but Caprisi got a soaking. He lit a cigarette.

'What was that about your brother?' Caprisi said.

'Nothing.'

'Didn't sound like nothing to me.'

'He's got a lot riding on Wall Street.'

'How do they know about that?'

'Word gets around. They were taunting me.'

'Is that why he came to see you?'

'My brother's too smart for jerks like them. He's not their type.'

'Sounds like a good guy.'

'He is.'

'We should have taken the money, though. Five hundred a week? That's what I call a wage.' Caprisi stretched. 'We're done here, right? We can go back to base, check in with the boss, see if he's going to reassign us.'

'How come you think we're done?'

'Lansky's not wrong. Their fix isn't against the law.'

'Last time I looked, murder was still a crime.'

'But they didn't whack Matsell. We can't prove it was a homicide and we've got no suspect.'

'Fixes still have victims.'

'They're not our problem.'

'You ever ask yourself why everyone is so keen for this to be a suicide?'

'I can think of a dozen reasons. How many do you need?'

'I have a hunch.' Quinn went around to the other side of the Gardner. 'Let's turn up the heat.'

'I don't like the sound of that. What kind of a hunch? And what do you mean – "turn up the heat"?'

But Quinn was already in the driver's seat and Caprisi had to leap in before he roared away.

CHAPTER TWENTY

QUINN HAD NEVER BEEN IN A NEWSROOM BEFORE, AND WAS surprised to find that the *Tribune*'s office looked pretty much like his own. It was a large, open-plan room, piled high with newspapers and documents, heavy with cigarette smoke. One journalist sat with his feet on the desk, a telephone earpiece pressed to the side of his head. Another pounded on his typewriter, his face distorted with the effort of composition. Quinn interrupted him. The man heard out the question and pointed to the far side of the room.

Jeremy Norton occupied a corner office with a brass nameplate on the door. He was on the telephone, too, so they slipped in quietly. He had his back to them, but turned long enough to frown at the intrusion, then carried on talking. The room was lined with framed copies of front pages. There was also a photograph of a woman and a group of children in front of a Long Island mansion.

Norton had his feet on the windowsill. He wore handmade shoes, thick red socks and fancy garters. He had a narrow face, with wild, curly hair and thick glasses. Quinn picked up a copy of the morning paper from his desk and leafed through it until he found Norton's column. 'The Street', it was headlined, 'by Jeremy Norton'.

> *Yesterday's market chaos is a signal to me that we may be on the verge of a once-in-a-lifetime buying opportunity. Others have said it. I have said it. But I'll say it again: the fundamentals of this economy are sound and the market will soon be heading squarely back into bull territory.*

Norton hung up the earpiece and whipped his feet away from the window. 'Good afternoon, gentlemen. Did you forget to knock?' Despite his Ivy League appearance, Norton's accent betrayed southern origins.

Neither Quinn nor Caprisi answered.

'Can I help you?'

'I'm Detective Quinn. This is my partner, Detective Caprisi.'

Norton smiled. 'Are you needing investment advice, gentlemen?'

'Not exactly.'

'Did you speak to my secretary?'

'She was on the telephone.'

Norton stood. 'Well, if you'd like to make an appointment, perhaps—'

'This is a homicide investigation, Mr Norton, so if you could spare a few minutes of your valuable time . . .'

'I see. And of course, if I can be of service, I'd be only too happy to oblige. But—'

'We'd like to ask you one or two questions,' Caprisi said.

'About Unique Investment Management,' Quinn added.

Norton blinked. 'Who?'

'One of its directors, Charlie Matsell, was pushed off a building on Wall Street yesterday.'

'I'm sorry to hear that.'

'You didn't know about it?'

'No.'

'We thought it would be the talk of the street.'

'Maybe you should speak to the metro desk. Now, if you—'

'Sit down, Mr Norton.'

'Excuse me?'

'Please take a seat. We could be a few minutes.'

'Gentlemen, I'm afraid I have a job to do.'

'Sir, just a few minutes and we'll be out of here.'

Jeremy Norton sat. He spread his hands and gave a weary Jeez-I-guess-all-the-good-guys-should-help-the-cops kind of smile.

Quinn grinned back at him. 'I'm real sorry, sir, I guess you'll probably think we're dumb, but my partner and I, we don't know too much about Wall Street. We need some advice.'

Norton looked at them indulgently.

'You didn't know these guys at Unique?'

'I don't believe so.'

'But if I told you what they appear to have been doing, you could explain it for us, right?'

'Perhaps.'

'We heard they made a fortune by ramping up the price of real obscure stocks, then selling out before they crashed.'

'I'm afraid I'd have to know the details before I could offer any sensible assistance.'

'But you've heard of guys doing that, right? It's what you might call common practice?'

'Not common practice, no.'

'But it's not against the law?'

'Not illegal, no, but—'

'Unethical?'

'Yes.' Norton leant forward. 'Gentlemen, with the greatest respect to you—'

'Hold on a second, sir.' Quinn pulled the sheaf of paper out of his pocket and placed it on the desk. 'One more question and we'll be out of here. Do you recognize this account number?'

Norton looked as if he might faint. 'I don't believe—'

'That's your account, sir.'

'No – I—'

'You've been taking money from Unique. We'd like you to tell us what they were paying you for.'

'I don't know what you're talking about.'

Quinn folded his arms. 'Be real careful, or this is going to get tough.'

'You've no right—' He reached for the telephone. 'I shall call my attorney.'

'What are you going to tell him? That you've been taking Unique's money to tip their stocks? And they've been paying you a handsome sum to do it?'

'I have no idea what you're talking about.'

'You want to know where all those dollars came from?'

'This is absurd.'

'The dough they offered you came straight from Lucky Luciano.'

Norton's eyes widened.

'So, if you'd like me to explain to your editor over there or, better still, a reporter on another newspaper why you've been getting two thousand dollars a month from one of the city's most notorious hoods, then the pleasure will be all mine.'

Norton's hand dropped away from the telephone. 'Unique is an investment house. I advise them.'

'Sure you do.' Quinn glanced at a photograph on the wall. The mansion, the fancy automobile: in these terrible moments, it was all under threat. 'Look, Jeremy, I'll be straight with you. We're not interested in your goddamned column or anything you put in it. You tell us what we want to know and we'll be out of here in a heartbeat.'

'I don't know anything about Unique.'

'What did they pay you for? You must know that.'

190

'I advised them. I . . .' He adjusted his glasses and breathed in deeply. 'I mean—'

'They invested in stocks and you tipped them?' Caprisi said.

'It's not illegal. I've broken no law.'

'But that's what you did?'

'Yes.'

'They got their friends on other newspapers to do the same so the price of the stock went sky high?'

He hesitated. 'Yes.'

'And then you all sold out, and it crashed?'

'Yes – no. The stock didn't always crash.'

'So, basically, we're talking fraud,' Caprisi said.

'No.' Colour was returning to Norton's cheeks. 'We picked stocks that had some potential to grow and—'

'What kind?' Quinn said.

'Companies that folk on the street had maybe over-looked. I do a great deal of research. We all do. They were good bets.'

'Any of the stocks you tipped higher than the day you sold them?' Caprisi asked.

'Well . . . I don't know. Maybe . . . I couldn't say.'

'What about the guys who invested their savings on the back of your recommendations, Mr Norton?' Quinn asked.

The journalist shifted in his seat uncomfortably.

'How did they approach you?' Caprisi said.

'I got a call.'

'From whom?'

Norton scratched at the leather on his desk top.

191

'It was Matsell and Moe Diamond who reeled you in?'

'Yes . . . yes.'

They watched him in silence. It sure didn't fit. You just couldn't imagine two-bit poolroom hustlers like Moe and his crowd pulling in a man like Norton. 'You never met Charlie Matsell, did you, Mr Norton?' Quinn asked.

'I've told you that—'

'You're lying. You never met him. Because if this was just about Charlie Matsell, you wouldn't be sitting here looking like you're about to soil your shorts. So you want to tell me who it was who reeled you into this fix?'

'I've just explained to you—'

'Try again.'

'I—'

'Spencer Duncan.'

Caprisi's head snapped around. Norton closed his eyes.

'So *that*'s what's scaring the living daylights out of you. In the middle of an election campaign, with Major La Guardia on the charge, your little fix links the mayor's office to a massive Wall Street fraud and organized crime in the shape of our friend Mr Luciano. And now one of your gang has been laid out flat. That's some story, right? You're a hack, Mr Norton, you tell me.'

Norton's hands covered his face.

Quinn didn't let up. 'Is the mayor in?'

'How in hell should I know?'

'What did Mr Duncan say? How did he reel you in?'

'I . . . can't talk about it.'

'My advice to you, Mr Norton, is to start talking right now, and do it fast.'

'I met him a couple of years ago at a conference on Long Island. He said there was a golden opportunity.' Norton's voice was tinged with bitterness. 'He suggested some of my colleagues were already onboard.'

'What did he ask you to do?'

'He said there was a chance to make some money, that they'd identified stocks which were undervalued or had potential.'

'Like everyone else on Wall Street?'

'They talked it up, said they had a pile of dough behind them and some contacts on the street.'

'Like Rosenthal?'

'They mentioned him.'

'And who else?'

'Wheeler on the *Times*. McGovern from the *Sun*.'

'What did they ask you to do?'

'He said they'd call up maybe two or three times a year and ask me to tip a particular stock heavily. The others would do the same.'

'That way you'd create a buying stampede?'

'Yes. Of course, the way the market's been, it's not been difficult.'

'And you made a whole lot of money from investing in the tips yourself?'

'It's not a crime,' Norton repeated. 'Others are doing it.'

Quinn turned back to the photograph on the wall. 'Did it surprise you to find Charlie Matsell had taken flying lessons?'

Norton winced. 'Yes. Of course it did.'

'Did you know who might have had a quarrel with him?'

'Half the world, I should think. He was a two-bit hustler.'

'What about Spencer Duncan?'

'What about him?'

'Do you have any idea how he got in on the act?'

'God knows.'

'Are you still in regular contact with Mr Duncan?'

'He came in a couple days ago.'

'What did he want?'

'Oh . . .' Norton threw his arms into the air '. . . to know I was still on the level. He asked me if I'd like to join their goddamned poker game. He said he had a real spectacular broad we could all use. Why in hell would I be interested in that?'

'What kind of broad?' Quinn snapped.

He shrugged.

'He didn't give you a name?'

'No.'

Quinn brushed a speck of dust from his jacket. He was careful to keep his voice level. 'Did he show you a photograph?'

'Of course not.'

'Did he say *where* this broad would be?'

'No.'

194

'A hotel, maybe?'

'How in hell should I know?'

Quinn was aware of Caprisi's eyes on his face. 'Thank you, Mr Norton,' he said.

'A hunch?' Caprisi yelled.

Quinn walked faster, but his partner kept pace. 'You're going to claim you had a *hunch* that the guy who strolled into Charlie Matsell's office that morning was the mayor's closest goddamned aide?'

'It was a hunch.'

'No, it goddamn wasn't.'

'Okay, somebody gave me a description of the guy.'

'Who?'

'A witness.'

'What kind of witness?'

'Martha.'

'And you didn't think to tell me about it?'

'She only talked about it last night. She didn't positively identify the guy, but there was a real accurate description. Cheeks like a bloodhound. It made me think of the way Duncan and the mayor spoke to us at the Plaza.'

Caprisi clutched at Quinn's sleeve. 'Hold on a minute, Detective. You've just landed us deep in the shit. As your new best buddy in there worked out, you've managed to explode a bomb in the middle of a real bitter election campaign.'

'We're detectives on a case, Caprisi. That's it.'

'No, no, no. We're two detectives officially *not* on a

case. And you just turned it into a suicide mission.'

'You want to pack it in? Go ahead. I never said you had to come along.'

'I'll tell you what I *don't* want to do. I have no desire to bust into Duncan's office to throw these allegations around, and if you're crazy enough to want to try you're on your own.'

'Okay.'

'No! Wait a minute.'

'Norton was on the level.'

'Sure, but Duncan may not be the only one who ends up wishing he'd kept his mouth shut.'

CHAPTER TWENTY-ONE

QUINN DROVE UPTOWN TOWARDS DUNCAN'S PLACE, AND BY the time they'd turned off Park Avenue the heavens had opened again. They found the house, killed the engine and sat watching the rain run along the edge of the sidewalk. A mother passed them, bringing two pretty daughters home from school. The girls skipped through puddles as day faded imperceptibly into night.

'We should drop this, Joe,' Caprisi said quietly. 'I promised I'd come along for the ride, and I have, but we should get out now.'

'It's too late for that.'

'It's never too late.'

'Are you scared, Detective?'

'Of course I'm goddamn scared. Why wouldn't I be? La Guardia has spent six months trying to prove the mayor is bent and we do the job for him in a morning. If this gets out, the mayor, the commissioner, Schneider and God knows who else will be out, and the shit dumped on our heads will make the tussle with Brandon and his boys seem like a picnic.' He paused. 'We're in way out of our depth.'

Quinn thumped the steering-wheel. 'Why did Luciano want to buy *us*?'

'I don't know and I don't want to. There's no need to make it our business.'

'Then what's the point of being a cop?'

'To win the battles you can win, not get whacked in the ones you can't.'

'You figure that's how it works?'

'I know it is.'

Quinn lost his train of thought in the neon lights and wound up with an image of Martha from the previous evening. He touched the edge of the photograph in his jacket pocket. 'I want to speak to Duncan,' he said, forcing himself to concentrate. 'Then we'll talk again.'

'I need some food.'

'In a minute.'

'Now.'

'Okay, okay.' Quinn fired up the Gardner and nosed it around the corner until he found a fancy-looking café.

Caprisi went in and got them a couple of thick sandwiches filled with bacon and melted cheese, and coffee in paper cups decorated with pink flowers. He wolfed his food like he hadn't eaten for a week.

'You're supposed to chew it first,' Quinn said.

'I missed breakfast.' Caprisi had a slug of coffee. 'She's beautiful, your sister.'

'She's not my sister.'

'I know. That's lucky, though, right?'

'How about you?' Quinn said. 'I saw the picture of your wife and son you keep in your wallet. What's your boy's name?'

'Andy.'

'After your brother?'

Caprisi shot him a warning glance. 'Who says I have a brother?'

'We talked about it before. I heard you had two and both were cops. I'm sorry if they—'

'Yeah, well, that's my affair.'

Quinn sipped his coffee. 'How old is your boy?'

'He's three.'

Quinn finished his sandwich. 'What are you going to do back in Chicago?'

'My father has a hole-in-the-wall grocery store. My baby sister's been helping him out, but he wants me to run the place.'

Quinn considered trading in his job to run a grocery store. He couldn't imagine not being a cop. 'Won't you miss it?' he asked.

'What?'

'This. Being a cop.'

'Are you kidding me?'

A Negro maid answered the door. She was dressed in a blue-and-white check uniform with a silver watch pinned to the bib of her apron. Light and warmth tumbled out onto the damp step and, inside, they could hear children laughing. 'Good afternoon. I'm Detective

199

Quinn and this is my partner, Detective Caprisi.'

'Come in – and wipe your feet!'

She pushed the door shut against a gust of wind. 'Stay here,' she said. 'Mrs Duncan don't like to have water on her carpets.'

She disappeared down the hall, leaving them to wonder at their surroundings. There was a thousand-dollar rug in front of them, with colours that glowed in the hall light. The painting on the wall looked like a European old master. A chandelier hung from the ceiling. Caprisi picked up a plate to check if it was solid gold. He grinned at his partner. 'Don't step on the carpet.'

A blonde woman rounded the corner and he put down the plate hurriedly. She was tall, with legs that appeared to stretch to her armpits. She wore a cream dress that hugged slim hips, many layers of beaded necklaces, embroidered stockings and enough makeup to keep a theatre company on Broadway for a month.

'Mrs Duncan?' Quinn asked. He followed the direction of her gaze to the trail of damp footprints. 'I'm sorry to trouble you, ma'am, but we're looking for your husband.'

Her frown deepened. 'So am I, Detective. So is half of Manhattan.'

'He's at the office?'

'No. He went to his tailor. He said he'd be no more than an hour and asked Elsie to bake a cake for the children's tea,' she answered, with a bitter smile.

'How long has he been gone?'

'More than three hours.'

'You've called his office?'

'Yes. He's not there and they don't expect him. What do you want to see Spencer about?'

Quinn took a step forward, careful not to put his wet feet on the rug. 'You seem anxious, ma'am. Is there a reason for that?'

'No.'

'You can try us.'

'Maybe he's got himself another girl. Maybe he went to shoot her.'

'I'm sorry?'

'He took a revolver with him.'

'Was that usual?'

'Spencer fears no man, Detective. I didn't even know he had one. If you'd like to wait, perhaps he'll grace us with his presence when he's done.' She glanced around for somewhere they could go that would not risk soiling something expensive. There wasn't anywhere.

'Ma'am, may I use your telephone?'

'If you must.'

Quinn moved to the hallstand. 'Would you have the registration number on his automobile?'

'Why do you want it?'

'Just a routine check, ma'am, to be sure there hasn't been an accident.'

'Yes.' She sank slowly onto an ornate chair. 'He only just bought it so the file is on his desk.'

'What make?'

'A swanky black Buick.' She smiled again. 'The kind the girls like.'

Quinn unhooked the earpiece and asked for Headquarters. The operator put him through to McCredie. Mae answered, and by the time he was connected to his superior, Caprisi stood beside him with a registration document for the Buick. 'Boss, it's Joe Quinn.'

'Detective. It's a good thing I'm not the Bull.'

Quinn had clean forgotten about the events of the morning.

'Everybody's talking about you, Detective. They all want to know where you learnt to be a prize-fighter.'

'It's a long story.'

'They're the kind I like. I'll buy you a soda some day and you can tell me about it.'

'Sir, we're at Spencer Duncan's place.'

'*What?* What in *hell* are you doing there?'

'Sir, there's more to this case than—'

'For God's sake, Quinn. Are you determined to follow Matsell off that roof?'

'Sir, Mrs Duncan is concerned about her husband. He went out three hours ago with a revolver and still hasn't come back. She seems kind of shaken up.'

'So he's got a new showgirl. You want me to break that to her, or can you manage it yourself? She ought to understand, she was once one herself.' McCredie sighed. 'For Christ's sake, Joe—'

'Sir, this is different. There's something not right.'

'Are you an expert on Broadway types, Detective?'

Quinn lowered his voice to a whisper. 'Duncan was mixed up with Charlie Matsell. He was the guy's last visitor. But there's more to it than that. Matsell was part of a Wall Street stock fix that connects the mayor's office to Lucky Luciano's boys. And now there's trouble. Trust me, it's—'

'Trust you? Right now, I wouldn't trust my own mother to piss straight.'

'According to the documents, the automobile's a black Buick. You want the plate number?'

McCredie grunted in frustration, but Quinn gave him the number anyway. He said he would call back. Quinn replaced the earpiece and tried to offer Mrs Duncan some reassurance, but her attention was fixed on the wall opposite. The children's voices floated to them down the corridor. 'Mind if I smoke, ma'am?' he asked. He lit up when she didn't reply.

He looked around him. The door was open to a bathroom. He could see a set of gold taps over an enamel basin. There were three kinds of soap in a bowl and a hand-towel draped neatly over a rail. Halfway down the wall, there was a portrait of Mrs Duncan in her Broadway prime, dressed for the stage. She was a beautiful woman.

Quinn smoked the cigarette to the stub, then looked about him for somewhere to get rid of it. Caprisi pointed at the floor, but Quinn shook his head. When he was sure it was out, he slipped it into his pocket.

The telephone rang. He snatched the earpiece.

'Quinn?'

'Yes, sir.'

'The Buick was called in five minutes ago. It was dumped at the eastern edge of the park by a hundred and second. It's a real mess. Get around there and keep the uniform boys away from it. I'll speak to the Bull. Don't tell the wife.'

'Sir.'

'And don't talk to anyone else. When the newspaper boys get a hold of this, they'll go nuts. I need to make some calls.'

CHAPTER TWENTY-TWO

THE BUICK STOOD JUST INSIDE THE BOUNDARY OF THE PARK, pulled into the side of the road and surrounded by dead leaves. Anyone passing would have assumed it was the scene of an illicit liaison and moved right on by.

The uniform cops were parked front and back. They'd put some tape around the scene and a couple walking down Fifth Avenue had stopped to see what was going on. Quinn offered his identification to the young officer in charge. He didn't look a day older than twenty. 'Sir, it's quite a—'

'You know who it is?' Quinn asked.

'No, sir.'

'If you see any newspaper boys you keep them well back, you hear?'

'Yes, sir.'

'Who found it?'

'A lady who lives up on a hundred and fifth. She was walking her dog. Her sons were fooling around and she told them not to look through the window, but they did. She went home and called it in. I've got her address if you want it.' The officer ripped the relevant page from his notebook.

'Turn your patrol car in here and keep the lights on,' Quinn ordered, 'but don't come across the tape.'

He did as he was asked.

Quinn put his head through the door, careful not to touch the sides, and cast a ghostly shadow across Spencer Duncan's ashen face. He got into the back of the Buick and crouched on the floor.

Duncan was sprawled across the seat. His pants were hooked around his knees, his groin exposed. There was a knife wound in his chest and a shallow cut across his throat. Quinn took out a handkerchief, covered his hand and prised apart the dead man's lips.

He sniffed gently, but could not detect chloroform.

Caprisi went around to the far door where he, too, could get a clean look at the body. 'Have you seen the driver?'

'He's on the floor in the front. A broken neck.'

He pulled back Duncan's jacket and slipped a hand into the breast pocket. He found a thin leather wallet and a dark comb. There was a clean handkerchief in his overcoat and a collection of nickels and dimes in his pants. Beside his feet was a screwed-up, blood-stained copy of the *Evening News*. A cigar protruded from an ashtray.

Quinn got out of the Buick and peered in through the front window. The driver had been hit from behind.

His head was thrust forward at a grotesque angle.

There was a flash behind them. Quinn and Caprisi turned. 'Hey!' one of the uniformed men shouted, but Quinn had already ripped the camera from the photographer's hand and shoved him back towards the tape.

'Easy, fella!' the man yelled, arms raised. He was tiny, with a brown derby and a brand new coat. He had a pinched face and a long nose that sprouted hair.

Quinn was tempted to smash his camera. 'What the hell are you doing here?'

'Easy, sir. Easy, Detective. I'm just doing my job.'

Reluctantly Quinn handed back the camera.

The guy breathed a sigh of relief. 'Say, you know what he was doing?'

'This is a crime scene.'

'That's one hell of a mess. You figure that's—'

'This is police business.'

The guy raised his camera again, but Quinn stood in his way. 'That's Duncan in the back, right?' the photographer persisted.

'Get behind the tape.'

'Aw, come on, Detective. Give me a break. You'll have half Manhattan here in five minutes. Just a few shots, right?' He reached into his pocket. 'Listen, I'll pay. Twenty each to you and your partner and a ten-dollar bill for the uniform guys.'

Quinn moved closer.

'Okay, okay . . .'

Brandon and O'Reilly pulled off Fifth Avenue and

turned into the park. Seconds later, the press pack screamed after them. The uniforms tried to hold them back, but they paid no heed until the Bull himself raised a hand, like Moses on the bank of the Red Sea. Quinn saw Caprisi smirk.

Brandon sauntered up to them. He had an overcoat draped around his shoulders and the brim of his hat pulled low to conceal the cut to his right eye. O'Reilly had a vivid bruise across his cheek. Brandon's gaze was steely. 'Have you taken a look?' Without waiting for an answer he moved towards the Buick and made O'Reilly hold his coat while he climbed in. He cast no more than a cursory glance over both victims before emerging to retrieve his coat and present himself to the waiting press. The flashguns popped and the newshounds hollered in unison. It reminded Quinn of the night he'd seen Ronald Colman arrive for a movie première on Broadway.

'It's definitely Duncan?' one journalist asked, louder than the rest.

The Bull nodded gravely.

'Is it true he's got his pants down?'

'What about the mayor?' shouted a second.

'Who do you think did it, Johnny?'

The Bull smiled. 'We've got some ideas, but you gentlemen will need to exercise a little patience.'

'You figure it could have been La Guardia?'

'No.'

'There's no love lost between him and Tammany.'

'Look for another angle, Jimmy.'

A new figure joined the throng. 'You told the mayor about this?' the man asked Brandon.

'When you gentlemen give us a minute, I'm sure we will.'

'You figure it was a broad?'

'It's too early to say.'

'But I heard he's got his pants down.'

'We'll put the word out, Sonny. I'm betting you won't have to wait too long.'

'Does his wife know?' The reporter had his hat cocked back and spoke more quietly than the others, who deferred to him. He and Brandon were evidently old acquaintances.

'Not yet. And don't you go telling her.'

'Used to be a showgirl, right?'

'If you say so, Sonny,' one of the reporters yelled. The others laughed.

'The chauffeur's dead, too?'

'Yeah.'

'You got a name for him?'

'Not yet.'

'You figure it's a gambling quarrel, like with Rothstein?'

'Who found him?'

'A broad walking her dog. We're not going to give you her name.'

O'Reilly raised his hand. 'Okay, gents. That's enough.'

'You figure they'll delay the election?'

As Brandon walked forward, the pressmen broke ranks for him.

* * *

Moments after Brandon and his travelling circus had swept away down Fifth Avenue, another saloon pulled quietly into the park. The chief of detectives got out and stalked towards them. McCredie's white hair curled over the collar of his blue overcoat, and his face was grey. The handful of pressmen who'd remained realized that they were witnessing a rare appearance by the legendary Ed McCredie and scrabbled for a photograph.

McCredie put his head through the door of the Buick. He remained motionless for a time, then stepped to the side and peered through the front window. As he did so, one of the press photographers let off a flash. 'Get these saps out of here,' he bellowed at the uniforms.

McCredie waited until the photographers had been hustled back behind the tape, scowling at them all the way. 'Have you told his wife?' he asked Quinn.

'I thought it was best not to. Just in case it turned out—'

'You did the right thing. Any idea why they pulled his pants down?'

'No.'

'You got a theory?'

'No, sir. Not yet.'

'You figure a woman could have killed him?'

'No, sir. She wouldn't have been powerful enough to get the better of both of them.'

McCredie turned back to the Buick. 'You think he was meeting someone?'

'It's possible. Matsell went up to the roof to see some-body before he hit the street.'

'What's the connection?'

'Matsell was pumping Charlie Luciano's money into a fix. They were getting a bunch of columnists to ramp stocks. Duncan was the guy who persuaded the columnists to sign up.'

'That sure is an unfortunate coincidence.'

'They were killed within thirty-six hours of each other. It's more than a coincidence.'

'One was a suicide, Detective.'

'Sir . . . I understand it's a sensitive issue, but we can't hold that line now.'

McCredie moved closer. 'Can't we, Detective?'

'Well . . . no.'

'Then let me tell you a few facts of life. We've just found the mayor's chief aide dead with his pants around his knees. Know what that spells?'

'Trouble, sir.'

'In the middle of an election, it spells the kind of trouble you can barely imagine. And you can bet your life the lines to City Hall are already burning hot. Make it a double homicide officially and we'll have a sensation. Schneider will roast the pair of us over a slow fire.'

'But, sir—'

'That's enough, Quinn.'

'Sir, there are other people connected to this fix. They seem real nervous. This may just be the beginning.'

'Who are we talking about?'

'Charlie Matsell's partners, Moe Diamond and Dick Kelly, tipsters like Jeremy Norton.'

'I'm not saying we drop it. I'm saying we need to keep it close. We have to box the political shadows. That's what Headquarters is about. Do you understand me?'

'Of course.'

'Let Johnny do what Johnny does. Whatever else we get, we'll keep to ourselves. Above all, don't talk to Schneider.' McCredie looked at the pressmen standing in silence at the edge of the cordon. 'You lads knock off now.'

'Sir, we can—'

'Get the fingerprint boys and the doc down here and then go home. We'll talk after line-up tomorrow.'

'Yes, sir. But if you want us to help tonight, we can—'

McCredie had already turned towards his automobile and his answer was lost in the roar of the Fifth Avenue traffic.

Quinn climbed into the Gardner.

'He's right,' Caprisi said. 'Schneider will nail us to a cross if we're not careful.'

'You mean if we tell the truth.'

'McCredie has to walk on eggs, Joe. Brandon will do almost anything to get into his chair.'

'Says who?'

'Valentine, for one.'

'But McCredie's the king. He's been here for ever. No one can touch him.'

'Times change. No one's bulletproof. What happens if Johnny the Bull cuts a deal with Schneider? Maybe he already has . . .'

'Do you figure Brandon invites his press pack to watch him take a shit in the morning?'

'I heard he doesn't shit.'

Quinn rifled through Duncan's slim leather wallet. He found three hundred dollars, a railroad timetable for Hartford and New Haven and a ticket for a prize-fight between Sandy MacDonald and Harry 'Kid' Brown at the Harlem Sporting Club the following evening. He passed it to Caprisi. 'Who goes to a fight alone?'

'A man with no friends.'

They watched the uniforms repel a couple of photographers who'd arrived late. 'It was the chest wound that killed him, right? So why did they cut his throat?'

Caprisi sighed. 'A struggle, maybe? There's no similarity in the method. Maybe the boss is right. We shouldn't jump to conclusions.'

'You figure he *is* right?'

'Well, no, but all the same . . .'

Quinn leant on the steering-wheel. 'What type of guy talks about *using* a woman?'

'What do you mean, Joe?'

'That's what Norton says Duncan told him. "We've got a broad you can use." '

'Joe, c'mon, they wouldn't be the first bunch of guys to hire a whore for the night.'

'No, but it's a real unusual phrase. If you had to nail a motive tonight, what would you say?'

'It has to be the Wall Street fix. That's the connection. There must be guys all over Manhattan sweating big losses.'

'Big enough for murder?'

Caprisi sneezed, took a moment to wipe his nose, then said, 'You're not in with your paycheck, let alone on margin, so what would you know? A guy who's gone in big on credit on the word of a couple of tipsters could now be staring ruin in the face. That'd be enough to make him sweat. And enough to have him think about murder.'

'What about the chloroform? What about Duncan's pants around his knees?'

'Maybe the guy's smart enough to want to throw us off the trail.'

Quinn fired up the Gardner. 'Let's go home.'

CHAPTER TWENTY-THREE

BUT QUINN DIDN'T GO HOME. AFTER HE'D DROPPED CAPRISI at the subway, he pulled the Gardner into a parking bay outside Centre Street. Their floor was deserted, but Mae was still hunched over her desk, correcting a report. There were dark shadows beneath her eyes.

Quinn sat on the edge of her desk. 'You okay?'

'I guess.'

'You should be out of here.'

'I have to check the Murray Street report. Schneider wants it first thing in the morning.' She stretched and yawned. 'I got that list for you. Delaware Photographic supplies four stores in town – one around here, the rest out in Brooklyn and beyond.'

'Where's the one around here?'

'List's on your desk. By the way, I persuaded Mrs Mecklenburg to go home. I got O'Reilly to talk to her and she seemed reassured that they were doing everything they could. She said she'd be back in the morning.'

'Thanks, Mae.'

'It was nothing, really. Poor woman. Can you imagine it?'

'I'd prefer not to.'

'When I got her downstairs, she started crying and I couldn't get her to stop. We spent an hour in the ladies' room and she was shaking like a leaf.' She glanced over his shoulder. 'Where's your partner?'

'He went home.'

'He's got a home? You'd never have guessed it.'

'Why?'

'Oh . . . he keeps himself to himself, doesn't he? I like him, though. I know the others wouldn't agree, but I figure you're lucky to have landed him.'

'Yeah.'

'Maybe he's not so lucky to have landed you, Joe Quinn.' Mae laughed. 'You're the talk of the office. About time someone taught the Bull some manners.'

Quinn grinned at her and went to his desk.

'Better watch your back, Joe,' she called after him. 'Their brains may be pea-sized, but they've got long memories.'

He picked up the sheet of paper she'd left for him. The Manhattan store was on the corner of Centre and Franklin. Quinn called a goodnight and headed for the street. A westerly wind blew a few spots of rain into his face as he pounded along the darkened sidewalk. It was the tail end of the commuter hour and shadowy figures still streamed towards the subway lights.

A small fat man peered at him through the drugstore window. 'I'm closed,' he shouted.

'One minute.' Quinn held up a finger. The owner relented and let him slip through the half-bolted door. Quinn slapped his hands together. 'Thanks. You won't regret it.'

The man bustled behind the counter. 'You'll have to be quick. I'm late for my daughter's ballet class. What can I do for you?'

Quinn leant forward with a quietly conspiratorial air. 'I understand you may be of assistance in the procurement . . . the production, maybe . . . of a certain type of photograph.'

'What kind of photograph did you have in mind, sir?'

'The intimate kind.'

The man glanced at the door. 'Did someone give you a personal recommendation?'

'Yeah, that's right. Real personal. I hear you might be able to arrange a studio shoot involving a group of—'

'No, sir. Hold on. I can certainly, for a fee, assist in printing a roll of film of a particular nature that you may wish to give me, but I'm afraid I cannot do more than that.'

'But you have a studio out back?'

'No, sir, I do not.'

'Ah, so you're a printer.'

'Yes. Now if you'd like . . .'

Quinn took out some of the pictures he'd found in Matsell's suitcase and spread them on the desk.

Hurriedly the man turned them face down. 'Please!' he said.

Quinn flipped them up again. 'I need to know if you printed these.'

'I have no idea.' He glanced at them. 'No . . . no.'

'You sure about that, sir? They're printed on the photographic paper you use.'

'How do you . . .' The man frowned. He tugged at the tips of his moustache. His eyes narrowed. 'There must be some mistake. I didn't realize this was the kind of thing you had in mind. This is a respectable business, a *family* business.'

'Did you print these?'

'No.'

He took out the photograph of Martha. 'What about this?'

The pharmacist's face went pale. He shook his head.

'Are you absolutely certain?'

'Yes. I've never seen it before in my life.'

Quinn bolted the door, turned the key in the lock and closed the shutters.

'What are you doing?'

'Nothing you need to worry about.'

'Who *are* you?'

Quinn took a pair of leather gloves from his pocket and put them on. 'What's your name, sir?'

'Nathan – Nathan Gregory.'

'Well, Nathan, that girl is my brother's fiancée, and he's not going to want to see her like that, is he?'

Nathan Gregory's eyes widened.

'So I have to find out who took that picture.'

'Yes – yes, of course.'

'And since you developed it, Nathan, that means I'm going to have to start by talking to you. And the quicker I get answers, the quicker you can be at your daughter's ballet class.'

'No – I didn't . . .' He backed away.

'It's printed on your paper.'

'There must be hundreds of stores that—'

'Four. Only one in Manhattan.'

'I've never seen it before. I swear it.'

Quinn moved behind the counter.

'I've done nothing wrong.'

'Who said you'd done anything wrong?'

'Who *are* you?'

'That doesn't matter.' Quinn closed the gap between them and gripped the printer's balls. 'You know what I have in my hand, Nathan?'

'Yes,' he squeaked. '*Yes.*'

'If you don't tell me what I need to know, I'm going to rip them right off. Have you got that?'

'Yes.'

Quinn smelt garlic on the man's breath. 'Who brought that photograph in?'

'I don't know— Aaargh! I don't! He never gave a name. No one ever does. I wouldn't have asked your name tonight – that's why people come here.'

'What did he look like?'

Tears ran down the pharmacist's cheeks. 'I don't know.'

'He was tall, Nathan? He was old?'

'Not tall, mid-forties, maybe . . . well-dressed. I – it's so hard to remember—'

'How long ago?'

'A week – no, two.'

'Do you still have the roll of film?'

'No.'

'But you remember what was on it, right?'

'No— Aaargh!'

'Think, Nathan.'

'I don't know. There were more pictures, but they were all the same.'

'Were there other people in the photographs, men?'

'No.'

'Think again, Nathan.' Quinn pushed the man's face towards the image. 'You can see a man's foot here, and in this corner, a hand. That's two men within reach of the girl and one behind the camera. So, who was in the other pictures?'

'I don't know! I swear it!'

'Think!'

'I – please—' He was choking, so Quinn released his head.

'Did you see any of the men? Were they visible in any of the other shots?'

'All the pictures were the same. They were just of the girl.'

'Were there any . . . acts like in this set over here?'

'No.'

'Are you sure about that?'

220

'Certain.'

'They were all of the same girl, lying on the same bed?'

'Yes.'

'Was she drugged?'

'I've no idea.'

'Did she look as though she might have been?'

'I don't know!'

'Did she have her eyes open? Look – here.' Quinn held up the picture in front of him. 'She has her eyes half closed. Were they all like that?'

'Yes – I believe so.'

'The man who brought the film to you, had he been in before?'

'No.'

Quinn put the picture back in his pocket and relinquished his grip on the pharmacist, who slumped against the wall and began to cry. Quinn stood over him. 'Now listen to me, Nathan. I am Detective Quinn. If the man who brought in this roll of film ever comes back to your store, you're going to call me. You'll ask to be put through to me at Centre Street, and if I'm not there, you'll leave a message with a lady called Mae Miller. Have you got that?'

He didn't answer.

'Have you got that, Nathan?'

'Yes.'

'When I come down here, you'll have the guy's name, his address and a picture-perfect description. And if you breathe a word of this to anyone, or you fail to call me,

I'll cut your balls right off and put them in this paper cup here. Is that understood?'

He nodded miserably.

'Just one more thing. In your professional opinion, Nathan, what kind of camera took this?'

'A Box Brownie.'

'You sure about that?'

'Yes. It's blurred. Studio portraits are of much finer quality.'

'Thank you. That's what I thought.' Quinn smiled. 'Have a good evening. And enjoy the ballet.'

CHAPTER TWENTY-FOUR

QUINN WENT TO MCGRAW'S PLACE FIRST, BUT IT WAS boarded up and shrouded in darkness, so he got back into the Gardner and headed north to Harlem.

The evening had barely begun, but the subway disgorged a steady stream of white folk dressed in black. Limousines and cabs stood beneath the lights of the nightclubs, and bejewelled revellers tripped over uneven sidewalks on their way between the two. There was a queue outside the Cotton Club. Quinn pushed his way to the front, which didn't impress the doorman. 'What do you want?'

'To see Owney Madden.'

'You got an appointment?'

'Tell him it's Joe Quinn.'

The man gestured to one of his colleagues, who disappeared up the stairs. A few minutes later, he returned to escort Quinn onto the floor of the nightclub.

Balloon lamps spilled dull light over crisp white

tablecloths. A troop of lithe Negro girls danced on the stage, but the evening hadn't yet come to life. Half the tables were empty.

Owney Madden sat beneath an artificial palm tree next to a giant African drum. A pair of waiters hovered close by. A pile of papers was spread in front of him and he was making entries in a leatherbound notebook. He looked up, but his manner was not as welcoming as it had been earlier. 'Take a seat, Joe.'

'I was looking for Moe, Owney.'

'Sure. Sit down.' He clicked his fingers at a waiter. 'What'll you have?'

'I'm okay.'

'Get my friend a Scotch highball.' Madden returned to his notebook. 'You should never run a nightclub, kid, you know that? Every sonofabitch is trying to steal from you. It's worth it, though, right,' he waved at the stage, 'just to have your pick of flesh like that?'

Almost at a run the waiter brought Quinn a Scotch. Quinn palmed him a dollar, but Madden snatched it away. 'Don't show me up.' He closed his book. 'I figured you'd be back.'

'Why?'

'Don't screw with me, kid. We both know why.'

'Did you hear about Duncan?'

'Yeah. A lot of people are going to be very upset about that.'

'Why?'

'Work it out.'

'Do you know who killed him?'

224

'If I did, you think I'd tell you?' Madden lit a cigarette and offered the case to Quinn.

They watched the dancers filter off the stage and the band stand up to acknowledge a ripple of applause.

'What's Luciano's connection to these killings, Owney?'

Madden kept his eyes on the last of the girls.

'You don't know, or you won't say?'

'What's that story about the goose that lays the golden egg? Like a fairy tale.'

'It's a fable.'

'Right. A fable. That's what it's like. You get it?'

'No.'

'If you have a goose laying golden eggs, maybe the goose doesn't always behave the way you'd like, but you've still got to keep it safe. That's Charlie's angle. That's our problem.'

'Who are you talking about?'

'You don't want to know, and if you ever find out, Charlie and his boys will have their say for sure. And, trust me, it's hard to swim in concrete boots.' He clicked his fingers at the waiter again. 'Hey, another drink for my friend here. And make it a large one.'

'Duncan was in on this fix, Owney.'

'So what? Wall Street's for suckers.'

'That means the mayor could be too.'

'You can't prove that.'

Quinn hesitated. 'There'd be nowhere to hide if it blows.'

'How's it going to blow? Are you going to blow it?'

'If La Guardia gets a sniff of it—'

'La Guardia! Don't talk to me about that prick. Mr Goddamn Honest-as-the-day-is-long-holier-than-thou-you'd-better-believe-I'm-going-to-be-mayor-of-this-city La Guardia. What's honest about refusing to talk to hardworking businessmen, eh? You tell me that. What's honest about refusing to even goddamn sit down with us?'

'You're Mayor Jimmy Walker's men, Owney.'

'We're businessmen, kid. What happens if he wins? What happens if some nut blows the little fix you're on to? Then Jimmy loses and all bets are off, that's what. So you need to be careful, *real* careful.'

'What was it the goose did that you didn't like, Owney?'

'That's enough, kid.'

'Did he and his friends use a girl in a way someone didn't care for?'

'I said that's enough.'

'We've got two bodies. My partner thinks they were victims of a Wall Street fix. I figure there's more to it than that.'

'Why don't you ask your pop? He was once king of the Centre Street cabal, right? Or is he too ashamed to talk about it?' Madden's eyes glinted. 'You keep out of it. That's my advice. And if you're as smart as I think you are, you'll take it. Your uncle is upstairs, sleeping it off. He's been shitting himself since yesterday afternoon.' He clicked his fingers a third time at the waiter. 'Show this kid up to the blue room and clean up if there's a mess. So long, Joe. Look after yourself.'

'Are you going to the Kid Brown fight tomorrow night?'

'For what? The Kid couldn't make that goddamn nigger Willard break sweat. Now if *you* want to fight, you give me a call. It's a whole lot safer than being a cop. And a whole lot better paid.'

Madden moved away from the table. Some of the customers tried to engage him in conversation, but he brushed them aside.

Moe Diamond was asleep in a small private lounge upstairs. The lights were off, bottles were strewn across the floor and the place stank of stale booze.

He was flat on his back, his mouth wide open. He was sweating and delirious, grumbling and muttering to himself.

Quinn reached out to touch him and Moe awoke instantly. Wide, frightened eyes stared unseeingly at him.

'Moe, it's me, Joe.'

'Oh . . . Joe.' He sat upright. 'That's good,' he gasped. 'I'm pleased to see you, Joe Quinn. That's all right.' He searched for an unfinished bottle, found one and gulped.

'Were you expecting someone else?'

'No. Yes. No. It's just that, er, I thought . . .'

'You're not making sense, Moe.'

He hung his head. 'Jeez, it was just a heck of a bad dream, you know?'

Quinn squatted down among the debris around him and cleared away a few of the bottles. 'You should go easy on this stuff.'

'It's too late for that.'

'You okay? You don't look so hot.'

'Well, that's a fine way to talk to your uncle Moe. I ought to clip your ear, whippersnapper.'

Quinn forced a smile. 'Is there anything I can get you?'

'An estate in Connemara with a harem of beautiful girls.'

'The journey home would kill you.'

'Nonsense, I'm as fit as a fiddle.' Moe tried to stand, but slumped back into the chair.

'You want me to get you some water?'

'Water? Pah!'

They watched one another in silence. Then Quinn said, 'What's going on, Moe?'

'There's nothing going on.'

'Owney says you're frightened.'

'Owney two-bit hustler Madden says that? Remember, Joe, it was me who introduced you to Rothstein. Now there was a man!' Moe picked up a glass from the carpet and poured a slug of whisky. 'Here, have a drink. To the old country.'

'The old country,' Quinn echoed, without enthusiasm.

'To Mr Pearse and the heroes of 1916. And let us piss for ever more on the grave of Mr Michael Collins. I knew him, conniving little fucker that he was. Not that you give two brass farthings, of course, but your father does and your mother did too, when she'd had a drink.' Moe seemed to realize what he'd said and lowered his glass. 'I'm sorry, Joe.'

Quinn nodded.

'I had to come to the funeral. You understand that, don't you? I know your old man claims he can't bear the sight of me, but she was a great woman.'

'I'm happy to hear anyone say so.'

'No, c'mon, I'm not just *saying* so. I know how it was, but . . . we all bear the guilt, Joe. We do.'

'How's that?'

'It was a tragedy what happened to her, so it was.' Moe's accent grew broader when he was in his cups. 'She was a great girl. Nobody wanted her to get hurt.'

'How did she get hurt?'

There was a long silence. 'It was just a shame she got sick, such a beautiful woman. Were you there with her at the end?'

'I guess so.'

'I'm sorry, Joe. Sure, it must have been terrible. Was there any warning?'

'I heard a cry and ran up to the roof. She was lying on the sidewalk.'

'You had no idea she was going to . . .'

'No.'

'Of course, you don't want to talk about it. I understand. She was a different woman those last years . . . Tragic. There's nothing anyone could have done. You mustn't blame yourself, Joe.'

'Charlie Matsell had a photograph of Martha in his desk.'

'So he should. She's a beautiful girl.'

Quinn took the picture out and dropped it onto the table between them.

'Good God,' Moe said.

'Have you seen it before?'

'No. God in heaven . . .' Moe raised his head. His eyes were wary.

'You know anything about it?'

'Of course not.'

'Look close and you can see at least three men around that bed.'

'Jesus, Joe. I can't see . . .'

'You know Jeremy Norton?'

'I know who he is. He's not much of a columnist, in my opinion, but—'

'He was in on your fix, just like Spencer Duncan. Duncan saw him a few weeks ago and asked if he'd like to be cut in on a real good broad they were going to *use*. Know anything about that?'

'I don't know what you're talking about.'

'Quit playing the innocent, Moe. It doesn't suit you.'

'And being a ball-breaker doesn't suit you. If your mother knew you were—'

'I'm guessing she never got to find out how you used to visit that apartment in the basement and stick your fat fingers down Martha's knickers.'

'For God's sake! To think of all the times I used to take you out and—'

'Something's been happening to make a guy mad enough to want to kill two men in two days. Both of them were in on your fix.'

Moe's cheeks were flushed with fury. 'Did your father put you up to this?'

'What's he got to do with it?'

'Did you tell him what I said last night?'

'Yes. He said you must have just got out of the asylum.'

'Did he? Well, you tell him tonight that if they come for me, he's next.'

'Why would he be next?'

Moe grunted something inaudible, got to his feet and stumbled towards the cupboard. He found what he was looking for, poured another glass and took a huge swig. 'Mr Holier-than-thou. Mr Oh-so-bloody-honourable. That's the biggest goddamned lie there is! I knew he'd put you up to this.'

'What're you talking about?'

'He's in as deep as the rest of us! He's just as much a part of it.'

Quinn felt pressure build in his head.

'You can work it out, kid. You're an intelligent boy. I'm not going to have him throwing the morality book at me.'

Quinn mopped his brow with a handkerchief. 'The old man's difficult sometimes, but he's the most honourable man I know.'

'Honourable men do dishonourable things, Joe.' Moe's eyes blazed. 'Then they like to pretend they're

231

paragons of virtue to conceal their shameful little secrets. He thinks he's better than the rest of us but he's not.'

'You're not making any sense.'

'Oh, yes, I am. Why do you think he took that girl in? Why did he pick Martha off the street? You ever asked yourself that? Look at her. I told you already. You can take a girl out of the Bowery, but you can't—'

'That's enough.'

'Your mother knew the truth and that's why she got sick, so I'm damned if I'll have him judging me!'

Quinn pocketed the photograph. 'He was there. That's what you're saying?'

Moe snorted. 'I'm saying I'm damned if I'm going to sit here and listen to you telling me *he*'s judging *me*!'

But Quinn was already on his feet. In the corridor he pressed his face to the cool stone wall and listened to the music of the jazz band drifting up the stairs. His heart was thumping like a jackhammer.

He made his way to the bathroom, shoved a cubicle door back against the wall and battled to stem the waves of nausea that threatened to overwhelm him.

'I say, old man, are you all right?'

Quinn straightened. A man with too much hair was bent over a line of white powder. 'Fancy a toot? It clears the palate.'

Quinn didn't answer.

'I said, fancy a toot? It'll cheer you up no end.'

'You're English?'

'Absolutely!'

232

'Ever been to this city before?'

'No!'

'Heard of a place called the Tombs?'

'Only just discovered the Cotton Club.'

Quinn took hold of the guy's shoulder, grabbed his hair and smashed his face on the marble surface. 'This is cocaine, I'm a cop, and the Tombs is the kind of place where boys like you get fucked from dusk till dawn, so beat it!'

The man's face was now as white as the powder that coated his bruised cheekbone. His leather shoes squeaked as he fled.

Quinn took a long, hard look at himself in the mirror. Hollow eyes stared back.

Twenty minutes later, Quinn parked the Gardner outside the front of the El station. He got out and stood on the sidewalk. The rain ran down the steel pillars that supported the train tracks and a group of young boys argued over a craps game. One caught sight of a familiar figure on the wooden steps and lurched forward with a cry. He had the umbrella up before his father's feet had touched the sidewalk. The pair set off, arm in arm, into the night.

Quinn went into the Italian store on the corner and shuffled around in the warmth until he found a Chinese parasol. He bought it, stepped onto the sidewalk again, put it up and listened to the rain pattering on its brittle exterior.

Another El arrived and unleashed its tide of

commuter traffic. Even the kids in the craps game looked up. 'Dad!' one cried. Then he, too, was gone.

The rain dripped onto Quinn's boots, but he made no move.

He could feel his father's hand tightening around his own. He could feel the warmth of his grip in the darkness . . .

'Joe?' Mae Miller was beside him, her forehead creased. 'Are you all right?'

'Sure.'

'Are you waiting for someone?'

'Er . . . no.'

Mae had a bag of shopping under her arm. 'I saw your father come off the El a few minutes ago. Aidan picked him up in that fancy new automobile.' Her smile faded. 'Are you really okay, Joe? You don't look well.'

'I'm fine.'

She seemed reluctant to move off. 'That was terrible news about Mr Duncan. The boss is in a real state. He was still there when I left, with the men from City Hall burning his ear.'

Quinn didn't answer.

'I'll see you tomorrow, Joe.' Her gaze lingered. 'Goodnight.'

''Night.'

CHAPTER TWENTY-FIVE

QUINN SLIPPED THE LATCH AND ENTERED THE APARTMENT quietly. The volume on the radio was turned up high and he recognized the relentless beat of the Melody Boys. He hung up his coat and dropped his keys into the bowl.

Martha sat by the window in semi-darkness, looking out at the night sky. She did not register his presence until he was beside her. Then her face lit up. 'Joe!' She glanced around him to check he was alone, then turned to the wireless and twirled the volume button. 'How are you? How was your day?'

'Long.'

'Did you get something to eat?'

'No.'

'There's some stew left. I'll heat it up for you.'

'Stay where you are. I'm not hungry.'

Quinn sat down near a photograph of his mother. Martha was standing by the wall, poised like a ballet dancer. She wore a simple cream pleated skirt. She had washed and curled her hair. 'Have you seen Aidan?' he asked.

'No. Didn't you look in at McSorley's?'

He shook his head and she wagged a finger at him. She sat down and put her feet on the window frame. Her skirt slipped above her knee. They watched a group of girls being upbraided by the night-watchman from the hat factory for playing potsy, a kind of hopscotch, on 'his' sidewalk. *I brek you hank 'n' feet* . . .

'Do you want a drink?' Martha asked.

'No.'

'Aidan has a new bottle of whisky. I know where he keeps it.'

The apartment was spotless. As usual, freshly starched shirt collars stood stiffly to attention along the dresser. The Santini grandchildren clattered up the stairs, singing as they went:

> *'Johnny on the ocean, Johnny on the sea,*
> *Johnny broke the sugar bowl*
> *And blamed it all on me,*
> *I told Ma, Ma told Pa,*
> *Johnny got a licking,*
> *Ha! Ha! Ha!'*

Quinn waited for the door to slam. A shout from their irate grandmother rose to the rafters.

A gust of wind rattled the windows and the rain

began again, in great sweeping arcs. The street-lamps rippled as the kids dashed for cover. Mrs Santini slapped young Paulo, who slipped on the stoop. The janitor's son, a small, slight boy with thick round glasses, was with him. He bore a striking resemblance to Mickey McIlroy, the least useful member of Quinn's childhood gang, who didn't like to play marbles, because it made his pants dirty, and refused to take off his glasses to fight. Aidan had made it his life's work to protect him, which meant that Joe had spent a lot of time fighting off Mickey's enemies.

'Did you see Sarah today?' Quinn asked.

'I found her on the roof. She said you'd let her stay there.'

'You believed her?'

'I know you're a soft touch. She was soaked to the skin, so I boxed her ears and took her back to the orphanage. I told her if I found her up there at night again, I'd bring her down to Headquarters and you'd lock her up.'

Quinn did his best to grin at her.

'I had to promise we'd take her down to Coney Island before the end of the week, so you'd better make sure you're here.' She spoke with the Irish lilt she'd picked up from his parents. 'What about you? Did you have a good day?'

He was silent for a time. Eventually he said, 'We found Spencer Duncan's body in the back of a Buick on the edge of Central Park.'

Her smile vanished. 'You mean . . .'

Quinn watched her intently. He didn't like her reaction. 'Yes.'

'But he's quoted in the paper.' She reached for the late edition of the *Evening News*, which had been tucked under a copy of the Bible. 'Here, look, "Bare Bank Books La Guardia Dares . . . Mayor Walker denied today he'd ever been photographed with Arnold Rothstein or Charles 'Lucky' Luciano and said it was 'absurd' to claim he was a friend of either man. His close aide Spencer Duncan suggested Major La Guardia's latest allegations were a sign of 'increasing desperation' and 'a sure sign he knows his cause is lost'." '

'He may have given a quote to the *News* but he's dead now.'

On the stairs the Santinis had begun their evening music practice.

'First Charlie Matsell, now his buddy over in City Hall,' Quinn said. 'Maybe you have an idea why.' He took out a box of cigarettes and offered her one. They listened to the Melody Boys and smoked in silence. Martha flicked through a magazine. When the song finished, she turned off the wireless. He noticed she'd left the page open at a shot of a long, sandy beach. 'You thinking of going away somewhere?'

'I often do.'

'Where would you go?'

'Sometimes I dream about that place on Coney Island. I can hear the rain on the tin roof and feel your mother's arms around me.'

They had found a kind of refuge at the *kuch alein* guesthouse after Martha's adoption, and had stayed on the island all summer, an unheard-of luxury.

'I felt safe there. At night, when it's dark, I can sometimes still smell her scent and feel my lips brush the skin of her neck. I wake up convinced she's there.'

Quinn suppressed a stab of nausea.

'I like to remember how she was then,' Martha said. 'Everyone was so kind to me. No one ever treated me like that before. Do you remember when you and I went to that fortune-teller in the gypsy tent?'

'It was a dumb idea.'

'Many children! I'd better get a move on, eh?'

Quinn avoided her eye. 'I guess . . .'

'Sarah told me she'd go to school for sure if we bought an apartment there.'

'You figure it's time to tell her that her father moved on long ago?'

'No,' Martha said. 'I don't think so. We should never tell her that. Sometimes hope, a dream, is everything.'

Quinn waited. 'It seems Charlie Matsell was fond of you. You ever consider going some place with him?'

Her eyes were suddenly cold, hard. 'You should go to McSorley's. They'll be expecting you.'

'I've got a picture of you naked, which I found in his desk.'

'Does that turn you on, Joe?'

'No.'

'Then don't mention it again.'

'There were other men in the photograph.'

239

'It's none of your business.'

Martha scooped up a sweater and headed for the door.

'Stay where you are.'

'Or what?'

'Those guys boast to their friends about *using* broads. They said a few weeks ago they were going to have a real special one they could *use*.'

'I'm going out.'

'Do you have anything to say about that?'

She tried to push past him, but he spun her around. 'You were screwing your boss?'

'You can't really believe that.'

'There's a picture of you naked on his bed.'

'I've told you – *it's none of your business*.'

'That makes you a suspect.'

'No, it doesn't.' Her tone was brittle. 'But it might make me a victim if you don't back off.'

'What's that supposed to mean?'

'You know what happened to Charlie Matsell and Spencer Duncan. You can see the kind of people they were. That's – that's what I found out. What do you think their friends are going to do if they hear someone's been shooting their mouth off?'

'You think this is Luciano's boys?'

'I don't know who it is. And I don't want to.'

'I've always said I'd protect you, but I can't unless you help me out.'

She stared at him. 'Will you protect me, Joe? You think that's what I want?' Her face was so close he could feel her breath upon his cheek. 'I used to worship you. You have no idea what it meant to me to be swept up by this family. Because you always had love and security, you can't imagine how it is to experience neither. I used to watch you skip past me up those stairs and dream of one day living in a world like yours. And when, miracle of miracles, it happened, I was so frightened I didn't dare speak for a month.' A tear glistened on her cheek. 'I followed you. I believed in you. But now I see you're like all the rest. This isn't about protecting me. It's about you – your ambition, your desire, your needs.'

'You can't pretend nothing's happening.'

'I'm not. I'm just telling you it's none of your business. You have no rights over me.'

'I don't claim any rights, but tonight this turned into a double homicide. I can't pretend—'

'Really? That's not what I heard.'

He stared at her. 'Who have you spoken to?'

'If you want to bring me down to the Tombs, go right ahead. Otherwise, I don't want to talk about it inside the walls of our home. And I certainly don't want it mentioned in front of Aidan. Is that clear?'

'Do you enjoy making a fool of me?'

'No one's making a fool of you.'

'How can you pretend nothing's passed between us?'

'Joe . . . I don't belong to you. I never have done. I'm marrying your brother.' She put on her cloche hat and stepped away from him. 'Now, go to McSorley's. If this is how it's going to be, I don't want to be alone with you here. You'll have to move out.'

He followed her down to the sidewalk. 'Martha!'

A bunch of older kids warming themselves around a packing-box fire whistled loudly as she darted past. Quinn growled at them. Martha skipped down the steps into the hole-in-the-wall.

Quinn forced himself to stride on.

CHAPTER TWENTY-SIX

THE DOOR OF MCSORLEY'S BANGED BACK HARDER THAN
he'd intended. The conversation dipped and heads
turned. The owner, Old Bill, raised a hand in ironic
salute as the hubbub resumed. He took down an
earthenware jug of the filthy 'near beer' he'd brewed in
the cellar since Prohibition had come into force ten
years earlier. It must have been freshly made, because
the smell of malt and wet hops was strong. It was mixed
with the habitual aroma of pine sawdust, pipe tobacco,
coal smoke and onions.

Quinn dropped a couple of coins on the bar. All
around him, between the cobwebs and the paint flaking
from the walls and ceiling, there were countless
mementoes of the past. There was a copy of the *New
York Herald* with a one-column story on the assassin-
ation of Lincoln and the edition of the *Times* of London
that carried news of the battle of Waterloo. There were
pictures of Lincoln and McKinley in heavy wooden

frames, and the area between the bar and the back bore portraits of jockeys, actors, singers and, above all, the men who had held sway at Tammany. Beside them, an engraving of the rebel leader Kelly being rescued by fellow members of the Irish Revolutionary Brotherhood in Manchester, England, hung in pride of place.

Like Leisler's oak, it made Quinn's father feel at home.

Quinn eased past a pair of customers standing at the bar and headed for the far wall. His father and brother always sat there. He put his jug on the stove, alongside theirs. In winter, they preferred to drink their ale as hot as coffee. It tasted just about palatable that way.

Neither his father nor his brother spoke. The atmosphere was sleepy, the air thick, and the rhythmic ticking of clocks seemed to slow time. Aidan picked up his jug, passed Gerry his, and they drained them. 'Hey, Bill,' he shouted, towards the bar, and the bartender raised a hand.

'Been home?' Gerry asked.

'Yes.'

'She wanted to know where you were.'

'I went to the El station to wait. I heard I just missed you.'

They were surrounded by friendly faces, but no one came near. 'We're thinking of taking a trip up to New Haven to see the football game, Joe,' Aidan said. 'A buddy's loaned me his new Duesenberg Torpedo. She's a beauty; a bright-red coupé. You want to come?'

'I don't know.'

'We're going on Saturday.'

'Aidan's got a bet on. He thinks Booth can win it on his own.'

'You didn't see him on those runs against Army.'

'Everybody and his kid brother is scoring against Army. I'll lay you five dollars Al Marsters'll block him out.'

Bill interrupted their discussion to place a pewter jug on the stove. Quinn reached into his pocket for some change, but the bartender wouldn't take it.

Aidan picked up a leather wallet and took out some papers. 'Joe, you just have to sign here.'

'What is it?'

'Your share of Mom's estate. It's only a few dollars, but I've paid Dad. I need to put the rest of the money into your account.'

Quinn scanned the page.

'You okay?' Aidan asked. 'You don't look well.'

'I'm fine.'

'They just need your signature.'

Quinn scribbled it, then pushed the paper back across the table.

'I spoke to Herman about the rent. He wanted a ten per cent raise. I told him to go to hell.' Aidan put the papers back in the wallet. 'I'll beat him down.'

'Aidan's persuaded Shipley to bankroll his first showroom,' Gerry said, his voice filled with pride. Shipley was an old friend who'd built up a successful auto-repair business.

'Maybe,' Aidan said. 'It's not for sure, but he called

me up today.' He glanced at his brother. 'I've a lot to thank Joe for.'

'His bloody snoring for a start,' Gerry said.

Quinn didn't laugh.

Aidan got up and headed for the men's room.

Quinn waited for his father to speak, but he was watching the fire and tapping his foot on the floor. 'I need to talk to you, Dad.'

'About what?'

'I need to talk to you outside.'

Gerry frowned. 'You've got something to say, son, say it here.'

'I'd rather it was outside.'

Gerry didn't move.

Quinn glanced about him. 'Did you ever get into any trouble with Moe?'

'What kind of trouble?'

Quinn hesitated. 'Something he said tonight.'

'About what?'

'About . . .' It was hard to find the right words.

'What?'

'That you were involved in something. Maybe it got out of hand.'

'What kind of thing?'

'It had to do with broads. He talked about Martha.'

Gerry went very still. 'What else did he say?'

'He said you played the good guy, but were as much a part of it as he was.'

'He was drunk.'

'Yes, but—'

'I hope he's not your witness.'

'I wasn't talking about a witness. I know you left Centre Street suddenly and I just—'

Gerry thrust his head forward. 'Now, you listen to me. Moe Diamond is a proven liar. He's a filthy, despicable human being and neither your mother nor I have had him in the house for more than a decade. If I'd had my way, he'd have been strung up from a lamp-post for daring to come to her funeral.'

'He was real worked up about it. He said you'd know what—'

'He's a *liar*. A fantasist. You either believe him or you believe me.' Gerry fixed him with a ferocious glare. 'That's it. There's no more to say.'

Aidan reappeared and landed heavily in his chair. 'Not breaking anything up, am I? No shop-talk. That's the rule.'

'Give us a minute, Ade,' Quinn said.

'I don't want to talk about it any more,' Gerry said. 'Is that clear?'

'Dad—'

'That's it. That's all there is to say.'

'About what?' Aidan asked.

'Leave it, Ade,' Gerry said.

Quinn sighed. 'Did you hear about Spencer Duncan?'

'Yes,' Gerry said.

'He was Charlie Matsell's last visitor. You know that?'

'Yes.'

'How?'

'Word gets around.'

'Did someone tell you what happened?'

'No.'

'He had a knife wound in his chest and a shallow cut to the throat. His pants were around his knees.'

Gerry sipped his ale. 'The cut to the throat is the mark of a vendetta. It's an old Sicilian tradition.'

Quinn heaved himself forwards. 'Did you know Charlie Matsell?'

'No.'

'It's just that if he was part of the same crowd that you and Moe were in, then—'

'There never was a crowd. And I said drop it.' He stared at his son. 'In fact, drop the case.'

'Why?'

'Because I've been around long enough to tell you that it smells to hell and back.'

'I can't just walk away.'

'You want to know how this ends? Sooner or later you'll hit the wall.'

'What wall?'

'The wall they've built around themselves and those who serve them. Just look at the names on the ticket. It's their world. Leave it to them. Join Ade in his show-room. He'd take you on any time.'

'Martha's involved. I can't just—'

'I've pulled her out. We should never have allowed her anywhere near them. Any of them.' Gerry kicked the door of the stove shut, so hard that the room fell silent.

CHAPTER TWENTY-SEVEN

MARTHA DIDN'T SAY A WORD, BUT HE KNEW SHE WAS STILL angry. The table was cleaned aggressively, plates banged down.

'You're mad at me.'

'How could I possibly be mad at you?'

'Dad won't give me any answers either.'

'To what? The eternal questions of life? The square root of fourteen million?' She turned to him. 'Are you going to say anything?'

'No.'

'Why not?'

'Because you *are* angry. And so am I.'

Quinn moved to the cupboard above the stove, took down Aidan's bottle of bootlegged whisky and a glass, then went to his room. He poured a huge measure, lit a cigarette, opened the window and sat on the edge of the bed. A few minutes later, he threw the stub into the court-yard, lay back and waited for the alcohol to take effect.

He listened to Martha outside his door. After a few minutes, the sound of crockery chinking ceased and she switched on the radio.

He killed the light, lay down and stared at the patterns on the ceiling. As teenagers, he and Martha had spent hours imagining what creatures might emerge from them in the darkness. He closed his eyes.

Suddenly the wireless was turned off and the apartment was silent. Quinn opened his eyes, but did not stir. He heard her soft footfall and saw a shadow beneath the door. He swung his legs off the bed.

He could see her bare feet on the uneven wooden floorboards beneath the ill-fitting door.

He heard her touch the door handle and release it swiftly. She paused a moment longer and then moved away.

Disappointment crowded in on him.

He heard a pot being boiled, the bathtub filled and, in time, water being scooped over her shoulders.

He reached for his jacket and took the photograph from the inside pocket. He looked at the half-tone shoes in the corner.

Water drained from the bath.

There was a long silence, and then he heard her outside his door again.

He waited.

Martha crept on down the corridor to her room.

Quinn drank two more huge slugs of whisky and waited for sleep. In a last conscious moment, he imagined her searching for those patterns upon the ceiling.

In their adult world, there was no pattern. Only darkness.

It was summer and the night was still. A faint breeze whispered up the stairwell.

Quinn joined his brother by the window. Their father was hunched over a bonfire in the courtyard. They watched him pick a dark suit and feed it to the flames. Aidan gripped his hand. 'What's happening, Joe?'

'I don't know.'

Tonight, once again, there had been no cheese or crackers on the table, no finely cut apples or homemade lemonade. Their mother did not sit, smiling, in the chair by the stove.

They heard only soft cries from behind locked doors.

There had been no music practice, laughter or gentle chastisement, just another day of tears, screams, anger, silence.

A door opened. They heard her in the corridor.

'Ade.'

They jumped onto their beds.

She crept in. She came to Joe first and wrapped soft arms around his neck. Her hair brushed his cheeks. 'Joe,' she whispered. Her face was still damp with tears. 'We shall just have to learn to forgive him. Isn't that what the good Lord teaches us?'

'What must we forgive him for?' Aidan asked.

'It's all right, Ade,' she said. 'You don't need to know. We must just believe in the power of forgiveness. That's all.' She shook him. 'Joe, are you all right?'

He turned to the wall.

'Joe?'

'Go away. It's your fault.'

'Joe, what have I done? You don't understand. Sometimes everything is not as it seems. I know you worship him, but—'

He covered his ears. 'La, la, la, la, la . . .'

'Joseph, stop it.'

But he did not wish to hear of fallibility and forgiveness. 'Dad,' he wanted to scream, 'Dad, Dad, Dad, Dad!'

'Joe!'

Gerry crouched over him, his face creased with anxiety in the half-darkness. 'Joe, what is it?'

'Dad?'

'You called me – you must have woken the whole building. Are you all right? You're soaked in sweat.'

He focused on his father's eyes, and as Gerry began to withdraw, he gripped his forearm. 'Dad, what am I going to find out? What was Moe talking about?'

Gerry tried to pull away, but Quinn held him. 'Please, whatever it is, you're still my father. Nothing can change that.'

'Joe—'

'Is that why Mom got sick? Is that what happened to her?'

'I don't want to talk about your mother.'

'Dad, I have to know. You can't expect me to walk away.'

252

'Then you're not my son.' Gerry Quinn stood. 'Then you're *not* my son.'

Quinn knew that Aidan was awake, but neither man spoke.

After a few minutes, Aidan was snoring, but Quinn struggled in vain for sleep. Unwelcome trains of thought led him nowhere he wanted to go. He tossed and turned on the straw mattress.

When he heard movement outside he got up, slipped out to the front room and closed the door behind him.

Martha stood by the window, her skin pale in the moonlight. He moved close enough to touch her, but she didn't turn. She ran her fingers down the window-pane and put her face to the glass, as she had in the *kuch alein* guesthouse on Coney Island that summer long ago. She wore a thin silk nightdress.

'What are you trying to do, Joe?'

'I'm not trying to do anything.'

'What is it that you want?'

'I want to know what he's frightened of. What we're all scared of.'

'We're not frightened of anything.'

'Then tell me why Mom got sick.'

'I don't know.'

'You don't know, or you just don't want to think about what we do know?'

'We don't *know* anything. I have no idea what you're talking about.'

'Why did she give up, Martha? Why did she fade

away? I never saw her touch a drop of alcohol before.'

Her face reddened. 'Before they took me in? Is that what you're saying?'

Only a hair's breadth separated them. A sheen of sweat glistened on her neck. 'Don't do this, Joe,' she whispered. 'You'll destroy us.'

'What use is a life based on a lie?'

'There is no lie!' Martha spun around. 'I've fought for this peace, Joe. Don't destroy it. If you do, I'll *never* forgive you.'

He held up the photograph.

She closed her eyes.

'Is that where Dad took you, Martha? Is that what he had in mind for you?'

She opened her eyes and slapped him. 'You filthy, despicable— You disgust me!' She shoved him in the chest. 'Get out of here.' She snatched the photograph and pushed it into his face. 'What the hell is wrong with you? Get out!'

Martha ran down the corridor and slammed her bedroom door so hard that the apartment shook. Quinn leant his forehead against the window.

'What's going on, Joe?' Aidan was still half asleep.

'Nothing.'

'I just woke up and heard shouting.'

'We were arguing.'

'About what?'

'It doesn't concern you.'

'Of course it does.'

'It was about the case I'm working on. She's not telling me everything she knows.'

'Leave her be, Joe, okay? We don't want your world coming into this house. She's my responsibility now, and however much I owe you, I'm going to make sure she's protected.'

Quinn went back to his bed. His head pounded and his throat was raw. There were still no patterns in the goddamn darkness. He got up again and put on his coat.

As he marched along the sidewalk towards the Gardner, he fought to stop himself looking back.

CHAPTER TWENTY-EIGHT

QUINN AWOKE TO A SHOWER OF NEWSPAPERS AND CAPRISI'S grinning face. He blinked up at the light, then rolled out from under the desk. His back was crooked and stiff and his mouth tasted like a skunk's breath.

'How can you fall out with your wife when you don't have one?' Caprisi asked.

'Very funny.'

'They charge, you know, for sleeping under a Headquarters desk.'

'I was working late.'

Caprisi raised an eyebrow. 'Sure you were.'

All the newspapers save the *Tribune* had devoted their front page to pictures of the previous night's crime scene. The *Sun* had an image of Duncan's body in the car. A large banner below its masthead claimed an exclusive. The others bore a photograph of Brandon talking to the press. They reported breathlessly that the NYPD's most seasoned and respected detective had been assigned the case. There were confident predictions that the matter would, therefore, soon be resolved. Two had the same headline: 'Mayor's Aide Slain'. The *World* claimed Tammany members were privately blaming supporters of La Guardia, with dark suggestions that an organized-crime syndicate may have been behind the murder.

No one linked it to Matsell's death.

Caprisi raised his arm and tapped his watch. 'We've got to go. You were dead to the world, so I left it until the last minute.'

Quinn stretched, then tried to tidy his hair and collar.

Caprisi handed him a cup of coffee. 'You're a mess.'

'Thanks.'

'Oh, Schneider came by. He didn't want to wake you, but he doesn't want either of us to mention what you found in Matsell's mouth at any meeting.'

'Why not?'

'He thinks it's . . . confusing.'

'Confusing?'

'Hell, I don't know, Joe. That's what he said. Take it up with McCredie, why don't you?'

They turned towards the briefing room. As they passed an open window, they heard the press baying for blood. McCredie was struggling to make his way through the throng. The questions came faster than they had the previous night. 'Is it La Guardia, Chief? What does his wife say? You think it could have been a broad? Have you spoken to the mayor? You think the Bull can crack it? How come his pants were down?

You figure there could be a La Guardia connection?'

McCredie finally made it to the side door, where a couple of uniformed officers shoved the mob back.

The briefing room was quieter than usual. Most of the detectives were digesting the morning's headlines. Neither Brandon nor any of his cronies was present.

Quinn and Caprisi took up their position at the back beneath the clock. It was just a shade before eight. Kitty and Mae stood by one of the large wood panels, smoking. They both held a cup of coffee. Mae had cut her blonde hair short. It suited her. 'We're going to install a bunk under your desk,' she told Quinn. 'You're lucky the boss wasn't in. You know how he hates people sleeping on the job.'

'You had a fight with your wife?' Kitty had a low cigarette voice. 'Or did you just pick one with yourself?'

'He hasn't got a wife,' Mae said.

'You got a sweetheart, Quinn?' Kitty asked.

'No.'

'So, you're available?'

They all grinned. Everyone in the joint knew Kitty was sweet on Mae.

Brandon and Hegarty, the press chief, strolled in together. Kitty stared at them. 'Jesus,' she muttered. 'What happened to those two?'

'Somebody taught them some manners,' Mae said. She smiled approvingly at Quinn.

Kitty picked up the message. She dropped her cigarette, ground out the stub and leant closer. 'So, what happened, lover-boy?'

'We had an exchange of views.'

McCredie swept into the room, trailed by the commissioner and Mayor Jimmy Walker.

'Okay, listen up,' McCredie said. 'You've seen the headlines. You all know the mayor here. Just in case some of you have been relying on the newspapers, let me give it to you straight: Spencer Duncan was murdered last night at around six. He had his pants below his knees and his private parts were exposed, but not molested. He had a cut to his neck, but he was killed by a knife to the heart. His driver was also murdered, but that's incidental. It was Duncan they were after.'

McCredie paused for effect. 'I don't need to tell you that the mayor wants and needs some answers. The press are pointing the finger at La Guardia, so things are about to get hotter.' McCredie glanced at Walker. The mayor nodded. 'The Bull heads this up. If anyone can crack it, he can. But I'm on the case, too. You can all miss line-up this morning. Get the hell out of here and work the streets. Turn over your stoolies, look in at some of the local precincts; keep your eyes peeled and your ears pegged to every goddamn sidewalk. If you hear something, call it in here to me or the Bull. Mae will be on the line. This has absolute priority over any and all other cases.'

McCredie stepped down. Mayor Walker took his place. Beside him, the commissioner adjusted the gardenia in his buttonhole and stroked the ends of his waxed moustache.

Walker surveyed the room as if he was about to make a presidential address. 'Spencer Duncan was a friend of mine, so I want these men caught quick. And, rest assured, when you have them, I'll make damned certain that every single one takes a walk to the Chair. I know your reputation and, as mayor, I've supported this department in every way I could. Now we have the press howling for a result and a mystery to which even Johnny Brandon hasn't yet got the answer. So, I want some action, and I want it now.'

Walker turned on his heel and stalked out, followed by the commissioner. Quinn saw Ed McCredie give the Bull a barely perceptible but ironic shake of the head.

They filed out in silence. Outside, the pressmen waited beside the mayor's silver-trimmed Duesenberg. The chauffeur already had the engine running.

At the end of the corridor, McCredie beckoned Quinn and Caprisi into his office. He'd already chalked a list of assignments on the blackboard, and leads that had to be followed. 'I want you to babysit the widow,' he said. 'She's upset, so you hold her hand, tell her we're doing everything we can. Keep those monkeys in the press away from her.'

'But, sir . . .' Quinn saw the surprise on Caprisi's face too. This was surely a job for some uniforms.

'You did well with the Matsell connection, but the Bull is onto it now. He'll take a look at the Wall Street fix as well.'

'Couldn't we get some uniform boys to take care of the widow?'

'No. He was the mayor's chief aide, for Christ's sake. I can't have this blow up in my face. Maybe it's just for today. Tomorrow we'll take another look.' McCredie squeezed Quinn's shoulder. 'You've done well, son. You're going places, even if the Bull does want to put you six feet under. But you're the new kids on the block and I need you to do this.'

'Sir, why doesn't Schneider want—'

'I don't care what Schneider wants. Mae!'

Caprisi turned towards the door, but Quinn remained where he was. 'Sir, can I have a word?' He glanced at his partner. 'In private.' Caprisi slipped out.

'What's this about, son?'

'My father.'

'What about him?'

'I'd like to ask a couple of questions.'

'Detective, we're rushed off our feet here. Can't it wait?'

'It'll take just a few moments.'

McCredie retreated behind his desk and lit a cigarette. 'Go on, son.'

'I'm curious you've never really talked about him. He worked here a long time. I figure you must all have known him.'

'We don't judge a man by the sins of his father. I told you that already.' McCredie blew out a thick plume of smoke. 'If we did, I'd be up Shit Creek and so would most of the other guys out on that floor. You seem like a smart kid. You're clever and you're a good man to have around in a tight spot. That's enough for me, so I'll stick with you even if you

261

have made mortal enemies of Johnny and some of the other boys.'

' "The sins of the father"?'

McCredie avoided his gaze. 'You'd better ask him.'

'He won't talk about his time here.'

'Hell!' McCredie stood. 'It's no big deal. He had a different style, that's all. He and guys like Johnny never hit it off. It came to something and your father bunked out. That was his choice.'

'Why did he leave?'

'I don't know, son. You'd have to ask him.'

'He didn't give a reason?'

'Not one that I recall.'

'Were he and Moe Diamond friends?'

'I have no idea. Diamond should be in an asylum.'

'That's what my father said.'

'Well, he's right.'

'But Moe gave me the idea that—'

'Forget Moe, son. I wouldn't trust him to tell me the time of day. I know your old man's a bit of a mystery. He always was a taciturn bastard, though a damned good cop. One of the best, in fact. He deserved his reputation, which you couldn't say for everyone around here. But maybe he just got tired, like we all do. Maybe he needed a change of scene. What I'm sure of is that you're young and keen, so you get out there and knock us dead.' McCredie rounded his desk and clapped Quinn's back. 'Just not as vigorously as you did with the Bull, okay?'

Quinn took the back stairs to the basement, where he found Maretsky picking his nose. 'Good morning,' Quinn said.

'I hadn't noticed.'

Quinn sighed. 'Let's look on the bright side, shall we? Is Yan about?'

'Not for an hour.'

'I need a favour. It's kind of urgent.'

Maretsky slipped from his stool. 'Go on, then.'

'I'd like to see all the homicide files from November last year until now.'

'Have you asked Johnny's permission?'

'I don't need it.'

Maretsky sucked his teeth. 'He still likes to know. I can get you the active list. If you want to take it further, you'd better talk to him. Why November?'

'It's when Charlie Matsell came back to the city.'

A few minutes later, Maretsky emerged with a list in his hand. 'Who do you want to know about? Most of the victims deserved everything they got. There was Rothstein, of course, still officially unsolved, then Mick "The Knife" Garraway three weeks later. There was our friend Dr Mackie over in Queens.'

'Dr Mackie?'

'He sent a couple of his elderly patients to the eternal hospital in the sky and mysteriously inherited their estates. Not very clever.'

'How did he kill them?'

'Arsenic. He's due to fry next week.' Maretsky

warmed to his theme. 'There was the Philadelphia Strangler, who murdered a bunch of people on the Upper East Side. He must be about ready to go to the Chair as well.'

'What about women?'

'Two of the Philadelphia guy's victims were women.'

'We're looking at the kidnap and assault of young women. Possibly even young girls.'

Maretsky looked down the list. 'No.'

'Nothing?' Quinn tried to hide his relief.

'I'm sure there were plenty of young girls murdered, Detective, all over Manhattan, but that doesn't mean the cases ended up here.'

'What about the Mecklenburg girl?'

'What about her?'

'How come her case is here?'

'There's an election on.'

'That's it?'

'It's Johnny's call. He and McCredie take whichever cases they want – or whichever the commissioner and Schneider tell them they want. It's all politics, Detective. You should know that by now.'

'What's the story with the uncle?'

'There's no file on him. They came and asked, but we don't have anything.'

'Where does he work?'

'Garage mechanic in the Bronx.'

CHAPTER TWENTY-NINE

AT DUNCAN'S MANSION, IT WAS LIKE NOTHING HAD happened. They encountered the same maid and the same fuss over dirty shoes and fancy carpets. As they stood in the hallway, they could hear children playing at the end of the corridor. 'You figure the mayor'll give me Duncan's job?' Caprisi asked.

'Jimmy doesn't employ Italians. Only decent, loyal, hardworking Irish Americans.'

'The masters of honest toil,' Caprisi said.

'Where do you figure the Bull and his friends'll go with this?'

Caprisi shrugged. 'Push around some dough, come up with a cock-and-bull shit story that'll play with the papers.'

As Quinn moved closer to the portrait of Mrs Duncan, she rounded the corner. She seemed weary but dry-eyed and drew on a cigarette in a long, ivory holder. She was wearing a tailored trouser suit and a hat, and didn't cut much of a figure as a grieving widow. 'You again,' she said to Quinn. This time there was no mistaking the way she sized him up.

'I'm sorry, ma'am, but—'

'There's no need to be sorry, Detective.'

'We've got to make sure that—'

'You're here to babysit me. How nice. Jimmy said they'd send somebody down. You want to wait here in the hall or . . .'

Quinn got the idea that this was, in fact, the only option.

'I'll get Elsie to make you a cup of coffee.' She turned to go.

'Actually, ma'am, would you mind if we take a look around?'

'A look around where?'

'Maybe your husband's study.'

'Why on earth would you want to do that?'

'Ma'am, this is a police investigation.'

'Are you going to rummage through my closets?' Her eyes flashed a challenge.

'If we could just look at your husband's study . . .'

'What do I have to fear?' She glared defiantly at Quinn. 'Isn't that right?'

Most of the doors off the hall were closed. The first they tried led to a darkened drawing room. Quinn flicked a light switch. Like the hall, the room was a monument to fine taste and great wealth. Luxuriant velvet curtains were pulled across tall windows. The carpet pile felt three inches deep. There were two long sofas, covered with a rich, red fabric, and a mahogany writing-desk. Another portrait of Mrs Duncan dominated the wall above the hearth. This time, she lounged seductively on an empty stage, the shoulder straps of her dress draped over bare arms.

Quinn turned off the light and closed the door. Caprisi had already gone into Duncan's study, which was sumptuously appointed in the style of a gentlemen's club. A brass ashtray stood at either end of a polished wooden desk. Bookshelves laden with weighty, leather-bound tomes filled one wall. Photographs hung on another. Quinn examined a picture of Duncan standing between Jimmy Walker and Grover Whalen at the tickertape reception for Charles Lindbergh after he'd flown non-stop across the Atlantic, then Duncan and the mayor at either side of Gene Tunney on the night he'd beaten Jack Dempsey to the world heavyweight title.

'Lucky bastard,' Caprisi muttered.

'Not so lucky now.'

Duncan's desk bore photographs of Mayor Walker in Havana, Paris and Berlin. The final picture was of Walker and Duncan with Al Smith and a fourth man Quinn didn't recognize. 'Who's that?'

'Al Blumenthal.'

The name was familiar. 'What's the connection?'

'He's one of the mayor's friendly millionaires.'

'How friendly is friendly?'

Caprisi sat down in the leather chair. 'How do you think he got to live like this, Detective? You figure it comes on a public official's salary?'

Quinn pulled open the central drawer of the desk. He found a selection of letters demanding payment for bills that were long overdue. One was from an automobile showroom for a brand-new Lincoln town car, which had been bought the previous spring but never paid for. Another was for a Plymouth coupé, a third for a Pierce-Arrow Roadster. There was a letter from Cartier, for the purchase of a diamond ring, and a second from Tiffany's for a ruby necklace. All the firms professed themselves certain the delay in payment had been due to an 'administrative oversight'.

Tucked beneath the pile was another photograph, a copy of the one of Martha he had found in Matsell's office.

Quinn tried to remove it, but Caprisi slammed his hand on it. 'Not this time.'

'It's my business.'

'Not any more it isn't.'

Quinn bent back his partner's fingers and slipped the photograph into his pocket.

'Now you're going to tell me what's going on,' Caprisi said, 'because it seems to me, Detective, that you know a hell of a lot more than you're letting on.'

'You've said you don't want trouble, so why don't you leave it?'

'Because you're my partner and I owe you.'

'You don't owe me anything.'

'In my neighbourhood, nobody stepped up to the plate for a guinea.'

268

'I'm real sorry to hear it, but you can consider your debt discharged.'

'It doesn't work that way. Also, I listened to your speech. Maybe you're right. I wear the badge, I should try to believe in it.'

Quinn watched a group of girls giggling on the sidewalk, and was reminded of Martha and the Santini daughters. He remembered how his father had watched her from the front room with his face pressed to the window.

His mind was playing tricks.

'I'll help you if you tell me how,' Caprisi muttered.

'What if the guys who are supposed to be protecting us are the ones we need to be protected from?'

'That's my line.'

'Maybe you're right.'

'No shit.' Caprisi's smile lit up his face.

'Luciano has top-level cover and he's looking after it.'

'Where did you hear that?'

'I dropped by the Cotton Club. Owney Madden told me Lucky will do what it takes to keep his man safe. The golden goose, he called him. What do you do, he said, if the goose turns bad?'

'Who was he talking about?'

Quinn raised his hands. 'You told me Valentine figured Schneider was calling the shots. Or maybe it's the Bull.'

'Unless you go higher,' Caprisi said. 'Look who Duncan was working for.'

'But do you figure the guys in the mayor's office are really in charge?'

'They can fire the commissioner, can't they?'

'But is the commissioner in control of men like the Bull?'

'I don't know, Joe.' Caprisi shook his head.

Quinn was pacing the floor. 'Moe Diamond was laid out flat in a room upstairs at the club. He was real shaken.'

'What about?'

'He wouldn't say.'

'But you can make a guess – and I reckon you already have.'

'I don't know what he's frightened of. Maybe it's like the story you told me. Some guy got his wife dumped in the East River and didn't like it.'

'So the guy fights back,' Caprisi said. 'Is that what you're saying? He wants to mete out a little justice to men who are *above the law*. First prize goes to Charlie, second to our friend Spencer Duncan. Meantime, Moe figures out his name is on the same ticket.'

'Maybe.'

'And Owney Madden's golden goose is on there with him?'

Quinn didn't answer.

'Which explains why Charlie Luciano and his boys are like cats on a hot tin roof. They lose the golden goose and their rackets fall apart. One weak link, and La Guardia cleans up. But why should we care, Joe? Even Duncan's wife doesn't mourn him.'

'We care because it's a crime.'

'A thousand crimes go unsolved in this city every day.'

'If we're right, there'll be other victims.'

'So you want me to bring out my handkerchief because a bunch of Wall Street crooks are shitting their pants? If they've been chasing broads and roughing them over, what the hell do we care if they get their just deserts? And if this goose gets fried, we'll have done the city a favour.'

'We care because it's the law, Caprisi.'

'*Do* we now? You believe everyone in this city is even close to being subject to the same law?'

Quinn turned away.

'Hold on a minute,' Caprisi said. 'I'm not finished. Some days, I figure you're an idealist and I like that. But sometimes you seem real naïve and that's not so good, because it means there's every chance you'll earn us both a ride out to Staten Island. And I'll tell you something else. There's no way on God's earth I'm going to leave my boy without a father.'

'You either believe in the law, Caprisi, or you don't. Maybe not everyone is guilty.'

'Maybe they're not and maybe the good Lord will forgive them.'

Quinn moved next door into a dressing room. It was furnished in similar style, with huge floor-to-ceiling closets and a couch along the opposite wall that doubled as a bed. Quinn opened one of the closet doors.

Caprisi stood beside him. 'So, why *do* we care, Detective?'

271

'Jesus . . .' The wardrobe stretched the length of the room and was full of suits. There must have been fifty, perhaps even a hundred. Beyond them, there were rows of matching sport jackets and striped pants, piqué vests, morning coats and top hats, then line upon line of ties. Rows of shoes stretched beneath the clothing. Quinn took out a couple of pairs. They looked as if they'd never been worn.

'Are you going to level with me?' Caprisi asked.

Quinn took out a suit. 'Hmm . . .'

'Don't tell me,' Caprisi said. 'Let me guess.'

Quinn checked the label. 'Jacob Zwirz.'

Caprisi wasn't about to be diverted. 'Joe, I'd like to help you. And, seeing the way you operate, I'd say you need a friend.'

'I've told you what I know.'

'Is that so? Then tell me again why we should give a damn if Moe and his friends are killed before sunset.'

'Because that's our job.'

'So you want us to get mixed up with these boys – with Moe and his golden-goose buddy, Luciano and his guys who're worried their rackets are about to go under – because it's our *job*?'

'Let's drop it.'

'Let's not. Where are you going to fly with those fists next, Joe? What are you trying to achieve?'

'We don't *know* anything,' Quinn hissed. 'You can't write Moe Diamond off because you don't like the cut of his suits. What happens if some of the guys on this ticket *are* innocent? That's what the law is supposed to

272

determine. Are we going to let a killer dance around Manhattan carving up whoever the hell he wants?'

'Why not? It seems like he's doing the world one hell of a favour.'

'I can't be straight with you,' Quinn said. 'I'd like to be. I know I should be. I appreciate what you're saying. I know the risks. I owe you an explanation. But I can't give it you. I don't know which direction the killer is coming from, or what his motive is, but I do know that some of the people in the frame could be innocent.'

'*Could* be?'

'Yes.'

'We're talking about that photograph, right?'

Quinn tried to avoid Caprisi's eye. 'Look, sometimes you can get caught up in something that really isn't your fault. Maybe it doesn't look good, but it can happen. So we can't just walk away. We . . . shouldn't.'

'Spell it out, Joe.'

'I can't.'

'Joe Quinn, I don't give two screws about this case, but I'd like to help *you*.'

'It's nothing. You're almost out of here. You have your world, I have mine. We should leave it at that.'

Caprisi took a deep breath. 'You say I'm a hard nut to crack. Well, let me tell you a true story. Maybe it'll help. My eldest brother was called Joe and you sure as hell remind me of him. He was smart, too, and head-strong. He joined the new Prohibition squad at Headquarters up in Chicago, but he wouldn't sign into the syndicate. One day, they decided he was more

273

trouble than he was worth and they sent one of their guys around to my parents' house and gunned Joe down on the doorstep. He died in my father's arms.'

'I'm sorry.'

'I'm not done. Here's the point. We know who killed my brother because he was a cop who lived only three streets away. He was Joe's friend. They used to be in the same gang when we were kids. But now he's a powerful detective and my father doesn't dare cross him. He passes him in the street every morning and raises his cap. He serves him coffee in the store and calls him "sir".'

'What are you trying to tell me, Caprisi?'

'You know exactly what I'm telling you. I'm ashamed of him. He's a coward. But he's still my father. He's my blood. More than that, he's old and frail and he needs me. After we got the news from Shanghai three years ago, I knew it was only a matter of time. There's no one else.'

Quinn felt the pain in his head again, deep behind his eyes.

'This is going to be a whole lot easier if you spell it out, Joe.'

Quinn took out the photograph of Martha. 'If you look hard,' he said, 'you can see two men in the picture, which means three in the room. But there were probably others.'

Caprisi examined it dispassionately. 'Who do you figure they are?'

'Charlie Matsell, Spencer Duncan and Moe Diamond

274

are top of my list. I guess Luciano's goose may have been there as well.'

'What did Moe Diamond tell you?'

'He asked me why we took Martha in.'

'And what answer did you give?'

'I didn't have one.'

'You figure this has something to do with your father? You think he's one of this group of men?'

'It's not possible.'

'But that's what Moe said?'

'It must be a misunderstanding.'

'Maybe Moe's lying,' Caprisi said quietly. 'From the look of him, I'd say it wouldn't be the first time.'

'Thanks.'

They sat in silence.

'It's okay, Joe.'

'It doesn't feel okay. I remember a time when everything was better, when it was good. I want to get back to that.'

'Don't we all?'

Quinn looked down at Spencer Duncan's shoes. He picked out a couple more pairs, loafers this time. As he crouched, he noticed a line of drawers along the bottom of the wardrobe.

The first was full of spats, the second bow-ties, the third suspenders and the fourth cufflinks. Quinn kept going along the row. The fifth had underpants, the sixth handkerchiefs (all neatly laundered and laid out), the seventh sock suspenders. Another had stud buttons for a dress shirt – hundreds of them.

The last drawer was locked. It was twice the width of the others.

'How are you with locks?'

Caprisi rolled his eyes, then took a small knife from his pocket and got down on his hands and knees. 'You sure you want to do this? If she tells the mayor, we're screwed.'

Quinn made sure both doors into the room were closed. Caprisi tried to pick the lock, without success.

'We'll have to force it,' Quinn said. 'The way she talks about him, I doubt she'll ever come in here again. Give me the knife.'

Caprisi held onto it. He used the short blade to try to force the drawer. It snapped. 'Now look what you've done. My brother gave me this.' He tried with the longer blade. It still wouldn't budge.

Quinn rifled the desk and found a letter opener. Together, they managed to splinter and force up the shelf above. 'Subtle,' Caprisi said as they surveyed the damage.

Quinn pulled out the drawer and placed it on the floor between them. He found a pair of gold cufflinks, beautifully engraved with Duncan's initials on each side. A silver heart-shaped pendant contained a lock of jet-black hair, and a pile of documents lay beneath it. They were mostly investment certificates. Nearly all the stocks had been bought through the same broker. There was no mention of Unique Investment Management, or of Luciano and Lansky's Olive Oil Company, but he did find a share certificate for Idaho Copper.

'What is it?' Caprisi asked.

'They've been in this business a long time. This was one of Rothstein's fixes eight or nine years ago. I read about it in Yan's files.'

Quinn unearthed a note from the Bank of America on Fifth Avenue acknowledging the deposit of a diamond necklace and five thousand dollars in cash. The final pages were covered with neat, handwritten figures. The first was headed 'Disbursements', but there was no sign of what the sums referred to. He showed them to Caprisi, then folded them and slipped them into his pocket. 'What triggered it?' he said. 'Why now? Why Matsell first? Why this Monday?'

'When was the photograph of Martha taken?'

'I don't know,' Quinn said. 'What about the Mecklenburg girl?'

They heard footsteps in the study and scrambled to replace the contents of the drawer. A moment later the maid was in the doorway. 'You're wanted on the telephone.'

Quinn followed her out to the hall. He picked up the earpiece. 'It's Schneider. Bring in the broad.'

'Mrs Duncan?'

'How many you got down there, Detective?'

Before Quinn could answer, the line went dead.

CHAPTER THIRTY

THE BULL'S TEAM LOOKED LIKE ALLEY CATS IN A CREAMERY. Brandon had his feet on the desk and was waving a newspaper with his own grinning face plastered across the front page. O'Reilly and the others sat in a circle around him, drinking coffee and smoking. Schneider hurried past them. 'Mrs Duncan, I appreciate this. We're real sorry to trouble you at this time.'

'I understand.'

He ushered her into his office.

The uniformed officer on the floor below was grinning from ear to ear. 'The Bull's sure hit the jackpot this time!'

Quinn lit a cigarette and offered him the packet. 'You're Ralph, right?'

'Seamus – Seamus Carrigan.'

'Are they in position, Seamus?'

'Sure are. Schneider said Mrs D was on her way, so we got them lined up. They ain't too happy.'

'Mind if we take a look?'

'Be my guest.'

'Which one is he?'

'Second from left. Seems pretty cool for a guy bound for the Chair.'

Quinn forced a smile. 'What's his name?'

'They call him Chile. Chile Acuna.'

Carrigan leant forward conspiratorially. 'They say he's a strong-arm guy, used to hang around the Bowery. They figure it's a carbon copy of Rothstein. Duncan fell out with this guy over a poker game and Acuna comes looking for his dough. One of the Bull's stoolies gave him the tip-off.'

Quinn and Caprisi stepped into the narrow corridor and pulled back the hatch. Chile Acuna was a sallow young man in a cheap suit and a slouch hat. 'Looks pretty relaxed, considering,' Quinn said. There wasn't a hood within striking distance of the Bowery who didn't know what it meant to be brought in by the Bull. Conviction always followed, guilty or not.

They heard voices and retreated down the corridor as McCredie and Brandon ushered Mrs Duncan through. The chief of detectives gave them a nod. 'You okay, boys?'

'Yes, sir. Just came to see how the real work's done.'

McCredie whispered a few words of reassurance to Mrs Duncan before he pulled back the hatch. She had to stoop a little to look through. 'Take your time,' McCredie murmured. 'There's no hurry. You've just got to be sure.'

They waited in silence. 'Yes,' she said. 'That's him. Second from left.'

McCredie slammed the hatch shut. 'You're certain?'

'Couldn't be more so.'

'You want to take another look?'

'No.'

'You're sure, ma'am?' Brandon asked. 'I don't like to press you, but with the newspaper interest and all . . . I mean, we know he's the guy, but—'

'I'm sure,' she said.

Quinn followed them out. 'You want us to take Mrs Duncan home?'

'No,' Brandon said.

'I'm all right, thank you,' she said. 'I have some business close by.'

'Are you sure, ma'am?' McCredie asked. 'Johnny here would be only too happy to—'

'I asked my driver to wait. But thank you for your assistance.' She glanced from one to the other. 'I'm glad the matter is resolved.'

Gloria Duncan made her way to the elevator. McCredie and Brandon followed at a discreet distance.

'I'll see you upstairs,' Quinn muttered to his partner.

'Where are you going?' Caprisi asked.

'I'll tell you later.'

Quinn whipped around to the Centre Street entrance in time to intercept her as she reached the Lincoln. 'Mrs Duncan? Would you have a minute?'

'For what?'

'Can I buy you a cup of coffee?'

She gave a tight smile. 'I've just identified my husband's killer, Detective. I'm not sure your timing is impeccable.'

'It's your husband I wanted to talk about.'

She tucked her handbag under her arm. 'Is that so? What more is there to say?'

'Mrs Duncan, I can explain.'

'Gloria,' she said. 'Mrs Duncan was my mother-in-law.'

Quinn smiled back. 'I'll call you whatever you want, ma'am, if I can just buy you that cup of coffee.'

Gloria Duncan spoke quietly to her driver and picked up a raincoat from the rear seat of the Lincoln. They walked a couple of blocks and took a table by a window in the corner of a diner. Quinn pulled the curtain half shut. 'Are you ashamed to be seen with me, Detective?' she asked. 'Or are you shy of the sun?'

He waved over a waitress and ordered.

'Are you married?' she asked.

'No.'

'You should be, handsome fellow like you.'

The waitress brought the coffee and they sipped it in silence. Now that they were sitting so close, Quinn could see the lines around her eyes.

'So, what is it you need to know so urgently?' she said.

'I wanted to ask a few questions about your husband.'

'So you said.' She brought out her cigarette holder and waited for him to strike a match. 'There's no great secret. I hated his goddamn guts and I don't care who knows it.'

'Ma'am, Mr Duncan has only just—'

'I thought you were interested in the truth, Detective.' She drew smoke deep into her lungs. 'Do you know his kind?'

'Well, ma'am, not—'

'God couldn't be any more arrogant. They rule the greatest city on earth, they're very rich men and they figure there is nothing – *nothing* – they cannot possess. And they might well be right.'

'Ma'am—'

'Gloria. Are you surprised, Detective, by what lies in a woman's heart? You shouldn't be. You look like you've been around the block a couple times. Why does a woman hate the man she was fool enough to marry?' She leant closer. 'He had a weakness for Ziegfeld girls, and I should know because I was one.'

'That why he was killed?'

'Not according to your superiors.'

'What did they tell you?'

'You mean they're not being entirely frank with you?' she said. 'Why, there's a surprise.' There was laughter in her eyes, and the same challenge she'd offered in the hallway of her home. 'They told me it's a ringer for the Rothstein case. My husband was lured into bad company. He got in too deep, lost out in a couple of big card games, and when they came to collect, he wouldn't pay.'

'Your husband was a very rich man, ma'am, but we

understand some of his possessions were never paid for.'

'He was arrogant, greedy and stubborn as a mule. And if you call me "ma'am" one more time I'll get up and walk right out.'

'So how does Mr Chile Acuna fit into all this?'

'They told me he was the gambler to whom my husband owed money.'

'And where had you seen him before?'

'He came to the house.'

'When?'

'The night before Spencer's death.'

'And they told you he was the killer?'

She concentrated hard on her coffee.

'And you believed them?'

She didn't look up. 'Yes.'

'You figure it fits?'

'I'm not sure I care if it doesn't. I told you, I hated his guts. I'm only too pleased he's dead. That way, I don't have to divorce him.'

'You should be careful who you share those sentiments with, Mrs Duncan.'

A waitress came to them and asked if they wanted anything to eat. They said no. Quinn watched her walk away, teetering on high heels. 'So who do you figure killed him?'

She shrugged.

'You really don't care, do you?'

'No.'

'Then why are you here?'

Now she looked at him. 'You're not part of their crowd, are you?'

'I guess not.'

'That sounds dangerous.'

'You said your husband had a weakness for Ziegfeld girls. Do you have any idea which ones?'

'No.'

'He had a mistress?'

'A great many, I should think.'

'Do you know who they were?'

'No.'

'Did he treat women well?'

'You mean did he treat *me* well?'

'Did he?'

'No. He was a bastard.'

'Rough?'

'Sometimes.'

'Can you think of anyone else who might have wanted to kill him?'

'Jilted lovers, angry fathers and brothers. Take your pick.'

'Do you have anyone particular in mind?'

'How about me?' There was suddenly real hurt in her eyes. 'I had more reasons than the rest of them put together.' She stood. 'May I leave you with the check?'

'Mrs Duncan—'

'*Gloria*, goddamn it!'

'You've never seen Chile Acuna before in your life.'

'Are you calling me a liar?'

284

'It's what they asked you to say. They took you aside and told you they had this guy nailed straight, that some stoolie had fingered him, they were sure it was on the level, but they needed you to identify him to be certain of a conviction.'

She froze. 'I think you should be careful whom you take to coffee in future, Detective. I can see you don't know much about the ways of this city.'

'But I'm right.'

'Being right won't make you popular.'

'Do you know a guy called Moe Diamond?'

'No.'

Quinn took out his wallet and flicked through it.

'If you're having trouble with the check,' she said haughtily, 'I'm sure I can help out.'

He dropped a photograph of his father on the table. Gerry was in uniform, standing outside the First Precinct station house. 'Do you know this man?'

She picked it up. 'Sure I know him. He's been around to the house a couple of times.'

'When?'

'I don't know. Does it matter?'

'It might. When was the last time you saw him?'

'A few days ago.'

'Do you know his name?'

'If I'd taken an interest in every gentleman who came to visit Spencer, I should have considered myself most unwise.'

'What did he do?'

'Spencer took him into his study, like he did everyone

285

else.' She picked up her handbag and managed to smile. 'Now you've probably had your money's worth, Detective, and that's certainly as far as I'm prepared to go on a first date.'

She stalked away and the café door banged shut behind her.

CHAPTER THIRTY-ONE

CHILE ACUNA SAT WITH HIS FEET ON THE DESK, SMOKING A cigarette. He showed not the slightest sign of unease. In fact, he seemed to be singing to himself.

Quinn touched Carrigan's arm and pointed towards the glass window. 'Mind if we have a chat with him, Seamus?'

Carrigan frowned. 'Sure, Joe. But . . . you should go tell the Bull – it's his suspect, right?'

'It's okay. We told the Bull already.' Quinn slipped into the interview room before he could be contradicted.

Acuna didn't budge, so Caprisi swept his feet off the desk.

'Hey!' The prisoner jumped to his feet.

'Sit down.'

Acuna fingered the brim of his hat.

Quinn reached down and flicked the light switch beneath the desk. 'Good afternoon, Chile. I'm Detective

Quinn and this is my colleague, Detective Caprisi. You can call us both "sir".'

'Kiss my ass.' Acuna snorted. He was an unattractive man, with greasy hair, narrow cheeks, an unshaven chin and dark, deep-set eyes; the kind of guy you'd leave the sidewalk to avoid.

'Want another cigarette, Chile?'

'I got my own.'

Quinn took one from his pocket and lit it. He threw the case across to Caprisi.

Acuna blinked rapidly as he scrutinized them both. 'You with the Bull?'

'Yeah.'

'Then how come I ain't never seen you before?'

'Just unlucky, I guess,' Caprisi said.

'I told Johnny all I know.'

'Johnny's a friend?'

Acuna frowned. 'He's a cop, for Christ's sake!'

'Known him long?'

'Everyone knows Johnny.'

'What do you do for a business, Chile?'

'Nothing much.'

'That's a fancy outfit for a guy who does nothing much.'

'I'm a gentleman of means and leisure.'

'So, you're a gambler?' Quinn said.

'A businessman.'

Acuna slid his feet back on the desk and Quinn made no move to prevent him. 'Where exactly do you conduct your business?' he asked.

'I got a place downtown.'

'Where?'

'That's my affair.'

'In the Bowery?'

'Maybe.'

'How long you been one of the Bull's stoolies, Chile?'

Acuna was on his feet. 'Jesus Christ, who said that? I ain't nobody's stool pigeon.' A muscle fluttered in his cheek. 'I ain't stooling for nobody, not Johnny or anybody else.'

'It's okay, Chile,' Quinn said. 'You're among friends.'

Acuna stared at them. 'Johnny's got me down here on a murder rap and you think he's a friend of mine?'

'Sit down.'

'You guys are crazy. I thought you said—'

'I said *sit down.*'

Reluctantly Acuna did so. Quinn saw Caprisi nod. 'You think it'll be Sing Sing?' Quinn asked. 'Or the Chair?'

'I ain't done nothing.'

'You seem pretty relaxed for a guy bound for the Chair,' Caprisi said.

'I told you, I ain't done nothing wrong.'

'What did they promise you, Chile?'

'Who?'

'The Bull and his crowd. What was it they promised?'

'I don't know what you're talking about.'

'Sure you do.'

Acuna leapt to his feet again. 'Who the hell are you guys? Is this some kind of Confidential Squad bullshit?'

'The Confidential Squad was disbanded,' Quinn said.

'Yeah? Well, you said you were from Johnny's mob, but I ain't never seen you before.'

'We're working another case, Chile, is all. You answer a few questions and we're out of here.'

'Like what?'

'Did you know Charlie Matsell?'

Acuna stepped briskly across and banged on the window. He shouted for the guard. Caprisi bent one of Acuna's hands behind his back and manhandled him to the chair. As he tried to get up again, Quinn stamped so hard on his toe that he squealed like a pig.

When he'd stopped yelling, he said, 'That hurt.'

Quinn struck him hard across the face. 'How about that?'

'Jesus!'

'Quit taking the name of Our Lord in vain.'

Acuna stared at him as if he were mad. 'I want to see the Bull!' He made another break for the door.

'Sit down.'

'I don't know who you guys are, but he'll cut your balls right off.'

'*Sit down!*'

Caprisi shoved the chair into the back of Acuna's knees and pushed him onto it. Acuna had dropped what remained of his cigarette and Caprisi stepped forward to tread it out. 'You answer a few questions, Chile,' Quinn said, 'and you can kiss us goodbye. So, let's try once more. What did they promise you?'

'I got no idea what you're talking about.'

'They said you'd have to take the heat for a few months, while the story was on the front page, but then they'd let the evidence drop at the prelim and you'd be out with a free hand?'

Acuna was silent.

'You figure they'll stick to the bargain, Chile?'

Quinn went out into the corridor and picked up a copy of the *Sun* from beside Carrigan's desk. 'Everything all right, Joe?' the officer asked. Should I call the Bull and just tell him that—'

Quinn closed the door on Carrigan and dropped the newspaper in front of Acuna. 'You seen your handiwork?'

Acuna glanced at it.

'Have you actually read this, Chile?'

He shook his head.

'You want to know what they did to the guy?'

'No.'

'They pulled his pants down, cut his throat and stabbed him in the heart. You know who he was?'

''Course I do.'

'Maybe you missed the fact that there's an election on. Some of the guys down at Tammany are saying La Guardia's behind it. Tomorrow you'll be on every front page. You figure it's all going to die down and they'll let you walk? Don't you know how much shit we were in after we failed to bust the Rothstein case?'

'I don't know anything about that.'

'They've set you up, Chile.'

Acuna blinked rapidly. The muscle in his cheek was still twitching.

'They have set you up *real* good. This morning we had the mayor in here, standing alongside the commissioner. So what does the Bull do? To prove he's still the biggest cog in the machine, he brings you in. Everyone knows you're a gambler and it looks like you've been settling a debt. Duncan's widow gives a positive ID. She says you came to her house to collect money from her husband, and when you discovered he wasn't there, you went looking for him.'

'That's bullshit. I never went to his house.'

'That's not what she says. And she used to be a showgirl so she'll lay it on real thick.'

'She's a lying bitch.'

'You've been set up, Chile. And, believe me, with a case like this, the bosses upstairs will be only too willing to buy the sting. Maybe Brandon meant what he said. But you figure he's going to be able to pull it off? You think you'll slip out the Tombs in six months?' Quinn shook his head. 'Her ID'll send you to the Chair, and you're a fool if you don't know it.'

'I ain't never been to her house.'

'She says different.'

'She's a dumb, lying showgirl b—'

'Then how come she picked you out?'

He frowned. 'What do you mean?'

'How come she picked you out, Chile, if she'd never seen you before?'

'I told you, she's a liar.'

'She picked you out because she'd been told to. The Bull wants to fix this case. He spun a line to McCredie and brought her in to pick you out. He told her they had the right guy, that her husband had been killed for a gambling debt and they just needed a positive ID to help them with the grand jury.'

'So what?'

'You still don't get it? You need to hire yourself a lawyer and real fast. Ask him if he thinks he can save you from the Chair. You imagine what she's going to be like as the grieving widow on the stand. "Yes, your honour, this was the man who came to my house. He frightened me." Take a look at yourself in the mirror, Chile. There isn't a jury in the land that wouldn't convict you. You're a walking electric current.'

Quinn stood. He checked there was no one in the corridor. 'Listen, we've tried to help you. I know you don't deserve to fry, but don't cry for me when they come for you.'

They were halfway into the corridor before Acuna took the bait. 'Who are you guys?' He was turning a cigarette lighter over and over with his right hand.

'Good luck, Chile,' Caprisi said.

'What are you working on?'

Quinn closed the door again and leant on it. 'You *are* a gambler, right, Chile?'

He didn't answer.

'You do some pimping, if you can find the right broads.'

'That's my business.'

293

'Did you know Charlie Matsell?'

'I heard he jumped.'

'So, you did know him?'

'I met him a few times. Doesn't mean I killed him.'

Quinn sat down again. 'Where did you meet him?'

'I ain't answering this bullshit. Johnny'll see me right.'

'We've been over that.'

'He's a good guy; everyone says so.'

'Chile, he's the star of the show. You're just another chorus girl. What does he care if you go to the wall?'

'He wouldn't do that.'

Quinn stood again.

'Okay.' Acuna sat back, palms open. 'I'll help you. I mean, what harm can it do? You're all on the same side, right?'

'That's good thinking, Chile.'

'So, what do you guys want?'

'We've been looking for a weak link. And I've got a hunch we've found it.'

Acuna laughed nervously, unsure whether this was meant as a joke.

'Tell us what you know about Charlie Matsell.'

'I don't know nothing.'

'Where did you meet him?'

'Some place around town.'

'Try again.'

'He sometimes took a hand.'

'Where?'

'There's a club called the Hellfire.'

294

'That's Luciano's joint. So, you, Charlie and Spencer Duncan used to meet up at the Hellfire?'

Acuna didn't answer.

'You had a poker game going?'

'Sometimes.'

'How often?'

'Couple times a week.'

'Did Lucky Luciano take a hand?'

'Not his scene.'

'The three of you would slip upstairs for a game?'

'Something like that.'

'They gave you a private room?'

He nodded.

'Lansky fixed it for you?'

'It was always the hostess, the Texan girl with the huge jugs.'

'Broads as well?'

Acuna shook his head. Maybe a little too vigorously.

'Tell us about the girls, Chile.'

'There were no broads.'

'You went somewhere else for that?'

'There were no broads. We took a hand, is all.'

'You smacked some of the girls around a little. That what happened?'

'I told you already, there were no broads.'

'That's not the way we hear it.'

'Then you don't know a damn thing.'

'You figure Spencer and the others went somewhere else to get their kicks?'

'How in hell would I know?'

'You got any idea where?'

'No.'

'But they went somewhere, right?'

Acuna glared at him.

Quinn leant back against the wall and put his foot on a chair. 'Something's not right here, Chile. We hear there's been trouble with some of the girls. A couple guys got a bit rough. It happens, right? Hell, maybe you were nowhere near. Shame if you took the rap.' He paused for a moment. 'You want to tell us where the girls came from?'

'How many times do I have to tell you? There *were* no broads.'

'So who else was in on the game?'

'A crowd. Not always the same guys.'

'Moe Diamond?'

'Yeah, Moe was there. He's a good guy.'

'What about Dick Kelly?'

'Sometimes.'

'Who else?'

'Jeez, I don't know. There were other guys to make up the numbers.'

'Like who?'

'I don't remember.'

'Were there any cops in the game, Chile?'

'No.'

'Are you sure about that?'

'Yeah, I'm sure.'

Quinn dropped the photograph of his father on the desk. 'You know this man?'

Acuna looked at it for a long time. 'Maybe.'

'Is that a yes or a no?'

'Yeah, I know him.'

'What's his name?'

'Gerry. Gerry Quinn.'

'You know he's my father?'

Acuna shifted in his seat. 'Yeah. I know.'

'Was he a part of this game?'

'Look, since Gerry's your old man . . .' he laughed nervously '. . . I mean, whatever the problem is, Gerry will sort it out. That's what I heard.'

Quinn brought out the photograph of Martha. 'You recognize this girl?'

Acuna bared his teeth.

Quinn bunched his fists and struggled to remain motionless. 'Where was the photograph taken?'

'I've no idea.'

'But you were there, Chile.'

'Who says I was?'

'C'mon, man, it's no big deal. She's just a broad, right?'

Acuna's eyes glittered. 'She's sure a beauty, ain't she? Must have been fun.'

Quinn cleared his throat. 'So who else was there?' He knew Caprisi was watching him closely.

'Who said I was there?'

'We know you were. Like I said, it's no big deal—'

'If it's no big deal, you don't need me to talk about it.'

'Humour us. Who brought the girl along?'

'I don't know, because I wasn't there.'

297

'You *were* there, Chile. Two of the guys who were in the room with you have already been sliced up, and Moe Diamond is shitting himself in the Cotton Club. Can't you see where this is going?'

'I ain't got nothing to say to you, man, but, hell, looking at that broad's pussy, I sure wish I had been—'

Quinn exploded from the chair and slapped Acuna hard across the face. 'Try again, Chile.'

'Jesus!' Acuna screamed, and tried to get to his feet, but he didn't make it to the door.

Quinn gripped him by the lapels and lifted him off the ground. 'Try again, you piece of shit!'

Caprisi came between them. 'Easy, Joe, easy. He's Johnny's man. We don't want to trigger World War Two here. Right, Chile?'

Acuna glared at him, his face livid from the impact of the blow.

'*Right*, Chile?' Caprisi forced Quinn's arms lower.

'You tell him to get the hell away from me.'

'Joe, easy.' Caprisi tried to break his grip. 'Let him go, Joe.' He forced Quinn back a pace. 'Listen, Chile, Joe here is real upset, so you need to help us out.'

'I ain't speaking to nobody but Johnny from now on.'

'Take a seat.'

'If he touches me again, I'll yell so loud they'll hear me in Queens.'

'Just take a seat.'

Acuna did so. Quinn didn't budge.

'Chile, you're a real smart guy,' Caprisi said, 'so just

think about this. Joe is right. Two of the guys who were in that room with you are already dead. Charlie Matsell went to meet a guy and took the quick way off the roof. Spencer Duncan got sliced up in the back of an automobile. Moe Diamond's frightened he may be next. Where does that leave you?'

Acuna's eyes flicked between them.

'C'mon, Chile,' Caprisi said. 'Don't you get it? You were in that room, so you're on the list. Someone is settling a score. You have to know that.'

'I ain't got nothing to say to you.'

'Monday they kill Charlie. Tuesday they kill Spencer. Who are they going to kill today?' Caprisi shook his head. 'They're your buddies, not mine.'

'I don't know what you're talking about.'

Caprisi grabbed Quinn's arm and yanked him towards the door. 'Okay, have it your way. But we'll be back. And if someone else goes under the knife without you talking, I'm going to allow my friend a free hand. Have you got that?'

Caprisi pushed Quinn out of the room, ignoring Carrigan's protests, and led him down the corridor. 'I thought you were going to kill him.'

'Next time.' Quinn shook himself free. He lit a cigarette and drew heavily on it, trying to pretend his hand wasn't shaking.

'He was there,' Caprisi said quietly.

''Course he was.'

'You're right about there being other girls.'

Quinn stubbed out the cigarette. 'I'm going to speak

to Yan. There must be some kind of pattern. I'll see you back upstairs.'

'Joe, hold on a minute—'

But Quinn did not look back.

On the way down to the Criminal Investigation Bureau, Quinn passed through the central hallway. Amy Mecklenburg's mother had resumed her position on the bench and the expression on her face drew him up short. Her eyes were hollow. 'Mrs Mecklenburg, it's Detective Quinn, Joe Quinn. I spoke to you yesterday.'

'Has there been any news?'

'Er, no, ma'am. Has no one come to talk to you?'

'Your friend, the lady, was with me. Are you working on the case?'

'No, ma'am. Detectives O'Reilly and Byrnes are still in the lead.'

'Your friend said that all . . . *most* detectives upstairs would be looking for Amy.'

'That's correct. They haven't found her?'

'She'll be worried now. Someone must have taken her in. She'll be cared for, won't she?'

'I sure hope so, ma'am.'

'I'm so frightened.' Mrs Mecklenburg began to cry again. Quinn watched her for a moment and put an arm awkwardly around her shoulders.

'Sometimes, in the night, I can hear her crying out for me,' she sniffed.

Quinn tried to think of something else to say. 'Is there anything I can get you?'

'No . . . no, thank you.'

'Are you sure?'

'Yes. I'll just . . . I'll stay here. I'm sure there will be some news soon.'

'Ma'am, you should go home. They'll call the moment they have anything.'

'No . . . thank you. I'll remain here.'

'Mrs Mecklenburg.' He sat down beside her. 'How long ago did your daughter disappear?'

'It was last Wednesday, in the morning. I told your colleagues, Detective. She was going to a new job. She was so excited. I sometimes wonder if they had cause to send her somewhere and she simply didn't have time to call.'

'Where was the new job?'

'I told your colleagues. It was on Broadway. They have the name of the firm. She was a stenographer. I called them when she didn't come home that night. They said she had never arrived. I . . . I didn't know what to do.'

'So, the last time you saw her was when you said goodbye to her that morning?'

'Yes.'

'Was there anything unusual? Did she appear pre-occupied? Had she made arrangements to meet anyone?'

'No. She was happy, *so* happy. She said it was a good job. It would allow her to . . . Since my husband died, Officer, we have not been . . . She was excited that she would be earning her own money and able to buy clothes. You know how young girls are . . .'

'How did she get the job?'

'She went on a course for two months at a school in Brooklyn. When she finished, she joined an agency.'

'Do you have the name of the agency?'

'No – I mean, it's in my book at home. I gave it to your colleagues.'

'You didn't see anyone following her after she left the house?'

'No.'

Quinn steepled his fingers. 'Did she ever go to a photographer's studio, Mrs Mecklenburg?'

'No . . . no.'

'She wasn't interested in modelling?'

The woman was clearly perplexed. 'No. Why?'

'It's probably nothing. I'm working on a case and thought maybe there might be a connection. Did she ever mention a man called Moe Diamond?'

'No.'

'How about Charlie Matsell or Spencer Duncan?'

'No . . . There was a boy called Charlie who lives down the street, but he . . . I know his mother. He's a charming boy. I couldn't imagine . . .'

'I understand that her uncle has also disappeared. Is it possible he's taken her on a trip?'

'I told your colleagues he's gone to see a friend in Syracuse for a few days. He's my brother. A good man. I don't understand why they have asked questions about him.'

'What's his name?'

'Peter Bruning.'

Quinn pressed her hand. 'Are you sure you want to stay here, ma'am? You'd be more comfortable at home and we could call when there's news.'

'No, I'll stay here. It can't be much longer. She'll be found soon.'

CHAPTER THIRTY-TWO

YAN WAS ALONE IN HIS OFFICE WITH A CUP OF COFFEE AND a doughnut. An early edition of the *Evening News* was open in front of him. He wiped sugar from his upper lip as Quinn walked in.

'What happened to Maretsky?' Quinn asked.

'I sent him home. He gets on my nerves.'

Quinn grabbed himself a stool. 'Is there any movement on Amy Mecklenburg, the girl who's missing in Brooklyn?'

Yan shrugged.

'They find the uncle?' Quinn asked.

'Not as far as I know.'

'How come they haven't got more guys on it?'

'They're focused on your business now. The Brooklyn precincts are doing the grunt work and chasing down leads on the girl.'

'Does it ring any bells for you, Yan?'

'Bells?'

'A pattern, maybe. Other girls missing in Brooklyn, anyone else being sent for a job and failing to turn up.'

He shook his head.

'Any idea where she might have gone?'

'Jesus, Joe, I don't know. Girls go missing in this city all the time. Maybe she met a guy and ran off to the west coast. She wouldn't be the first.' Yan finished his doughnut. 'Is that all you came down for?'

'I could use your help on something.'

'Go on.'

'This case we're on, Johnny figures he's got it wrapped up, but we think he's on the wrong track.'

'And what's the right track?'

'These guys, the ones who are getting killed, have been in on some girls being assaulted. Could be the guy out there is a husband or a brother. I asked Maretsky to check out homicide cases for a match, but there's nothing.'

'So what can I do?'

'Yan, I'd call around myself, but you know the filing guys in the precincts – you talk to them the whole time. There has to be something. Maybe the girls were drugged. That would explain the chloroform. Perhaps some guy in the precincts has spotted a pattern—'

'Hold on, Joe. I have hundreds of requests coming through here every day and only the Russian to help me this week. And this is the Bull's case. Hell, I can see the way you're thinking, but tomorrow's front pages have been written.'

'But it's bullshit and you know it.'

'Johnny's been around a long time. He knows a thing or two.'

'It's bullshit.'

'Mind who you say that to, Joe. Big high-profile case in the middle of an election . . . Johnny's an ambitious man. The guys on the top floor are on the way out and everyone knows it. He can do himself some favours with City Hall if he handles it right. You need to watch your back.'

Quinn poured himself a jug of water and went to his desk. He picked up the Matsell file and flicked it open. Caprisi had pinned a photograph of Matsell's body to the front of the first report. Quinn read through the witness statements twice, then turned to the pictures of the scene of Duncan's murder. He tapped the file against his nose.

'Calculating your losses?'

Quinn swung around. 'What losses?'

Mae leant against the table, arms crossed. 'Are you so absorbed in your work, Detective, that you don't know Wall Street's in freefall?'

'It's always in freefall.'

'No, this time it really is. The boss figures it's all over for shares.'

Quinn turned back to his notepad.

'Aren't you interested in what Johnny has to say to the reporters?'

'What's he saying?'

'He's the star turn at a press conference. Everyone

went down to hear how he'd cracked the case in record time.' She laughed. 'You know how he loves the limelight.'

He smiled back at her, then reached for the phone and asked the operator to put him through to the fingerprint bureau.

'Detective Quinn, Homicide.'

'Ah, Detective Quinn, already a legend.'

'Who is this?'

'Zac Kroner. We haven't met, but if we do I'll bring my gloves. About time someone taught the Bull some goddamn manners.'

'You find any prints inside the Buick last night?'

'Not a single one. Hundreds from the dead guy and his driver, but no one else.'

'So, he had gloves on.'

'Yeah.'

'He's a pro.'

'Well, he's no fool.'

Quinn replaced the earpiece.

Mae was still standing next to him. 'Trouble?'

He stood up and stretched his arms. 'This is one strange place.'

'Have you only just worked that out? McCredie's all right, but some of the others . . .'

'He must know what goes on.'

'I guess he doesn't miss much.' She glanced over her shoulder. 'But someone like Johnny Brandon gets results and that's worth a lot. If a few unsavoury elements come with it, perhaps that's a price worth paying.'

'You think McCredie'd let a case go the wrong way even if he knew Johnny's story didn't add up?'

'Not in the end. But he's got Schneider on his back, so in the short term it'll get ugly.'

Caprisi rounded the corner. 'It's already ugly.'

Quinn nodded. 'There were no prints in the Buick.'

Caprisi slumped into his seat. 'So, the guy's a ghost. He can get onto the roof of a building and off again without being seen. He can get in and out of Duncan's car without a trace.'

'And Duncan was waiting for him.'

'How do you know that?' Mae said.

'He was carrying a piece. His wife said he'd never packed one before. And why else would anyone be waiting in Central Park?'

A group of stenographers clattered past. 'I know it's a hell of a coincidence,' Mae said, 'but are you sure these two murders are connected? The way I hear it, Duncan had a whole bunch of enemies.'

'Like who?'

'Like pretty much everyone he ever crossed.'

'What about Matsell?'

'I don't know. Maybe that was suicide.'

'It wasn't,' Caprisi said.

'They're messages,' Quinn said. 'First the chloroform in the mouth. Then the cut to the throat.'

'Who for?' Mae asked.

'The men who have their names on the ticket.'

'What are you saying?'

'Someone out there knows exactly what they mean.'

'But none of those details have been in the papers.'

'They don't need to be,' Caprisi said, 'if the people they're intended to reach are right inside this building.'

Quinn watched Mae's face pale. 'We should go and listen to the Bull.'

CHAPTER THIRTY-THREE

THE BULL STOOD AT THE EDGE OF THE PODIUM FLANKED BY McCredie and the commissioner. Mayor Jimmy Walker, hands slipped into his pockets and hair slicked neatly back, stood behind a bank of broadcast microphones. Most of the reporters sat in serried rows and the walls were lined with photographers. Quinn had to shove past a couple of latecomers to get a decent view. O'Reilly and Byrnes stood by the exit, watching him intently.

'I thought Byrnes was in Syracuse,' Quinn whispered to Caprisi.

'I think you're right, Jack,' Mayor Walker told one of the reporters. 'We've moved on since Rothstein and this proves it. I said at the time it hadn't been handled well. When the occasion arises, there's no one prepared to be a stronger critic of this department than I – and these men know it. When a crime attracts the attention of our friends in the press, it's real important we nail it fast or people lose faith in their police force. I'm open about that. But under Commissioner Whalen and Ed McCredie, with top-rank detectives like Johnny, the force has never been in better hands and this case shows it.'

Hegarty, the press chief, fiddled with his red suspenders and nodded gravely. He still had a bruised cheek from the fight with Quinn the morning before.

'You figure he'll go to the Chair?'

'That's not a matter for me,' the mayor said.

'You going to hand Johnny a medal?'

Mayor Walker gave a wide grin. 'I believe he already has a chestful.'

The Bull didn't smile.

'You think Chile Acuna acted alone, Johnny?'

'As I've already said,' Brandon replied testily, 'we've known Acuna a long time. We've watched him. He has a record of this kind of argument. We know that, like the Rothstein case, it was high-stakes play. Duncan wasn't making good his debts, so Acuna lost patience.'

'He didn't need an accomplice?'

'In our opinion, he did not.'

'He overpowered two guys, one in the front and one in the back?'

'He was armed and he's a dangerous man.'

'More ammunition for La Guardia, Mr Mayor?'

'If Major La Guardia and his friends would like a less efficient police force, then sure it is.'

There was a sycophantic laugh.

'I heard there was a connection to another case.' All

eyes turned to the new voice, which came from a small, dark-haired reporter close to the back. He wore tiny round glasses and a crumpled coat, the collar half turned up and shoulders white with dandruff. 'There was a guy who jumped off a building in Wall Street on Monday, right?' The reporter consulted his notebook. 'Name of Charlie Matsell. He was another part of this poker game?'

'We don't believe there's a connection,' the Bull said.

'That wasn't my question. I asked if they were part of the same poker game.'

The Bull glowered at him. 'I'm not aware that they were.'

'I heard you thought this guy Matsell was murdered.'

'You heard wrong.'

'One of your rookies figured there could be a connection.'

'I don't know who you've been speaking to, Mr Goldberg, but your information is not correct. We have had a number of detectives working on the case, as you'd expect with an incident of this kind. One was sent to check out whether there was a link. There wasn't.'

'Why did you think there might be?'

'We didn't.'

'If you didn't think there could be,' Goldberg continued, 'then why did someone need to go and check it out?'

There was a moment's silence as the Bull fought to control his anger. 'I can see you've never run an investigation, Mr Goldberg. We follow many leads

312

that prove ultimately to have no bearing on a case.'

'Yeah, but my point is, why did you ever think there *might* be a connection?'

The Bull stared at him. 'I believe I've answered your question, Mr Goldberg.'

'You haven't.'

'Mr Goldberg,' Mayor Walker interjected smoothly, 'you've had your say. Now, if you gentlemen have your story, we have a city to run.'

'What about the photograph?'

Heads turned.

'Which photograph?' McCredie said.

'I heard Duncan had a picture of the mayor with Rothstein and Lucky Luciano out on the realty development in Queens.'

'Mr Goldberg—'

'You know what Major La Guardia says: Rothstein got that sewer dug in and managed to put up forty-eight houses, block after block, without being troubled by building inspectors.'

'Mr Goldberg,' McCredie said, 'this is a press conference about the murder of the second most important man in the city. If you'd like to make political accusations—'

'I heard that's what you thought it was about.'

McCredie took a step forward. 'We're here to talk about a crime.' He had lowered his voice an octave. 'If you'd like to make politically motivated accusations, Mr Goldberg, for your friends in the Republican camp—'

'They're not my friends.'

'And neither will we be if you continue in this manner. Right, that's it, gentlemen. Thank you for coming.'

As the press conference broke up, cameras flashed and reporters broke off into small huddles. Quinn shoved his way through the throng, past the payroll department, *en route* to the back stairs.

'Detective Quinn?' Goldberg wiped his glasses. 'Mind if I ask a few questions?'

'No. I mean, yes, I do.'

Caprisi slipped away. Quinn tried to follow him.

'It'll just take a few minutes—'

'Mr Goldberg—'

'Call me Joshua. I just wanted to ask—'

'Mr Goldberg, you've had your press conference. I don't have anything else to say.'

'But you believe there's a connection with the Matsell case.'

'I don't know where you're getting your information, but I have nothing to add.'

'That's right, though?'

'I'm just a small cog. You need to talk to the Bull.'

Goldberg pushed his glasses back onto the bridge of his nose. 'Don't take me for one of those other schmucks, Detective. I've got a real good bullshit detector and Johnny Brandon sends it right off the scale every time he opens his mouth. So, you want to tell me what's really going on?'

'No, thanks.'

'We could help each other.'

'I doubt it.'

The reporter took a card from his wallet and shoved it into Quinn's top pocket. 'Think about it. You can call me, day or night.'

Quinn had barely got through the door upstairs when Johnny Brandon thrust him back out into the stairwell. Through the open doorway, he could see the mayor and Commissioner Whalen inside McCredie's office.

'You and your little guinea friend been talking to that snivelling shit Goldberg? You've got a nerve, kid.'

Quinn shook his head.

'You'd better wise up. Keep going like this and I'll have you busted out of here so fast your little dancing feet won't touch the ground.'

'Sure, Johnny.'

'Don't you "sure, Johnny" me. I was busting cases in here when you were sucking your mother's tit.'

O'Reilly stepped into the stairwell. 'Come on, Johnny. The boss wants you, and this kid ain't worth your breath.'

The Bull adjusted his tie and followed him back into Homicide. Quinn joined Caprisi at his desk. They glanced across at the group huddled in McCredie's office. 'You figure someone's trying to set us up?' Caprisi said.

'Why would anyone want to do that?'

'You tell me. How in hell did Goldberg know so much? Did you speak to him?'

'Never saw him before.'

Caprisi passed a softball from one hand to the other and back again. 'If a newspaper got a hold of that picture . . .' He whistled quietly. 'The mayor, Rothstein and Luciano . . . City Hall goes bang! Someone in here is singing to the press. The Bull's got nothing to gain, nor big Ed McCredie or any of the other guys on the top floor. They've got to figure it's us.'

'What do you suggest we do about it?'

'I'm just saying it doesn't look good.'

'That's helpful.'

'Always glad to be of service.'

'I'll talk to McCredie.'

'That's not such a smart idea. Not now. It's too soon to resign. Besides, things are going so well, with all the new friends you've made . . .' Caprisi pulled open a drawer and lobbed the softball inside. 'You sure know how to complicate a guy's life.'

'You could always go back to the Rat Squad.'

'Cheap shot.' Caprisi was no longer smiling. 'I'll tell you something. When I was with Valentine, people in here used to spit in my face. Now some even call out good morning when they pass.'

'We don't get paid to make friends.'

'But we sure as hell don't *have* to make enemies.'

They looked at each other.

'I thought you joined Valentine because you believed in him,' Quinn said.

'I did, but I joined to get to Headquarters.' Caprisi pulled over his chair. 'Listen, Joe. You stepped up to the plate for me with the Bull and I appreciate that. I'm your guy now. But we don't have to make enemies of everyone in the building.'

'I'm not *trying* to offend anyone.'

'You don't have to try.' Caprisi laughed. 'Hey, that's life. You take two steps forward and one back. I told Sandra last night there were at least a dozen people in here who didn't want to spit in my face now, but maybe I should reconsider.'

'I'm sorry.'

'It's not your fault. Well, it is, but I won't hold it against you.'

They watched Schneider join the crowd in McCredie's office. The Bull had his back to them, leaning against the glass.

Caprisi lit a cigarette, sucked in the smoke and blew it towards a ceiling fan. He watched it spiral slowly upwards.

CHAPTER THIRTY-FOUR

DR CARTER SAT WITH HIS FEET ON THE WINDOWSILL, reading a copy of the *News*, a glass of bootlegged whisky in his hand. He wore a thick woollen sweater against the cold.

'Afternoon, Doc,' Quinn said.

Carter didn't return his smile. He folded the newspaper, took a slug from his glass and went to replenish it. He picked out a couple of ice cubes from a red box. 'The case is closed.'

Quinn walked over, removed the glass from Carter's hand and poured the contents down the sink. 'It's okay, Doc. Just give us a couple minutes.'

'What do you want?'

'We'd like to talk about the new friends you've got in your refrigerator.'

'I've nothing to say.'

Quinn shoved past him.

Duncan and his driver lay side by side on the slab.

Duncan's skull had been sliced open and his brain exposed. The metal slide and the floor beneath it were spattered with tiny specks of flesh, bone and blood.

'You want to fill us in, Doc?' Caprisi said.

'On what?'

'Did you find any chloroform in Duncan?' Quinn said. 'That's why you cut his brain open, right?'

Carter glowered at them. 'Whose side are you gentlemen on?'

'We're all on the same side here.'

'*Is that so?*'

Quinn sighed. 'Doc, if you want to call McCredie, go right ahead. But it's every shoulder to the wheel right now.'

'What's your angle?'

'We want to see if there's any similarity in the method. We have to write up a final report on Matsell and confirm there are no connections with Mr Duncan's murder.'

'There aren't.'

'Then just talk us through what you've got and we can close the file.'

'There's nothing to say.'

'So, no chloroform in Duncan?'

'None.'

'You sure about that?'

'Certain.'

Quinn peered at the two bodies. Duncan was close on a foot taller. His cheeks sagged even more markedly in death than they had in life. Quinn circled the slab. He studied the cut to Duncan's throat and the purple bruising around the stab wound in his chest. The driver did not appear to have a mark on his body.

'How did the chauffeur die?' Caprisi asked.

'Asphyxia.'

'He was strangled?'

'No.'

'He was hit?'

'With a lead pipe.'

'How do you know that?'

'Because it's my job and, despite appearances to the contrary, I'm good at it.'

'Sure you are, Doc. We've seen that.'

Carter poured himself another drink and slumped against the windowsill. He sighed heavily. 'Have a seat.' Neither man budged. 'Come on, I'm sorry. This job gets to me, some days. Dead men make lousy company.'

Quinn reached for the whisky glass. 'Doc—'

'I'm all right. Take a seat.' He held up the glass. 'Will you gentlemen join me?'

They shook their heads as they sat down.

'Shame. You know, I probably shouldn't tell you this but I have a fatal weakness for anyone who actually shows an interest in my work. You ought to go far. You won't, of course, because—'

'Doc . . .'

'All right! Was it cold last night?'

Quinn looked at his partner. 'Not that I recall.'

'Was it warm?'

'Not at night.'

'Exactly. Mr Evans here was hit with a lead pipe, which crushed several of his vertebrae and caused swift asphyxia. The surface coating of the pipe has rubbed off on the back of his neck and on his shirt and jacket. Lead only does this when it's warm and, as you say, it wasn't a hot night.'

'Doc, forgive us, but—'

'There's only one conclusion that can be drawn.'

He had laid down a challenge. Quinn tried not to let his irritation show.

'He had it in his pocket,' Caprisi said.

'He may have done, but that, in itself, wouldn't have been enough.'

Quinn listened to the clock on the wall. It had just gone three. He watched the second hand move slowly around the dial. 'The automobile was warm,' he said. 'He'd been sitting there a while.'

'Exactly!' Carter looked gleeful. 'Very good, Detective! I'd say he must have been there fifteen minutes or more.'

'So, it was a rendezvous. Duncan sat chatting to the guy and had no idea what was coming.'

'One assumes so.'

'What were they talking about?' Caprisi asked.

'I'm a pathologist, Detective, not a clairvoyant. But here's another thing. What else does one have to conclude about the lead pipe, if it's warm enough to shed a surface coating?'

'It's soft,' Quinn said.

'Well done, Detective. No wonder the Bull's looking

to his laurels. It's too soft to achieve the result he wished for.'

'What does that mean?' Caprisi asked.

'It means that you're dealing with a guy who knows a thing or two. An amateur would assume that a lead pipe is the perfect instrument for the job. But he has it in his pocket for fifteen minutes or more in a warm car and it softens up. He pulls it out to strike his target only to find that it merely injures, not kills.'

'So he used something else as well,' Quinn said.

'If I were a betting man, I'd say he'd put an iron rod down the centre of the pipe and welded it in place, to be sure he would achieve his desired objective.'

'For which he'd have needed a workshop.'

'Probably.'

Quinn got to his feet again and walked around the bodies. 'If you're right, he must have broken the chauffeur's neck with one swift, clean, unexpected blow. But what happened next? He asked Duncan to pull down his pants?'

Carter shrugged.

'He still had the lead pipe in his hand. Why did he pull a knife?' Quinn turned to Caprisi.

'He's lost the element of surprise,' Caprisi said. 'Duncan's a big guy. Maybe he feels he needs something more.'

'But he strikes the chauffeur in a flash. With the reverse blow, he can crush Duncan's skull, so we have to think he wants Duncan to know he's going to die and he wishes to put that mark on his throat.'

'For what purpose?' Carter asked.

Quinn gripped Carter's shoulder. 'Thanks, Doc.'

The canteen was only half full, but the air was thick with the smell of damp leather and cigarette smoke. A large group of uniforms had laid out their winter jackets on one table while they ate at the next. Their laughter echoed in the cavernous room.

Roast pork and beef stew were on the menu, and something that might have been chicken.

Caprisi ordered a peanut-butter sandwich, cut from thick slices of white bread, and took a Fig Newton from the self-service counter. Quinn poured himself a cup of coffee and paid the man at the till, whose moon face was as expressionless as Elmo Lincoln's, Hollywood's 'Tarzan of the Apes'.

Caprisi took his tray to a bench in the corner furthest from the entrance. Hegarty sat nearby with a reporter from the press conference, his knees wide apart and his great stomach pressed against the table. He spoke in hushed tones, making his points with short, agitated thrusts of a pudgy index finger. The reporter listened intently and made notes on a small pad.

'What do you think he's selling?' Quinn asked, but Caprisi was too busy shoving the peanut-butter sandwich down his throat to answer. 'Didn't your mother ever tell you to chew your food?'

Caprisi finished the sandwich, licked his lips, then picked up the Fig Newton. 'Aren't you hungry?' he said.

'No.'

Caprisi pulled off his boots. His feet stank.

There was a roar of laughter from the uniform crowd. One threw a boot at another. Quinn watched Hegarty get up and head for the doorway. He shot a glance in their direction. 'Was Hegarty ever a cop?'

'You must be kidding,' Caprisi said. 'He was a lousy hack from the gutter end of the yellow press until they decided to make him a lousy press officer with a yard of attitude and ideas way above his station.'

'Whose idea was that?'

'Some Tammany genius. Who else? Now he fancies he's a big player in your Irish gang.'

'Not my gang. Not any more.'

Caprisi grunted in agreement. The uniform party broke up and spent a couple of noisy minutes putting on their uniform jackets and wet leather boots, then stamped away down the corridor. A pair of cleaners appeared with mops and brooms.

'I asked Yan to canvass his friends in the precincts, see if anyone can spot a pattern of assaults. Maybe guys who've used chloroform to drug girls and take them into a poker game . . .' Quinn sat back. 'Where do you *get* chloroform?'

'A drugstore, I guess. Or a hospital – a surgery.'

'We should go back to our friend Chile Acuna and see if there was a doctor in the poker game.'

'You mean you'd like me to?'

'One of us should. Otherwise we'll have to work our way through every drugstore in Manhattan.'

'I'll go. I reckon you should leave Chile to cool off until the morning. You're not going to break him tonight.'

Quinn took out Duncan's wallet. He pushed across the ticket to the MacDonald–Brown fight. 'Who goes to a prize-fight alone?'

'You asked me that already. Maybe he was meeting a friend.'

'Maybe.' Quinn pocketed the ticket.

The cleaners had reached their table. They wiped the floor in sweeping, useless arcs.

'What you going to do, Joe?'

'About what?'

'Your father.'

'What would you do?'

'I wouldn't jump to any conclusions. Maybe it's a misunderstanding, like you said. Have you spoken to anyone about it?'

'Like who?'

'Anyone who knew him in here.'

'I talked to McCredie.'

'I meant guys who worked alongside him. Who were his partners?'

'I don't know. They never came to the house. There was a guy called Marinelli from Vice, but he died a few years back.'

'There must be a record.'

'It was a long time ago.'

'But they can tell you what kind of guy he was. Maybe that's what you need to hear.' Caprisi pulled his boots on. 'Where are you going to sleep tonight? Under the desk again?'

'Very funny.'

'No, I'm serious.' He handed over a scrap of paper with an address scrawled across it. 'You'll have to sleep on the couch and put up with my wife's cooking, but if you need somewhere to rest your head, you'd be welcome.'

'I appreciate that, Caprisi. Thank you.'

'If you're going to accept my hospitality, you'd better call me Tony.'

'Sure . . . Tony.' Quinn folded the piece of paper and slipped it into his pocket. 'Thanks.' He headed for the door.

'Joe, there's one other thing. Do you know what happened to the dough in Matsell's suitcase?'

'What do you mean?'

'It's just Schneider keeps going on about it. He wants to know exactly who's had sight of the case since we took it away from Matsell's suite in the Plaza.'

'Why?'

'He won't say. He's just real insistent about it.'

'What have you told him?'

'I reckon I had sight of it pretty much the whole time, bar a few seconds here and there until I went home that night. And then you handed it over to McCredie, right?'

'Right.'

'He wants a goddamned report, so that's what I'll put in it.'

'Sure. Thanks . . . Er, good.'

326

CHAPTER THIRTY-FIVE

QUINN RODE THE ELEVATOR TO THE TOP FLOOR AND walked along the highly polished corridor beneath the dome to the section next to the commissioner's office. He knocked once and put his head around the door. He had come here on his first day to sign in and hand over the photograph for his file. A younger, prettier woman now sat behind the reception table.

'Hi. I'm Joe Quinn from the main squad.'

She smiled. 'I know all about you.'

'Is that good or bad?'

'It depends which way you look at it. Can I help you, Detective? We're about to close here.'

'I need to look at a file.'

'Then you'll require written permission from your boss.'

'Okay.' He shot her an apologetic grin. 'It's kind of urgent.'

'It always is, but the answer is the same. Not without

the written permission of a manager. Those are the rules. You'll have to get Schneider or Ed McCredie to sign it off for you.'

'This is . . . private.'

She went to get her coat. 'It may be, but there's nothing I can do about that, however much of a hero you've made yourself.'

'It's a favour for my dad. It's only his file I want. He needs to send something to one of his ex-partners and he's forgotten the guy's address.'

Her resolve weakened. 'All right . . . but I shouldn't.'

'Thank you.'

'Stay here.'

She walked into the vault and disappeared. 'Quinn, G., right? Gerry?' she shouted.

'Yeah.'

'Which partner?'

'He gave me the impression he only had one.'

'There are three listed here. Tony Pigniatelli, Sean Murray and Stefan Yanowsky.'

'Yanowsky?'

'You know Yan. From down in the CIB.' She came out, file in hand. 'Are you all right, Detective?'

'I'm fine. Yan . . . Dad must mean Yan's address.'

She took a piece of paper from the tray beside her and scrawled on it.

'Mind if I take a look at the file?'

'I do, yes.' She snapped it shut and handed him the address. 'He may be your father, but rules are rules.' She smiled at him again. 'There's nothing in it anyway, apart from the front sheet. Someone must have cleaned it out.'

'Is that standard procedure?'

'He did leave more than a decade ago, and quite a few of the old files are like that,' she told him. 'But no, it wouldn't happen today. That's all I'll say.'

By the time Quinn reached the basement, Yan had his coat on. 'Joe, hold your horses. I said it would take me some time.'

Quinn watched him tidy his space and switch off the lights. Yan appeared not to notice as he went to pick up his briefcase from the counter.

'I'll get back onto it first thing in the morning. You're not even assigned, for God's sake!'

'Is there something you forgot to tell me, Yan?'

'About what?'

'About my father.'

Yan opened his case and slipped in a few loose sheets of paper. 'What did you have in mind?'

'He was your partner. You were a detective on the main squad.'

'He tell you that?'

'No. I've just taken a look at his file upstairs.'

'Who gave you clearance?'

'No one.'

Yan flicked the last of the switches in the front lobby. He led Quinn into the corridor, closed the door and turned the key in the lock. 'Let's get the hell out of here.' He strode down to the double doors and out into the alley at the back of the building. The wind whipped their ears and blew the trash in tight eddies.

Yan strode ahead, his overcoat billowing. They didn't talk until they'd slipped into a booth in a basement speakeasy off Broadway. The table was sticky, the décor a gaudy red. A kid sprinkled fresh sawdust on the floor. 'Joe, your old man doesn't like to talk about it, and he doesn't care to have others do so on his behalf. That's just the way it is and I have to respect his wishes.'

'Why doesn't he want to talk about it?'

'He's a hell of a modest guy.'

Quinn searched Yan's beaming face. With every fibre of his being, he wanted this to be true. 'What was he like?'

'Straight. Tough. He knew how to take care of himself.' Yan's smile widened. 'Like father, like son.'

'I'm nothing like him.'

'That's what you think. Others see it different. Sure, he had a temper. I'd say you have your mother's temperament.'

'You knew her?'

'Yeah. She was a spirited and beautiful woman. I was real sad to hear what happened, Joe. That's . . . I guess it was . . . I mean, hell, it's a private affair. But your old man was the best cop we ever had. I'm not saying he played everything by the book. There were a few guys who took a trip to the morgue rather than the Tombs, but the city was none the worse for it.'

A waiter brought over a bottle of whisky and two glasses. Yan poured as a jazz band struck up in the next-door room.

'Why did he leave?'

Yan raised his eyebrows. 'Why does anyone leave? He got tired.'

'Of what?'

'You can see how it is, Joe.'

'How what is?'

'You know how these things play out. This case you can do. That file comes out all right. A jerk takes a walk to the Chair. Then you hit a wall, and if you can't work around it, you have to retreat.'

'That's what my dad said.'

'He was a man of honour so he was never going to last for ever. The brightest lights in here often burn out.'

'What burnt him out?'

'There was no single thing. It wears you down. If you get some nice little armed robbery by a bunch of guys with no connections, it's great. You're everyone's hero. But if the men turn out to have political cover, it's complicated. Your dad was a huge figure, so no one was going to tell him to his face he couldn't do something, but evidence would go missing, witnesses would clam up or disappear. It's hard when you have to fight your battles in here as well as out there on the streets, especially when you're not sure who you're really fighting against.'

'Who did he think he was fighting against?'

'I don't know, Joe. Maybe he didn't either. In a lot of ways he kept himself to himself. If he had suspicions, he sure didn't share them with me.'

'What about you?'

'Me? I left the force and went straight for a while.' Yan grinned. 'Then I needed a proper job. The big fellow upstairs was good enough to have me back.'

'Do you still see my father?'

'It's been a while. Tell him I was asking after him.'

'Did you get along?'

Yan didn't reply immediately. Eventually he said, 'He wasn't an easy guy and there's no point in saying he was. He was always damn sure he was right and he saw the world in black and white. But I admired him more than any other man alive.'

Quinn lit a cigarette and drank some whisky. It was potent and burnt the lining of his stomach. 'Did you know Moe Diamond?'

'I heard the name.'

'Was he a friend of my father's?'

'Not that I'm aware of.'

'You never saw them together?'

'No.'

'They pretend to hate each other, but I'm guessing the true story may be something different.'

Yan frowned.

'Do you think my father could have been . . . ' Quinn gazed into his glass. The whisky was making his head spin. Suddenly he wanted the oblivion it offered. He took another gulp.

'Do I think your father could have been what?'

'It doesn't matter.'

'C'mon, Joe, it's obviously troubling you.'

'It's nothing.'

'Well, you might as well spell it out.'

'Compromised.'

'In what way?'

'Do you think he could have been using his position to hide something?'

'Like what?'

'A crime.'

'What kind of crime?'

'Look, forget it. It doesn't matter.'

'I've got to say I'm surprised at you, Joe.'

'Yeah, well, honourable men aren't always what they seem.'

'This one is.' Yan leant forward, elbows on the table. 'Sure we made mistakes, but he put himself on the line for me more than once, and if it wasn't for him, I wouldn't be sitting here. You're a good kid and I'll help you out any way I can, but I'm not going to sit here and listen to you badmouth him.'

'Maybe he fell in with people after you left.'

'He dominated any crowd he was ever in. He'd never let himself be pushed around by anyone. Somebody's been poisoning your mind, Joe, making up some—'

'My mother got sick. Nobody made that up.'

Yan was stony-faced. 'Okay, so she was your mother. Families have arguments and I don't want to get involved, but I'll tell you something that's beyond doubt. Your old man was a damn straight, honourable guy, so you need to take a long hard look at whoever is feeding you this horseshit.'

CHAPTER THIRTY-SIX

IT WAS PAST CLOCKING-OFF TIME. A COUPLE OF stenographers were still huddled around the wireless outside the safe and loft division, but otherwise the office was deserted. Rain hammered on the windows. Ceiling fans pummelled the damp air. The wail of a siren rose from the street. Quinn watched a couple of traffic cops weave down Broome, their rear lamps dancing like fireflies in the half-darkness. Office lights still burnt bright all down Centre Street, but the sidewalks were packed with people heading for the subway and the trolley-buses groaned under the weight of passengers. A pair of dark automobiles nosed out of bays marked 'Official Cars Only'.

Quinn moved along to McCredie's office. The blinds were down. He knocked once and, when there was no reply, nudged the door open.

The place smelt of whisky and cigars. The ashtray overflowed and the desk was heaped with files. The

334

Amy Mecklenburg posters lay undisturbed in the corner. Quinn picked one up. A bright, happy girl grinned at him.

He glanced at the photographs nailed to the wall. One was marked 'Headquarters Squad, 1918'. Gerry Quinn and Ed McCredie stood in the centre of the frame with their arms around each other. He could just about make out Yan in the same gathering, close to the back, next to Johnny Brandon. Another showed the chief of detectives in China, with his arm around a man who looked extraordinarily like Caprisi. They stood next to a rickshaw, in front of a wide river. Above the photographs were police shields from Shanghai, Hong Kong and Formosa.

'He was a good cop.'

Quinn swung around to find McCredie beside him. 'Yes, sir. I was just thinking he looked a lot like Caprisi.'

'I meant your father.'

'Oh . . . yes.' Quinn realized he still had the poster of Amy Mecklenburg in his hand and tossed it back on the pile. 'I thought you were going to put these up today, sir. I mean, a week on.'

'They've found the uncle.'

'And the girl?'

'Danny's working on him.'

'So they haven't got her?'

'Not yet. But Danny will break him tonight. And I wouldn't hold your breath for good news, son. Hell, this is the New York Police Department. Like I told you, we don't believe in fairy tales.' McCredie put on his coat

335

and picked up his briefcase. 'Have you got a minute, Detective? I'd like to buy you a cup of coffee.'

'Now, sir?'

'Yes, now. You busy?'

'No. I only just went . . . Of course.'

'Get your coat. It's clocking-off time, so you won't want to come back.'

Mrs Mecklenburg sat on the same bench but her head was bent, as though she was in pain. She did not appear to see them pass. Quinn didn't ask whether she had heard the news from Syracuse.

They strolled along the sidewalk against the tide of commuters, with careworn faces, pressing for home. A trolley-bus screeched to a halt, narrowly missing a line of pedestrians, and insults were traded.

The door of the café banged shut and they slipped into a booth adjacent to the one Quinn and Gloria Duncan had occupied earlier in the day. The trumpeter Jabbo Smith's 'Take Me To The River' was being played on a wireless behind the counter. McCredie ordered ham and eggs over easy, Quinn a cup of black coffee. When it came, he spooned in sugar.

'When did you arrive at Centre Street, sir?'

'Before Noah entered the Ark. And before that shit Schneider, which is how I've managed to survive. I know a few tricks he still hasn't quite mastered.'

McCredie lifted the curtain and glanced out of the window, then put his briefcase on the table and flipped the latch. He took out a piece of paper. 'Have you seen the report your partner gave Schneider?'

When Quinn shook his head, McCredie turned the sheet around and pushed it across the table. He waited while Quinn digested it. There was nothing surprising. 'Is something wrong?'

McCredie lit the stub of a cigar and sat back. 'You've worked hard to get here, son.'

Quinn didn't know if this was a question or a statement. 'Yes, sir.'

'According to records, you first applied for an attachment two years ago.'

'That's right.'

'You've waited longer than you might have expected to, given your precinct reports. You figure they were holding your father's experience against you?'

'No,' Quinn said warily.

McCredie puffed at his cigar. The waitress brought the ham and eggs and he palmed her a dollar bill with a wink. She slipped it into her pocket.

McCredie shovelled the food into his mouth. 'You lost out on the market?' he mumbled.

'I've never bought any stocks.'

'I'm down a grand on the day. I'll be working till I'm goddamn ninety.' He pointed at the report. 'You've got to be careful with this stuff, son. You understand me?'

'No, sir, I—'

'Schneider wants you out.'

'Why?'

'He thinks you're a hothead. I say you've got balls.' McCredie leant forward. 'You're smart, kid, and strong.

I can use a cop like you. Hell, you might even help me stop Schneider, Fogelman and all those bastards in Vice taking over the force. But look out of the window at the faces of those schmucks traipsing home. What do you see in their eyes?'

'Rainwater.'

'*Defeat*. They've been piling in on margin like every other sucker in this country. And they've all been dreaming of a house on the prairie or a beachside home in Florida. Tonight they're staring ruin in the face. Have you thought about that, son?'

'No, sir.'

'Well, you should. A good cop is aware of the environment in which he lives and of the events that swirl around him.' McCredie wiped up the remains of his egg with a hunk of bread. 'Now, if you're smart enough to have kept your dough in a plain old savings account, then I congratulate you on your foresight. But you need to take a look at the faces out on that sidewalk and think about this report.'

'I'm not sure I—'

'I'm trying to do you a favour, Detective.' McCredie prodded the paper. 'What your guinea partner has written here is enough right now to blow this city sky high. People are spooked. The market's falling. Dreams are dying. There's panic on Wall Street, even if you and your friend have your heads too far up your backsides to notice. The House of Morgan has not stepped in. Washington is nervous. The commissioner wants the Riot Squad to ring the district at the crack of dawn.'

McCredie's green eyes were fixed on Quinn. 'How much do you figure these people trudging home tonight need to know that the second most powerful man in the city, the mayor's chief aide no less, has been in bed with a bunch of cheap guinea hoods to buy off the respected writers upon whose analysis they have faithfully invested their paycheck and plenty else besides?'

'I see.'

'Good, because what you should know is that Schneider has spent his entire life kissing the ass of every politico and Wall Street swell he thought might do him some good. You put something like this in front of him and he flips out. And that means I have to save your hide.'

McCredie slipped the sheet back into the briefcase and closed it. He pushed away his plate and relit his cigar. 'That's it, right? We're done.'

'Yes, sir,' Quinn agreed. 'Thank you.'

'Wrong, son. You want to tell me about Goldberg?'

'There's nothing to tell.'

'Schneider thinks different – and so does the commissioner. Johnny wants to put your eyes out. How long have you known the guy?'

'I don't know him.'

McCredie stared at the clock on the wall. Smoke from his cigar drifted towards the counter. He opened his briefcase again and took out another document. 'This was compiled by the commissioner's new Red Squad.'

A photograph of Martha was pinned to it, a copy of

an old studio portrait his father had commissioned for her eighteenth birthday. It must have been lifted from their apartment. The report itself ran to four pages. They had clearly been following her for weeks.

'Some people say she's your sister and some your girlfriend. Which is it, Detective?'

'Neither.'

'Then what shall we call her?'

'She's my adopted sister and my brother's fiancée.'

McCredie smiled. 'Good. Because that means you can drop her. This girl is trouble. She's a Communist.'

'A socialist.'

'You tell me anyone in Commie Russia knows the difference? She's a troublemaker – labour reforms, picket-line agitation, some bleeding-heart goddamn refuge for street kids and, worst of all, she's in with La Guardia.'

'I didn't know Major La Guardia had become a Communist.'

'Don't play the smartass with me, son. I'm all that stands between you and a lifetime back in the precincts.'

'I'm sorry, sir.'

'Tell me about her.'

'What do you want to know?'

'She's a Communist, right?'

'No, she's not.'

'That's not what it says here, son.'

'She wears her heart on her sleeve. She had a tough upbringing. She considers herself fortunate to have been . . . rescued. She feels passionately that she should spend

340

her life helping others.' Quinn thought about this. It was certainly what he wanted to believe. 'She's . . . I guess you'd call her an idealist.'

'What's the difference between an idealist and a Communist?'

'She's not interested in politics. She's interested in human beings.'

'She works for La Guardia.'

'Not any more. And she only worked for him for a short time.'

'Take a look at the file, son. She's met him half a dozen times in four weeks.'

Quinn turned the page and scanned the rest of the report.

'You understand our concerns?'

'Not really, sir, no.'

'Then you need to wise up. We all know La Guardia would make common cause with the devil if it suited him. So Schneider reckons he put your sister – or whatever the hell she is – into that firm to steal documents that could be used to link the mayor's office with the Wall Street fix.'

'That's absurd.'

'It's real, son. That's how politics in this city works. And if she or her boss weren't feeding material to Goldberg and his masters at the *Sun*, then Schneider figures it must have been you.'

As McCredie took back the file, his eyes rested on the photograph pinned to the front. Then he slipped it into his briefcase. Louis Armstrong's 'Ain't Misbehavin'' was now being played on the wireless and a waiter turned up the volume. McCredie put his face to the window and waved at someone on the other side of the street. The lamps on an automobile flickered into life and, a moment later, a dark town saloon pulled out of one of the official bays and cruised to a halt outside. 'Did you hear what else happened today, son?'

'No, sir.'

'The commissioner confirmed to us privately upstairs that he's going to stand down after the election. Schneider wants his job and he's spent the last year telling City Hall *I'm* the problem. The word is he's done a deal with the Bull. If Johnny supports his bid to go upstairs, he gets my job. In the next few days, Johnny adds the Red Squad to his empire, which means this file and a whole bunch of others formally become his responsibility. So, we have to play a smart game here, and right now you're out on the left field. Do we understand one another?'

'Yes.'

'You've got to watch your step. If a jerk like Goldberg gets wind of the Wall Street fix your guinea friend just wrote up, we're deep in the shit.' McCredie sighed. He put on his hat. 'After you've been here a while, you'll learn that survival's the real deal.' He stood and shunted the table back. 'My advice is to dump the broad. A good-looking Headquarters detective like you should be able to hook any woman he wants.' McCredie slipped on his raincoat and plucked his cigar from the ashtray.

'Sir, what happens if the murders of Matsell and Spencer Duncan *are* connected?'

'They're not.'

'But suppose we're wrong. Two guys have been murdered in two days, so what happens if it *is* the same killer and he has other victims in mind, maybe other men who are connected to the mayor?' He saw a flash of doubt in McCredie's eyes.

'That's not going to happen,' he said.

CHAPTER THIRTY-SEVEN

IT WAS FIGHT NIGHT IN HARLEM AND THE BUCKS AND swells of New York's twilight world had cruised well north of the roaring forties. Limousine headlamps the size of searchlights backed up from the sporting club. Bejewelled women and dandies tripped up the steps into an auditorium packed to the rafters.

It smelt of sawdust, sweat, cheaply brewed ale and cigarette smoke. Wiseguys yelled odds from their booths. Negro kids darted up the aisles with cigarettes, sweets and fight programmes. Quinn found his seat – the three next to it were empty – then walked one row along, climbed to the back and bought a bag of boiled sweets and a programme.

The first fight was between Johnny Logan and Luigi Marsillo. The purse was two thousand dollars and a percentage of it was being donated to the Olympic boxing fund. Quinn cracked his teeth on a boiled sweet and watched the fighters warm themselves up. Logan looked stronger and fitter and was the four-to-one favourite, but Marsillo's manager was Vic Raymond, and Pete Hartley was in as referee.

So, you could bet your life it would be Marsillo.

Quinn dabbed the sweat from his brow. The heat beneath the steel rafters was ferocious.

The bell sounded and Johnny Logan danced into the centre of the ring. Both fighters ducked and wove for a few seconds, then Logan hit his opponent so hard he went down. Marsillo was stunned. Vic Raymond surged against the ropes and roared his anger, jumping up and down like he was dancing on coals. Since he was barely five feet tall, weighed more than two hundred pounds and had a round face with only two teeth showing, the effect was comical.

Marsillo got to his feet. He kept his opponent at bay until the end of the round, but next time out got knocked flat twice in quick succession. He tried to fight back. He went down once in the next round and twice in the one after. The crowd began to roar for the fight to be called off or Johnny to finish him. Vic Raymond screamed synthetic abuse at the referee, his face twisted with fury.

Quinn took off his jacket and sat on it. He kept half an eye on the empty seats.

The bell sounded the final round. Quinn watched Marsillo for signs of fatigue. He was holding up well, given he'd hit the canvas half a dozen times. Logan was tiring and Marsillo got a couple of decent jabs to his jaw. One caught the corner of an eye and drew blood.

From this distance, it didn't look too bad, but the referee saw his chance and was in like lightning. Logan tried to shove him off, but Hartley clung on and waved for the medic. It took them only a few seconds to decide the fight should be called off.

The crowd erupted. Bottles were thrown. Abuse was hurled at Hartley and Raymond. Marsillo shrugged on his robe and was bundled from the ring.

Quinn sucked another sweet.

The main bout pitted Sandy MacDonald against Harry 'Kid' Brown and as the two fighters emerged, a tall, elegant blonde climbed up towards the empty seats. Despite the heat in there, she was wrapped up in a shiny new raccoon coat.

The new referee announced the bout to loud cheers.

Quinn moved down to join her. 'Mrs Duncan.'

Cool blue eyes scrutinized his face. 'Detective. What a delightful surprise.'

He handed over the ticket he'd found in Spencer Duncan's wallet. 'I was curious to see what kind of a guy went to a fight alone.'

'As you can see, he would not have been alone.'

'I thought you hated his guts, ma'am.'

'It's Gloria – for the last time. And who says I didn't?'

The bell went. They watched Sandy and the Kid exchange blows.

She waved at a kid and palmed him a hundred-dollar bill. 'Place it on Sandy and bring me the ticket.' She peeled off another note. 'This is for you.'

'You might want to go for the Kid,' Quinn said.

'You know something I don't, Detective?'

'Yeah.'

She nodded to the boy to indicate he should go with Quinn's advice, then turned back, brushing his leg as she did so. 'Is this what you expected to find, Detective?'

'No.'

'Then there are more surprises in store for you.'

'What kind?'

'You'll see.'

She lit a cigarette. One leg rested easily against his. The tempo of the fight tailed off and the two men circled each other. Sandy MacDonald was managed by Champ Segal, who was on his feet yelling something at his fighter or the referee, maybe both. The Kid stepped in and knocked MacDonald flat.

The crowd roared. Men waved their hats.

A couple entered the auditorium, the man in a baggy suit and a black Stetson. He bowled forward like a bull elephant. The tall, graceful woman glided after him in a simple pleated white skirt and sweater. Fiorella La Guardia took the seat next to Quinn. He had a strong, lived-in face, resolute rather than handsome, with a square jaw and bright blue eyes. Quinn took the proffered hand.

'I guess you must be the detective. We weren't expecting you.'

Martha sat alongside Gloria Duncan. She avoided Quinn's eye.

Sandy MacDonald was on his feet again. He charged

at the Kid and flailed ineffectually at his upper body. He'd deteriorated dramatically since Quinn had last seen him fight and there seemed little need of a fix. MacDonald opened himself up with an unwise thrust at Brown's jaw and the Kid knocked him flat again.

'What brings you here, Detective?' La Guardia said.

'I was thinking perhaps I should ask you the same question, sir.'

'I like a good, clean fight.' La Guardia wasn't smiling. 'That what we've got here?'

'No, sir.'

La Guardia turned to his right. 'Did he tell you who to wager on, Gloria?'

'He said I should go for the Kid.'

'Then he's a smart man, maybe the kind we can do business with. What do you say, Mr Quinn?'

'It depends what kind of business you're in.'

'A fine answer.' La Guardia ran a hand over his jaw. 'Well, it's simple. I don't want to prove that the mayor is a liar because I want to take his place. I want to prove it because he *is* a liar and the corruption he encourages is a cancer that's destroying this city.'

The bell sounded for the end of the round and Champ Segal darted into the ring to retrieve his fighter. MacDonald looked close to the end of his strength. He staggered and slumped onto the stool. Segal poured a bucket of water over his head.

'They should give the guy a break,' La Guardia said, 'or the Kid will kill him.'

'What line of business *are* you in, sir?'

The politician placed his Stetson on his knee. 'I'm a debt collector, Detective.'

'What kind?'

'The kind that operates for the city of New York.'

'Whose debts do you collect?'

La Guardia gave him a thin smile. 'Are you telling me, my friend, that you've never asked yourself how the mayor, on a salary of twenty thousand a year, manages to travel the world first class, for months at a time, in the style of an oil millionaire?'

'That's not really my affair, sir.'

'Are you sure about that?'

'I'm a city detective.'

'You're a New Yorker. You're a citizen of this town.'

'Yeah, but—'

'What if there was a connection with a case you were working on? Would it be your affair then?'

'Is there?'

La Guardia laughed. 'Why do you think your department, with all its swanky automobiles full of celebrity cops, couldn't crack the Rothstein case? The city's most notorious gambler and criminal is gunned down on the sidewalk and we still can't pin it on a single damn hood.'

The bell rang again and MacDonald stumbled out. The Kid looked reluctant to put him out of his misery.

'This is goddamn murder,' La Guardia grumbled. 'Someone should put a stop to it.'

MacDonald went down flat.

'You figure it's a coincidence,' La Guardia said, 'that

Mr Albert H. Vitale, magistrate, Tammany hack and friend of the mayor, borrowed twenty thousand dollars from Rothstein a week before his death, which he had no means of paying back?'

'Major—'

'What I'm saying to you, my friend, is that the mayor is bent.'

'Sir, why are you here?'

La Guardia watched MacDonald clamber to his feet. He sucked his teeth. 'Martha tells me you're an honest cop. Is that true?'

'Yes, sir.'

'Are you part of the cabal down at Headquarters?'

'No.'

'You turned them down?'

'I don't recall an invitation to join them.'

'You ever had your hand in the till?'

'No.'

'You figure we can trust you? Martha says we can.'

'It depends what you're asking me to do.'

'Another good answer.' La Guardia took a bag of pistachio nuts from his pocket and offered them along the line. Nobody accepted so he cracked a few from their shells and put them into the corner of his mouth. He watched MacDonald and the Kid dance around each other. 'Gloria's been helping us, Detective. If someone hadn't killed him, her husband might have been here tonight, sitting right where you are – with me.'

'Why?'

'If you want to break a cabal, you need evidence. To

get evidence, you need to find someone willing to break ranks. It looked like Spencer Duncan was going to come over to us and maybe bring a few others with him.'

'Who?'

'He was dead before he could give us a name.'

'Spencer Duncan was willing to turn state's evidence?'

'We believe so. Perhaps you're aware that there's a photograph of Jimmy Walker and Rothstein together at that realty development in Queens. Enough in the current climate, I'm sure you'll agree, to finish him off and bring the entire edifice tumbling down around him. We know it was in Charlie Matsell's suite at the Plaza.'

'When?'

'Less than a week ago. Now Matsell and Duncan are dead. Can that be a coincidence?'

The fight reached the end of its penultimate round and a fair proportion of the crowd got to its feet to urge MacDonald to quit.

'You work out a way to help us before this election is done,' La Guardia said, 'and I'll make you the goddamn chief of police.'

'Sir, are you telling me Spencer Duncan was murdered because he was prepared to turn against his friends?'

'It sure seems like a hell of a coincidence.'

'It does. And it's real interesting, but we believe this guy was coming from a different direction.'

La Guardia shrugged. 'It's your show.'

'How did you find out about the photograph of Rothstein and the mayor?'

'I think that had better remain our business.'

Quinn glanced at Martha. 'There's an allegation you put someone into Matsell's office to try to uncover the connections.'

'Who said that?'

Quinn hesitated. 'It came from Headquarters.'

'Who?'

'It's what they think on the top floor. They asked me how in hell Goldberg had found out about the picture.'

Martha stood and darted down the stairs. As he made to follow her, Gloria Duncan grabbed his jacket. 'We'll be in the Cotton Club,' she breathed.

CHAPTER THIRTY-EIGHT

MARTHA RAN DOWN TOWARDS THE ENTRANCE. QUINN caught her by the cloakroom. 'Where are you going?'

'Home.'

They were no more than inches apart. Her skin glowed in the half-light.

'What are you really doing here?' he said.

'You can see perfectly well what I'm doing.'

'It doesn't take a genius to work out who La Guardia put into that office to dig his dirt for him.'

'So, that confirms it. You're not a genius.'

She tried to leave, but he held her tight, his fingers digging into her flesh. 'You were screwing Matsell and Spencer Duncan so you could turn in the mayor?'

'You're hurting me.' Martha shook herself free. This time she got ten or twenty yards down the street before he forced her into a doorway. Light from the street-lamps glinted off hurt, angry eyes.

'I found another copy of that photograph of you on

the bed in Spencer Duncan's drawer. Is there anyone in town who hasn't got one?'

'You didn't get one.'

'Did La Guardia ask you to screw these men, or did you decide to do that all by yourself?'

She stared at him, open-mouthed. 'Sometimes I can find it in my heart to truly hate you.'

'If Aidan finds out about this . . .'

'Let's not pretend this is about Aidan, because that makes you look pathetic.'

'Tell me about the photograph.'

'Why? What does it matter what some sad old men wanted to do to me?'

The blood pounded in Quinn's head. 'Did he take you there?'

'Who?'

'Don't play games with me, Martha.'

'Charlie Matsell asked me to go for a drink in the Plaza. The next thing I remember I was waking up on a bed with Sarah scratching my ear.'

'He drugged you?'

'He put something in my drink.'

'Did they—'

Her eyes flashed. 'I don't know.'

'You must.'

Her face crumpled. 'Please, Joe . . .'

'You must know, Martha.'

'I . . . Joe, I—'

'We have to . . . know.'

Tears trickled from the corners of her eyes. 'I don't

know who they were, Joe. I could only hear voices. When I woke, I felt so terribly sick. Sarah was whispering in my ear. She helped me get dressed and we crawled into the corridor.'

'Do you know who was in that room?'

'No.'

'But you heard voices?'

She didn't answer.

'When did this happen?'

'Two weeks ago.'

'Exactly?'

'Yes. It was a Wednesday night.'

The sporting-club crowd spilt into the street. Limousine drivers gunned their engines and pressed forward. She swayed against him, then held him tightly. Lips brushed his neck. 'Now I *am* tainted.'

'No.'

'I wash myself and wash myself, over and over again.'

'It's not your fault.'

'Maybe it is.'

The wind and rain, the hubbub of the city, curled around them.

Without warning, she withdrew from him and darted between the automobile lights.

'Martha!'

She didn't stop. He watched her go, until the night had swallowed her.

Quinn turned back towards the club, limousines jostling for position outside its entrance. Horns sounded. Shouts were drowned by the nearby El. He slipped his hands into his pockets. A few drops of rain splashed on his face. A door opened and the music of a jazz band escaped. A man's voice rasped into a microphone.

Quinn spun around again and worked his way through the automobiles. He began to run.

Martha stood in the middle of the street, trying to hail a taxi. He caught her and pulled her close. Her cheeks were damp with rain. 'Let me take you home,' he whispered.

'It's better I go alone, Joe, you know that.'

'What harm can it do?'

'Please . . .' She pushed him away, but did not let go. 'Joe, do you remember the guesthouse in Coney Island, the tiny attic? The first time your mother got drunk and Aidan and your father were out, you took me up there to hide. There were polished wooden floorboards and the smell of cinnamon because it was where the man who owned the house kept the spices for his store. You must remember, Joe.' Her eyes implored him.

He nodded. The memory lived with him.

'You kept me safe there. I cried and you held me. We looked up through the tiny window at the stars. That was happiness, Joe. That's where I've always wanted to be.' She moved closer. 'But I can't hide from myself. There is no refuge. It's like they say. You can take a girl out of the Bowery, but never the Bowery out of a girl.'

'Martha . . .'

'Please, Joe, let me go.' She hurried away down the

356

sidewalk. She waved at a dozen taxis, then one swerved through the traffic.

As she passed Quinn, her face was pressed to the rain-swept glass.

CHAPTER THIRTY-NINE

THE COTTON CLUB WAS PACKED TO THE RAFTERS. Hundreds of white swells from uptown jammed the corridors and crowded around the big circular tables beneath African masks and giant artificial palm trees. The bongo drums pounded. A chorus line of nubile light-skinned girls danced to Duke Ellington's steel band.

Quinn forced his way to the bar and ordered a cocktail. He drained it, then ordered another, downed it and lit a cigarette. The girls were pretty, slight and young. A couple looked barely old enough to be out so late. A trumpeter stepped forward for a solo. As the piece reached a crescendo, the rest of the band joined in and the crowd clapped. The girls' legs flew higher.

Quinn mopped his brow. He ordered another cocktail and drank it. He dropped his change on the floor, but in the crush, didn't bother to pick it up.

The chorus girls took a break to rapturous applause and the band left its trumpeter on stage. The tables turned in on themselves and the hubbub echoed off the domed ceiling.

Quinn took off his jacket, draped it over his arm and slid along the wall. He stopped a waiter. 'Where's Moe Diamond?' He had to shout. 'I'm looking for Moe Diamond.'

He kept moving, scanning the crowd. After a few minutes, he glimpsed Moe on the far side of the room. He walked over and touched his arm. Moe shot him a furtive glance, then, 'Oh, Joe, it's you.'

'We need to talk.'

'Later, maybe.'

'Now.'

Quinn bundled him through an exit to a dark corridor by the cloakrooms, where a startled grey-haired man in evening dress had second thoughts about the need to relieve himself.

'Let go of me, Joe.'

'What did you do to her?'

'I don't know what you're talking about.'

'You and your buddies at the Plaza. What did you do to her?'

'Joe, c'mon . . .'

Quinn gripped his uncle's neck and tightened his fingers.

'Aaargh! For God's sake – it wasn't my idea, I swear it.'

'Whose idea was it?'

'Joe, you know what they say: you can take a girl out of the Bowery—' Moe gasped.

It took Quinn a massive effort of will not to shut the man's windpipe completely. 'Tell me what happened, who was there, what you did.'

'Joe, I can't.'

'Every man in that room is marked, Moe. On Monday, Charlie Matsell. Yesterday, Spencer Duncan. Who's going to be cut up today? Have you worked that out yet?'

'I know we're marked!'

Quinn grabbed his lapels. 'I always hated the way you looked at Martha. Now I know how Mom got sick.'

'Martha wasn't *why* she got sick, Joe. Martha was *because* she got sick.'

Quinn sensed movement behind him and whirled around. Owney Madden was flanked by two of his bodyguards.

'That's enough, Joe.'

'Leave us alone, Owney.' He turned back to Moe. 'What do you mean, she was *because* Mom got sick?'

'I said, that's enough.' Madden nodded at one of his men. 'Take Moe upstairs and make sure he stays there.' He waited until they had disappeared before he spoke again. 'For just one guy, you're causing a lot of trouble. My advice is to quit screwing with us,' he stepped aside, 'and go get yourself a cocktail. It's on the house.'

'He's a frightened man, Owney.'

'Maybe he is.'

'He deserves to be frightened.'

'Maybe he does.'

'Somebody's gunning for him.'

'For all of them, it seems, but that's not your business.'

'If you tell me why, I can help.'

'You can't. Go get yourself a drink. You look like you could use one.'

Quinn returned to the bar, ordered another cocktail and watched the line of chorus girls onstage. Then he spotted Gloria Duncan. She sat between a slew of fancy-looking men and women, but they talked over or around her for her eyes were fixed on him. She got to her feet and glided over, cool in a straight evening gown with an elaborate beaded overdress. Her blonde curls had been expensively set. She wore thick makeup, which hid the lines around her eyes, and bright-red lipstick. 'You're hot,' she said. She reached into his pants' pocket, took out a handkerchief and dabbed at his brow. She put it back, pushing her hand deep. Then she reached up to his collar, loosened his tie and undid his top button. 'That's better. May I buy you a drink?'

'I've had one.'

'So I see.' She clicked her fingers at the bartender, who hurried over with a bottle of champagne and two glasses. He popped the cork and poured.

'Where did Major La Guardia go?' he said.

'Home. I don't think this is his scene, do you?'

'How do you know him?'

'Does it matter?' Her eyes seemed to mock him.

'Sure it does.'

'He was once a decent *pro bono* lawyer and I was a girl who needed one.'

'He asked you to turn your husband in?'

'He didn't need to.' She leant closer and pressed her lips to his ear. 'You want my advice, Detective, drop the case and ditch the girl. She's trouble.'

'Why?'

'Just do as I say or the big man will eat a guy like you for breakfast and spit out the bones.'

'Who is the big man?'

'He's the guy even Spencer was scared of.'

'Do you have a name?'

'If I knew it, I wouldn't be sitting here.'

Quinn took a handful of papers from his pocket. He showed her the page headed 'Disbursements'. 'Is this what La Guardia wanted?'

'Have you been stealing documents from me, Detective?'

'Did he explain what these figures meant?'

'Throw the detective switch, Detective. It doesn't turn a girl on.'

'Answer the question and I might.'

'Spencer called them his insurance. Who got what and when. When we were lovers he said I should give them to the newspapers if anything happened to him. Should I do that now?'

'Where did the money come from?'

'Now you're not being so bright. Where do you think it came from?'

'I'd like to hear it from you.'

'You wouldn't have to walk far from your desk to find the source.'

'It came from Centre Street?'

'That was where it went. I didn't say it came from there.'

'Where did the money go? There are no details here.'

She smiled. 'Spencer may have been many things, Detective, but stupid he was not. He kept the really important stuff in his head. He could have told us which bank account on which day, had he so wished.' Gloria touched her glass to his and drained it. 'You've lost her, do you know that?'

For a moment Quinn was silent. The steel band struck up again. His temples throbbed in time with the music. 'I don't think I ever really had her.'

Gloria put down her glass and took his hand. He resisted. 'C'mon. Even detectives can dance, can't they?'

They spun around the floor, her body pressed to his. Expensive French scent wafted over him. Her fingers caressed his back. Her lips brushed his neck.

He shut his eyes. 'I have to go,' he said.

'No, you don't,' she murmured. 'Neither of us has anywhere to go.' She drew him closer. Her cool, moist cheek seemed to take the fire from his. Quinn's head swam. Sweat from his brow trickled into his mouth. She brushed his lips with hers.

The pressure in his forehead eased.

She slowed the pace. Her fingers skipped lightly across the back of his head, soothing where they touched. Then she slipped her hand into his and led him out of the club into the street. 'There's a place I know,' she said.

She paid no heed to his indecision. She led him two blocks and through an archway beneath a flickering sign saying 'Paradise Alley Hotel'. Half the bulbs on its illumination board had been smashed. She pushed a ten-dollar bill across to an attendant and took a key.

Halfway down a moonlit corridor, she ducked into a room with a simple wooden bed and crisp sheets. The walls had been newly whitewashed. He took in a Bible and telephone before she drew him to her again. Her lips tasted of champagne and cigarettes. Her hips and thighs moulded themselves to his.

They swayed together. Immaculately honed finger-nails gouged at his neck until they drew blood. She bit her lower lip and ran her tongue along the tip of his. Her breath quickened and she tugged at his shirt, then skilfully worked the buttons on his pants and tugged him free.

Quinn closed his eyes as she took his hand and guided his fingers beneath her dress, from the smooth silk of her stocking and the intricate lace of her garter belt to the bare flesh between.

He pushed her back against the wall and pulled the dress above her waist. She spread her legs and drew him closer.

As they slid together, he pulled back.

He let go and stepped away from her. He took in her eyes, the crumpled dress, the crimson garter belt and the tantalizing patch of dark hair that sprouted beneath it.

'No,' he muttered. He buttoned his pants and reached for his jacket.

'Come back,' she hissed.

As he stumbled blindly away her voice echoed down the corridor. 'Damn you,' she yelled. '*Damn you to hell.*'

CHAPTER FORTY

QUINN WOVE HIS WAY ALONG THE RAIN-SLICKED SIDEWALK through fight-night stragglers still making their way home. He took in only blurred faces and distant voices. Back in the Gardner, he laid his forehead against the steering-wheel and pressed his eyes with his thumbs until the pain became unbearable. His fingers smelt of her.

He heard himself humming the lullaby his mother used to sing to Martha on the stoop of the Coney Island guesthouse.

> *Mama's going to buy you a brand-new toy,*
> *It's going to give you hours of joy.*

He switched on the engine and turned south. He barely registered the passing street-lights until he drew up outside the front entrance to the apartment. He went through to the courtyard and climbed the stairs to the roof, then walked to the edge and looked down. An accordion was playing close by. Windows were opened and closed. Snatches of conversation and argument carried on the night air. Dogs barked. A few old men sat out front on the stoops. They smoked cigars and talked in hushed voices.

'Sarah?'

He checked her den and found only a hunk of bread.

'Sarah?'

He climbed over the brick divide and walked through line after line of washing. 'You're not in trouble. I just need to talk to you.'

He looked behind the roof-light and the makeshift store. He climbed over the next divide. 'C'mon, Sarah, it's important. We need to talk.'

He moved around the roof again, quicker this time. He tried the door of the store. It was locked. 'Open up, Sarah. I know you're in there.'

Nothing stirred.

'Open the door. Please . . .'

He waited.

'Sarah . . . *Sarah!*' He slapped the outside wall of the store. 'I don't know why in hell we ever picked you off that street.'

Quinn reached down and ripped off a piece of wood cladding. He tried to jemmy the door open. It broke. He forced the tips of his fingers into the gap. The door was old and rotten, and gave way easily.

She sat on the floor, knees pulled up to her chest. Her

eyes glittered and her cheeks were damp with tears. 'Did you mean that?'

'What?'

'The thing you just said.'

'Of course I didn't.'

'Then why did you say it?'

'You were with her at the Plaza, weren't you?'

'Did she tell you that?'

'I asked you if you'd followed her and you said no. It was important.'

'She told me not to tell anyone, especially not you.'

Quinn sighed and stepped back. 'Come on, out of there.' He lit a cigarette, went to the lip of the roof and sat with his legs over the edge.

She joined him.

'You look cold,' he said.

'I'm used to it. You don't look real well.'

'I'm fine.'

'You look kind of crazy.'

'I'll take that as a compliment. Thank you. Now tell me what happened. From the beginning. Leave nothing out.'

'What happened where?'

'At the Plaza.'

'She went for a drink with that man.'

'Why did you follow her?'

'I was bored. They make you drink milk at the orphanage in the evenings and sing stupid songs.'

'What happened?'

'She sat there, talking to him. She didn't look like she

368

was having a good time. I couldn't understand it, because she told me he was a horrible man.'

'Then what happened?'

'She got up to go to the bathroom. I saw him put something in her cocktail. I tried to stop her, but she came back and drank from it, and he carried her to his room. He made it look like he was being a real gentleman.'

'Did anyone else help him?'

'No,' Sarah said. 'I didn't like that man. When she was away from the table, he stared right at me.'

'So you followed them?'

'I watched which floor the elevator rode to. Then I went up the back stairs.' She looked at him sheepishly. 'Sometimes, if I'm hungry, I go to the kitchen in the Plaza and take food from the room-service trolleys in the corridor or outside the rooms. Nobody ever uses the back stairs. You could walk up and down there for a month and no one would see you.'

'How did you find out which suite she was in?'

'I crept along the corridor. Behind one door I could hear men laughing.'

'Which door?'

Sarah shook her head. 'I – I didn't know what to do. I listened at the keyhole. The men were still laughing, but then their voices grew fainter so I tried scratching on the door. She didn't answer. I called. I thought she might be . . . I was frightened. I called her name, but I guess she couldn't hear me, what with the drugs and all. I thought the door must be locked, but I tried the handle and it opened.'

'What did you see?'

'She was . . . I . . .'

'She was on the bed?'

'Yes.'

'They had stripped her? '

Sarah hesitated. 'Yes.'

Quinn cleared his throat. 'Where were they sitting, the men?'

'In the next room. The door was open. I could hear them talking. There was a whole lot of smoke. I crawled to the bed and tried to wake her. I was scared – I didn't know what they'd do if they found me. I tried to pull her off the bed, but I wasn't strong enough. I spilt some water in her face, but she still didn't wake up. She made a noise and that frightened me more. So then I tried to hurt her. I put my hand over her mouth and I pulled her hair. She woke up and I whispered to her.' Sarah was talking faster now. 'I found a coat – there was a pile of coats, so I took one for her and put it around her and we ran. She kept falling over. We went down the back stairs and out by the kitchen. I helped her and we escaped. She was sick in the back of the taxi – sick again and again – but I was glad I helped her. She helped me and now I've helped her.'

'You did so well, Sarah. Without you, she'd be dead now.'

Sarah's face went white. 'Do you think so?'

'I'm sure of it.'

'I'm sorry I didn't see the men. I know that's what you want. I heard voices but—'

'It's okay. Can you remember which floor the suite was on?'

'The fifteenth. It took us a long time to get down the stairs. Martha was sick and she had to stop so many times. I was frightened that when we got to the bottom, they'd be waiting for us.'

'You can't recall the number of the suite?'

'I – I wasn't looking at the numbers.'

'Did you see anyone else on that floor? A bellman, maybe, a waiter?'

She shook her head again.

Quinn took a last drag of his cigarette, flicked it high in the air and watched it spin down and fizzle out on the street. 'Close your eyes a minute, Sarah, and think yourself back to that room. Try to tell me what you can see.'

She squeezed her eyes tight shut.

He put an arm around her shoulders. 'Don't try too hard. Walk along that corridor. Now ease yourself through the door and tell me what's there.'

'I can see smoke from the next room, like fog. I can see a suitcase, open, and there's money inside . . . a lot.'

'What else?'

'I don't remember. There were pictures on the wall.'

'Take a look at the pile of coats. How many were there?'

'I don't know.'

'Was it a big pile? Were they spread around the room?'

'They were . . . spread.'

'Were there many of them?'

A couple of tears trickled out between her eyelids. 'I don't know. I can't remember.'

Quinn stared into the darkness. 'You know the coat my father wears – old and blue, with a black leather collar? Did you see that there?'

'No.' She opened her eyes. 'Why do you ask?'

'You didn't see it?'

'No, but—'

'Has he talked to you about this?'

She wiped her nose on the sleeve of her sweater. 'Yes.'

Quinn's heart was beating fast. 'What did he ask you?'

'He asked if I'd ever followed her.'

'What did you say?'

'I told him no.'

Quinn took her hands. 'Sarah, don't talk about this – not to anyone, you understand?'

'Will you take me to Coney Island tomorrow?'

'Probably not tomorrow, but soon.'

'We haven't been for an awful long time.'

'A week.'

'I know, but . . . Martha must come, too.'

'When have you ever known her turn down a trip along the boardwalk?'

'She likes it, doesn't she?'

'She feels safe there.'

'Why?'

'It's a long story.'

'I'd sure like to hear it.'

'My mother took us there for a whole month the

summer Martha came to us. We hired a couple of rooms in an old guesthouse and we went on the beach and swam. At night, she would wake up and my mother would sing lullabies on the porch to comfort her.' Quinn thought about what Moe had told him. *Martha wasn't* why *she got sick. Martha was* because *she got sick.* 'It's okay to be afraid, Sarah. We're all afraid sometimes.'

'She's never taken me . . . to that place. That guest-house place. She talks about it all the time, but she's never taken me there.'

'She wanted to buy it a few years ago. It was a crazy idea. It went to some realty developer for ten times the money we had.' He stood up and dusted himself down.

A couple strolled along the street below. The girl slipped a hand into the crook of her lover's arm and laid her head on his shoulder. Quinn could hear their laughter as they skipped up the steps to the apartment building.

Sarah took his hand. 'Poor Joe,' she said.

CHAPTER FORTY-ONE

THE WINDOW TO THE MAIN BEDROOM IN HIS PARENTS' apartment was closed, so Quinn walked down to the courtyard and climbed back up the stairs. On the top landing, he caught his breath. No light seeped from beneath the door. He turned into the apartment and stood outside the box-room. Gerry's bed was empty.

'Dad?'

He knocked softly on the door of his parents' room and turned the handle. It wouldn't open, so he fumbled above the lintel for a key, turned the lock and stepped inside. He lit a candle on the dressing-table and sat in an iron chair by the bed. He picked up a studio portrait of his mother and Martha. Their smiles were fixed for the photographer.

Quinn dropped it on the white bedspread. As a very young child he would sometimes sit here in the after-noons and watch his mother sleep. He could see her beautiful face now.

The door creaked and his brother came in. Aidan closed the door behind him and sat on the bed.

'Don't,' Quinn said. 'You know how Mom hates to have the place messed up.'

Aidan rubbed his hands uneasily. 'You shouldn't joke about it.'

'Why not? It's the only thing we have left. Where's Dad?'

'Out late, I guess.'

'Did you sell him the new model?'

'No.'

Quinn picked up the photograph of Martha and his mother and put it back on the dressing-table. 'Do you miss her, Ade?'

'I miss how she was a long time ago.'

'Like I said, we never talk about it.'

'No, we don't.'

Quinn looked out of the window at the shadows on the courtyard wall. 'You remember how it was when we were kids – I mean just little kids – when we used to come home from school after stopping off for a fight and she was mad at us for doing that, but she was always smiling and there were crackers, cheese and cookies on the table.'

Aidan didn't answer.

'Do you remember that, Ade?'

'Sure.'

'Did you ever wonder what Mom really thought about taking Martha in?'

'Joe . . .'

'You ever ask yourself why Dad took her up to New Haven and down to Washington, not us?'

'I don't know what you mean.' Aidan sighed heavily. 'Do we have to talk about the past?'

'It never goes away, Ade. We just try to bury our ghosts.'

'But I ask myself why *you* always have to imagine a dark side to everything. Mom was sick. She died. We all knew she was sick. Why do you want to make something more of it?'

'Why did Mom get sick, though? You never answer that question.'

'No, and I don't understand why you have to either. What does it achieve?'

Quinn gave a rueful smile. 'Maybe I ask too many questions.'

'No one wants you to be a cop at home.'

The candle flame flickered. 'Do you remember when we used to talk about everything, you and me and Dad, all of us?'

'We used to talk about ball games, Joe. It just seemed like everything.'

'Maybe, but now we don't talk about anything. We can talk about going up to see Booth run out against Army or taking a trip up to see the game at New Haven, but everywhere else the ghosts get in the way.'

'Only because you insist on seeing them.'

A clock on the mantelpiece marked the long silence that followed.

'Don't let her go to that office again, Ade. She'll listen to you. In fact, you should persuade her to stay at home until all this blows over.'

'Why?'

'Just tell her.'

'That doesn't sound like much of an explanation.'

'The men she worked for are dangerous – more dangerous than Lucky, Meyer and their friends. One of them may be the most influential man in this city. La Guardia put her into that job to spy on them but they chewed her up and spat her out. She's lucky to be alive.'

'Are we talking about the mayor here, Joe?' Aidan's voice was heavy with sarcasm. 'You figure you've finally hit the big-time?'

'Do as I ask, Ade.'

Aidan stood. 'I'll talk to her.' He paused. 'This is from Aunt Margaret.' He dropped a postal card onto the bed. 'She wants us to go up and see them before the wedding.' Aunt Margaret was their mother's only sister.

'What did he do with her things?'

'Who?'

'Dad. What did he do with Mom's letters and photographs? Did he burn them all?'

'I don't know. I doubt it.'

'Did he ever ask us if there was anything we'd like to keep?'

'He's been in a lot of pain, Joe. Don't blame him for that. I'm going to bed. I hope you wake up in a better mood.'

Quinn blew out the candle. Pools of moonlight splashed across the ceiling. He stared at the silhouetted picture of his mother and the crucifix beside it.

CHAPTER FORTY-TWO

HE DROVE UPTOWN AND PARKED THE GARDNER OUTSIDE
the front entrance to the Plaza. The doorman was about
to instruct him to move it when he caught Quinn's
expression and rapidly changed his mind.

A pretty blonde girl stood behind the reception desk.
He opened his wallet. 'Detective Quinn from Police
Headquarters. I need to speak to the manager.'

'Sir, may *I* help?'

'I talked to him the day before yesterday about a
homicide. An English guy.'

'Mr Templeton?'

'Sure. Could you have him come down?'

'Sir, Mr Templeton is not here.'

'Then ask him to come in.'

'He no longer works at the hotel. He left town
yesterday.'

'For where?'

'He didn't say.'

A man with a broad forehead and receding grey hair appeared behind her. He had evidently been listening to the conversation. 'I'm the duty manager, sir. Perhaps I can help?'

'Where's Templeton?'

'He's left our employment.'

'Why?'

'I'm not sure I know, sir.'

'Where is he?'

'I'm afraid I have no idea. He didn't leave a forwarding address. Perhaps he intends to return to London. I know he has family there.'

'You're kidding me.'

'No, sir.'

Quinn took the man's arm and marched him into the room behind the desk. He closed the door. 'You mean to tell me that the manager of this hotel has been allowed to walk out in the middle of a homicide investigation?'

'Yes, sir. I mean, he's left. That's all I can say.'

'Was he fired?'

'I understand that the management board has been shocked by the abrupt nature of his departure.'

'What's your name?'

'O'Grady, sir. Michael O'Grady.'

'From the North, right? Belfast?'

'Armagh. But we've been here twenty years.'

Quinn took a step closer. 'You know what went on up there in Charlie Matsell's suite, Michael?'

'Yes, sir.'

Quinn's eyes narrowed. '*How* do you know?'

'I overheard part of the conversation your colleague had with Mr Templeton last week.'

'Which colleague?'

O'Grady frowned. 'I couldn't say.'

'Was he in uniform?'

'Yes.'

'Was he from Headquarters?'

'I don't believe Mr Templeton asked him which department he represented.'

'What did he want?'

'To know who had been in Mr Matsell's suite on the Wednesday night prior to his visit. He asked whether anyone had delivered food to the room.'

'And had they?'

'Yes, sir. Room Service had delivered a tray of sand-wiches early in the evening.'

'Is the waiter here tonight?'

'He left for California at the end of last week.'

'Had he planned to leave?'

'I don't believe so.'

'Didn't that strike you as odd?'

'Yes, sir, it did. The staff . . .'

'Go on.'

'The word among the staff is that he was given some money. He certainly seemed in a hurry to leave.'

'Do you know what actually went on in Mr Matsell's suite, Michael?'

'Not precisely, sir. I understood there to have been an incident.'

'Did the officer tell you that?'

'Yes.'

'Did he explain what kind of incident?'

'No.'

'But you guessed?'

'I really wouldn't like to say, sir.'

'Would you tell me what the officer looked like?'

O'Grady frowned. 'It's hard to say. He was in uniform.'

'He was an older man?'

'Yes. He was stocky, about your height. Irish, too. There was certainly a hint of the old country in his accent.'

'Thank you, Michael. You've been most helpful.'

Quinn stood on the Plaza's front step and breathed in the night air. He took out Caprisi's address and tapped the card against his sleeve. He lit a cigarette and sucked in the smoke. A cop's uniform was the best disguise in the world. No one ever remembered the face. He turned towards the shadows of Central Park.

He couldn't see any sign of the Gardner and looked for the doorman, but got no more than four or five paces before he felt the unmistakable pressure of a gun barrel in the small of his back. 'Keep moving, Detective,' a man growled.

He was bundled down the steps and into the back of a cream saloon that cruised up alongside the kerb. The engine roared and the automobile screeched away down Broadway, a man on each running board.

Quinn pushed himself upright in the deep leather seat.

'Good evening, Joe,' Meyer Lansky said.

'Not any more.' Quinn eased himself forward.

'Don't even think about it,' Siegel warned. 'Lucky just wants to talk.'

'What kind of talk does he have in mind?'

'Not the kind you need to worry about,' Lansky said. 'Someone's screwing with us, Detective, and we don't like that.'

'What's it got to do with me?'

'You're in the middle, and that ain't a comfortable place to be. Did you sell that dope to Goldberg?'

'No.'

'Are you sure about that? The boys at Headquarters say different.'

'I'm sure.'

'She's your broad, though, right?'

Quinn sighed. 'What is it you want, Meyer?'

'We want to protect our interests. Are you going to help us do that? Or would you prefer to take a ride out to the island?'

The driver swung the saloon onto the Bowery. The city's flotsam and jetsam poured in and out of the flophouses and salvation missions. As they reached the thieves' market, between Houston and Delancey, the lights turned red. A couple of jewellery and watch salesmen approached Quinn's window, oblivious to the men on the running boards.

Quinn glanced from side to side. 'Relax, Detective,' Siegel drawled.

But Quinn knew how road trips to see Luciano usually ended. As the car jerked away from the lights, he lashed an elbow into Siegel's mouth and threw open the door. The guy on the running board tipped onto the street and Quinn was through. He rolled once on the tarmac, sprang to his feet and was immediately lost in the crowd. He heard shouting behind him and a burst of gunfire. He did not look back.

Tyres screeched and more shouts pierced the cacophony of the night. Quinn knocked over a raincoat banner outside a second-hand store, almost flattened a pair of men who staggered from a flophouse and swung into a salvation mission.

It was packed. It smelt of unwashed bodies and cigarette smoke. Onstage, a preacher intoned drearily beneath a large wooden cross, a Bible clutched to his chest. Men sat on rows of long benches in front of him. Most were fast asleep.

Siegel and one of his men appeared in the doorway. Quinn sprinted onto the stage, past the startled preacher, and out through a door at the back.

He found himself in a narrow corridor, filled with the aroma of onions and cabbage. He sprinted to the kitchen. Siegel yelled at him to stop, but Quinn threw himself across a wide metal table, catapulting a pile of dishes onto the floor. He dived out of the window as machine-gun fire peppered the walls.

He was in a backyard. He reached for a decrepit metal fire escape. Siegel shouted again and bullets pinged off the metal struts. The staircase rattled. Quinn reached the roof of the building and leapt over the parapet.

He ducked beneath a series of washing-lines and scuttled down a ladder into a courtyard. It appeared deserted, but as his foot touched the ground he felt a searing pain in the back of his head and fell to his knees. A man stood above him, machine-gun raised. He pointed the muzzle at Quinn's chest. His eyes were barely visible beneath the brim of his hat. 'Get up,' he said.

Quinn took a few paces back. 'Where are we going?'

'You don't need to know.'

Quinn glanced over his shoulder, then up at the roof. The guy followed his gaze and Quinn took his chance, swinging his right leg in a high arc. The gun barrel slewed skyward. Quinn smacked him with a straight right to the jaw, then a left and right to the belly and nose. But the guy was tough. He staggered back, raised his weapon and, when the magazine clicked empty, flipped it around and swung the butt.

Quinn ducked, but he wasn't quick enough to dodge the kick to his groin that followed. He doubled up in pain and spun into the wall.

They sized each other up. Siegel's man had lost his hat. He had a bald head and scars across both cheeks. His nose was broken and half his teeth were missing. He was twice Quinn's size.

The guy picked up a broken bar from the metal stair. The first swing caught Quinn across the shoulder. He rolled with the blow and staggered to his feet again. The pain was agonizing.

'You going to come quietly?' the man asked. 'Or you want me to take you in a box?'

'I'll come quietly,' Quinn said. 'It's easier that way.' He edged forwards, nursing his damaged shoulder, but as soon as he was close enough, he struck with a lightning right jab. The man stumbled and Quinn punched twice more. He finished with an upper cut and the guy went down.

There was an open door beside the man's prone body, but Quinn figured that way led straight to Siegel and his friends. He forced a window on the opposite side of the courtyard and slipped through it. He found himself in a men's room at the rear of a second-hand clothes shop. He heard voices in the yard. He slid between racks of clothes, which smelt of damp and decay. He looked out of the window and saw Siegel's driver by the door of the automobile. The Bowery down-and-outs stood and stared.

Quinn heard voices again. He went to the far side of the store and climbed to the top of the fire escape. From there, he was able to jump across to the next building.

He looked back at the uneven rooftops and the angry sky, heard more shouts from the direction of the Bowery, then an automobile roaring away. He sat on the edge of a roof, dangling his legs over the side, then lay down, eyes closed against the pain in his shoulder.

CHAPTER FORTY-THREE

HALF AN HOUR LATER, HE SLUNK THROUGH CHINATOWN, dead beat. By the time he reached Canal Street, he was sure he was not being followed, but slipped into one of the convenience stores to check. He looked through rows of brown-paper fans, incense sticks, black slippers and butterfly kites. He smiled at the inquisitive old man behind the counter. The rear of the store was packed with shark fins, squid, blubber and roasted ducks hanging from long metal hooks. The cloying smell caught in his throat.

He stepped outside again and lingered by a group of men playing mahjong. Copper foils tinkled in the breeze.

He hurried past a line of restaurants, turned into a narrow doorway and climbed to the top floor. There was no sign on the battered wooden door and no bell. He knocked once. 'Who is it?' Caprisi called.

The door opened. 'It's late,' Quinn said. 'I'm sorry.'

'You're damned right it's late. I'd given up on you.'

'I'll go.'

'Don't be a fool.' Caprisi took hold of his arm and yanked him inside. Quinn winced with pain.

'Christ,' Caprisi said. 'What the hell happened? You've got blood on your shirt.'

'It's nothing.'

'Oh, yeah?' Caprisi took his arm, gently this time, and led him to the front room. 'Sandra!'

A slight, pretty, dark-haired girl appeared. 'Joe, this is my wife. Sandra, this is Detective Quinn. You'd better get a bowl of hot water and some iodine.'

A small boy, the spitting image of his father, poked his head through a doorway and gazed at the newcomer. 'Get to bed, monkey,' Caprisi said. The child withdrew, but popped out again once his father's back was turned. Quinn winked at him.

Caprisi seated him in a wooden chair. 'What happened?'

'Somebody wanted to take me for a ride.'

'Who?'

'Meyer Lansky and Ben Siegel.'

'Christ.'

'I didn't like the look of the place we were headed.'

'They still searching for you?'

'Maybe.'

'What did they want?'

'I don't know.'

'They follow you here?'

'I lost them in the Bowery.'

'You sure, Joe?'

'I'd never have brought them here, Caprisi.'

'Of course not.' Caprisi pursed his lips. 'Sorry, Joe.' He followed his wife into the kitchen.

The front room was tiny, but a tall window offered a view of the street. It was open a fraction. The curtains were shabby and worn, the upholstery and carpets threadbare. There was a small table in the corner and a cheap print of Niagara Falls. A crucifix took pride of place above the fireplace. There was no wireless set. No books or magazines.

When Caprisi returned, Quinn pushed himself to his feet. 'I'll go,' he said. 'I shouldn't have come here.'

'Don't be a fool, Joe.'

'Maybe they *are* still looking for me.'

'Sit down. Sandra will never let you back out there.'

Caprisi forced Quinn into his seat. Sandra knelt before him with a bowl of hot water and a cloth. She unbuttoned his shirt and cleaned his graze with brisk, unselfconscious movements. Up close, she looked tired, the skin around her eyes pinched and tight. Her husband poured two glasses of whisky.

'What did they hit you with?' Caprisi said.

'An iron bar.'

Sandra squeezed the cloth into the bowl.

'How did you get away?'

'I ran.'

'Do you run as fast as you fight?'

'Faster. I'm a natural-born coward.'

389

'Your trouble, my friend, is that you're nowhere near coward enough. What did they want?'

'I've no idea.'

'What did they say they wanted?'

'They didn't.'

'What do you *think* they wanted?'

Quinn looked out of the window at the black night. 'They're worried that this group of men will fall apart and their rackets will go with it.'

Sandra finished her work and buttoned his shirt.

'Thank you,' Quinn said.

She smiled and retreated to the kitchen. Caprisi lit a cigarette and offered him the packet. They listened to her clearing up. After a few minutes, she hurried down the corridor. 'I've left the sheets out.'

'It's all right,' Caprisi said. 'I know.'

'I'm sorry it's not very comfortable, Joe. I said perhaps you could have little Johnny's bed . . .'

'I'll be just fine right here, ma'am. It's a whole lot more than I deserve.'

'Thank you for looking after him,' she said, and gestured to her husband. 'I know it's not easy, and I—'

'Goodnight, woman!' Caprisi said.

'Mind you don't keep our patient up too long,' she added. 'He's tired.' She went out and pulled the door to.

Quinn took a sip of whisky, settled into the chair and stretched out his legs.

Caprisi saw his boy and scolded him, but the kid ran forward and leapt onto his lap. Caprisi ruffled his hair. 'This is my partner, Joe Quinn.'

The little boy stared at him with wide eyes. He didn't dare speak. Caprisi kissed him on both cheeks and sent him on his way again. 'To sleep, this time!' he demanded.

'Don't tell me,' Quinn said. 'He wants to be a cop.'

'I'm trying to put him off.'

'So did my dad, but it didn't work.'

They sipped in silence. Quinn didn't want to think about his father any more. 'Is that a picture of one of your brothers I saw on McCredie's wall?'

'Yes.'

'How come they knew each other?'

'McCredie went out to Shanghai in 'twenty-five to teach them how to fight organized crime, but he was the guy who ended up getting the lesson.'

'How long was he there?'

'A couple months.'

'They were friends?'

'They were shot at together a few times. It's not the same thing.'

'When was your brother killed?'

' 'Twenty-six, just before I left the precincts. I wanted to cut it at Headquarters to make him proud.' He smiled bitterly. 'But who wants to work in a place where your colleagues spit at you in the morning, or where Johnny the Bull and his friends can kick the living daylights out of you and walk away? Without you, would I even be here tonight?'

Quinn hadn't realized the legacy of the Rat Squad still preyed so heavily on his partner's mind. 'Someone else would have helped.'

'No, they wouldn't, Joe,' Caprisi said quietly. 'At times like this I just need to remind myself there's a world far away from Johnny, Charlie Luciano and the whole damned lot of them.'

'How much longer do you have before you're out?'

'Two months, all being well.'

'What needs to be well?'

Caprisi swirled the liquid in his glass. 'You're not interested in Wall Street, are you, Joe?'

'Not much.'

'Try to keep it that way. Once upon a time people like you and me didn't even know what a stock market was.'

'You've a lot riding on it?'

'Dumb, eh?'

'I don't know. Maybe not.' Quinn leant forward. 'Are you all right? You don't look well.'

'I'm fine.'

'Come on, man. We're in this together. If there's something on your mind . . .'

'There's nothing on my mind.'

'That's not the way it looks to me.'

Caprisi drained his glass. 'Every morning I wake up feeling sick. And that never goes away. At night, I sit here and drink until I'm too numb to care any more. Maybe I should thank you. This investigation is the only thing that's kept me sane.'

'The market always comes back, doesn't it? Isn't that what they say?'

'Perhaps, but if we could predict the future, we'd all be rich.'

'How deep in are you?'

Caprisi smiled sadly. 'Joe, my dad doesn't want me to be a cop any more. He's lost two sons and it's broken his heart. Like I told you, he's asked me to get out, come home and run the family store. He's old, tired and needs to take it easy. He deserves to, despite what I told you. And I want to do that for him. My little sister helps him with the place and we could run it together. Sandra doesn't like it here and is sick of me being a cop. She wants to go home, too. I've told you what I think of life in Centre Street, my partnership with you aside.'

'So what's to stop you?'

'Times have been hard up there. My dad hasn't run the place too well. There's debt, a lot of it. The store and the diner have to be spruced up, and I need to clear the loans and get the sharks off my dad's back.'

'So you put your savings into the market?'

Caprisi bit his lip. 'Everyone said it was a one-way bet. I shouldn't have listened. Maybe if I was as obsessed with my work as you are, I wouldn't have had time to take any notice. The trouble is, Joe, once you're in you can only go deeper. I lost some dough. There was bad luck and a few dumb choices, courtesy of our friend Jeremy Norton and his buddies. So then your broker says go in on margin and hit this big and you'll make it all back and more . . .'

'And have you?'

'No. I went in, but I haven't won.'

'But it'll come back.'

'Maybe, but not in time. My broker called me in. If

393

the market doesn't turn up tomorrow, then I guess . . . The truth is, I'll be finished, Joe.'

'But you can't have everything you've got on the market.'

'Everything and more. We're fools, all of us. The whole damned world went mad for a few moments there and now we're going to pay for it.'

'What will you do?'

'I look at my boy, I look at Sandra, and I just don't want to think about it.'

'We can do something. Lean on your broker, buy some time.'

'I already did. He's hurting too, Joe. It's the way it is.' His face was ashen.

They listened to Sandra in the bathroom. 'Does she know how deep you're in?' Quinn whispered.

'Not yet, but she knows we don't have two cents to rub together.'

'You figure you should tell her?'

'I can't bring myself to. She's been looking forward to going home for a year.'

'Maybe we can find a way to help.' Quinn breathed deeply, then met his partner's eye. 'Tony, I'm real sorry. I took some of that dough from Matsell's apartment.'

'I know.'

'But you needed it more than I did. You could have taken it. I stole it to help my brother. But,' he waved his hand around the apartment, 'you have a family and—'

'Joe, it's okay, really.'

'I'll turn myself in to Schneider in the morning.'

'Don't be a damn fool. Schneider will assume it was McCredie and they'll blame each other, same way they always have. No one will know.'

'*You* will.'

'I'm your partner.'

'And that's enough?'

'In this case, it is.'

'I'll find a way to help you. I can—'

'It's all right, Joe. It's my problem.'

'No. It's our problem.'

Caprisi got up and went to the window. An argument had broken out in the apartment below and a piece of crockery shattered against a wall. A woman began to cry. 'I'm sorry about your dad, Joe.'

'It's okay.'

'What are you going to do?'

'I don't know. Part of me is terrified to discover he isn't the man I thought he was. But mostly I just don't want him to be next on this guy's list. I don't want him to die.'

'Maybe it's not as bad as you think.'

Quinn touched his forehead. 'You know, sometimes I have this pain behind my eyes. It hurts so bad I think I'm going crazy.'

'How did you get mixed up with the girl?'

'Which one?'

'The one you're in love with.'

'Jesus.' Quinn stared at his feet. 'One day, you come home and you suddenly realize you're disappointed she's not there. You miss the way she lights up a room.

Hell, you even miss the way she scowls at you sometimes. But it's complicated. *She's* complicated.' He glanced at the empty glass in his hand. 'The booze is loosening my tongue.'

'Are you going to walk away?'

'Yes. No. Maybe. I don't know.'

Quinn felt tired and drunk. Caprisi slipped the glass from his hand and took it to the kitchen. 'I understand, my friend. Maybe more than you can imagine. But you need to sleep.'

Quinn lay down. Fatigue tugged at his eyelids. 'I'm glad they teamed me with you,' he said. 'I'm real glad they did that.'

After a few minutes, he felt Caprisi put a blanket over him, and he sank slowly into a deep sleep.

'C'mon, Detective!' He was being shaken violently. '*Wake up!*'

It took him a moment to work out that Caprisi was standing above him in the semi-darkness. He tried to sit up. His neck and shoulder ached.

'We have to get our backsides over to the abattoir on First and Forty-second. They say it's a goddamn mess.'

CHAPTER FORTY-FOUR

CAPRISI HADN'T BEEN KIDDING. THE AUTOMOBILE, A SHINY
new bright-red Chrysler seventy-seven, stood in a rancid
alley amid the crates and stench of rotting carcasses. In
the glare of the Gardner's headlights, its interior looked
like an abattoir too.

Dick Kelly was twisted against the side window, his
nose pressed to the leather trim. Moe Diamond was
sprawled on the seat beside him. Both men had a gash
to the throat, similar to Spencer Duncan's. And their
tongues lay in a pool of blood at their feet.

Quinn stepped away from the Chrysler, head pounding like a tractor's engine, and moved towards the
entrance to the alley. 'Tell the uniform boys to set up a
cordon,' he said. 'If the press get near this. . .'

'Sure.'

'Where's Brandon?'

'They couldn't find him. That's why they called us.
McCredie's on his way. He was out on Long Island.'

Quinn watched his partner issuing instructions to the uniforms. He grabbed a torch from the Gardner and clambered into the back of Moe's automobile. He moved his nose as close as he could to the men's swollen mouths. Shit, it was early. And his head hurt.

He couldn't detect a hint of chloroform.

He crouched down and flicked the torchbeam from one face to the other. He gazed at Moe's fleshy cheeks and wide eyes.

'Easy,' Caprisi said from the doorway. 'The print boys'll go nuts if we screw anything up.'

Quinn ignored his advice. 'There won't be any prints,' he said.

He took Kelly's wallet from an inside pocket and handed it to his partner. He checked the rest of the suit and waistcoat, but found only a watch. 'Look at this.' He held the jacket open and pointed at the label. 'It's this guy again.'

'If I ever need a new suit, I'll know which tailor to avoid.'

Quinn checked Moe's clothes, but there was no label on the overcoat and he couldn't get a look at the suit without slipping on blood.

'Leave it, Joe,' Caprisi said.

Quinn stepped out and switched off the torch. There was a chill in the air and they stamped their feet.

'Should we talk to your father, Joe? Offer him protection?'

'No.'

'But you said last night you didn't want to see him—'

398

'I know what I said.'

There was a commotion by the entrance to the alley as McCredie's chauffeur-driven automobile nosed through the cordon. The boss stepped out and strode towards them. He grabbed the torch from Quinn's hand, then thrust his head into the back of the Chrysler. 'Jesus Christ!' he whispered. He surveyed the scene for a minute or more before he handed back the torch. 'He's cut their goddamn tongues out! Who the hell is this guy? Quinn?'

'Yes, sir?'

'Who is he?'

'We don't have a suspect yet, sir.'

'Well, that's helpful. Let's start at the beginning. Are these two dead men from the Wall Street fix?'

'They're Matsell's partners.'

'Somebody lost a pile of dough and figured he'd make these guys pay for it?'

'We don't believe that's the motive, sir, no.'

'Why not?'

'Nobody cuts men up like that over a stock fix. However . . .' Quinn trailed off. He glanced at his partner. 'However much pain it might cause.'

'So what *is* it about?'

'What they did after Wall Street.'

'Which was?'

'They liked to play cards, maybe gamble a little. We're looking at how some of those evenings ended up.'

'And how *did* they end up?'

'They liked to "use" broads. That's what Norton told us. Not all of the girls were bought and paid for.'

'They were white-slavers?'

'I don't know how to put it, sir.'

'Try.'

Quinn peered into the rear of the automobile. 'They used drugs to kidnap the girls and assault them.'

'You got a witness?'

He hesitated. 'Yes.'

'Who is she?'

'Well, sir, she hasn't said she'll go on the record yet, so—'

'Who is she?'

'I'm afraid I can't tell you that, sir.'

McCredie sighed. 'Why does that not surprise me? I wouldn't put her on the stand, son, if I were you. You want to tell me why he ripped out their goddamn tongues?'

'It's a message,' Caprisi said. 'Just like the others. Joe was right about that. The chloroform, the cut to their throats . . .'

Quinn's eyes rested on Moe's leg, which protruded from the door. 'This is different.'

'It looks pretty much the damned same to me, son,' McCredie said.

'It's been made to look the same.'

'What's that supposed to mean?'

Quinn looked from Caprisi to McCredie and back again. 'The first two murders carried a warning they all understood – chloroform for the drugs they used on the girls and the mark of Sicilian vengeance upon their throats for what they had done.'

'Where did you hear that?'

'My father told me.'

'Since when did this become a family affair?'

'It hasn't, sir.'

'These men have had their necks slashed too. What's the difference?'

'The cuts here are deeper than the one on Duncan. And I don't think the way the tongues have been cut out fits the pattern.'

McCredie scuffed his boots impatiently on the ground. 'Why in hell not?'

'The first two murders were about revenge. This feels like a warning.'

'What kind of warning?'

'Against talking. To us, maybe, or anyone else.'

'Was Moe Diamond singing to you?'

'No. But he was rattled. Maybe somebody thought he would. Maybe he was going to.'

'You're reading a lot into this, son.' McCredie wrinkled his nose. 'It stinks.'

'It's an abattoir.'

'I can see that! Okay, first up, we keep the press back this time. Don't let anyone through and make sure Johnny doesn't either, when he bothers to show up. Tell him that's a direct order. I'm sure you'll enjoy passing it on. Then check out the abattoir.' McCredie kicked the side of the automobile. 'What in the hell were they doing here?'

'How did he get them into the back of the Chrysler?' Quinn asked, more quietly.

'What kind of question is that?'

'It's the same question. Diamond and Kelly knew what was coming to them, so how did their killer get them into an automobile? How did Duncan's killer get close to him? Why did Matsell go up to the roof to meet his murderer?'

'Maybe the guy's a ghost.'

'Or the next best thing.'

'Which is?'

Quinn paused. 'I was just thinking aloud.'

'Go on, son.'

'Well . . . I was just . . . How about a cop? Or maybe *cops*.'

McCredie gawped at him. 'Say that again.'

'The only thing we know for certain is that one of the guys seen bending over Matsell's body was an officer in uniform.'

'Have you got any evidence for this theory, or is it idle speculation from your cop-hating friend here?'

'It's just an idea. But once someone's got used to the fact that cops are around, all they see is a uniform. They don't register a face. And who is the one person a guy about to get whacked *doesn't* suspect? A cop.'

'Sir,' Caprisi said, 'do you want us to—'

'Just get on with it. That's what I want. And there's no public connection to be made between any of these killings.'

'We can't hold that line,' Quinn said. 'We've got four men from one poker—'

'I know that, Detective. Don't tell me my job. I'm just instructing you to keep your mouths shut until I tell you otherwise. You work directly to me. I want everything kept as tight as a duck's ass. Don't talk to Schneider. Don't talk to Johnny.'

McCredie stalked off towards his automobile. A few seconds later it screeched away.

Caprisi slipped his hands into his pockets. 'Imagine what the jackals in the press are going to make of this. Why do you think the killer changed his method?'

'Maybe he didn't.'

Caprisi's brow furrowed. 'You've lost me.'

'Maybe it's not the same killer.'

'Joe, c'mon.'

Quinn stared at Moe's automobile, deep in thought.

'I don't want to push it,' Caprisi said, 'but should I go talk to your old man?'

'No.'

'It's just maybe now he'll—'

'I said I would. Let's clean up here and get the hell out.'

Inside the abattoir gates, men in thick winter coats and dark woollen hats had gathered by the water's edge. They watched a barge swoop down the East River and glide into a berth. A wooden ramp was lowered against the concrete pier and a couple of hundred lambs were driven down it into a dilapidated shack. A damp wind blew in off the river, but it was not enough to banish the putrid odour of the shack. As a wooden gate swung shut, two lambs made a break for it, but the only avenue of escape was across the concrete courtyard and into the slaughterhouse. A couple of men chased them back and wheeled the gate shut.

Quinn strolled over to the nearest, who did not acknowledge him. 'Where's the boss?'

He gestured at a balding man who stood at the end of the pier.

The boss didn't seem surprised to see them. 'You got here, did you?' he asked.

'It was your men who found them?'

'Hey! Easy there!' Another ramp was lowered onto the pier and a herd of calves driven into the shed. The supervisor ticked the board in his hand and waved at the skipper of the barge. 'You're early!' he yelled. The guy waved back. 'Makes a goddamn change.' The supervisor turned to his men. 'Are they in yet?' He pointed at the gaping doors of the slaughterhouse.

'No, boss.'

The guy examined his clipboard. 'I didn't expect to see you until at least lunchtime,' he told Quinn.

'Murder is still a crime, even in Manhattan.'

'Murder?' The guy frowned. 'Who said anything about a goddamn murder? They stole our truck. I called it in – one green model-A Ford pick-up. I know that if some big city swell ain't involved none of you boys is interested, but I pay my taxes.'

'When was it stolen?'

'I told them already. I came in an hour ago and saw it wasn't there. So it was—'

'Have you got the plate numbers?'

'Of course I goddamn have! I told you, it was my truck!'

'Give them to me.' Quinn turned. 'You hear that, Caprisi? We've got something.'

'I'll check it out. Why steal a pick-up? After Duncan, he just melted into the night.'

'It's not the same guy.' Quinn nudged his partner towards the Gardner. 'Come on. Let's get out of here.'

CHAPTER FORTY-FIVE

QUINN DROPPED CAPRISI AT THE OFFICE, THEN CARRIED ON down to the First Precinct. He couldn't find his father in the station house but tracked him down twenty minutes later on the steps of the Subtreasury Building.

Gerry was surrounded by a crowd of expectant faces, hushed and anxious in the dawn sunlight. Hundreds of people were already jostling for sight of the Exchange, but the street was almost silent. It reminded Quinn of the moment before a ball game, when the batsman strides out from the dugout, swinging his arms one final time before attempting to snatch victory from the gaping jaws of defeat. 'Not much longer to wait,' his father said, then waved at one of his men. 'McGrady! Over the other side. Down by William Street.'

Quinn could smell the fear in those around him. 'When does it begin?'

'Soon.'

'Which way will it go?'

406

'Who in hell knows?'

'Dad, I need to talk to you.'

'It's not a good time, Joe.'

'Please.' Quinn took his arm and led him down Nassau Street. He searched for a café, but Gerry shook him off. 'What is it, Joe? What do you want?'

'Moe's dead. They found him this morning, up by the abattoir. He'd been stabbed and . . . Dad, they cut his tongue out.'

The light went out of Gerry's eyes. 'Some would call that a fitting end.'

'He was in Owney Madden's place last night. Dad, he was terrified. He asked if I'd passed on his warning to you.'

'What do you want me to say, Joe? What are you looking for?'

'I want you to talk to me.'

'About what?'

'I need to know the truth, Dad. I know it's not good.'

Gerry flushed. 'I hope you can back that up, son.'

'You mean you want *evidence*? You're my father, for God's sake.'

'You don't understand.'

'We're talking about a crime, a terrible crime. What is there to understand?'

Gerry's shoulders sagged. He seemed older suddenly. 'Please, Joe, I beg you, let this go.'

Quinn saw the guilt in his father's washed-out eyes and vomit rushed to the back of his throat.

'Please, Joe. You're my son.'

Quinn stumbled through the crowd to the Gardner and slumped into the driving seat. His vision blurred. 'Damn you, Dad,' he whispered. 'Damn you to hell.'

He made the journey slowly to Centre Street and parked in an official bay by the front entrance. He remained at the wheel of the Gardner as the early-morning commuter crowd flooded towards City Hall.

Mrs Mecklenburg walked haltingly down the front steps and shuffled off towards Broadway, a broken woman.

He watched a few drops of rain roll down the windscreen and smoked a cigarette to the stub. His hands shook. He got out of the Gardner and glanced again at Mrs Mecklenburg's receding figure as he headed back into Headquarters.

Upstairs, he found wooden boxes stacked two deep beneath his desk. There was a note. 'You wanted cases,' it read, 'so here they are. Yan.'

Quinn sat down. He tried to drag himself back from the abyss, but every nerve end was on fire. He flipped through one or two files. Some were as thick as his thumb, and packed with closely typed reports. The faces of long-lost daughters stared up at him. Amy Venning, aged seventeen. *Missing*. Sadie MacLeish. Twenty. Homicide. Body found in a trash bin in the Bronx. *Unsolved*.

Mae appeared at his side, a cup of coffee in one hand and a newspaper in the other. 'What happened this morning?' she asked.

'About what?' He gripped the edge of the table to stop his hand shaking.

'The call-out. Diamond and Kelly . . .'

'It was a mess.'

She gave a low whistle. 'The boss went straight upstairs and hasn't been back.' She dropped the newspaper on Quinn's desk. 'Be warned, some of the guys don't like this. They're saying it's down to you.'

Quinn took in the headline. 'Slain Walker Aide: Link to Wall Street Fix. Conspiracy to Ramp Stocks Cheats Millions.'

'Jesus,' Quinn said. 'How'd they get that?' He read the article and checked the byline. 'Where does Goldberg get this stuff? Did the boss mention it?'

'No.'

'Does he know about it?'

'It's front-page news, Joe, hardly a secret. It may explain his temper.'

'Is there any news on the Mecklenburg girl?'

'I don't think so. I was looking for the case file, but it seems our friend Mr Byrnes took it away with him.'

'I thought that was a capital offence.'

'It is.'

Caprisi returned to his desk. Quinn flipped over the newspaper and tapped it against the table top. 'Is Doc Carter in?'

'Already hard at work,' Caprisi said.

Quinn got to his feet and picked up his jacket. Caprisi followed him to the rear stairs. 'What did your father say?'

'He didn't say anything. He asked me to leave the case alone.' Quinn quickened his pace to bring the discussion to a close.

'That's it?' Caprisi asked.

Quinn walked still faster.

Their footsteps echoed down the long corridor in the basement. The building seemed unnaturally quiet so early in the day.

Doc Carter was humming to himself. He was bent over Moe Diamond's body with a saw in one hand and a scalpel in the other.

'Happy in your work, Doc?'

'Very funny, Detective.' Carter straightened up. 'You know, I've started to enjoy our encounters, which probably isn't healthy for either of us.'

'Why's that?'

'You can probably guess.'

'How far have you got?'

'Not far.'

'You want to tell me what you've found?'

'You'll have to wait for my report.'

'C'mon, Doc,' Quinn said. 'I can see you already have something you're bursting to tell me. There were two killers this time, right? Two different knives?'

'Very clever, Detective.' Carter put down his tools. 'How did you know?'

'Moe and Dick were nervous as hell. One guy couldn't have taken them on.'

Carter moved to the sink and washed his hands. He picked up a towel. 'Permit me to observe that you're sometimes a little too clever for your own good.'

'What else have you observed?'

'Nothing. That's it, as you suggest. Two different knives. The larger one was used to kill Moe Diamond and was thrust in hard and deep. The other was smaller. If it hadn't pierced his heart, it might not have killed Mr Kelly.'

'So what are you saying?'

'I'm not saying anything. Those are the facts.'

'It was a professional hit?'

Carter hesitated. 'It's not an attractive proposition, is it? For any of us . . .'

'But that's what you're getting at.'

'Both men were killed cleanly, Detective. The rest of it,' he waved a hand in the air, 'pure theatrics.'

'Moe Diamond was already dead when they cut his tongue out?'

'I'd say so.'

'And the cuts to their throats are deeper than Duncan's?'

'Correct. I think that calls for a drink, don't you?'

'Doc, it's real early.'

'Never too early.'

Quinn moved to the window. 'You think one of the knives could have been used on Duncan?'

'No. The shape and trajectory of the incisions are quite different.'

'Which means Moe and Dick were killed by somebody else?'

Carter pursed his lips. 'Let's just say that the man

411

who murdered Spencer Duncan was an amateur. Both these guys have gone for a single thrust straight to the heart. They knew what they were doing. They've killed before. They'll probably do so again.'

'Maybe our friend Major La Guardia is to blame.'

'What do you mean by that?'

'Oh . . . nothing. Thanks, Doc.'

'Don't mention it.'

Quinn and Caprisi stepped into the corridor. 'What's La Guardia got to do with this?' Caprisi said.

'I saw him at the fight last night. He's trying to expose the mayor. That's why he sent Martha to work for Moe.'

'Moe was talking to La Guardia?'

'I figure he was half a bottle short of talking to anyone who'd listen.'

'So they decided to shut him up?'

'And send a pretty clear signal to anyone with a loose tongue.'

'Now maybe it's your dad's turn, Joe.' Caprisi clutched at him. 'When are they going to decide it's time to shut *us* up, too?'

Quinn shook himself loose and started walking.

'Please, Joe,' Caprisi called after him. 'This has gone far enough. We can't go on like nothing's happening.'

Quinn turned and saw the fear in his partner's eyes. 'I never asked you to come along for the ride.'

'But I am along. So now, please, tell me you have a plan. Because otherwise I know how this is going to end.'

'They wouldn't risk taking us out.'

'The hell they wouldn't! We're nobodies. No one outside of Centre Street even knows we exist. Risky is taking out Johnny the Bull. Hellish risky is taking out Ed McCredie. But nobody gives a damn about us.'

'They will.'

'And how are you going to make that happen?'

'I'll work something out.'

CHAPTER FORTY-SIX

CHILE LAY ON HIS BUNK, SMOKING A CIGAR. 'HEY! WHAT'S the deal with you guys? Don't you even give a man a drink?'

'Shut up, Chile,' Caprisi said.

'Sit down,' Quinn snapped.

Acuna perched on the edge of the bunk. His jauntiness suggested that, since their last meeting, he'd been offered reassurance.

'You heard about Moe and Dick, Chile?'

'What's there to hear?'

'They're dead.'

'Yeah? Says who?'

'Says the two big knives that got stuck in their chests. Their bodies were in the back of an automobile alongside the abattoir.'

Acuna's mouth gaped open. Clearly he didn't think this was good news. '*Moe*'s dead?'

'Dog meat.'

414

Beads of sweat sprang to Acuna's brow.

'The way we see it, Chile, you're more or less the only guy in that poker game who's still alive and kicking.'

'I didn't do nothing,' he whined.

'You all did *something*,' Quinn said.

'Who's the big man, Chile?' Caprisi said.

'The Bag Man?'

Quinn frowned. 'No, he said the *big* man.'

'Jesus . . .' Fear glinted in Acuna's oily brown eyes. 'I don't know.'

'Then who is the *Bag* Man?'

'I don't know. I guess I heard you wrong.'

'This guy was cut in on your games, right? That's why there was never any trouble.'

'Where's the Bull? I wanna speak to the Bull.'

'Let's slow down here,' Caprisi said. 'We've got to break into your game, Chile. You understand that. Someone's killed Charlie and Spencer, Moe and Dick, so it doesn't take a genius to know that your seat at the table isn't too comfortable right now. Who else took a hand?'

'We've been over this a hundred times already,' Acuna squeaked. 'I told you, Moe, Dick, Charlie and Spencer.'

'Who else?'

'No one else. Sometimes they'd grab a few guys who were hanging around the club. There was no one regular.'

'What about the game at the Plaza?'

'I told you before, I've never been to the Plaza in my life.'

Caprisi perched on the edge of the desk. 'What did Moe and the guys talk about?'

'I don't remember.'

'You were there.'

'The usual kind of stuff.'

'And what was that?'

Acuna touched the ends of his inconsequential moustache. 'Sometimes they'd pick a few stocks.'

'What did they say about them?'

'Hell, I don't know. Does it matter?'

'It matters.'

'This was a good buy, that was a piece of shit. I didn't take it in. I wasn't interested.'

'You're a gambling man,' Quinn said. 'Did you and Moe talk about going up to Saratoga?'

'I never liked the horses.'

'Charlie Matsell only rode in from Cuba a few months ago. You talk about that?'

'No.'

'He got around a bit. You know why?'

'Maybe it was while they were all away.'

Quinn took a step closer. 'Away where?'

'I don't know, wherever it was.'

'You said, while they were *all* away.'

'Did I?' Acuna squirmed.

'Where did they go?' Quinn said.

'Search me.'

'But they went somewhere, all at the same time. They got the hell out of the city and travelled overseas?'

'I guess so, yeah.'

'Why did they go away, Chile?'

'I don't know. I didn't know them in the old days.'

'They were on the run?'

'I never said that.'

'Did they say why they went away?'

'No.'

'How long ago did they come back?'

'I don't know, man. I swear it.'

Quinn offered Acuna a cigarette. He accepted. They smoked for a moment in silence.

'Moe was scared, Chile. His friends were dying. You figure he could have been tempted to shoot his mouth off to La Guardia?'

'I don't know what you're talking about.'

'He was a troubled guy. Maybe he was looking to save his worthless hide or to salve his conscience. After all, you guys are hardly to blame. You're just passengers, right? None of it was your idea. You didn't get much of the dough from the fixes and you didn't really want to use the broads. You couldn't *stop* any of it.' Quinn waited. 'So who was it Moe was going to blow the whistle on? The Bag Man?'

Acuna looked as if he was about to faint.

'We're headed for the pre-line-up meeting,' Quinn said. 'You know what I'm going to nail on the board? Mr Chile Acuna says the guy at the heart of the fix is the Bag Man and he's ready to blow the whistle on him.'

'No!' Acuna leapt to his feet. 'You're crazy! They'll kill me!'

The Bull barged into the room. He took off his fedora

and threw it on the table. He looked from Quinn to Caprisi and back again. If they'd been dog excrement on the sidewalk, he'd have accorded them more respect. O'Reilly and Hegarty lurked in the shadows behind him. 'Detective Quinn,' Brandon said. He motioned towards the door.

Quinn followed him into the corridor.

'Scram, Seamus,' Brandon instructed the duty officer. Carrigan needed no second bidding. 'What are you doing with my witness, Quinn?'

'He's *our* witness, Johnny.'

Brandon shook his head, as if Quinn had gone stark staring mad. '*Mr Brandon* to you, Detective. And Chile Acuna is *my* witness.'

'Whatever you say, Johnny. Hey, Caprisi, let's go.'

'Hold on a second.' Brandon led Quinn further down the corridor, out of earshot. His deep blue, matinée-idol eyes scrutinized Quinn's. The cuts from their fight were less evident, but still pleasingly visible. 'What's wrong with you, Quinn? Don't you even *want* to be one of the guys?'

'It depends what that involves.'

'We respect each other's work here.'

'I heard that respect was a big thing with you, Johnny.'

'At least your old man knew which side he was on.'

'I'm beginning to figure that out,' Quinn said.

'Then be careful how you tread.'

Brandon made to leave, but Quinn stopped him. 'Is the Mecklenburg girl now officially a homicide?'

'Which girl?'

'You know damned well which girl. She's been gone more than a week, and now you've found the uncle, it should have been reassigned from Missing Persons to Homicide. I'd like to see the file.'

Brandon's face was stony. 'Talk to McCredie.'

'The file isn't on the shelf.'

'That's McCredie's problem.'

'You figure there's any chance she's still alive?'

'What do you think, Detective?'

'Did *you* find the uncle?'

'Talk to Byrnes.' Brandon's face contorted with anger. 'This is a jungle, Detective, and you need to work out real soon who are the biggest goddamn beasts.'

The Bull pivoted on his heel and they watched him go.

'What did he want?' Caprisi asked.

'The name of my tailor,' Quinn said. 'Look, do me a favour and go find Mrs Mecklenburg. I just saw her leave the building. Maybe Mae knows where she's headed.'

'Why?'

'Just bring her in here.'

'Why, Joe?'

'Because we've been real *dumb*. We figured it was all about *this* year and *this* poker game. We never thought about what might have happened before they ran away to Cuba.'

'I don't get it.'

'The Mecklenburg case has been bugging me from the

419

start. A girl goes missing but they don't put it out on the wire. It's not in the newspapers. You ask yourself why?'

'It's a family issue.'

'The hell it is. I'll bet you a dime to a dollar she's already dead and has been for a week. When Amy Mecklenburg goes missing, everyone south of Schneider wants to play it down. Hell, it's election time. But someone knows there's more to it than that.' Quinn clasped his partner's shoulder. 'I'm sorry, Tony. It's been staring me in the face. We have to find the mother.'

CHAPTER FORTY-SEVEN

YAN WAS READING THE GOLDBERG PIECE TOO. 'DID YOU GET the files? I couldn't see any involving chloroform.'

Quinn gritted his teeth. 'Yan, I made a mistake. We need to go further back.'

'How much further?'

'You should start with the summer of 1919.'

'Why?'

'It's when you were still my father's partner.'

Yan hesitated. 'What am I looking for?'

'The same thing. A missing girl, a homicide.'

He was gone a few minutes. 'Nothing.'

'Why doesn't that surprise me?'

'What do you want, Joe?'

'I'd like to know if there was some kind of pattern that summer, maybe a sequence of young girls being abused, or going missing, or winding up at the bottom of the East River.'

'I said, what is it you want?'

'I'm just trying to—'

Yan's expression had clouded. 'Don't fool with me, kid.'

'Okay, Yan. I just want to know the truth about my father.'

Yan sat down heavily. 'And what would you say if I told you that isn't so smart?'

'You said he had nothing to hide.'

'We all have something to hide. You find out the truth about him and you'll find out the truth about some others. And they won't think twice about shutting you up.'

'Who are we talking about?'

'If I knew that, I wouldn't be standing here.'

'You do know. You know damned well.'

Yan brushed his palm to and fro across the wooden desk top.

'Mind if I pull one of the Rothstein files?' Quinn said.

Yan shrugged. 'You know where they are.'

Quinn ducked under the barrier and walked down the corridor to the rogues' gallery. It took him a few seconds to locate the file marked 'Rothstein/Gambling Commission/Bag Man'.

The first item was an article from the *New York Times*, stamped October 1913 and yellowed with age. It exposed a 'secret gambling commission' operating at 'the highest level' within the city. It detailed the yearly graft paid to the protection rackets and listed the different operations and their respective yields.

Poolrooms, 400, at $300 monthly	*1,440,000*
Crap games, 500, at $150 monthly	*900,000*
Gambling houses, 200, at $150 monthly	*360,000*
Gambling houses (large), 20, $1,000 a month	*240,000*
Swindlers, 50, at $50 a month	*30,000*
Policy	*125,000*
Total	*$3,095,000*

According to the *Times*, this colossal figure had been paid to the 'secret gambling commission', which was composed of the head of one of the city departments, two senators, the director of the poolroom syndicate and a senior official at Police Headquarters known as the Bag Man, who was responsible for the collection and distribution of the take. Quinn got out the papers he had taken from Spencer Duncan's house.

Under the heading 'Disbursements' the figures were bigger, but they were broken down into smaller denominations. He decided that the top line recorded what was coming in, while the numbers running down the side related to what was going out, and to whom.

'What are you looking for?' Yan asked.

Quinn folded Duncan's papers and put them back in his pocket. He returned to the file. It was packed with witness testimony about the case of Lieutenant Charles Becker, who had been executed for murder. 'What has this got to do with Rothstein?'

'Valentine's first Confidential Squad put it together. They wanted to detail where Rothstein and his like came from.' Yan took the file from him. 'In the old days, the Bag Man was the link between the underworld and the guys sitting up at Tammany Hall. He took in the rake-offs and oversaw the distribution of the take.'

'So who was he?'

'Bill Devery, while he was chief. When he went, Lieutenant Becker took over. After the *Times* blew the whistle it was all over for the cops so Rothstein stepped into the breach. He oiled the wheels the same way the Bag Man had done. He provided political connections for the underworld strong men and kept the cash flowing into the pockets of the Tammany sachems. In theory, the cops were cut out.'

'Only in theory?'

Yan slipped the file back onto the shelf. He took the whisky bottle from its hiding place. 'You want a drink?'

'Rothstein was a smokescreen. Nothing changed.'

Yan poured himself a glass. 'You have a suspect, kid?'

'Yes.'

'Who is it?'

'A cop. Or maybe someone who was once a cop.'

'Do you have any evidence?'

'It's a crime, Yan. Whatever the reasons, it's still a crime.'

'I don't know what you're talking about.'

'You do, Yan. It's because of the Mecklenburg girl. When she went missing, you knew it had started again.'

'Forget it, Joe.'

'Something happened when you were working with my old man. That was when the arguments at home began and he was in the courtyard at night burning his suits. You knew what was going on. Moe and the rest of the gang had to lie low for a while, but now they're back in business and you weren't about to let it happen again.'

Yan's eyes burnt into his. 'You don't know what you're getting into.'

'Is my father next on the list?'

'He knows the risk! He always has. Listen to me, Joe—'

'The Bag Man runs it. He's the guy at the heart of this everyone is trying to protect. Who is he, Yan? Is it Johnny?'

'Listen to me.' Yan held up his thumb and forefinger, a razor's breadth apart. 'You're this close to oblivion, so you need to wake up. I don't want to see you go under. You need support. You need allies. Do you have any reporters in your pocket?'

'No.'

'Then get some! Everyone else has. Have you spoken to Johnny?'

'Why in hell should I want to do that?'

'I'm trying to help you, kid.' Yan picked up the bottle of whisky.

'You won't get away with it,' Quinn said.

'Get the hell out of here. I've helped you all I can.'

CHAPTER FORTY-EIGHT

CAPRISI SAT BY A WIRELESS. EVERYONE IN THE ROOM WAS listening.

'Crowds have gathered here on Wall Street to witness this extraordinary spectacle ... There are reports already of despair and suicide as men struggle to come to terms with the scale of their losses. The tickertape runs behind, way behind, as brokers deal with an avalanche of orders to sell, sell, sell ...'

Quinn's eyes were on Caprisi's hunched shoulders.

'There's something close to panic.' The pitch of the announcer's voice had risen. 'Chaos and confusion reign as America comes to the conclusion all at once that the time has come to sell, sell, sell ...'

Quinn went over to his partner and Caprisi smiled weakly at him.

A stenographer flew past. 'I heard there's been a riot outside the Exchange,' she whispered.

Quinn took a seat. 'Did you find Mrs Mecklenburg?'

Caprisi gestured at McCredie's office. Quinn stood again. He saw Mrs Mecklenburg bent over in a chair, flanked by McCredie, Schneider and Brandon. Mae was trying to comfort her.

'They found the girl's body?'

Caprisi nodded.

'Where?'

'Nobody's saying.'

Quinn sat down again. He put his head in his hands and tried to block out the broadcaster's shrill commentary.

Mae came out of McCredie's office, walked over to him and massaged his neck and shoulders.

'Where did they find the body?' Quinn said.

'I don't know.'

'C'mon, Mae.'

'It was dragged out of a canal. Apparently they didn't fasten the rocks properly into the canvas.'

'Where is she now?'

'That's what they've been arguing about. Schneider doesn't want Doc Carter to perform the autopsy.'

Quinn made to stand up, but she wouldn't let him. 'Take it easy, Joe. It's not pretty in there. And they're a little angry with you this morning.'

Quinn's eye fell again on the newspaper headline and the Goldberg byline. 'Do me a favour, will you, and tell me where the body goes? If it does end up with Carter, give me the nod as soon as it's through the swing doors in the basement.'

'I'll try, Joe.'

'Thanks.' He eased her fingers off the back of his neck and went to the bathroom. He ran a basin of cold water and scooped it over his face. He reached for a filthy towel and dried himself. Then he examined his reflection in the glass. His eyes were red with fatigue, his cheeks gaunt and haggard. Stubble coated his chin. He looked like the kind of guy you'd cross the street to avoid.

Quinn stepped out into the corridor and let the door bang shut. He listened to the noise from the main floor: the hammering of typewriter keys, the low whine of wireless sets and the murmur of conversation. It was just possible to make out the traffic on Centre Street far below.

He picked up his coat, walked down the stairs and hurried to the nearest drugstore phone booth. It took the operator a few minutes to put him through to the right desk at the *Sun*.

'Goldberg here,' a distant voice said. 'Who is this?'

'Quinn. Detective Joe Quinn.'

There was a momentary silence. 'I wondered when you'd call.'

'You caused me some trouble with that piece this morning. The guys in here think I'm giving you the dope.'

'I didn't mean to cause you any discomfort. Maybe we should talk. Perhaps I can work out how to keep it away from you.'

Quinn tapped another nickel against the glass. 'I can give you half an hour. But it's a two-way street.'

'Of course. When?'

'Now. And it needs to be somewhere no one will see us.'

'There's a café on the corner of Lafayette and Houston. I've never seen a cop there. If you arrive first, take a seat at the back, away from the windows.'

Quinn put down the receiver. His hands were shaking again. He stepped out onto the sidewalk and turned north. By the time he got to the café, Goldberg was already in the corner, half hidden behind a cloud of smoke. He held up his mug of coffee and waved at a waitress to indicate she should bring another.

They shook hands. The reporter adjusted his spectacles.

They waited for the waitress to bring the coffee. 'You think it'll stop raining soon?' Goldberg said.

The waitress arrived. 'You want anything else, boys?'

They shook their heads. Quinn gave her a dollar and she left them.

'I heard you found the body of the missing girl,' Goldberg said. 'You got any details on the case? It sounds interesting.'

'You'll have to call Hegarty.'

Goldberg smiled. 'Okay, Detective. I get it.' He leant back. 'You asked for a two-way street. What is it you want to know?'

Quinn flipped his copy of the paper so the headline was face up. 'Slain Walker Aide: Link to Wall Street Fix. Conspiracy to Ramp Stocks Cheats Millions.' He pushed it across the table. 'Who's giving you this stuff?'

'I can't talk about that.'

'It's La Guardia, right?'

'You can guess all you like, but it's confidential, same as it would be if anyone asked about this meeting.'

'La Guardia knew about this fix long before Matsell's body flopped onto Wall Street.'

'You sure of that or just guessing?'

'I'm sure. And so are you.'

Goldberg stubbed out his cigarette and took off his glasses. He had dark, intelligent eyes. 'If you're asking me in my capacity as a City Hall reporter, I'd say Major La Guardia knows about a lot of things. But *proving* them is another matter altogether.'

'Did you know he'd been trying to hook Spencer Duncan?'

'Wouldn't you, if you were in his position?'

'You figure Duncan would have turned in the mayor?'

Goldberg gave a short, mirthless laugh. 'What would he have said? You think our friend Jimmy knew about the fix? Of course he didn't. He's too smart to *know* about anything. He floats along on a cloud of eau-de-Cologne, while guys like Spencer run along behind to pick up the tab. Laughing Boy Jimmy is a symptom of the problem, but not the problem itself.'

'So who is?'

'I thought you'd have worked that out by now.' Goldberg twirled his glasses. 'You want to run a racket, you need to square off the cops, right? And there are big rackets in this town. Even if La Guardia got rid of Jimmy and shoehorned himself into City Hall, he'd still have to break Centre Street.'

'Who does he have to break?'

'You're the detective, Mr Quinn.'

'So that's who Lucky Luciano pays off?'

'Lucky Luciano and all the other slime,' Goldberg said. 'But what would I know? I'm just a reporter looking for a story. So, you want to give me some dope on your case? You got a suspect yet? Spencer Duncan was quite a target.'

Quinn sipped his coffee. 'No.'

'What about our friend Mr Chile Acuna?'

'Forget it.'

'So? You must have something.'

'Spencer Duncan kept a list.'

'What kind of list?'

Quinn took out the papers and pushed them across the table. 'He called it his insurance policy.'

Goldberg looked through it. 'There are no real details. It could be anything.'

'We have a witness.'

Goldberg scrutinized him. Quinn wondered if he could tell he was bluffing. 'What kind of witness?'

'Someone who can tell us where the money came from and into whose accounts it was paid.'

'So?'

'It was collected in Centre Street from the rackets. Spencer Duncan made sure the men in City Hall got their take.'

'So these numbers are all for guys at City Hall?'

'Yes.'

'Who?'

'I can't tell you that.'

'But you've got names?'

'Sure.'

'Who's your witness?'

'I can't tell you that either.'

'Is he willing to go on the record?'

'Yes.'

'Before a jury?'

'Yes.'

Goldberg whistled. 'These are monthly payments?' Quinn nodded. 'Jeez, they're big numbers. Have you spoken to La Guardia?'

'No.'

'You should.'

'I'm a cop, not a politician.'

'Yeah, but you're going to be a cop in need of friends if your buddies find out this is what you're on to.'

'I hope I just made one. Are you going to write it?'

Goldberg's eyes narrowed. 'Yeah. I'll have to be a bit circumspect with the detail because you haven't given me any, but you're a Headquarters cop and you've said you're on the level, so sure. It's a hell of a tale. You should speak to La Guardia, though. When this hits the stands, they'll figure out where it's come from and they'll destroy you.'

'They'll try to do that anyway.'

Caprisi was still hunched over the wireless set. He hadn't moved a muscle. Mrs Mecklenburg and

McCredie, Schneider and Brandon had not budged from the corner office either.

'Tony, we need to go.'

'Listen, Joe.'

'I can hear. We'll take a look, see what's going on.'

'Everyone's waiting to be assigned. The boss wants to move some of the guys onto the Mecklenburg murder. We're meeting at half past.'

'Maybe we'll be back by then,' Quinn said, without conviction.

Caprisi went to get his coat. 'Where are we headed?'

'I told you. Wall Street.'

'Yeah, but you're not in the mood for sightseeing. I can tell.'

'I want to visit a tailor.'

'A new suit. Just what I need,' Caprisi said.

Quinn couldn't get the Gardner anywhere near the Exchange: the whole area was sealed off by uniform cops and filled with a rapidly swelling crowd.

They parked up and wove past a succession of white, dazed faces, picking up snippets of hushed gossip as they went. *Organized support is coming . . . Morgan and the banks are going to buy at lunchtime . . . Did you sell . . . ? I heard Lehman Corp and Blue Ridge are down twenty-five each . . . No one will give any more margin . . .*

Some mounted cops appeared anxious, their horses skittish and ill-tempered. A handful of photographers had reached the front of the crowd and a motion-picture crew was setting up on the steps of the Subtreasury Building.

A man stumbled out of the Exchange like a bomb victim, his collar torn open. As he passed, a woman took off her wedding ring and threw it at him. 'You want more margin?' she yelled. 'Here's your margin!' The ring hit him just beneath the eye, but he gave no sign of having noticed.

'You okay, Tony?' Quinn asked.

Caprisi did not respond.

Quinn left his partner where he was and worked his way around the crowd towards the entrance to the Exchange. People spilled from every brokerage-house doorway. Those at the back craned their necks for a glimpse of the action.

Quinn pressed his face to a window. Everyone was shouting and trying to reach the clerks' booth. They yelled at the young kid managing the green quotation board, but he was too shocked to reply. A clerk stood up, telephone receiver in hand. 'Radio at fifty-two,' he yelled, and the crowd gasped.

The news travelled like the wind, out of the brokerage house and along the street. A Chinese man shoved past, a dead cigar glued to his lips. 'The sonofabitch sold me out,' he muttered.

Quinn edged forwards.

'Montgomery Ward is down to *fifty-five*,' a voice rasped beside him. It came from a tall, stooped man.

His wife was fashionably dressed in a fur-trimmed coat,

and her expression said it all. 'What about Westinghouse?' she hissed back.

'I couldn't see.'

'Then get back in there.'

'There's no way in. It's hopeless.'

'Tell them who you are!'

The man removed his Homburg to reveal a rim of grey hair soaked with sweat. 'We should stand pat. That's what he told us.'

'He called in the margin!'

'Selling out is for pikers. If we stand pat, we'll be okay.'

The woman turned her sour face and looked through Quinn towards the Exchange.

He retraced his steps and found Caprisi by a brokerage-house window. He had to shake him hard before he took any notice. 'Let's get the hell out of here.'

'I have to stay.'

'Come on. It'll do no good. You'll just torture yourself.'

'Radio is down fifteen and still falling.'

'I heard.'

'Even US Steel's heading south and I've got a packet of it.'

'Tony, if you can gain anything by standing here, then do. If not, let's get away.'

'Look at it, Joe. Look at what's going on.'

'I can see. There's a stampede, but maybe the herd will switch direction this afternoon. There's nothing you can do.' Quinn took his arm and led him firmly towards the Gardner.

As he fired the engine, Caprisi's eyes were still locked on the Exchange. 'I'll be a cop until I die,' he said.

Quinn checked the address of the tailor and turned east onto Cedar Street. 'What made you such an optimist all of a sudden?' he asked, but his partner wasn't in the mood for anything that resembled levity.

It took them a little time to find the tailor. The brass plate saying 'Jacob Zwirz' was tiny and nailed to a wooden panel on the left of the door. His shop was at the south end of the Swamp, sandwiched between a leather merchant and the old Beekman tavern. It was deceptively spacious, with bolt upon bolt of cloth stacked along each wall. There were photographs of famous clients – 'tailor to the stars', a sign announced beneath them – and pride of place was given to a picture of Jimmy Walker in a brand new morning suit and spats.

Zwirz was a wiry old man with a mop of unkempt grey hair. Quinn watched him convince an uncertain customer that a particular cloth would suit him perfectly. Once the man had left – satisfied, having dithered for an age – Zwirz turned his attention to the new customers. 'Gentlemen, how may I be of assistance?'

Quinn took out his wallet. 'I'm Detective Quinn, and this here is my partner, Detective Caprisi.' The air of welcoming bonhomie evaporated. 'We'd like a word in private, Mr Zwirz.'

'Yes, of course.' The tailor made a show of taking out

and examining his gold pocket watch. 'Perhaps I could come down later.'

'I'm afraid our business can't wait. Do you have somewhere we can talk?'

'But I have an appointment with the mayor.' Zwirz gestured at the photograph on the wall.

'Then he will have to wait.'

'But—'

'He won't mind,' Caprisi said quietly. 'Maybe you heard his aide was murdered?'

Zwirz puffed out his cheeks. He draped a protective arm around the young boy behind the counter. 'This is my son, Joshua.'

Quinn and Caprisi nodded.

'You man the shop,' he said to the kid. 'I will only be a few moments.'

Zwirz led them up a flight of stairs so narrow that Quinn almost had to turn his shoulders sideways. 'He's a good boy, my son,' Zwirz said. 'I tell him over and over again the secret of our business: never forget a face. A father must guide his son in this world. Is that not so?'

Quinn offered him an unconvincing smile.

'Do you have children, Detective?'

'No.'

'One day, perhaps.'

They reached a small room lined with leatherbound ledgers. There was a table at its centre and a small desk upon which stood a photograph of Mayor Walker arm in arm with Charles Lindbergh.

'You make all Jimmy's suits?' Quinn asked.

Zwirz grunted as he searched a drawer.

'Then you must be a rich man.'

The tailor sat down and pointed at the two seats opposite him. 'Would you like something to drink?'

'No. Thank you.'

Zwirz took down a bottle and three glasses from the cupboard in the corner and poured them some liquor anyway. 'Naturally, I'm a great supporter of the police department,' he said.

'You make the commissioner's suits, too?' Caprisi asked.

'As a matter of fact, I do.'

'You must be getting along nicely.'

'Not any longer.' Zwirz flicked a switch on a box wireless. He twisted the dial until they heard the steady drone of an announcer. He sucked his teeth.

'You also made suits for a man called Charlie Matsell,' Quinn said.

Zwirz blinked. 'I don't recall the name.'

'Well, here's a couple more for you to think about. Early this morning, we found Dick Kelly and Moe Diamond in the back of an automobile parked at a meat-packing plant on the East River. Like Charlie Matsell and Spencer Duncan, they were wearing suits tailored by Jacob Zwirz, and both are very dead. Do you see the connection?'

The tailor turned towards the solitary window.

'What we'd like, Mr Zwirz,' Caprisi said, 'is for you to tell us what you know of these four men.'

The man sighed. 'I said it would come to this. When men are greedy, people get angry, though perhaps they keep it to themselves. But over the years, it burns and burns.' He shook his head. 'There are always so many fools. Listen to the radio today. Greed is king. We all get rich, they say! Hah! I tell you, nobody gets rich for nothing! What am I supposed to tell my son? "Of course we can get rich, Papa," he says. "Everybody's doing it – the shoeshine boy, the stenographers, the tram drivers and the steamboat captains. We'll never have to work again!" Well, never, never again will I fritter away the money I slaved for all my life in such foolishness.' He banged on the table. 'It is madness. The only way you get rich is by hard work, day after day, year after year.' Suddenly Zwirz seemed deflated. He replaced his glasses. There were tears in his eyes. 'Sometimes it is better not to delve into the past.'

'That's not a luxury we can afford, sir,' Quinn said.

'They were gangsters, hoodlums! Who could forget them? They walked in here so cocksure and arrogant, as if they owned the place. I had never seen them before, but suddenly they wanted twenty suits and ten over-coats, and they wanted them by the weekend and, oh, they would pay double or triple or whatever I wished. The dollars poured out of their pockets and I told them it was not about the money, it was just not possible to—'

'When was this?'

'Years ago.'

'When exactly?'

Zwirz blew out his cheeks. 'I cannot recall.'

Quinn glanced at the line of ledgers on the shelf behind the tailor's head. 'Perhaps you could allow us to check your records.'

'No, Detective. Those are confidential. I cannot—'

'We'd be extremely grateful for any assistance you can give us.'

'But many of my clients are private individuals. Very private.'

'Sir, we don't wish to cause you any trouble.'

The tailor rose slowly to his feet. He selected a ledger, opened it, and ran a finger over column after column of neat entries. 'Here . . . January the second, 1919.'

'They all came in together?'

'Mr Duncan was first. He introduced the others. You can see that I have written down their order. Mr Diamond wanted ten suits, four overcoats . . .'

'How did they get so rich?'

'Ah, Detective, if I turned away every man whose honesty I questioned, I would be a poor fellow indeed. I am a tailor. No more, no less.' Zwirz closed the book.

'Mind if I take a look?'

The tailor's shoulders sagged. Quinn prised the book out of his grip and flicked through the yellowing pages. It wasn't long before the same characters appeared again. 'Mr Diamond,' it read, 'Plaza Hotel, Central Park South, 5 thick woollen suits, two overcoats.' The entry noted the type of cloth, the measurements for the suits and, of course, the prices charged. 'How long did they keep ordering like this?'

Zwirz raised his hands, palms upwards.

'Who is this man here? Dr O'Brien? Did he come in with the others?'

'Yes.'

'He was part of the same group?'

'I believe so.'

'What was his Christian name?'

'Liam.'

'When did you last see them?'

'I could not say.'

'Months or years?'

'Years.' Zwirz's expression betrayed heartfelt contempt for those men and their flashy, hoodlum ways. 'I did not miss them.'

Quinn paused. There was something he couldn't put his finger on. These men were low-level gangsters, of course, and Zwirz must have suspected the provenance of their money, but that alone didn't explain his profound unease. Quinn looked at the shelf of leather spines. He ran his finger along to the gap, replaced the ledger and removed the one next to it.

Matsell, Diamond, Duncan, O'Brien and, to a lesser extent, Kelly appeared frequently through the spring of 1919.

Then, in May of that year, Quinn came across another name: Arnold Rothstein. 'You knew Rothstein?'

Zwirz gazed at them with hollow eyes. He spent a few seconds methodically cleaning his glasses. 'It was a long time ago.'

'But you never forget a face.'

Zwirz pushed his glasses back onto the bridge of his nose. 'Detective, I am a respectable businessman.'

'So, it's not a connection you advertised?'

'I cannot refuse a client.'

Quinn turned a few more pages. One day that summer, all five men – Matsell and his buddies, including O'Brien – had turned up together. Zwirz had written 'night fitting' in the margin. But the chronology was out of sync. The date – 22 June – had been written in after a handful of July entries.

The tailor chewed his lip. 'My book-keeper was ill,' he said.

' "Book cost . . ." What does this mean?'

Zwirz waved his hand. 'I couldn't tell you.'

'You don't know what's in your own accounts?'

'Some material for a customer, perhaps. I would sell at cost only.'

There was a soft knock and Zwirz's son poked his head around the door. 'Papa—'

'Not now.'

'But Mr—'

'Ask him to wait.'

They listened to the boy's footsteps fade.

'Can you think of anyone who would want to kill these men?' Caprisi said.

'Half of Manhattan, I should think.' The tailor stood, scooped up the ledger and put it back on the shelf as carefully as his shaking hands would let him. 'Now, please, I ask you both . . . I have a business to care for. My son . . . you understand . . .'

'Tell me about Dr O'Brien,' Quinn said.

'He came in with the others. I measured him and—'

'Was he tall or short, fat or thin?'

'Tall. I made his suits and he came in to collect them. That was all.'

'Do you have an address for him?'

'No.'

'Are you sure? This is very important.'

'I am sure. Now, please, I have answered your questions. I know nothing more, so I ask you to leave me in peace.'

Quinn and Caprisi followed the tailor down the stairs and went outside into a sudden burst of fall sunshine. Caprisi lit a cigarette and leant against the bonnet of the Gardner, legs crossed. He tossed the pack to his partner. They smoked in silence.

Quinn watched a trolley-bus sweep past. A picture of a grinning Jimmy Walker was emblazoned on its side. '*Your* mayor,' it read, 'for *your* city.'

'Wait a minute.' Quinn threw his cigarette away and turned back into the shop.

The tailor shrank away from them, alarmed.

Quinn brushed past him and led the way up the stairs. By the time Zwirz caught up, flustered and out of breath, Quinn had the ledger open. 'You want to tell me why this entry is not in chronological order?'

Zwirz looked old and ill.

'And a *night fitting*?'

'Detective, please . . .'

'Who comes for a night fitting?'

'It was a special arrangement, but not uncommon. My clients are busy men, so it is often easier for them to come at night.'

'How often have you written "night fitting" in these records, Mr Zwirz?'

'Detective—'

'This is the only time, right?'

'Perhaps.'

'You want to tell us the real reason that this is out of chronological order?'

'I did tell you. My book-keeper was ill. When this happens, I find it hard to—'

'This is an alibi.'

The tailor tried to steady himself and sat down on a stool.

'What you have here is an alibi for these men.'

'No – I—'

'Tell us what happened on the night of the twenty-second of June, Mr Zwirz.'

'I don't know what you're talking about.'

'Mr Zwirz, please. You're an old man. I don't want to have to march you out of here, past your son and your next important customer, into the Tombs. Someone asked you to construct an alibi for a crime. Who was it?'

The tailor did not answer.

'What is "book cost"?'

'I have told you already.'

Quinn flipped over a couple of pages. He bent closer. At the bottom of the column was the entry:

'Delivery, book cost suits: 23a Seventh Street, 10c'.

He sat down and momentarily closed his eyes.

'I'm sorry, Detective. Your father seemed to me a good man.'

Quinn breathed in deeply. He glared at the tailor. 'What did he ask you to do?'

'It was a long time ago.'

'*He* was the one who asked you to fix the alibi?'

Zwirz seemed utterly defeated. 'He said there had been some trouble and might be much worse to come. He asked me to place this entry in my book and to make sure I stuck to the story we had agreed. I said I was happy to help the department. Those were darker days, you understand, even than these in which we live now. He did not want new suits . . . would not be measured for them. But I made them all the same.' His expression brightened. 'It is good to have friends, is it not? That is something I always say to my son. It is good to have friends.'

'What do you think he meant by "trouble"?'

'I was not invited to discuss it further.'

'When did you last see my father?'

'I have not seen him since.'

The sun glinted hard off the Gardner's coachwork.

'I'll see you back at the office,' Quinn said.

Caprisi kept a discreet distance. 'Joe . . .'

'Go down to the CIB and ask Maretsky to dig out any unsolved crimes from the twenty-first to the twenty-third of June 1919. And see if you can pull a file on Dr

445

O'Brien. If he's still practising, we should be able to nail him fast. Oh, and don't say anything to Yan.'

'Why not?'

'Because he was my father's partner.'

'*Yan* was?'

'Yes.'

'When?'

'From all the things he hasn't told me, I'd say it was around the twenty-second of June 1919.' Quinn sat behind the wheel of the Gardner.

Caprisi put his head through the window. 'Just take it easy, okay? Don't assume the worst.'

'Why not?'

'Because he's your father and things aren't always as they seem.'

'Aren't they?'

Quinn gunned the engine and roared off, leaving his partner standing forlornly upon the sidewalk.

CHAPTER FORTY-NINE

THE BUILDING ON SEVENTH STREET WAS QUIET IN THE DEAD hour of the day. The only sound was of mothers scrubbing laundry in the rear stairwell or down in the yard.

Quinn slipped into his father's apartment. The front room was neat and clean. He unlocked his parents' bedroom door and stepped inside. He pulled open every drawer, but could find no trace of his mother's possessions. The postal card from Aunt Margaret was still on the bed and he glanced at it again. He tried to cast his mind back, but his memory was hazy. He tapped the card on the palm of his hand.

He pulled over a chair. He could hear his father's voice now. *Your mother will never throw any damned thing away* . . . He flipped the hatch to the roof and heaved himself into the attic. He found a trunk of old clothes, shoes, ice skates, uniform jackets, even a pair of shinty sticks. The box in the corner was the one he'd been looking for. He dragged it to the hatch and lowered it to the floor below.

It was full of photographs, prints and his mother's letters. There were scenes of the Falls Road in Belfast, pictures of the docks with giant cranes, and numerous studio portraits of distant relatives whom his mother had tried to bring to life in childhood stories. There were pictures of himself and Aidan. There were pictures of Martha.

He found a postal card from his father depicting the Tower of Victory at Saratoga in upstate New York.

Dear Joe,
This is the monument we talked about. I'm sorry I
could not bring you. One day it would be good for us
to come here. Martha is well and has enjoyed the trip.
We will be staying at your aunt Margaret's house near
Albany tomorrow night and shall be home shortly
afterwards. I hope all is well with you.
Your loving father,
Gerry

Quinn picked up the letters. Almost all had been written by Margaret, his mother's sister. He removed those with a 1919 postmark and hunched over them. He found one dated July of that year.

I am sorry, my dear girl, that you have had such a
dreadful time. Of course I respect your desire not to
discuss details – what is marriage, if not an island,

after all? – though I certainly do not accept that it would mean I could never look at either of you the same way again. I am your sister and have we not been through so much? What is it you could tell me that might conceivably alter my view of either of you?

I am distraught to hear you say Gerry's actions have brought such shame to your door. Are you sure you do not exaggerate, my love? Of course I adore you, but you have, as you know, always been a truly passionate person, inclined to rush to judgement. Can it really have been so bad?

Quinn folded the letter away and opened the next.

Why do you not come up to see us? You could bring the boys; from what you say, Gerry would barely miss them and I am sure they should enjoy the trip. I'm sorry again for your travails, my dear, and pleased and heartened that you should say you have been saved by your faith.

God forgives all those who truly seek his mercy. I shall pray for you. Please do not distress yourself so. I am sure that whatever has come to pass cannot be – simply <u>cannot</u> be – as bad as you seem to suppose. Since you have given me no details, I can offer little comfort in that regard, but all men are prone to actions on occasions which they later come to regret. <u>Do not let it destroy you</u>.

Quinn put away the letters.

After a few minutes, he leant forward again and flicked through the pile until he found one written in January 1920.

My dearest Catherine,
I received your latest letter today, which I must confess left me entirely lost for words. If I understand you correctly, you have decided, at Gerry's urging and insistence, to adopt a half-starved, ragamuffin girl from the basement of the apartment building whom he found trying to sell herself on the streets of the Bowery (and whose mother is herself a lady of ill-repute).

When I told Sean last night, he was as stunned as I am. If this is a simple act of charity, then we can only commend you in the warmest terms; but, my dear, have you thought it through? Is this girl not already damaged? Can you offer her anything more than temporary shelter, for which she may return only heartache and pain? What will the boys make of this intrusion? Will they not inevitably be jealous of the energy she is bound to suck out of you?

My beloved sister, I do not wish to offer criticisms and difficulties. I have urged you often enough to come and visit us this year – if one cannot talk to a sister, then with whom can one share troubles? – but I urge it upon you now with greater force than ever. You always had our mother's impetuousness and generos-ity, whereas I was burdened with Father's caution and prudence, but please allow us now to offer some sort of counsel. I cannot imagine what Gerry's motives can

have been for such a bold and radical step, but we
both urge you to proceed with the utmost caution and
only make the step absolute and irreversible when you
are both <u>sure</u> this is what you want – and what the
boys want too.

Quinn folded the letter and replaced it. Out of the window, dark clouds hovered over the cluttered rooftops.

The First Precinct building was a forbidding granite structure that glowed white in the morning sunshine. A small group of reporters leant against its stone walls or lounged on the steps.

Quinn turned right inside the entrance and found his father seated at a raised dais in the corner, some distance from the duty officer and the sawdust-strewn hallway through which the flotsam of the district was marched. He sipped from a giant mug of coffee. All around were shields from forces within the continental United States and mementoes – nightsticks, revolvers and uniform badges – of days gone by. It reminded Quinn of McSorley's, and perhaps that was no coincidence.

It was quiet. Most of Gerry's fellow cops had been drawn to the corner of Wall and Nassau. He looked up. 'Good morning. For the moment, it seems, the end of the world may have been postponed.'

'I'd like to talk to you.'

'Shoot.'

'In private.'

'Joe, please. We've been through this—'

'I've spoken to Jacob Zwirz.'

Gerry Quinn pushed himself to his feet and closed the ledger. He led his son through to the kit room and banged the door shut. 'So, the witch hunt goes on.'

'There is no witch hunt. There's a multiple homicide investigation and everything, every trail, every hunch, leads right back to you.'

'What did old man Zwirz say?'

'He told me you'd fixed an alibi for Charlie Matsell and his friends for the night of the twenty-second of June 1919.'

'Did he tell you why I did that?'

'No.' Quinn waited. 'I thought perhaps you could.'

'It would do you no good.'

Quinn felt his cheeks redden. 'Were you part of their game, Dad?'

'No.'

'I don't believe you.'

'That's your choice.'

'You have to tell me.'

'I don't *have* to do anything.'

'You cannot—'

'I don't want to talk about it because it's the past! Sometimes you have to come to terms with what you've done and move on. The truth isn't a passive object. It has a life. It has a capacity to inflict wounds.'

'Why did you take Martha in?'

Gerry's normally ruddy features were now a ghostly white. 'What do you mean?'

'I've read Aunt Margaret's letters to Mom.'

452

'Where did you find them?'

'In the attic. You didn't destroy everything.'

'I haven't destroyed anything.'

'You burnt the suits.' Quinn watched his father's face. 'That was the summer Mom got sick. Why did we take her in, Dad?'

He didn't answer.

'Why Martha? There must have been thousands of girls like her all over the city.'

'We passed her every day on the stairs. She was sinking. You could see it in her eyes.'

'What did you do that summer that Mom was so ashamed of?'

'Joe, I've asked you already – I've begged you to—'

'Why was it you took Martha down to Washington and up to New Haven?'

'You'll destroy us.'

'What is there left to destroy?'

'There is life. Yours. Mine. Aidan and Martha's.' Gerry shook his head. 'I'd like to talk to you. I'd like to tell you everything. I always have. But if I do so now, I'll be signing your death warrant as sure as if I pulled the switch on the Chair.'

'Don't hide behind that.'

'Then you've learnt nothing! Leave this! Leave Headquarters! Join Aidan in his showroom before it's too late. For God's sake, leave it all behind.' Gerry turned on his heel and the door slammed behind him.

Quinn leant his head against the wooden panel. He could hear himself breathing.

453

* * *

Quinn tried to light a cigarette on the stoop, but it was impossible in the damp wind blowing off the river.

The Gardner pulled up and the passenger door swung open. 'Get in,' Caprisi said.

Quinn did as he was instructed.

'You okay?' Caprisi asked. 'Because you sure don't look it.'

He didn't answer.

'The commissioner's just called a press conference and you're the star turn.'

'Not now.'

'Joe, if we don't go to this press conference, we'll be off the force this afternoon and probably wrapped up in the Tombs. The press have got hold of what happened to Diamond and Kelly and the mayor has issued express instructions that you're to be found and brought to him immediately. And the really swell news is that the man sitting in the front of the Buick over there is Ben Siegel.'

Quinn turned. There were three men in the automobile. 'How long have they been there?'

'About ten minutes.'

'Are they waiting for us?'

'I'd say so.'

'How did they know we were here?'

'You tell me.' Caprisi pulled out a revolver and checked the chamber. He gave it to Quinn. 'Let's hope they don't start shooting, because if they do I don't rate our chances.'

Siegel got out and stood on the far running board.

He gazed at them over the roof of the Buick.

Caprisi pressed the starter button, shifted the Gardner into gear and gunned it away. He kept going straight, to minimize their exposure to the side of the Buick, but Siegel turned his vehicle around and sat on their tail.

Caprisi handed Quinn a folder. 'I checked with Maretsky. There are no unsolved cases between the twenty-first and twenty-third of June 1919. But take a look at this. It's the file on our friend Dr Liam O'Brien.'

Quinn gazed at his father's handwriting on the sheet of paper in front of him.

1/9/1919

Liam O'Brien's recruitment agency in Brooklyn, the Stenographers' Association, has been closed down with immediate effect. O'Brien has been struck off the medical register and is no longer allowed to practise as a doctor anywhere in the continental United States. He should remain a prime suspect in all cases involving the sexual assault of young women or their procurement for prostitution rackets.

'Mae has already looked. There's no one under that name still registered to practise in the city. I've asked her to put it out on the wire, but I'm not going to hold my breath.'

'Amy Mecklenburg was on her way to a new job when she went missing,' Quinn said. 'Her mother said she'd got it through an agency.'

CHAPTER FIFTY

THE MAYOR WAS CAMPAIGNING OUT IN QUEENS. LONG
Island City snaked along the East River and Newtown
Creek and was packed from end to end with factories,
whose harsh and grimy outlines cut through a soot-
laden sky, labyrinthine streets criss-crossed by elevated
lines, railroad yards and bridge approaches. The air
shook with the thump and clatter of trains and trucks.

Caprisi pulled up the Gardner on a stretch of deserted
land by the canal. Barges ploughed through the oily
waters, almost nose to tail, laden with coal and raw
materials in one direction and crates of freshly manu-
factured goods in the other.

Ben Siegel's Buick slid to a halt across the street. He
got out and leant against the hood.

There were plenty of sleek automobiles in the narrow
parking strip, including the mayor's Duesenburg.
Newsmen lolled on the steps of a large red-brick building, Homburgs tilted as they scanned first editions of

the *Evening News*. The sign on the door hung askew from a single nail. It read: 'Long Island City Community Centre'.

One of the reporters scrabbled to his feet as Quinn approached. 'Here's the guy.'

Hegarty, the commissioner's press spokesman, was smoking a cigar in the hallway. 'What in hell kept you?'

Quinn was shuffled into a side room strewn with empty coffee cups and tumblers. It stank of furniture polish, cigars and whisky. Hegarty slammed the door. The mayor was flanked by Commissioner Whalen and a man called Kenton from the district attorney's office. 'Ah, the man we've all been waiting for,' Walker said. 'Ready for this?'

'Well, sir—'

'Talk to the guys here while I freshen up.' He flashed Quinn a dazzling smile. 'Joe, this case will be the making of you. You'll be as famous as your father!'

He slipped out, followed by the commissioner. Hegarty and Kenton crowded in. 'You know what you've got to do?' Hegarty asked.

'Well . . .'

Hegarty picked up a copy of the *News* and held up the sensational front-page account of the monumental Wall Street plunge. He folded it over to reveal the banner headline on page two: 'Rothstein/Luciano Photograph Could Sink Mayor's Bid, Claims La Guardia; Campaign Wide Open.'

'Do you get the picture?' Hegarty asked, his puffy cheeks flushed with colour.

'No.'

'Your job here, Detective,' Kenton explained patiently, 'is to tell the hoodlums out there that this photograph does not exist, that you have seen no evidence of it and you believe the entire story was invented to throw us off the killer's scent. Otherwise La Guardia is going to win this election and we'll all be screwed.'

'Have you got that?' Hegarty said.

'It's a press conference. I'll answer the questions they put to me in as truthful a manner as I can.'

'What in hell is that supposed to mean?'

'It's okay,' Kenton said. 'You haven't seen this picture, have you, Joe?'

'No,' Quinn said.

'Is there any evidence it exists?'

Quinn hesitated. 'No.'

'Do you have a witness who has seen it and is prepared to go on the record?'

'No.'

'In other words, all we've got is hearsay. Nothing that would stand up in court. So just pretend you're on the stand.'

'Hold on a minute . . .' Hegarty said.

'Sean, we've no choice. If we don't kill this story, we might as well kiss the election goodbye.' Kenton took hold of Quinn's shoulder. 'You do understand that, don't you, Joe?'

Hegarty glanced at Caprisi. 'What about the guinea?' he asked.

'Better Joe goes up there alone,' Kenton said.

Hegarty nodded. 'Okay, let's roll.' He pushed open the swing doors and strode into the packed hall. He took his seat behind a long wooden table on the podium.

Caprisi was at Quinn's shoulder. 'Smells like a set-up.'

'I know.'

Hegarty beckoned Quinn to the chair next to his. A moment later, the mayor and the commissioner made their own entrance. Walker gave the crowd a generous wave and the flashguns popped. He sat down and took the microphone. 'Now, I won't keep you folks long because I know why you're here today, but I'd like you to stop a moment to take in your surroundings. Five years ago, this community centre did not exist. Like many other services all over the city, it was brought to you by an administration committed to improving the lives of each and every citizen it represents.' He wagged his finger. 'Whatever our opponents would have you believe, the people who live in these boroughs, men and women who expect a decent return on their hard-earned tax dollar, know a socially responsible and honest administration when they see one.'

Walker almost caressed the microphone. 'Now, I'll bet there isn't a single man or woman in this room who isn't affected by the unfolding market correction taking place today. So I'd also like to take this chance to affirm my own personal faith in the future. This is the greatest stock market, for the greatest city, for the greatest country on earth – and, as a consequence, I have advised my own stock broker to utilize this momentary madness as a giant buying opportunity.' Walker smiled again. 'I know what some of you are thinking: I'm not taking advice from a man who knows how to spend a dollar better than he knows how to save and invest one, but mark my words, you will not regret following in my footsteps . . .'

Walker's gaze swept the room. 'Now, we've all heard it said that there's been some cynical fuelling of the atmosphere of uncertainty in order to buy stocks at bargain-basement rates. I cannot comment on that, but I'll say this to my opponents. Let's deal in truth. Let's deal in facts. Smears serve no one, not the bankers on Wall Street, or the politicians in Washington, or the good, honest, hard-working man whose interests we have striven night and day to represent.'

Few of the reporters were bothering to take notes. Some continued to read their newspapers or glanced idly around the room. 'Okay,' Hegarty said, as he took the microphone. 'Questions. Put your hand up and state which organization you represent.' He pointed. 'Damian Connor.'

The man stood. 'Where's this photograph?'

'Which photograph?'

'C'mon, Sean. Don't play us for fools. La Guardia says the photograph exists and it proves the mayor's in the pocket of organized crime. He claims it's what these murders are all about. The kid there has been looking into it, right?'

460

Hegarty turned to Quinn. He pushed the microphone across the tabletop. 'We've no hard evidence there ever was a photograph,' Quinn said.

There was a brief silence. 'So, where'd the rumour come from?'

'I have no idea.'

The reporter looked at him. 'That's it, Detective? That's all you've got to say?'

'Mr Connor, we've got five dead bodies and a killer with a penchant for carving up his victims. Isn't that enough of a story for you?'

'Do you figure they're political murders? These guys were all friends of Mr Duncan, right?'

'There's no evidence that was the motivation and plenty to suggest it wasn't.'

'You figure there'll be more victims?'

'It's possible.'

'What's the connection?'

'We're still working to establish that.'

A man at the back got to his feet. 'So, you've never seen this photograph?'

'No.'

'Where did the rumour come from?'

'Mr . . .?'

'Donaldson, from the *News*.'

'Mr Donaldson, we've chased up every lead we can find. None of them has ever led to this mythical picture. The only people I hear talking about it are you good gentlemen.'

A man coughed. Feet scuffed the wooden floor.

Jimmy Walker leant towards Quinn. 'Nice work, kid, you're slaying them.'

Another newsman stood up, a slick, good-looking guy, with a well-oiled moustache and a gut that suggested he'd shared a few too many lunches with Sean Hegarty. 'Billy Burke, from the *Mirror*. Say, Detective, you're new to this, right?'

'I've not been at Headquarters long, that's correct.'

'And you're old man Quinn's boy?'

'I am.'

Burke tapped his notebook against his leg and moistened his lips. 'What I hear is that your broad was playing hot lips with Matsell and Spencer Duncan and she had the photograph.'

Quinn glanced at Caprisi, who stood by the door, then along the line of men beside him, but they all avoided his eye. 'I don't know where you're getting your information from, Mr Burke, but you're plain wrong on every count.'

'Matsell's stenographer is your broad, though, right?'

'No. She's not.'

'So that wasn't the two of you together last night at the Harlem Sporting Club?'

Quinn felt his face redden. 'Mr Burke, do you have a point to make here?'

'And she's the girl who's alleged to have had the photograph of the mayor getting cosy with Rothstein and Lucky Luciano.'

Sean Hegarty moved towards the microphone. 'Make your point, Billy.'

'I was just trying to figure out if young Prince Charming here was really the guy to be staking this out. I mean, if his broad used to work with La Guardia, we've got to ask ourselves whether—'

'Detective Quinn is running a murder inquiry, Billy. If you've any questions on the politics, save them for the mayor. That's what he's here for.'

Jimmy Walker smiled again.

'We've said all we're going to on the photograph,' Hegarty said. 'Detective Quinn here has been on the case from the first morning and he's never seen or heard of this damned picture. He's the guy who knows, so we've just got to accept what he says. Let's move on. Yes . . .'

Goldberg got to his feet. 'Did you know they were going to set you up here, Detective?'

'For Christ's sake, Goldberg,' Hegarty said. 'You're banned from these press conferences until you can ask a straight question.'

'I'll take it,' Quinn said. 'It's not a question of being set up. But people are understandably nervous, so I wouldn't be surprised if some had taken the opportunity to try to compromise me with Mr Burke here.'

There was another silence. Someone coughed. Billy Burke looked furious.

'Why are folk nervous?' a voice called from the back.

'This investigation is leading to some uncomfortable places.'

'What kind of places?'

Quinn let them wait. 'We believe that what lies at the

463

heart of this murder case is corruption at the very highest level of the city's administration. In the course of the investigation we have uncovered pay-offs from organized crime that have lined the pockets of some of our most powerful and influential men. So, yes, of course they're nervous.'

'Who?'

'At this stage, I'm afraid I cannot say. The investigation is ongoing.'

'Are you talking about City Hall?'

'I must ask you to be patient.'

'Do you have evidence?'

Quinn stood. 'Gentlemen, that is all I have to say.' In the quiet that followed, he noted Jimmy Walker's grey face. And then the crowd was around him, shoving and pushing and yelling questions all the way to the door. Hegarty held them back. 'That's enough!'

Quinn and Caprisi slipped through the back exit to the Gardner. 'Let's get the hell out of here before they lynch us,' Caprisi said. As they turned onto the road, besieged again by photographers, Siegel got back into his saloon and pulled out behind them.

'Congratulations,' Caprisi said. 'That went real well.'

'Thank you. I think so.'

'I hope to God you know what you're doing, Joe, because the way I see it you just declared World War Two.'

CHAPTER FIFTY-ONE

THE CROWD GATHERED OUTSIDE CENTRE STREET WAS sullen and silent. A mounted squad was saddled up on the sidewalk and ready to go. An emergency squad, kitted out with shields and batons, loaded themselves into the back of a truck. As Caprisi nudged the Gardner into a parking bay, three motorcycle cops roared off downtown, sirens blaring. One bumped the Gardner's hood. Caprisi shouted after him and heads swivelled.

Inside Headquarters the central hallway was teeming with cops. Some spoke in hushed whispers, but most gazed motionless at newswires posted on the board. A wireless had been wound to full volume in the corner.

Caprisi joined the throng and wouldn't move. Quinn walked on without him. He headed for the back stairs, but before he put his foot on the first step he heard a scream echo through the corridor below, then a second, still louder, like the cry of a wounded animal. He ran down to find Mae with her arms around Amy

465

Mecklenburg's mother. The woman convulsed un-controllably. She screamed again. This time, the echo seemed to last for ever.

Quinn edged forwards. The smell hit him first: a cloying, toxic combination of ash and decay. He looked through the laboratory door to see a pile of bones laid out on the metal table. He made out a half-burnt shoe. Carter stood beside it with hollow eyes.

Quinn turned to approach Mrs Mecklenburg, but Mae held her in a close embrace and warned him off with a shake of her head.

A group of men, including several uniformed officers, stood outside McCredie's door. Schneider watched from behind the glass wall in his office, like a spectator at a ball game.

Quinn tried to approach McCredie, but the chief of detectives indicated, with a curt wave, that this was not a good time. He turned towards Byrnes's desk in the corner, but could see no sign of the Mecklenburg file. He approached Schneider. The deputy commissioner ushered him in. 'What is it?'

Quinn closed the door behind him. His eyes rested on the photograph of Schneider's wife on the shelf above the desk.

'Have you been feeding Goldberg again?'

'No, sir.'

'I heard about the press conference and there's a rumour over at the *Sun* that he has a big story for the morning. Do you know what it is?'

'No.'

'You want to tell me what kind of evidence you have about corruption at City Hall?'

'I'd rather keep it to myself. It's . . . sensitive.'

'I bet it is. I could order you to tell me.'

'And I could refuse.'

'You have balls, Quinn, I have to give you that. If you survive this, who knows? You could even make it to chief of detectives one day. But it's a mighty big "if". What do you want?' Schneider thrust his hands in his pockets.

'Do you have any briefing notes on the Mecklenburg case?'

'Why?'

'Because Byrnes never seems to be in the office and I can't find the file.'

'I have it right here. I have to brief the commissioner in ten minutes. You've probably heard they've found the body, or what remains of it. They tried to burn it first, then dropped what was left in a canal. What is it you want to know?'

'I'd like the name of the agency Amy Mecklenburg got her job through.'

'Why?'

'There's a pattern. A group of men used the agency to identify and ensnare Miss Mecklenburg. They've done it before, perhaps many times, and they'll do it again.'

Schneider went to the other side of the desk. He opened a drawer, took out a file and threw it across to him. 'Be my guest. It's on the front sheet.'

Quinn hesitated. He glanced through the report then turned the file over to check who had already signed for it.

Danny Byrnes
Johnny Brandon
Courier Dept
Danny Byrnes
Ed McCredie
Danny Byrnes
Deputy Commissioner Schneider

'The courier department?'

'It means it was signed out to a precinct overnight. They must return it by dawn.'

'Which precinct?'

'You'd have to check. Whichever the girl is from, I should think.'

Quinn noted down the name and address of the recruitment agency.

'Satisfied?'

'Yes, sir. Thank you.'

'I've not had much in the way of briefing from you on this case, Quinn. Is that because McCredie told you to cut me out?'

'No, sir.'

'You're a poor liar. And you forget how long I've been around. I guess he told you I was set on doing him in so I could claw my way up to the commissioner's chair.'

'No, sir. He didn't say that.'

'I'll bet he did.' Schneider moved to the other side of his desk and sat down. 'I'll tell you something, Quinn. The commissioner is going to step down all right, but I wouldn't take the job even if it was all that stood between me and eternal damnation.'

'I'm sorry to hear that, sir.'

'I doubt it. There are people who are looking out for you. Did you know that?'

'Not exactly, sir, no.'

'From your behaviour, I'd say you haven't guessed who they are.'

'I'm just trying to get my work done and go home.'

'I admire your single-minded pursuit of this, even if your motives are frankly transparent. But I feel compelled to say that the odds remain stacked against you, whatever you may have told your new friend Mr Goldberg.'

'Why is that, sir?'

'If a group of powerful men have kept a secret for more than a decade, you'd have to wager that they're going to carry on keeping it, wouldn't you?'

'What is the secret?'

'Don't play the fool with me, Quinn. You have an idea already, but it's the tip of the iceberg. Men in this city have got away with murder, quite literally, for longer than I care to think. They're protected by the system. And all we can do is keep shuffling the cards.'

Quinn thought of Mrs Mecklenburg's cries in the corridor below. 'Is that all we can do?'

'For the time being, yes. To smash a cabal, you need someone to break ranks.'

Quinn looked at his superior. 'Duncan was going to turn state's evidence.'

'Probably.'

'Moe Diamond and Dick Kelly might have threatened to do the same.'

'You may be right. What do you make of our friend Mr McCredie over there? Do you trust him?'

'Yes.'

'In a way that you don't trust me?'

'Sir, you're the deputy commissioner.'

'Don't insult my intelligence, Quinn. This isn't about a tag on a desk. I suppose he asked you how I managed to afford an estate out on Long Island.'

'I don't recall him mentioning it.'

'He told you I spent my time kissing the backside of every politician this side of Washington in the hope of preferment once the commissioner is on his way.'

'No, sir, he didn't say that.'

'I don't blame you, Detective. Why trust a Jew over a good, hard-drinking man from the old country?'

'Sir, I don't know what you're talking about.'

'Yes, you do, Quinn. These men generate enough wealth to buy God. They probably already have. Only if we unite will we stand a chance of defeating them.'

'How are we going to unite, sir?'

'Just keep me informed and remember what I said. I know what you're doing. If you need help, you know where to find me. And think about this. Your father was the best – and the straightest – detective we ever had in here. But we all make . . . mistakes. We all have . . . emotions beyond our control.'

'You're not his son.'

'No, but you are. And it's hard. Believe me, I under-stand that better than you might imagine. If you want help, Detective – I mean *really* want it – you know where to come.'

Quinn closed Schneider's door quietly behind him. When he reached his desk, the deputy commissioner was still watching him.

Quinn picked up the telephone and asked for the courier department. 'It's Joe Quinn here from the main floor,' he told the woman who answered the call. 'I need to check something.'

'Of course, sir.'

'Last week, the Mecklenburg briefing file was signed out overnight to you. Where did you send it?'

'Just hold on a minute, sir, and I'll check.'

Quinn waited, still aware of Schneider's penetrating gaze. The woman came back on the line. 'It went to the First Precinct, sir. It was addressed to Gerry Quinn.'

He cut the connection.

CHAPTER FIFTY-TWO

BEN SIEGEL LOCKED ONTO THEIR TAIL THE MOMENT CAPRISI nosed the Gardner into the afternoon sunshine. His men no longer stood out on the running boards, but they made no attempt to hide their pursuit.

'What do you figure they're going to do?' Quinn asked.

'They want to show us their stamp collection.'

'That's very funny, Caprisi.' Quinn rested his head against the leather door pillar. 'This could begin to get on my nerves.'

'Relax. If they were going to kill us, they'd have done it already.'

'That's real encouraging.'

The recruitment-agency address in the Mecklenburg file was on Sands Street. It was a low, dirty white building sandwiched between a flophouse and a Filipino restaurant. The air was charged with the aroma of spices and roasting coffee from the nearby factories

472

and the Manhattan skyline loomed in the distance beyond the East River, like the backdrop of a Broadway set.

The grimy cobbled street was still damp from the rain and its sidewalks almost deserted save for a few sailors who idled in the afternoon sun. Jackhammers pounded from the salvage pontoon close by inside the Navy Yard.

The office was deserted. There was a small discoloured area of brick by the door where a sign had been jemmied off and the windows had been boarded up. Quinn broke down the door, but the interior had been stripped of its contents: there were no desks, chairs, pinboards, notices or filing cabinets.

The owner of the Filipino restaurant didn't know who had operated there. Neither did any of his neighbours.

'Byrnes gave the wrong address?' Caprisi suggested.

'Probably.'

Quinn circled the interior once more. Out of the window he saw an old woman reading a newspaper in her garden. Behind her was one of the ugly frame houses La Guardia had condemned so vociferously during his campaign for office. She reminded him of his grandmother, wrapped up in a black shawl and thick hat.

Quinn hummed the Irish rebel song she had sung to them as children. More or less his first memory was of the day she had shuffled through the immigration pens at Ellis Island, muttering curses at the new land that rose like a mirage across the water. She had only lasted a week before dying peacefully in her sleep.

'What next, Joe?' Caprisi asked. 'If we start trying to trace every missing girl in the last fifteen years, we'll be here until hell freezes over.'

'We have to be able to find out what happened on the twenty-second of June 1919. You can clean the files, but not the public record.' Quinn turned for the stairs.

'Joe, are you sure you're ready for this?'

'Ready for what?'

'You think you want to know the truth about your father. I understand that. But are you certain you're ready for it?'

Quinn stopped dead. 'What do you mean?'

'Sometimes it's better not to know.'

'It's never better.'

'I wish I didn't know who killed my brother. I wish I didn't know that my father doffs his cap to him every morning.'

'That's different.'

'No, it isn't. I'm just advising you to think about it before it's too late. I'm frightened for you, scared for both of us. And I have been, right from the start.'

'And I've always told you, there's no need to make it your affair.'

'It's too late for that.'

'It's too late for everything. They've found the Mecklenburg girl's body. All that was left of her was a pile of bones and a burnt shoe.' Quinn looked at his partner. 'Go take a look at the girl's mother in the corridor, Tony, then tell me I have a choice.'

Quinn kept his foot hard on the gas pedal all the way up Fifth Avenue.

Newspapers and periodicals were stored in a dingy room on the ground floor of the library. Quinn shoved his badge at the assistant. She wasn't impressed. 'How may I help you?'

He explained what he wished to see and was directed to a seat. Caprisi had disappeared.

The woman returned with newspapers piled high on a wooden trolley. Quinn had chosen only copies of the *Evening News* and the *Sun*, but the library had every edition, so he ended up with a mountain of paper. Caprisi returned, took a seat and helped himself to a slice of the pile.

'I'll take June and July,' Quinn said. 'You take August.'

Caprisi pulled the newspapers closer and set to work. Quinn turned to the twenty-second of June 1919, but he could find no reference to a missing girl, an abduction or a murder from that day or any of those that immediately followed it.

He read everything, every item of news, however brief, in every column.

The room was warm, the air heavy. He searched for hidden significance in every headline. '$15,000 For Girl Attacked at Fifteen', ran one. 'A verdict of $15,000 has been awarded against a man who attacked the girl two years ago and is now serving seven years in prison as a result.'

Twenty minutes later, he lingered over 'Sold Sister to White Slave Ring, Syndicate Agent's Kin Tell. U-S.'

'Greedy for what were called "commissions",' it read, 'at least one member of New York's shame syndicate sold his own sister into white slavery.'

Quinn spun the newspaper around so that Caprisi could look. ' "The operations of the syndicate",' he read aloud, ' "were revealed by the arrest of Albert Lucks, held under charges that he had conspired to transport young women to Boston, Philadelphia, Detroit and St Louis. Evidence that the gang was organized on the principle of a Broadway booking office was found by investigators during a raid of the office of men suspected of being Lucks' accomplices in Coney Island. Bookers, who made the rounds of dancehalls, were paid $500 for their recruiting efforts." '

Caprisi pushed the newspaper back. 'It doesn't mention a recruitment agency.'

Quinn took out his notebook and scribbled down half a dozen details. He turned the pages faster. A British airship made the first two-way crossing of the Atlantic, and Dempsey thrashed Willard to take the world heavyweight title in Toledo, Ohio.

He stopped. 'Rice Arrested', ran a headline, 'as Attorney General Alleges Wall Street Fix over Idaho Copper'. He flipped back to a story that had caught his eye a few days previously. 'Rice under Fire, as Investigators Probe Wall Street Fix over Columbia

Emerald Company'. He turned a few more pages. 'Idaho Copper Sound, Claims Finance Director Matsell. No One Will Lose a Dime. Rice Denies $25,000,000 Profit'.

'Tony, look at this.' Quinn ripped out the relevant pages and passed them over. 'I saw this a few days ago in the CIB files.'

'So what?' Caprisi said.

'That's why they had money spilling out of their pockets at Jacob Zwirz's place.'

'How does that help us?'

'The CIB must have a file on this fix, right?'

Caprisi leant back. 'There's nothing here, Joe, is there? Admit it.'

'Maybe they kept it out of the newspapers.'

'C'mon!' Caprisi threw up his hands in exasperation. 'I need something to eat.'

'Not now.'

'Yes, now. Because now is when I'm hungry. There's a café opposite. I'll see you there when you finally admit defeat.'

Quinn watched him leave and started turning the pages again. After half an hour, he had found nothing. He returned to the twenty-second of June. He flipped the pages over more slowly this time, but still nearly missed the story. It was at the very bottom of the City pages in a 'News in Brief' column: 'Rice Link to Missing Brooklyn Girl'.

Police last night acknowledged a girl reported missing in Brooklyn two months ago had been on her way to a job at the Idaho Copper Company when she disappeared. Rice's lawyers told the *News* last night that their client had been cleared of any connection to the girl's disappearance, which police still believe is 'domestic' in nature.

This has nothing to do with Idaho Copper, which remains sound, Finance Director Matsell told the *News*.

Quinn turned over the pages for the days and weeks that followed, but could find no further reference to the disappearance on the City pages or anywhere else. He ripped out the article and darted across the road to the café. Caprisi was eating steak and fries in a booth by the window.

'Okay, but there's nothing in our files,' Caprisi said, after he'd read it. 'I asked Maretsky to check twice. There are no missing girls and *no* relevant homicides from June 1919.'

'A girl disappeared in Brooklyn. She was on her way to a new job. The cops tried to write it off as a family issue. The similarities are overwhelming.'

'You don't have a name.'

'I'll find one.'

'How? There's no file, and there's no name in that article.'

'I'll call every precinct in Brooklyn and ask them to check their records.'

Caprisi pushed away the last of his fries. 'Jeez, you're a persistent bastard.'

478

The waitress came to take Caprisi's plate. 'You boys want anything else?'

Quinn ignored her. The sleek Buick was parked across the street. 'We should find the cops who worked the Idaho Copper case.'

'Let's talk about something else.'

'What do you figure Ben Siegel wants?'

'I don't know, but I've a feeling we're about to find out.' Caprisi tapped on the window. Siegel was striding towards them. 'Relax, Joe.'

The door banged shut. Siegel took off his Homburg and nodded at the waitress. 'A cup of coffee, doll.' He chucked his hat into the centre of the table and slipped in beside Caprisi. 'Good afternoon, gentlemen.' His blue eyes were fixed on Quinn.

'How long do you plan to trail us around?'

'As long as it takes. We've interests in common, Joe.'

'Like what?'

'Charlie Matsell was a friend of mine.'

'Is this what you do for all your friends?'

'No.' Siegel's flawless face was devoid of expression.

'So what is it you want?'

'We want you with us.'

'I'm a lowly Headquarters cop. What can I do for you?'

'Don't fuck with me, Detective.' They stared at one another. 'I don't know what's wrong with you, Quinn. There isn't another cop in Manhattan who'd fail to make the right decision on a case like this.'

'What decision is that?'

'Make it clear you're with us, or we'll have to conclude you're against us.'

Quinn sighed. 'I'll be sure to tell La Guardia that's your take.'

'Screw La Guardia.'

'Listen to me, Ben. You're a two-bit hustler and I'd like to see you rot in hell, but you don't *need* to make this your affair. If there's a shakedown coming at Headquarters, you're better off out of it. Wait to see how it pans out and you can hook up with whichever side wins.'

Siegel frowned. 'You figure there'll be a shakedown in Centre Street?'

'You know it.'

Siegel thought about this. 'We've got a system.'

'You've got a guy who's more trouble than he needs to be. You pay him enough, right? So who needs to be cleaning up after a man like that? There are better . . . arrangements. It's time for a change.'

'Is that a pitch?'

'It's a statement of the obvious.'

'Lucky doesn't like change.'

'Then he's not as smart as I thought.'

Siegel picked up his Homburg. He glanced at Caprisi, then at Quinn. 'You've got a broad to worry about, Joe, so you need to listen to me. If you're not with us, you're off this case. Do you understand?'

'I don't know if I speak your language, Ben. What is it I'm supposed to understand?'

'Your partner here can translate for you.' Siegel

stood. 'Take it easy, Cap.' He chucked a ten-dollar bill on the table and turned on his heel. Quinn watched him climb back into the rear of the automobile. The driver roared away.

Quinn grinned. 'Take it easy, *Cap*?'

Caprisi didn't answer.

'You figure Lucky Luciano is acting on his own, or taking orders from Centre Street?'

'Luciano wouldn't take orders from anyone. If his man in Headquarters goes down, he'll find another.'

'Ben Siegel didn't buy that pitch.'

'If it ain't broke, don't fix it.'

'So what was that all about?'

'They're worried. Any kind of change is bad for business. That's all it is to them.'

CHAPTER FIFTY-THREE

QUINN STARTED WITH A CALL TO THE 60TH PRECINCT. THE
captain there didn't seem in any hurry to assist him, and
as he worked his way through the list, precinct by
precinct, neither did many of the others. In each case, he
had to pull rank and invoke McCredie's name, sometimes the mayor's too, in order to have someone sent
down to check the files. He watched the clock. People
drifted home, though small groups still huddled around
wireless sets like shipwreck victims and spoke in hushed
whispers.

Caprisi concentrated on the report he was typing.
Eventually he got up and slipped out. He didn't bother
to tell Quinn where he was going.

A meeting in McCredie's office broke up and most of
the detectives gathered around the wireless set on Mae's
desk.

Quinn turned his back on them. 'Missing persons
1919, right?' a voice said, at the other end of the line.

'Okay, I've got the list.' The man was out of breath from his trip down to the basement. Quinn checked which precinct he'd just telephoned. It was the 76th, down near Red Rock. 'Sir, half of these people will have turned up two hours after they were reported gone. You know how it is – a husband stays out late drinking, a wife runs off with some guy she met on the subway . . .'

'Give me the names, the girls only.'

'There's plenty of 'em.'

'Are there any from June?'

'There's no dates here, sir, just the names.'

'I have a pen.' Quinn pulled over his notebook and rubbed his eyes.

'Okay. Higgins. Myers. Clarke.'

'You got the first names?'

'Yes, sir. Susan Higgins. Sinead Myers. Jane Clarke. Mary Hohenstraat – Jesus, that's a mouthful. Sadie Foreman. Alice Hempelman . . . No, sorry, Hempelhof. It's handwritten, this list. Mannie . . . I can't read that one. Mannie Jones. Yes, Mannie Jones. Ruth Scher. Diana Hobhouse. These are girls from all over Brooklyn, sir. I don't know why the other precincts didn't have a list, they sure should—'

'Hold on. Did you say *Scher*?'

'Er . . . yes, sir. Ruth Scher.'

Quinn flicked back through his notes. The name was familiar . . . Yes, the Plaza: the note in Matsell's suite at the Plaza. 'Mr Scher called again . . .'

'When did Ruth Scher go missing?'

'Sir, there's no dates here. Like I said—'

'Well, check, would you? See if you have anything else.'

The man huffed and puffed. 'Is this going to take long, sir? There's a line of folk at the desk.'

'It's real important.'

Quinn watched the second hand make its way slowly around the clock face.

'Okay, sir. Ruth Scher, right?'

'Yes.'

'You're in luck. It was our precinct. She was reported missing the twenty-second of June 1919. That's all we have. We passed it on to Headquarters and you took the case.'

'June the twenty-second? You're sure?'

'That's what it says here.'

'Do you have an address?'

'Henry Street, twelve twelve.'

'Why did we take the case?'

'I've no idea. Like I said, we passed it on. You'll have to check your files.'

'We've lost them. That's the problem.'

The officer snorted in disgust. 'It says here "suspected white slave abduction". That's all.'

'Where was she abducted?'

There was a momentary silence as the man turned a page. 'She went for some stenographer's job uptown and never came back.'

'Who was the job with?'

'An agency sent her.'

'Which one?'

'It doesn't say.'

'Where did she go?'

'Some mining company ... Here it is ... Idaho Copper. Don't ask me where in hell that is. That's all we've got. Ruth Scher missing, reported by her father—'

'What was his name?'

'Abe.'

'Thanks.' Quinn cut the connection. He stood and went to look for his partner. He checked the cloakrooms and ran down to the canteen, but there was no sign of Caprisi anywhere.

By the time Quinn reached the area above Red Rock, dark clouds had squeezed out the last wisps of blue sky and rain thundered down so hard he had to keep his nose pressed to the windshield. It kept on misting up, so he steered with one hand and wiped the condensation from the glass with the other. The numbers were hard to see. He got out once, only to find he was at least fifty houses short. By the time he was back in the driving seat, he was wet through.

The front of the Schers' house had been newly painted sky blue. The tiny garden was well cared-for. He waited a couple of minutes to see if the rain would slacken, then gave up and ran for the steps.

He knocked, but there was no answer. He crouched and opened the letterbox. He could see a line of coats in the hall, but there were no lights on inside.

He ducked back out into the rain. There was no way around to the rear of the house on either side so he rapped on a neighbour's door. After an interminable wait, an elderly woman opened it a crack.

'I'm Detective Quinn.' He fumbled for his badge.

The door yielded a fraction. 'I haven't seen your sort in a while,' she said.

'I'm real sorry to trouble you, ma'am. I was looking for Abe Scher.'

'Oh.' She peered around the corner. 'Is he not at home? I saw him this morning, I'm sure I did.'

'He still lives here, then?'

'Yes . . . Well, he's alone now, of course, since his wife passed away.' She leant closer. 'So sad . . . such a cruel blow.'

'Do you know where he might be?'

'No.' She shook her head. 'Is everything all right? I mean, Abe is usually home at this time, so I don't know if . . . Perhaps he's gone up to Albany. I believe he has a sister there. Oh, Lord, has there been some news?'

'I'm afraid not, no.'

The woman hesitated, as if about to invite him in, but she thought better of it and swung the door shut. Quinn lingered on the porch. He caught sight of a black saloon rolling down the hill. Its driver seemed unsure of his route.

He crossed to the Schers' home and knocked louder. Rain bounced off the sidewalk and ran in rivulets along the edge of the tarmac. The saloon came to a halt.

He turned to the door and examined the lock, then forced it open with his shoulder, the sound of splintering wood camouflaged by the rain.

The hallway was a monument to understated good taste. It reminded him of the way his mother had decorated their apartment. There was a bookshelf full of leatherbound volumes and a wireless.

The kitchen was immaculate. Someone had ringed 1 November on a wall calendar and written 'Albany?'.

Quinn called up the stairs.

The only sound was the drumbeat of the rain on the tin roof.

He reached the landing and called again. He nudged an open door and stepped into a spacious bedroom that had been turned into a shrine. Every inch of every wall was covered with photographs and mementoes. They had been arranged chronologically, moving from baby pictures through bunched teenage curls to the shy smile of a girl on the cusp of womanhood. There was a candle on the shelf above the bed, which had burnt down to its base, and a rosette with gold ribbons. In the centre of the tableau was a picture of the girl in a white blouse and jacket.

She had a kind, trusting face.

'Can I help you?'

Quinn spun around. An old man with white hair and spectacles watched him from a wicker chair behind the door.

'I'm real sorry. I didn't know anyone was here.'

'Are you going to rob us?'

Quinn fumbled for his wallet. 'I . . . Detective Quinn, from Headquarters.'

Abe Scher bent forward and examined the photograph. Then he scrutinized his intruder. 'You look like your father.' He sat back. 'I assume I'm right in thinking he is your father?'

Quinn nodded and gestured at a photograph of the little girl with her arms around a sheepdog. 'What happened to your daughter, Mr Scher?'

The old man did not reply. He sat up straight, his face expressionless. 'We're still waiting for you to tell us that.'

Quinn picked up a new candle from a pile on the shelf, put it into the glass holder and lit it. They watched the flame catch, then settle. 'I'm going to be straight with you, sir. I don't know about your case. I should, but the file is missing from Headquarters and no one, including my father, is willing to talk about it. I'll understand if you never wish to hear from a single one of us again, but if you'll do me the honour of telling me what I need to know, I may be able to assist you.'

'It's too late for that.'

'Sir, I give you my word that—'

'Your promises are worth nothing here. Ruth was just a girl, Detective.'

'What happened, sir?'

'One day perhaps you and your colleagues will be kind enough to tell us.'

'I mean, what were the circumstances of her disappearance?'

Abe Scher stared at the photographs on the wall. They listened to the rain. 'On a clear summer morning, she left to make her way in the world. She was a trained and highly competent stenographer and she had just signed up to a new agency. She was due to catch the El uptown for an interview for her first job. She was as cheerful as a lark. I took that photograph, then stood on the porch and watched her all the way to the crest of the rise. I never saw her again.'

Abe Scher's fingers scratched at the chair. 'The police came, first the uniformed officers from the local precinct and then the men in trenchcoats and Homburgs from Headquarters. They told us they'd find her and it would be all right. They said it would be better not to talk to the newspapers because that way there was a greater chance they would find her alive. Three weeks later, they discovered her body. She had been incinerated. Only her jawbone was left. I identified her from the buckle on her belt.'

'I'm sorry, sir.'

'Why are you sorry? It's not your fault.'

'What did they—'

'I don't rightly know what they did, Detective, but I'll tell you this. I can conjure the power of nightmares even in the sunshine of a golden summer's day.' He smiled. 'Of course, I've had no one to distract me since Mary passed away. What do you think? Did she cry out for us, did she beg them to stop? "Can you take me back to my mom and dad now?" Maybe she prayed for a miracle – that we would find her, that the door would open suddenly and the nightmare would end. But life isn't like that, is it, Detective? In the real world we know not to believe in miracles.'

'I meant . . . what happened after you found her body?'

'More detectives came. At first there were dozens, but the numbers dwindled over time. Your father led the investigation. He was a kind man. Mary liked him. We both knew that if anyone could find Ruth's killers, it would be him. He said he had a suspicion as to who might have been responsible and, complicated as it might be, he would bring the men to justice.'

Quinn swallowed hard. 'But that didn't happen.'

'No, it did not. Your father's visits became more infrequent and then, one day, he stopped taking my calls. I went down to Centre Street to see him, but I was told he was busy. Eventually, I was informed that he had been transferred back to a precinct and the case had been marked "unsolved" in the file. There was nothing more they could say. It was his decision, I believe.'

'What was?'

'To close the file.'

'Who told you that?'

'We had our friends. Your mother came by to see us. I don't remember exactly when, perhaps a year later. She said she was sorry. She stood where you're standing now and cried. I couldn't get her to stop. I didn't understand the cause of her empathy, of her sorrow. Perhaps she, too, had lost a child.'

490

'No, sir.' Quinn shook his head. 'No.'

'She was a beautiful woman. Is she well, Detective?'

'She died a few months ago.'

'I'm sorry to hear that.'

Quinn turned to the pictures on the wall. 'What did you do, sir? I mean, after they closed the case.'

'I took it to every place in town – to the DA's office, to Tammany, to the newspapers. Nobody was interested.' Abe Scher looked at him. Tears stood in his eyes. 'I told Mary when she slipped away that we would receive justice one day, but she didn't believe me any more.' Now his ravaged cheeks were wet.

'I'm sorry, sir.'

'Everyone is sorry, but such pain cannot be shared.'

'I'd like to help you.'

'It's too late for that. What are three broken lives to anyone, Detective? We're just so much flotsam that has long since drifted on by.'

'I'm not my father, sir. I believe I can help you and I'd like to try.'

Abe Scher sighed. 'What is it you wish to know?'

'Can you recall which Headquarters detectives worked on your case?'

'There were so many. They came and went.'

'You can't remember anyone else?'

There was a loud crack from below. Quinn stood. 'Were you expecting a visitor?'

Abe Scher shook his head.

Quinn stepped onto the landing, walked downstairs and to the front door.

A trail of damp footprints led from where the rain bounced off the porch. He swung around. The barrel of a revolver pointed directly at him.

CHAPTER FIFTY-FOUR

'WHAT IN HELL ARE YOU DOING?'

'It's over, Joe.'

Caprisi's eyes were cold, his gun arm steady.

'I looked for you at the office,' Quinn said.

'Put your piece on the table.'

'Why?'

'Do as you're asked.'

Quinn took out his revolver and placed it very slowly on the tabletop. Caprisi's gun arm had begun to shake.

Quinn studied his partner's anguished face. His heartbeat slowed. 'It's Luciano and Siegel, right? "Take it easy, Cap." I should have guessed,' he said. 'You don't have to do this. I know you're in a fix, but we'll find another way.'

'It's too late for that.'

'It's never too late.' Quinn moved towards him. 'C'mon, man, we can sort this out.'

'Stay where you are, Joe. I made a deal. And nobody breaks a deal with Luciano. You know that. I've got no choice but to bring you in.'

Quinn took a seat by the bookshelf. 'What do they want?'

'Owney Madden has kept them at bay, Joe. You owe him your life. He still figures he can talk you out of it. They'd just like to keep things the way they are.'

Quinn pointed at the ceiling. 'You want to explain that to Ruth Scher's father?'

'I have a family to protect,' Caprisi said.

'So did Abe Scher.'

'There's nothing I can do about that. We have to go now.'

'What are they going to do with me?'

'I don't know. It's not for me to decide.'

'I'm your partner.'

'I know that. But . . . those days are gone now. I'm sorry, Joe.'

Quinn pulled the front door open. A bolt of lightning split the sky. 'Get into the back,' Caprisi shouted against the rain.

There was another man in the automobile. He trained a revolver on Quinn's chest.

The Buick eased off, nice and slow. Rain pummelled the windows.

'Where are you taking me?' Quinn asked.

'Uptown.'

'When did you make the deal?'

'Joe, please don't ask any more questions. It's – it's over now. I can't say any more.'

Quinn was overwhelmed by sadness.

They came to a halt outside the Central Park Casino, where the traffic was backed up for half a block as taxis and limousines disgorged men in tuxedos and silk hats. Quinn was swept into the lobby. They stepped into a dazzling ballroom fashioned from black glass. The din of conviviality was punctuated by the pop of champagne corks, the rattle of ice in cocktail shakers, and the rumble of a steel band.

The mayor sat dead ahead of them, belly up to the bar, pants hitched high above shiny shoes, ringed by glittering lights and cronies. He wore white spats and a dark suit, and tapped a charcoal fedora with the tips of his fingers.

Caprisi took Quinn's arm and led him around the edge of the dance-floor where Betty Compton, the mayor's girlfriend, twirled with a handsome, dark-haired man beneath a ceiling that groaned with gold leaf. Her bobbed hair curled inwards at the nape of her neck and she wore a sleek, close-fitting magenta dress. Next to her Gloria Duncan was in cream silk, with diamonds trickling down her cleavage. She watched him pass without a word.

The air was violet with cigarette smoke and waiters hurried past, carrying silver trays packed with champagne glasses and colossal brandy balloons.

Owney Madden sat alone, flanked by a pair of showgirls who scuttled away as Quinn was wheeled in front of him. 'Joe.' Madden offered his hand. 'I'm glad you could make it.'

'Good of you to invite me.'

'I knew you'd be sore about that.' Madden clicked his fingers. 'What will you have?'

Quinn shook his head.

'Scotch for the gentleman.' Madden ignored Caprisi. 'Take a seat, Joe.'

'I'd rather stand.'

Madden lowered his voice an octave. 'I said take a seat.'

Quinn did as he was instructed and contemplated the Scotch that was placed in front of him. 'What do you want, Owney?'

'I've always looked out for you, Joe.'

'I know that.'

'You're a good boy and I'd like you to stay with us. I don't want you to have to take a ride out to Staten Island.'

'What have I done wrong?'

'What have you done right? You're making some of my friends nervous and they've asked me to have a word with you, to see if something can be worked out. If you'd been prepared to help *us* find the killer . . . But now it's gone too far.'

'Don't you trust the police, Owney?'

'Are you kidding me?'

'What do you want me to do?'

'I'd recommend taking a long vacation, all expenses paid.'

The ice clinked in Quinn's glass as he swirled the amber liquid.

Madden lit a cigarette. 'We'll give you ten thousand to see you on your way and we'll put you on the payroll when you come back, if that's what you want. If not, we won't trouble you again.'

'Is that all?'

'And you give me your word you'll *never* come back to this case. Is that a deal?'

'What happened today that made you want to pull me in?'

'Joe, I'm trying to do you a favour here.'

'Who is the man you have to protect?'

Madden bristled. 'Be careful, Joe.'

'He's the guy who keeps the show on the road for you, right? You don't need to speak to the mayor over there, because the Bag Man – or whatever you call him now – looks after your rackets and takes in the graft.' Quinn glanced at Jimmy Walker and his cronies. 'He makes sure *they* get their cut.'

'If you figure the mayor takes our money, then you're not so smart.'

'Who is he, Owney? Schneider? The Bull? Or is it someone else?'

'I need to know if you buy the deal.'

'I'm asking myself what the Bag Man and his cronies did that made someone want to cut them up so bad.'

'Joe—'

'There was a little girl in a small house in Brooklyn—'

'That's enough.'

'So what did they do, Owney? They screwed her and dumped her body in an incinerator – then got a taste for it?'

Madden's eyes were flinty.

'Is that what you're trying to cover up? You've got to chase your guy across town like a nursemaid to clean up his mess? Is this how you want it to be?'

'If you play ball, Joe, we'll make you a rich man – richer than you ever dreamt of. If you fuck us over, then Ben and the guys will have their say. There'll be nothing more I can do for you.'

'So your golden goose, your Bag Man, gets his kicks from tearing up young girls and you have to put up with it, because he keeps the wagons rolling?'

'That's enough.'

Quinn was only inches away from him. 'You think I care about your threats, Owney? You want to know what it feels like to find out your father's one of them . . . a rapist, a murderer? You can all rot in—'

'Your *father*?' Madden was startled. 'Gerry Quinn? Give me a break. Your old man was almost as stubborn a fool as you.' His face twisted. 'Sure we had to buy him off the Ruth Scher case, but you know how we did that? He had a son he truly loved, a strong, fit, smart kid who could knock seven bells out of all comers on any canvas across America. A son he used to tell everyone he was real proud of. We gave it to him

498

straight, Joe. Play ball or find the kid at the bottom of the Hudson.'

Quinn was finding it hard to breathe. 'But that's not—'

'He was a father. He made the right choice. Don't look so shocked. He was a goddamn pain in the ass. Like you, he ignored the warnings. We couldn't let him nail the Scher business and he drove a hard bargain. We had to promise we'd make sure nothing like it happened again – but how in hell am I supposed to control these scum-balls?

'So here it is, the same pitch. Find your broad and get out of town. You have until sundown tomorrow. In six months, if you want to come back and give me the reassurance we need, we'll talk about it.'

Quinn got up, but Madden grasped his jacket. 'The decision has been taken. Your time is done, Joe. Don't screw me over on this. The others didn't want to give you this break.'

'Is that what it is, Owney?'

'Yes, my friend. That's exactly what it is.'

CHAPTER FIFTY-FIVE

THE CAB DRIVER WAS THE TALKATIVE KIND. 'THE CEMETERY over in Greenpoint? You want me to go via the East River? There was a trolley-bus turned over down the end here. Jeez ... Those trolley-bus drivers! Think they're kings of the road ...'

Quinn's head lolled on the leather seat as the rain-soaked sidewalks gave way to smudged images of the Brooklyn seaboard. They hurtled down Delancey Street and rolled onto Williamsburg Bridge. The night air was thick with the rhythmic clatter of tugs and ferries ploughing through the choppy waters below.

The driver bore left and headed north on Kent, past a line of dilapidated piers and abandoned warehouses that stretched to Newtown Creek. The light was poorer. Crumbling tenements were squeezed between factories, lumberyards and gas-storage facilities. A few lone figures trudged through the tall iron gates on their way home.

The driver crossed the creek and let the taxi ride down towards the cemetery.

Thunder rolled across a gunmetal sky and a flash of lightning cast the pawn shop on the corner in sharp relief. A gust of wind lifted a discarded newspaper the length of a block. A solitary automobile tracked the wet pavement.

Quinn pushed his hands deep into his damp pockets and ducked into the cemetery. It was pitch black this side of the stone archway and his feet slipped on the wet turf. He wiped the rain from his face and turned up his collar. Silhouetted on the brow of the hill ahead of him he saw a hunched figure.

'Dad?' He bent down, draped an arm round his father's shoulders and pulled him close. 'Christ, you're soaked through. How long have you been here?' Quinn swung around, so that he was between his father and his mother's headstone. Gerry's face was blue with cold. The rain streamed down the deep lines across his forehead. His eyes were dull and lifeless. 'You're freezing.'

Gerry said nothing.

'Why didn't you tell me, Dad?'

Gerry put his hand over his son's. It was like ice.

'You did it for me. I know you did it for me . . .'

Gerry Quinn tightened his grip. Cold wet fingers interlocked with Quinn's own.

'I'm sorry, Dad.'

'It's all right, my son.' They held each other against the wind, until Gerry released him and bent forward to remove a couple of stray leaves from his wife's grave.

501

Quinn hooked an arm beneath his father's and pulled him to his feet. He helped him to the sanctuary of a stone shelter in the centre of the graveyard, from which paths stretched like the arms of a cross. Gerry wiped the water from his face and shook it off his fingers. The distant lights of the shipyards glinted in his eyes. Quinn was close enough to feel his father's breath on his face. 'It'll be the death of you,' he said.

'Maybe that would be a blessing.'

'Don't talk like that.'

Quinn lit two cigarettes and handed one to Gerry. An aircraft buzzed overhead, its lights dimly visible through the gloom. Another roll of thunder crashed through the sky.

Gerry smoked his cigarette to the stub. It fizzled and went out as he flicked it onto the turf. 'I guess you found Abe,' he said.

'He was sitting in his daughter's room, surrounded by memories.'

'Do you know what they did, Joe?'

'Not all of it.'

'They choked the life out of us all, that's what they did. Ruth Scher was just a girl, shy, nervous, none too pretty, but she was real excited that day. The sun was shining. It was going to be one hell of a morning. They'd told her she was headed for a good job uptown. Her parents waved as she walked up the rise. Then, on the other side, our friends pulled up in an automobile to offer her a ride. Why should she refuse? They were the guys she knew from the agency and it would be quicker that way. She'd have time to look into a few store windows on Fifth Avenue.'

Gerry breathed in hard. 'So they drugged her and took her to a house a couple of blocks away from where her parents lived. They abused her, all of them in turn. They strangled her and shoved her body in a furnace. And then they laughed at us. No fingerprints, no witnesses. They *laughed*.' Gerry stepped out into the rain and faced his son, water dribbling down his face again. 'What could I tell you, Joe? What could I tell your mother? What was there to say?'

'It wasn't your fault, Dad.'

'It was *my* case. Abe Scher looked *me* in the eye and asked for his daughter's killers to be brought to justice. When you wanted to know about life in Centre Street, how could I tell you what a coward I'd become?'

'You've never been a coward in your life.'

'Are you sure about that? I killed your mother as sure as if I'd pushed her off that building myself.'

'That's not true.'

'You don't know.'

'Dad . . .'

'I should never have told her the trouble I was in. After that, she wanted to know every damned detail and it made her sick.'

'That's why you took Martha in.'

'I thought it might help . . . put something back. Your ma wanted to meet Ruth Scher's parents. She wanted me to go back on the case. We fought. Sometimes she got better for a while. How was I supposed to explain this world to her? Why would I want to?'

'Who's the Bag Man?'

'Do you think he's dumb enough to reveal himself?'

'You must know.'

'That's not how it works. He's like a shadow. One of the cabal's acolytes will sidle up to you. He makes his pitch, lays it on the line. "Who's the boss?" you ask, but he just smiles. They all know and you know how far up the line the sewer runs. If they want to nail you or your wife or your sons, there's no one and nothing can stop them. They keep the cash flowing through to Tammany, and the fat politicians, who have their snouts deep in the trough, cover their backs. They don't tell you who the Bag Man is but, then, they don't need to. In your heart you know, from the first moment you walk through that door.'

'Schneider.'

'Schneider? Can you imagine him shooting the breeze with Hegarty, O'Reilly or the rest?'

'How come he's so rich?'

'He's a sensible fellow. He married an heiress. He has no need to hide his wealth.'

'What about the commissioner?'

'Grover Whalen? He doesn't have the first idea what's going on. No, this came over from the old country, and that makes our shame all the greater. McCredie runs the place, doesn't he? He always has.'

'When you heard about Amy Mecklenburg,' Quinn said quietly, 'you knew it had begun again.'

Gerry didn't answer.

'You had the file sent over. The details were all there – a recruitment agency, the set-up that it was a family affair . . .'

'I knew she was dead by the time I got the file.'

'And you had to do something before another girl got caught in their net. You'd promised to kill off Ruth Scher's case if the perpetrators were scattered to the four winds and nothing like it happened again. They'd reneged on your deal, so you killed Matsell first because he was the easiest to get to.' Quinn paused. 'You pushed him off that roof.'

'I should have roasted him over a slow fire.'

'You told Duncan you knew who was after him. Why wouldn't he trust you of all people, a cop they'd bought off years ago? You arranged to meet him at the edge of the park.'

'I'm sorry about the driver.'

'Moe and Dick would have been next in line, until they saved you the trouble.' Quinn rubbed his temples. 'The rest of them have to figure it's you.'

'They suspect me. They suspect Yan. They suspect Schneider. They were hoping you would help them out, but now they're afraid you'll expose them for what they are.'

Gerry took out a pack of cigarettes, lit one and retreated to the bench inside the shelter. He stamped his feet on the concrete floor and kicked the clumps of earth back onto the gravel path. 'You remember the way Mom used to send you down to the El station with that stupid Chinese umbrella?'

505

'They were the best times.'

'You ever wonder why I mostly asked her to send Aidan?'

'Of course.'

'I loved you, kid, but Aidan and I, we just talked about ball games. You asked about real stuff. Was it true what they said about the Fifth Avenue diamond thief? How about the stick-up guys over in Brooklyn?' Gerry looked at him. 'And, pace by pace, you forced me to ask myself what use was a cop if all he did in a city like this was to put away the stick-up men.'

'I liked just being there.'

'And I liked you to be there, but everyone wants to believe he's a hero in his own story. The hatred, the way you see yourself, it turns you inside out. It poisons everything.'

'It's okay, Dad.' Quinn smoked his cigarette and ground it out on the concrete floor. He wanted it to be okay. But the wreckage of the past weighed them down. He leant against the pillar and tried to press away the pain behind his eyes. 'What are you going to do?'

'I have to finish what I started. I owe that at least to your mother.'

'Mom's dead. You owe it to her to get away from here. We can load up Aidan's new model tonight—'

'And go where?'

'Hell, I don't know. They need cops in Detroit, don't they, and Philadelphia and Los Angeles?'

'I'll never leave this city, Joe. This is my home. It's not just your mother. I owe it to you, to Aidan and Martha, to Ruth Scher and Amy Mecklenburg, and to the other victims our friends in Centre Street have yet to select. You think I could just turn my back on all that?'

Quinn stared out at the night sky. 'I can help you.'

'This is not your fight.'

'It belongs to all of us.'

'No, Joe. It belongs to me.'

Silence settled between them. The city seemed to have receded beyond the graveyard's cold embrace.

'Martha told Aidan she couldn't marry him,' Gerry said. 'He doesn't know where she is.'

'Do you?'

'I figured you might.'

Quinn avoided his father's gaze.

'Be careful, Joe. It would destroy him. You know that, don't you?'

'I guess I've always known.'

A figure appeared at the cemetery gate and walked up the hill towards them. He moved swiftly, head bent and face concealed beneath the brim of his hat. Quinn didn't realize it was Caprisi until his partner was right in front of him. The rain spilled off the brim of his fedora. 'You've got to get out of here, Joe,' he said. 'The guys at Centre Street have overruled Madden. They're spooked by what you said at the press conference. They've decided you know too much – and they want your girl. They've heard we're after Liam O'Brien and they think she may have seen some of the faces at the Plaza.'

A couple of automobiles screeched to a halt outside the cemetery. Doors slammed and dark figures swarmed towards the gate. As they moved under the light by the entrance, Quinn caught sight of Hegarty and O'Reilly.

'Go,' Gerry said. He pushed his son into the shadows.

Caprisi shoved a set of keys into Quinn's palm. 'Take the Gardner. I left it out back.'

'Move,' Gerry said. 'We need to go now.'

CHAPTER FIFTY-SIX

THEY SLID ON THE WET TURF ALL THE WAY TO THE EAST gate and the gloomy sidewalk beyond it. Quinn got into the Gardner beside his father, started up and nudged it down the lane.

As they crossed Newtown Creek, a black Buick pulled out behind them. It came on fast, so Quinn flashed up his headlamps and accelerated along Meeker Avenue. He swung right at the junction and headed towards McCarran Park. Keeping his foot hard down, he slewed past the incongruous domes of the Greek Orthodox Church and wove through Williamsburg and Stuyvesant Heights.

Gerry turned back to watch their tail. 'Two men inside,' he said.

'Where do we go?'

Gerry glanced at the road ahead, then back over his shoulder. 'We'll have to face them. Head for the Bush

Terminal.' He took out his revolver and checked its chamber.

Quinn skirted Prospect Park, then drove back west towards the Bush Terminal District. The streets were narrower here, and sailors and pierhead workers were still about on the damp sidewalks. The stores and restaurants bore mostly Scandinavian names and Quinn flattened a large billboard for the *Nordisk Tidende* newspaper as he rode onto the kerb to avoid a group of revellers.

He slowed as he approached the terminal.

'Keep going,' Gerry said.

Quinn drove past the railroad sidings and along the line of the piers, where a stream of figures still ran between the steamships and the giant steel and glass loft buildings that stood alongside them.

'Pier four,' Gerry said quietly. 'Go to the end and spin around.'

Quinn turned right and drove down the pier. There were fewer ships berthed here and the last few loft buildings along the row stood in darkness. He swung the Gardner into a warehouse, turned it around and killed the lights.

They waited. Quinn watched his father's granite face. He could see why Yan had been pleased to have this man beside him.

Gerry wound down the window. 'Don't let them get away from the automobile,' he said.

The Buick rode to a halt. One of the men opened the door to get out. 'Now,' Gerry whispered. 'Now!'

Quinn gunned the Gardner's engine and stamped the pedal to the floor.

The automobile roared and lunged forward. It screamed out of the warehouse and slammed into the side of the Buick. Quinn hit the steering-wheel with the force of the impact, but kept his foot on the gas. The Gardner roared still louder as the shrieking wail of metal against metal rent the night air.

The man had rolled clear. He hollered in alarm and swung his machine-gun up in a slow arc. Gerry put his arm out of the window, took aim and loosed off a single shot. The dark figure crumpled.

The driver of the Buick grasped too late what was happening. He struggled to get across to the other side of the automobile and escape, but the Gardner was powerful and shifted the Buick to the edge of the pier. 'Keep going!' Gerry yelled.

Quinn pitched the Buick straight into the icy water.

He reversed up, killed the headlamps.

The silence was deafening.

They got out, walked to the edge of the pier and watched the Buick slide beneath the dark water. They waited to see if the man would free himself and break the surface, but the ocean swallowed its metal gift without a murmur.

The sea was still again. They heard the hoot of a steamship coming into dock further down the wharf.

'Should we call the cops?' Gerry said.

'I heard they don't like to get their feet wet.'

They returned to the Gardner and drove back

towards the terminal entrance. As they inched through the Norwegian colony outside its gates, a group of sailors blocked their path. They were singing loudly, drunk and good-humoured. One or two bashed the hood. Gerry raised a hand and smiled. Just beyond them, he tapped Quinn's shoulder to ask him to pull over. He opened the door. 'Where are you going?' Quinn asked.

'Find Martha, Joe. If they get to her, nothing will have been worth anything.'

'What are you going to do?'

'Finish what I should have started a long time ago.'

'I'll come with you.'

'You and I will travel better alone.'

'Dad—'

'Joe, you know what they tried to do to Martha in that hotel room.' Gerry's eyes were cold. 'I need you to make sure they don't find her.'

'If we hooked up with La Guardia and Goldberg, we could bust them wide open.'

'It's too late for that.'

Gerry stepped out of the automobile and slammed the door. Quinn leant over and wound down the window. 'Yan and I have a place to go,' Gerry said, 'so don't worry about us tonight. Tomorrow it will be over.'

And before his son could say another word, he had melted into the crowd.

Quinn parked in a narrow alley by West Fifth, next to the bath-house where they had once changed for the beach. The rain had eased, so he stepped onto the boardwalk and followed the lights back towards Manhattan. Even at this time of night, Coney Island was a huge discordant cacophony. The crowd shuffled to the music of two dozen jazz bands in dance halls and honky-tonks. The air was thick with the aroma of popcorn, cotton candy, Jewish potato cakes and frankfurters. Couples strolled arm in arm and children scampered through the shadows.

He made his way past the penny arcades, chop-suey parlours, carousels, bath-houses, shooting galleries and freak shows which popped up one after another all the way down the strip. He looked into the store where Martha had liked to buy custard pies and screwballs, then turned right into Luna Park, past the big saltwater pool that lay beneath a ride called the Dragon's Gorge. He got on board and, as the carriage hit the top of the first rise, surveyed the crowd below.

He saw a fleet of sleek automobiles roll down Surf. The convoy came to a halt and a dozen men got out and moved into the crowd. O'Reilly and Hegarty were in the lead.

When the ride came full circle, he climbed out and hurried back to the boardwalk. The crowd was thick, the cries of the barkers more insistent. A lurid billboard advertised the waxwork Chamber of Horrors and cries from revellers on the Loop-o-Plane carried on the wind.

He caught sight of Hegarty's fedora and quickened his pace. He reached Feltman's and looked through the window at a group of Bavarian folk singers dancing the *Schuplatt'l* on a makeshift stage. He turned. A ferry had tied up at the pier. Two kids on roller-skates crashed into him. 'Hey . . .'

Hegarty scanned the crowd behind him with two of his men. Others joined them, their heads bent close in conversation.

They split up again.

Quinn dodged through the shadows and ducked into a dark lane beyond the steamboat pier. He kept moving until the noise of the seafront faded, then leant against some wooden boarding to catch his breath.

He navigated his way around a series of tight corners to a row of ramshackle wooden houses with wide balconies. Number thirty was boarded up. Blue paint peeled in great strips from neglected walls. A sign saying 'Long Island Realty' had been pinned to the door. He climbed over a makeshift barrier onto the porch.

The bench where they had once sat and waited for the rain to cease had been broken. The little palm tree had gone and the lamp above was covered with spiders' webs. The sign announcing this was a *kuch alein* guest-house had faded with age. The door had already been forced. He eased it open and stepped into a hallway with black-and-white flooring and walls of varnished burlap.

In the half-darkness, the place seemed suddenly to reverberate with their laughter. He could see the sand from the beach between their toes, the wooden spades and metal buckets. He could smell the potato cakes and cotton candy.

He could feel her hand in his.

A shutter banged in the breeze.

He moved to the bottom of the stairs and climbed noiselessly. On the top floor, a breath of sea air cooled his cheeks.

Uneven boards creaked beneath his feet.

She stood by a window. Lights from Luna Park lit her face. Her skin was damp with rain.

The sound of a ship's horn drifted up from the Narrows. As children, they had listened to his mother in her more lucid moments conjure from this window an exotic world far beyond these shores in the passage of the great steamships: spruce from Norway, figs from Egypt, tea from China . . .

The lights blinked. Screams carried on the night air.

'Don't come in here, Joe,' she said.

'They're looking for you. They believe you can identify some of the faces in that room in the Plaza.'

'Then they'll find me sooner or later. Please don't come any further.' He ignored her. She faced him, dark eyes searching his. 'I can't destroy him. I . . . can't. You know that. You must know that.'

He came closer still. Her breath caressed his cheek. They leant against each other. He could feel her heart beating. Her hand sought his. She wove their fingers together, then rested her forehead against his lips. 'God, Joe . . .'

Quinn heard voices. He caught a glimpse of Hegarty's fedora on the pavement below. O'Reilly was right behind him.

'This is what the guy was talking about. These are the *kuch aleins*,' O'Reilly said. 'My sister used to own one.'

'Did we get a number?' Hegarty hissed.

'No.'

'Then we'll have to check the whole damned row.'

Quinn heard the crunch of a boot on the porch and the creak of the front door. He pulled Martha close against the wall. She slipped her arms around him. Doors were opened and closed on the ground floor. They heard whispered voices, then footsteps going down into the basement.

They waited. She slid behind him and he could feel the thump of her heart in his back.

The men returned to the ground floor.

Boots scuffed the stairs. Martha's fingers gripped Quinn's ribs. He fumbled for his revolver, looked up and spotted the trap-door to the attic.

He slipped his revolver back into his coat, put a finger to his lips and pointed up at the hatch.

Martha cupped her hands for his foot. She was strong and just held his weight, swaying as he strengthened his grip on the edge of the frame. He pushed up the hatch and slid it back.

They heard footsteps in the corridor.

One of the men was in the next room.

Quinn pulled himself into the loft, then swung around and stretched out his arm. He hauled her up by the wrists until she had her elbows on the ledge, then lifted her through the gap.

One of the men was in the corridor again.

Quinn pushed her out of sight but didn't have time to get the hatch back into place.

They heard footsteps below them. 'You figure we should check up there?' O'Reilly said.

'Forget it. We'll be here all night.'

One moved to the window. 'You smell that?' O'Reilly asked. 'It's like a lady's perfume.'

'Maybe you can smell yourself,' Hegarty said. 'You always did stink like a tart's boudoir. C'mon. We've got the rest of the row to check.'

A few moments later, the front door banged shut. Quinn closed the hatch. The attic was no longer tall enough for them to stand in, but otherwise nothing had changed. Even the polished floorboards still smelt of cinnamon. The place was warm, clean and cosy. Moonlight spilled through the window at the gable end.

He caught a glimpse of Hegarty and O'Reilly as they passed along the alley to the house next door. There were muttered voices and another door banged.

Martha came alongside him. They listened to the footsteps and hushed voices until they were confident that the men had reached the far end of the alley.

Quinn sat back against a beam. Martha knelt beside him.

'I recognized one of the voices,' she said, and shivered.

'They've gone,' he said.

Her body shook violently. 'They're never gone.' There were tears in her eyes. 'I can always see them in my head. When I woke up in that room, I felt so sick.

My head swam. Sarah was whispering in my ear. "Martha, wake up. Wake up. Martha, wake up. Wake up . . ." The room was spinning. Then I tried to sit up and I saw myself – saw what they'd done – and I heard voices . . . The fear . . . it's like . . . it eats away your soul.'

He touched her gently. 'It's okay, Martha.'

'No – no, it's *not* okay. In the night now I can see them in that doorway, smell the smoke, hear those voices and feel their fingers on me. I . . . My God, Joe, it makes my stomach churn. I knew what they'd wanted, what they'd take. I knew what would happen, what they wanted to do, what they were going to do . . .'

She crumpled into him.

He wrapped his arms around her.

Martha cried as if she would never stop. He held her tight and tried to smooth away her sorrow.

'It's *me*,' she said. 'It's because of who I am.'

'No,' he whispered. 'Life is about where you reach for, not where you began.'

'My mother . . . I used to see her. I used to see her come downstairs with those men and—'

'Stop it, Martha.'

'But it's like they say, isn't it? You can take a girl out of the Bowery but—'

'That's enough. The past is past. It means nothing now. You escaped. You've made yourself magnificent – difficult, outspoken, courageous and bold. It's why I love you, why I always have.'

His declaration hung in the air.

They heard the hoot of a distant steamship.

Martha's lips touched his cheek.

She was as still as stone. 'When we lay on the boards here,' she breathed, 'I used to look out of that window and paint pictures of your face in the stars.'

'That's very poetic.'

'I loved you too, Joe.'

His heart pounded against his ribs.

'I felt safe here. I wanted to stay here, right here, always.'

She cupped his face with her long, cool fingers.

She brushed his forehead with her lips and then, very slowly, very gently, his eyelids and nose. She slipped astride him and kissed him deeply, caressing his neck and throat.

She eased her dress up her thighs and whispered, 'Did you dream of me like this, Joe?'

She loosened his pants, then undid the buttons down the front of her dress and slipped it off. She was almost naked. Her long, graceful body glowed and her breasts were high and proud in the moonlight. She lowered herself upon him with agonizing slowness, her breathing ragged now. 'Joe,' she whispered, 'Joe . . .'

When it was over, they lay curled together, listening to the clatter of the rides and looking up at the stars. Her breathing slowed and she relaxed in his arms.

Voices rose from the street, then fell away. Quinn watched the lights of a ferris wheel. A steamer hooted in the Narrows, drowning the voices of the revellers. He could hear his mother: 'The *Conte di Savoia* steams up river, wine from Capri, olive oil from Spain, figs and dates from North Africa . . .'

He sought patterns in the shadows, but did not dare move lest the careless brush of an arm let the world back in.

CHAPTER FIFTY-SEVEN

LATER, QUINN COVERED THEM WITH HIS RAINCOAT AND they lay together, limbs entwined, her warm body pressed to his. He slept fitfully and awoke long before dawn. He sat back against the beam, her head on his lap. He watched the light creep into the corners of the attic. A mouse scampered along the floorboards, looked at him, then scurried back to its hole.

He listened to the first steamboat dock at the pier. Despite the hour, a Victrola horn spilled 'When You and I Were Young, Maggie' along the alleyways below them.

He noticed her eyes were open. She had been watching him.

He waited for her to say something, but after a few minutes she sat upright. The raincoat slipped from her body and she pulled on her dress with unselfconscious ease. The ease lovers feel. 'Joe . . .' she began, but stopped and sat down again, cross-legged.

He could tell she was already retreating: her armour had been restored with the dawn.

He buttoned his shirt and pants and stood. 'I have to go,' he said.

'You have to go where?'

'Please stay here.'

She frowned, her expression suddenly brittle and wary. 'I need to find Dad.'

'I'll come with you.'

'No. Please stay. You're safe here. We'll come back for you.'

'You'll never persuade him to leave, Joe.'

'I have to,' he said simply.

'What about ... the others?' Shame prevented her saying Aidan's name. Or perhaps he imagined that.

'All of us.'

'Sarah?'

'All of us.'

He waited for her to contradict him, but she swept the palm of her hand to and fro across the floorboards. 'I'll only be a few hours. Please stay here.'

He reached the hatch. 'Be careful, Joe,' she said.

'I shouldn't have let him go.'

'I can't ... I mean ...' She wavered. 'You understand, don't you?'

Quinn held her gaze for a moment, then swung himself down through the hatch to the floor below.

He avoided the Gardner in case they had a man watching it and searched the alleys further along

Surf until he found an automobile he could steal.

By the time he was on the road, the rain was lashing down with renewed ferocity. He leant closer to the windshield and navigated his way through Brooklyn to Prospect Park.

West of Sixth, grand mansions gave way to small, down-at-heel brownstones squashed between industrial plants and warehouses. He drew to a halt in a narrow alley that stank of fish and brackish water. Netting spilled from the backs of pick-up trucks and was tacked up high to the red-brick walls. He could hear men still dancing to balalaikas in a basement speakeasy three doors away.

Quinn rapped once on a flimsy wooden door. The rain trickled down his neck. A fisherman shot him a wary glance. 'Stefan Yanowsky?' Quinn asked. 'Is this where the cop lives?' He waited, but the fisherman did not answer.

Quinn put his shoulder to the door and climbed the narrow steps to a first-floor apartment with windows high in the roof. The main room boasted a stove, a table and three chairs, and the Dodgers' four National League pennants tacked to the walls above photographs of Nap Rucker, Babe Herman and Dazzy Vance. Alongside them was a shot of Yan, grinning at the entrance to Ebbets Field with the pennant from 1920 pinned across his chest.

Quinn moved along the wall. He found another photograph of Yan, this time with two young kids in front of the miniature boathouse on the other side of

Prospect Park. They clutched a model yacht, which now stood in the centre of the sideboard.

There was a key-rack, neatly marked. Three hooks were empty: 'House'; 'Buick'; 'Boathouse'.

Quinn returned to his automobile and drove through to the south side of Prospect Park. He left the vehicle at the kerbside as the sun broke momentarily through the clouds. Then he ran through strolling families to the boathouse.

The door was locked and he had to smash a window to get in. From the discarded whisky bottle and rolled-up blankets he knew immediately that this was where they had spent the night. His heart beat faster.

He stepped back outside, observing the bank of thunderclouds that had regrouped in the east for another assault on the city.

Back at the automobile, he got in, turned north and kept the pedal down hard, hammering his horn as he careered through the teeming streets. The traffic jammed around City Hall Park and Quinn drummed his fingers in frustration as he watched shadowy figures stream from the subway. Shoeshine boys on the side-walk yelled themselves hoarse to compete with the screeches of El trains in the rambling shed on the Brooklyn Bridge approach.

He reached Centre Street and slid into an official bay.

Lights burnt through the gloom. A newspaper vendor stood beneath his umbrella. 'Scandal of City Hall "List"', ran the banner headline on the board beside him. 'Cops Uncover "Proof" of Corruption at the

"Highest Level"'. The byline was Joshua Goldberg's.

Quinn skirted around to the rear entrance that led straight to the CIB. An ambulance screamed to a halt beside him and its doors were flung open. Quinn rounded the corner. A rope cordoned off the alley. He pushed past a crowd of onlookers. The doors to the basement corridor were wide open.

He saw a white wall smeared with blood. He saw Schneider, Caprisi and Doc Carter.

Yan lay spreadeagled across the floor, another body beyond him.

Quinn saw a marble-white face, a thread of spittle hanging from pale lips. For a moment, he stood frozen in the doorway.

'Dad . . .' He knelt. Gerry's pale blue eyes stared back at him. His face was grey, his skin clammy. 'Where are you hit?' Quinn pulled back the sheet gently to reveal his father's bloodstained stomach. Doc Carter had bound it tight, but blood still seeped through.

'Not much longer, Joe . . .' His voice was faint.

'Dad, the ambulance is here.'

'Listen to me.'

Quinn leant closer.

His father's face was distorted by the effort of speech. 'Did you find her?'

'I found her, Dad. She's safe.'

The worry eased in Gerry's face. 'Look after them. Look after Aidan. He needs you. You understand?'

'Of course.'

'Take them away from here, son. Begin again.

Somewhere new. The battle here is lost . . .' Gerry closed his eyes against the pain.

Quinn took his hand. 'Dad, hold on.'

Gerry smiled weakly. 'It's okay, Joe.'

'Hold on.'

'I'm so . . . proud of you, my son.'

'Dad, please . . .'

'It's time.' He tried to smile again, but the pain was too great. 'I'll see your mother and we'll talk about . . . what might have been. I'll see Ruth Scher . . . tell her . . . how sorry I am.'

'Dad, you looked after us.'

Gerry stared at him fiercely and raised his head. 'Don't take the same road.' His face twisted. 'You understand?' Passion flared in his eyes for a few more seconds, but then the light faded and he sank back.

'Dad?' Quinn gazed at his father's motionless face. Silence enveloped him. 'Dad?' He wrapped his arms around his father's blood-soaked body and pressed his cheek closer to the failing heart. Blood seeped through the sheet onto his forehead. 'Dad, please . . .' He held him tighter. 'Dad . . . please . . . I'm sorry, I'm here. Don't go . . . not now . . .'

Schneider knelt beside him. 'Joe, let the medics through.'

'Dad . . . I'm sorry, so sorry . . .'

'Joe . . .' Quinn didn't budge, so Schneider grabbed him beneath the arms and pulled him to his feet. 'There's nothing more you can do.'

The hallway was silent. The ambulance men, the

uniform cops, Schneider, Caprisi, Doc Carter, all stood as still as statues.

Quinn shrugged himself free of Schneider's grip. He turned and punched a hole through the door beside him, then smashed it off its hinges for good measure. Caprisi and Schneider tried to take hold of him. 'Steady, Joe!'

Suddenly Quinn's legs turned to water.

'Steady.'

There were hushed whispers further down the corridor.

Quinn shook himself free and plunged through the door to the stairs. 'Stop, Joe!' Schneider called.

Quinn heard footsteps behind him, but burst onto the central floor like a raging bull. Silence fell and anxious faces turned towards him. McCredie's door was shut, his office shrouded in darkness.

Schneider caught Quinn's arm and guided him down to his own office. Caprisi was alongside him. He closed the door behind them. 'He's not here, Joe,' Schneider said. He picked up a copy of the *Sun* and dropped it on the desk. Quinn stared at the headline: 'Scandal of City Hall "List"'. He moved to the window and watched the rain bounce off the sidewalk. He could hear the water pelting against his mother's parasol on the journey back from the El station. He could hear his father's voice. 'You asked about real stuff . . . And, pace by pace, you forced me to ask myself what use was a cop if all he did in a city like this was to put away the stick-up men . . .'

'Joe, we can help each other,' Schneider said.

'How?'

'With your list, we can destroy him. He knows it. We've never run them this close. We're ready to move. We can do a deal with them, Joe. We can finish him.'

'We can do a deal?'

'Sure.'

'What in hell's that going to change?'

'You're full of rage. I understand that—'

There was a knock on the door. 'There's a call for Joe,' Mae said. She glanced at each man in turn. 'It's . . . He said it was urgent.'

As Quinn passed Mae in the doorway, she squeezed his hand. He picked up the telephone on her desk.

'I'm sorry about your father, son.'

Quinn clenched his teeth.

'Hegarty . . . some of the other boys, they can get a little out of hand. They panic, you know. They'll have to be punished. I give you my word on that.'

Quinn took a quarter from his pocket and turned it over and over in his hand.

'Your father was an honourable man. Nobody denies that. I once had a deal with him. I was sad it didn't hold, but I understand that, with your mother's death, maybe things looked a little different.'

'I'm touched by your concern.'

'We can do a deal, Joe. Nobody wants a fight.'

'What kind of deal do you have in mind?'

'You've got some papers that don't belong to you, something our friend Mr Duncan shouldn't have kept and that his dumb showgirl wife should never have handed over. We'd like them back.'

'What do I get?'

'Like I said, son, nobody wants a fight. If there's anything else you need, we can talk about it.'

Quinn took Duncan's list from his pocket. Johnny Brandon was watching him intently from across the floor.

'We should meet,' McCredie said. 'There's a good place in Brooklyn, a warehouse down in the Navy Yards. We can work something out.'

'I'll meet you on Wall Street, by the Subtreasury steps.'

'I don't think so, son. Half the city's on Wall Street today.'

'You don't say. Be there. And be sure to leave your dogs at home.'

'Maybe, in a few days, we can think about—'

'I've arranged to meet Goldberg at noon. If I don't show, he'll get a copy, along with one or two little extras. I'll make sure to include your confession to the murder of my father.'

'I'm not sure I like your tone, son. And the goddamn Sub treasury steps are out. There are several thousand half-crazed suckers crawling all over them.'

'Then I'll see you on top of the building where Matsell worked, the roof of number eighty. In one hour.'

'You think I'm stupid enough to believe it won't be a set-up?'

Quinn glanced at Brandon again. 'You want the list? You've got one hour. Make sure you come alone.'

Quinn cut the connection and returned to Schneider's office, where the deputy commissioner and Caprisi sat.

Johnny Brandon crossed the room. His eyes were like chips of ice. 'You're finished, all of you. You know that, don't you? This time it's over.'

Quinn closed the door behind him.

CHAPTER FIFTY-EIGHT

HALF AN HOUR LATER, QUINN HEADED SOUTH. AS HE PASSED through City Hall Park, a cloud of starlings and black-birds darkened the sky, gathering for winter migration. The birds came in so hard that the traffic ground to a halt. They bumped and scratched at the hood, wind-shield and roof as they sought places to rest and forage. When they left a few minutes later, the street was strewn with the corpses of those that had keeled over from exhaustion or starvation.

Some of the birds had flocked above Wall Street, but the assembled throng paid little heed. Newspaper bill-boards yelled yesterday's calamity in bold type: *STOCK MARKET CRISIS OVER. Stock Houses Survive Worst Day in History; MANY STOCKS DOWN DESPITE RALLY AFTER 12,894,650 SHARE PANIC! SENATE TO PROBE FINANCIAL SYSTEM. Losses 3 Billion More; Morgan stems stampede.*

The shoeshine boys and street urchins were huddled

around newspapers or glued to the translux brokerage windows, an illuminated reflection of the moving ticker tape. While yesterday's panic had stimulated hysteria, the whispers of new losses were now met with up-all-night fatigue. Tour buses were backed up along South Street. Their occupants strolled along damp sidewalks to record the disconsolate scenes for their picture books back home. Four or five hundred men from the First Precinct station house stood patiently by. Between them, the street sweepers attempted to clear up the debris from yesterday.

Quinn walked into number eighty.

There was a translux in the hall so nobody paid him the slightest attention. He stepped into the elevator, rose to the top floor and emerged into the gloom of the morning sky.

A seaplane skimmed the surface of the East River and spun back towards the downtown skyport on pier twelve. He trod across the gravel to the edge of the roof. The crowd stretched away below him towards the Exchange, where newsmen jostled for space. Film cameras rolled.

'It's not a good place to jump.'

Quinn turned. McCredie stood a few yards away, hands thrust deep into his pockets and a cigarette clamped to his lips.

He was not alone.

Martha was behind him, handcuffed to the rail, her face bruised and bloodied.

Quinn took a pace towards her.

'Stay where you are, Joe.' McCredie motioned towards the street. 'Take a look down there.'

Aidan stood on the far pavement. His was the sole face tilted skywards. He was surrounded by men with bulging raincoats.

'There's no escaping us, son. You should know that by now.' McCredie smiled. 'But, like I said, we don't want a fight. In fact, you could say we owe you a favour. We were scratching our heads about who in hell had our number when you figured it out for us: a cop. Of course! It had to be your old man. If you hadn't been so smart, Joe . . .'

'You remember Ruth Scher, McCredie?'

'Sure I do.' He flicked his cigarette over the lip of the roof. 'But we're not here for a history lesson.'

'Was she the first girl you killed or just the first we know about?'

'What is this? Confession time?'

'She was *sixteen*.'

'So she got in out of her depth. There are hundreds of dames with tight little tits all over this city begging for a shot at the big-time. Just ask your girlfriend here.' McCredie's smile became a leer. 'Screwing your brother's woman, Joe? Now that *is* dirty.'

'How many of you were there when Ruth was torn to pieces?'

'She was just another broad!'

'She was a girl. She was Abe and Mary's only child, their pride and joy.'

'Yeah? Then they should have educated her better in

the ways of the world, because she cried the whole god-damn time,' McCredie snapped. 'What is it with guys like you? We've been creating the greatest business the world has ever known. You get offered a nice big cut of the action, and for doing what? Nothing. *Not a damn thing*. All you have to do is sit on your fat ass and stay in line while we make you richer than any of the suckers down there could ever dream of. Tell me, honestly, what the hell do a couple of broads matter?'

'They matter to their families. They matter to their friends. They mattered to my dad. And they matter to me.'

'I don't think so.' McCredie acknowledged the Bull with a tilt of his head as Brandon emerged from the doorway.

The Bull trained a revolver on Quinn's stomach. 'Okay, son,' McCredie said, 'this has been a real swell discussion, but I'm tired of the small-talk. If there's a deal to be done, let's do it.'

'You figure I'm naïve enough to think you'll let me walk away from here?'

'You're a real smart guy, Joe. You can work out the score. You let me take a look at those papers and get them into safe hands and I don't give two bits what you do.'

'You just confessed to the murder of a sixteen-year-old girl.'

'Did I, son? Well, blow me down. But, hell, if you figure the fate of some girl who wouldn't stop crying and wouldn't keep her mouth shut when we were screwing her is going to change anything in this city, you're more of a fool than I thought. Duncan's indiscretion will cause us discomfort while this election is running and Major La Guardia continues to make himself a pain in the ass, which is why I'm prepared to offer you a deal, but that's all. Now if we could get on with—'

Quinn started to move towards Martha.

'Stay there!' McCredie moved two paces closer. 'We've written the script for you, son. You busted the case. You went out on a limb and trailed our killer to a distant, lonely place. We'll find some hustler who needs to be put six feet under and you'll walk away from his corpse a hero. We do the deal and I'll go down these stairs now and start spinning the story for Billy and his gang. All you have to do is play your part and you'll be as big a star as your old man. That's what you want, isn't it? But remember this. You work for the New York Police Department. And we don't believe in fairy tales.'

Quinn continued to walk towards Martha.

'Last chance, kid.' McCredie glanced at Brandon. 'Take him, Johnny.'

Brandon didn't move.

'Finish him.'

McCredie turned to stare at the Bull. 'What are you telling me here, Johnny?' His laugh rang short and hollow. 'After all these years, you've found your conscience?'

Brandon still didn't move.

'What are you saying, my friend? You've sold me out,

is that it? You've sold me out to that prick La Guardia? You've done a deal with the kid here?'

'Yeah, I sold you out.'

'You son of a bitch. After all I did for you?'

Quinn closed slowly on his quarry.

McCredie blanched. 'You reckon you're changing the world, Joe? Is that it? Forget it!' They circled. 'If Johnny's done a deal it's to give himself the keys – and that's all the goddamn change you'll ever see.'

Quinn took another pace towards him.

'Come on, son, don't—'

Quinn hit him.

McCredie stumbled back. He clutched his jaw, startled by the insolence. 'Jesus,' he said. But he recovered fast and parried the follow-up. He was good and quick, but his time was past. Old bones and guile were no match for Quinn's speed and strength. McCredie absorbed a punch to the stomach and one to the shoulder, but another clean right to the jaw sent him reeling back.

McCredie shook his head and came forward again, but Quinn pummelled him with blow after blow. He staggered back. By the time they reached the lip of the roof, McCredie was beat. He looked groggy and uncertain on his feet. 'Joe, one minute.'

Quinn smacked him in the mouth so hard that he teetered on the edge of the roof, arms flailing, then crumpled.

He fell awkwardly and scrabbled to hold onto the parapet. 'Joe – please . . .'

Quinn stood above him, motionless. He saw the fear in McCredie's eyes.

The Bull came alongside him. He lowered his revolver. 'Goodbye, Ed,' he said. 'It's been swell knowing you.' He fired a single shot through McCredie's forehead.

There were shouts from below. The crowd surged down from the Exchange. A whistle blew.

Quinn looked down into the street. A man lay on his back, face up to the glowering sky. His derby had landed rim up, and as the rain came once more, it started to fill with water.

CHAPTER FIFTY-NINE

THE WIND TUGGED AT QUINN'S HAIR AND COAT. THE RAIN cooled his cheeks. He looked down again. McCredie appeared to be floating on a sea of umbrellas, arms outstretched.

Aidan stood motionless on the far side of the street.

Quinn crossed the roof, took out his revolver and fired a shot through the metal link of the handcuffs.

Her tears were wet upon his cheeks as he carried her into the stairwell. Halfway down she wriggled free. She kissed him hard, her body moulded to his and her arms tight around his neck.

He picked her up again. She didn't struggle. As they emerged onto Wall Street, the crowd spilled forward. A whistle blew to keep them back. A flashbulb exploded in the gloom.

Quinn saw Aidan at the front of the throng. He was close enough to see the hurt and fear in his brother's eyes. He forced himself forwards and placed Martha gently in Aidan's arms. She would not release him, but he broke her grip.

'Joe,' she called. 'Joe!'

A newsman shouted, 'Mr Quinn? Detective!'

He walked towards South Street, the breeze fresh on his cheeks. A lone tree rustled beside him, but all he could hear was the sound of the rain on an old Chinese parasol.

Reporters crowded in. He recognized Billy Burke from the *Mirror*.

'Detective, I hear it was you who bust this open. McCredie was the Wall Street Killer, right? You cornered him? What did he say before he fell?'

Quinn turned into South Street.

'Just one line, sir,' Burke shouted. 'It's a hell of a story – multiple homicide, the killer one of the most powerful men in the city, a struggle high above Wall Street. It was about this list, right? McCredie was overseeing the take for City Hall? Spencer Duncan and Moe Diamond were going to go on the record for La Guardia so he had them rubbed out? Detective, c'mon, we'll make you a hero.'

Quinn did not break his stride.

'C'mon, Detective, just a line!'

He walked faster.

'Detective, a single line!'

Quinn turned on him. 'I'm a detective from the New York City Police Department,' he said. 'And we don't believe in fairy tales.'

ACKNOWLEDGEMENTS

Thanks to: Bill Scott-Kerr, brilliant publisher and friend; Mark Lucas, the greatest agent there is (who slaved long and hard on this novel with me); my fantastic mother Sally for research assistance; my inspirational wife Claudia for too many things to list . . .

The God of Chaos

By Tom Bradby

1942. THE NAZI hammer is about to fall on the beleaguered city of Cairo. As tension mounts, a key British officer is found brutally murdered. Nobody can fathom the motives behind the killing, and it is certainly the wrong time to start asking questions.

Former New York cop Joe Quinn is a maverick whose methods run against the grain of the British military police. But he is tasked with uncovering the truth and in spite of the circumstances determines to do so – in his own way. Is this merely a straightforward case of espionage or something rather more intimate?

'Bradby's best book yet . . . Enjoyable
and atmospheric'
SUNDAY TELEGRAPH

'Bradby has the talent of a reporter but the
heart of a storyteller'
DAILY MAIL

'The kind of historical fiction that may send
you back to the real history books to learn more'
WASHINGTON POST

9780552151450

The White Russian

by Tom Bradby

St Petersburg 1917. The capital of the glittering Empire of the Tsars and a city on the brink of revolution, where the jackals of the Secret Police intrigue for their own survival as their aristocratic masters indulge in one last, desperate round of hedonism.

For Sandro Ruzsky, Chief Investigator of the city police, even this decaying world provides the opportunity for a new beginning. Banished to Siberia for four years for pursuing a case his superiors would rather he'd quietly buried, Ruzsky finds himself investigating the murders of a young couple out on the ice of the frozen river Neva.

In a city on the brink of revolution, and pitted against a ruthless murderer who relishes taunting him, Ruzsky finds himself at last face to face with his own past as he fights to save everything he cares for, before the world into which he was born goes up in flames . . .

'Unfailingly evocative . . . Reminiscent *Gorky Park*'
THE TIMES

9780552149006

The Master of Rain

by Tom Bradby

'An immensely atmospheric, gripping detective story with just the right mixture of exoticism, violence and romance'
THE TIMES

SHANGHAI. 1926. EXOTIC, sexually liberated and pulsing with life, it is a place and a time where anything seems possible. For policeman Richard Field, it represents a brave new world away from the past he is trying to escape. His first moment of active duty is the brutal and sadistic murder of a young White Russian woman, Lena Orlov. The key to the investigation seems to be Lena's neighbour, Natasha Medvedev. But can he really trust someone for whom self-preservation is the only goal?

With the International police force riven with rivalries, it is soon clear that Field must make his own way through the investigation. And in a city where reality is a dangerous luxury, Field is driven into the darkness beyond the dazzle of society to a world where everything has its price and the truth seems certain to be a fatal commodity . . .

'Nigh on impossible to put down . . . This intelligent thriller brings Shanghai to life as *Gorky Park* did for Moscow'
TIME OUT

'Rich, dark, atmospheric, this fine novel captures time and place perfectly. A great crime story that ends up in a place you won't predict'
LEE CHILD

'The atmosphere and menace of Twenties Shanghai are brought to vivid life as the backdrop to this gripping tale'
DAILY MAIL

'*The Master of Rain* is that rare thing: a truly epic crime novel, brilliantly researched and superbly executed'
JOHN CONNOLLY

'Does for Shanghai what Raymond Chandler did for Los Angeles – stylish and cool – debauchery at its most elegant'
TIME MAGAZINE

9780552147460